STAY WITH ME

THE PI GUYS

BOOK 1

S.E. HARMON

First edition published 2014, Second edition 2019

In memory of my mother, Sylvia Ann.

1

A good PI would never spend stakeout time to play *Tap Tap Revenge* on his iPhone. But I like to consider myself an adept PI, one that can multitask. So I felt no guilt as my fingers flew dexterously over the screen. It was either that or watch the guy one house over, who either seemed to be fixing an old beater of a car or going for some sort of beer drinking record.

Damn. I could go for something cold right now. "Drew, why didn't we bring beer?"

Always the patient sentinel, my partner sat relaxed, as if we hadn't been sitting here for three hours. His fingers drummed lightly on the wheel. He ignored me, as he was wont to do. I was well aware that beer on a stakeout was probably irresponsible. But dammit, I could operate a camcorder whether I was sober as a judge or loose and relaxed. I didn't bother to explain to his cold profile.

You didn't need to see his "Army for Life" tattoo to know he was ex-military. Drew was a real hoorah motherfucker who'd been honorably discharged after an injury in the field. If that convoy ambush hadn't left him slightly deaf in his left ear, he'd probably be wearing combat boots and fatigues right now. His more anal military tendencies made him an amazing PI. He could probably sit in this car in his slacks and French-cuffed shirt, straight and pressed, for a decade or more.

I glanced down at my tan cargo pants and Jack Daniel's T-shirt. We couldn't be more different, and not just in mode of dress. His by-the-book approach was a good foil to my wild-card personality and made us good partners. If Drew was searching for a crafty way to enter a house, I probably already had my elbow through the back door glass.

"I need a smoke," I said.

"Like you need a gun to your head," Drew finished my already finished statement, and that was that.

I scored a not too shabby 96 percent on my game and briefly hit the sleep button.

"Good God, Drew, can we turn on the A/C? The leather is sticking to my ass like glue."

"We look too conspicuous if the car is running," he said, giving me the shut-up-I-know-what-I'm-doing look. "People pay attention to an idling car. You can't even tell we're in here."

"They'll be able to tell when they box up our well-done skeletons," I whined.

I rolled down the window a quarter inch, just a crack, hoping for relief. I met only hot, sticky air. Florida weather in July gave no quarter, not even for sun worshippers like myself.

I fanned myself for a bit, looking around the street for the hundredth time. Alton Street was wide and treelined, with the same type of homes dominating both sides of the street—large ranch houses. The street was the picture of normalcy. Mr. Fix-it scratched his head with a wrench next door as I checked the front of the sprawling white ranch house yet again. No activity. Two ponytailed young girls giggled in the driveway of our target house—they'd been giggling now for two hours. Only the Lord above knew why.

As a few kids tumbled past, yelling for no reason I could discern other than the fact that they had mouths and lungs, I rolled the window back up. I was grateful the windows of Drew's low-slung black Mazda were darkly (illegally) tinted. Kids were a decidedly nosy bunch and made excellent tattletales to suspicious mothers and fathers.

"Is that CLS550 still there?"

Drew snorted. "You'd think someone would know not to do surveillance in a Mercedes."

I eyed the flashy silver car parked neatly on the curb, only four doors down. Drew was right. You needed a car that was at least neighborhood appropriate, so that it would blend in. It was a nice neighborhood, but no one here drove that kind of car. He was a bogey. Out of place.

"You think Blake hired a second team to watch us?" I asked.

"If he did, they are definitely on the wrong track, seeing as how we're behind them."

Looking back at the neatly manicured lawn with the crazy rooster lawn ornament (and picket fence for God's sake), it was hard to believe we were there to bust the lovely Mrs. Blake for something seedy. She had, however, been in the backyard for over an hour.

"Maybe she gardens," Drew murmured, his timing making me jump a little.

"I wish we could have eyes on her," I said. "There are a lot of things you could be doing in an enclosed backyard."

"Swimming. Gardening. Barbequing."

"Screwing someone in a lawn chair?"

"I'll take a little of option four. And three."

I checked the photo in the file again, looking down at her smiling, round visage. Wispy bangs fell into her sweet brown eyes as she charmed the photographer with her smile—front two teeth slightly spaced apart, as if she didn't have enough charm. She looked exactly what she was—a forty-one-year-old mother of three who lived in the hell that was suburbia. Okay, I was ad-libbing there. She probably thought it was the *joy* of suburbia.

"Probably drives a minivan even," I guessed.

"Dodge Durango," Drew said casually, not even asking where my thought pattern originated.

Well, that still fit the profile, then. Moms were driving SUVs now.

Big sport utility monsters that carted their kids around in the lap of luxury, replete with DVD players and headphone sets. When I was a kid, I either played the license plate game, listened to my Walkman until the batteries died, or played gin rummy until cards were thrown and someone was called a "damned dirty cheater." Or we tried to see who could get the other kid in the most trouble without actually making my dad pull over to beat us both. I couldn't help but think that if we'd gotten to watch *The Suite Life of Zack and Cody* (had it existed back then) while drinking Capri Suns, we'd probably have been more pleasant kids.

"I've got two more of these today," Drew said, rolling his shoulders. "Let's hope they're as uneventful."

Cheating spouses was our number one requested service. It was not only a reflection of the current state of marriage but also damned depressing. If I had to hear one more husband or wife, married since the beginning of time with 2.5 kids and a mortgage, tell me about his or her suspicious inkling about a spouse's new cologne, I was going to lose it. Really.

Tonight's contestant on Let's Catch a Cheating Bastard fit neatly in that profile. Mr. Blake with the large glasses, as lean and sparse as his spouse was round, had earnestly told me his tale of woe. And wonder of wonders, I'd barely managed not to roll my eyes clear out of my head. It was just that typical. "But that's so cold, Mac," you might say. And I would say that once you enter the private investigator phase of your relationship, it's pretty much over anyway, isn't it?

They made our jobs easy—most women already knew. They just wanted the proof. They wanted the pictures to rub in his face. They wanted the bitch's *name*. Nine times out of ten, their suspicions came to fruition, usually spurred by a behavior change. *He's eating right nowadays. He's wearing contacts now*. I'd even had one strange woman give me the mistress's phone number and name. *I just want to know what he's leaving his family for*, she'd lied to me (and herself), her eyes burning with fervor. *Is that weird*?

Yes. Yes, it was.

The men were a different bag of chips altogether. They were

wrong *most* of the time. *I just want to know who she's banging*, our last enlightened caveman had groused about his wife and mother to his lovely twins. Turns out she was banging the *Oprah Winfrey Show* before slamming the dry cleaners, and then finally getting hammered by a BerryBlast Coolatta on the way home. In other words, a big fat nothing. But what did I care? I got paid either way. I only wished I could let Mrs. Caveman know that he didn't trust her as far as he could throw her.

I stuck Mrs. Blake's picture back in the folder and pulled out my digital camcorder. Since we were working on Mr. Blake's dime, at some point I knew we were destined to follow this woman to the bookstore, a Starbucks, maybe even cool our heels while she browsed a super Target, before finally following her to pick up her 2.5 kids at daycare. All right, it was three—Emily, Taggert, and Taylor. Our only break was that the huge blue Dodge Durango would be hella easy to tail.

"Time is 1:15 p.m.," I murmured in the general direction of the mike before recording four time-stamped seconds of the stationary Dodge Durango.

For my own purposes, I panned out to get the tags of the CLS550 still kissing the curb. I was pretty sure he was a PI by this point, and I was getting annoyed. "Amateur." Iclicked off the camcorder. "This will make scintillating footage for Mr. Blake later on."

"You always hope they're right," Drew said, popping the tab on a Red Bull.

I stared at him for a moment. "What's that supposed to mean?"

"Ever since you dumped Trevor. Love lost, and all that nonsense. Or maybe it's just that misery loves company."

"That's a miserable thing to say," I said, glaring at the camcorder in my lap.

Drew shrugged.

Just because I decided Trevor and I were better off enemies than lovers didn't make me bitter. The fact that he then decided he was more into breasts than he'd formerly thought? Yeah, that made me a little tart, I won't lie.

"Or maybe it started before Trevor even. Maybe it was—"

"Don't." I knew exactly who he thought it was, and I didn't want his name mentioned. Nick was a failure I kept close to my heart, even more of a failure than the Trevor thing. Which said quite a bit.

The green micro numbers on Drew's dashboard clock ticked past three. My mind was itching with being still. I wanted to walk around the block. Sleep. Eat something.

"Toss me the Cheetos," I demanded.

Drew aimed the bag at my head, and I caught it just in time. I opened the bag violently, and Cheetos flew into the console, making Drew holler at me. I threatened to rub Cheetos dust on his slacks, which settled him down quickly enough. I slowly picked the artificially orange pieces off the dash, eating them one by one, knowing it would annoy him.

He managed to ignore me for three minutes before I heard a low, measured growl. He turned slightly in his seat, giving me more back than profile. The stress alone sent him running an unnerved hand through his black hair, messing up his low pony, and when he released his hair from the tie, I briefly wondered why we had decided messing around was such a bad idea. He kept his hair slightly long, long enough for a pony that hit mid shoulder blade. His time in the military made him determined to never get a buzz cut again, and he was, quite simply, a hair whore.

"You should leave it down."

"You should finish eating those Cheetos out of my cup holder before I go insane."

I glared at the clock, stuffing more orangey goodness into my mouth. *Not* from the cup holder. This was pretty much it. Mr. Blake got off at four and home at five, like clockwork. So if Mrs. Blake wanted to get her groove on, she had a small window to get it done.

At 4:46 p.m., our patience was finally rewarded, as a woman in a blue sweat suit and a high ponytail moseyed out the door. I pressed record on my digital cam and watched her on the tiny screen as she checked the mail, threw away a few circulars, and pulled the trash can in from the curb. She waved the handful of mail at Mr. Fix-it.

Then she waved the ponytailed girls in and shut the door behind them.

"Well, that was certainly worth it." I saved my sarcastic aside for when I clicked the camera off.

Drew shrugged. "See? Looking for dirt."

"I don't care," I said, annoyed. "We get paid either way. And just for the record, we still have a few more days of reconnaissance to do."

The CLS550 hadn't moved an inch, and suddenly I was incensed enough to do something about it. I jammed a baseball cap on my head and crammed on my aviators.

"Blake has a lot of nerve, hiring two PIs to watch this nonexistent show."

Drew snorted. "We're not entirely sure that's another PI."

"Don't you want to know for sure?"

"We'll run the tags," Drew said, pressing the ignition start button. "Don't do anything crazy."

My right leg was already half out the door. "I have a better idea."

"I hope that better idea doesn't involve walking up to the car of a complete stranger," Drew called out the window as I shut the door. "Mac—"

"Just keep the car idling, okay? Be back in five."

He muttered something I didn't care to catch and rolled up the window. Disapproval was written all over his face before the tinted glass sealed the interior of the car, but I couldn't care less. After four hours of being cooped up in the front seat with Drew, it was too nice to finally stretch my legs. I meandered—not slowly enough or quickly enough to attract attention. Pearls of sweat were rolling down the back of my neck before I even reached the bogey.

I leaned over and tapped on the tinted glass. The window rolled down, and I was surprised by the clean-cut guy that eyed me suspiciously. He had a typical corporate image, even sitting in his car, suit jacket discarded and tie loosened. He was ridiculously good looking, something I realized I had no business noticing. Black hair, thick and silky, a little overlong. Smooth, creamy skin looked as if it would be soft as butter.

I leaned back and forced myself to focus. Who cared how hot he was? He was on our turf. "Blake gets home at five, you know. No need to sit here all night."

"Blake?" He looked at me blankly, blinking those big sky-blue eyes. Even his glasses made him look good. "Who is Blake?"

"Is that the way you're going to play it?"

"I'm not Blake." He started to sound annoyed. "My name is Jordan Channing, actually."

Uh-huh. Sounded about right. Last time I checked, they weren't giving away Benzes on the street corner. He probably had the perfect corporate Barbie girlfriend with matching accessories and a sweet Barbie Dreamhouse. Even if I was wondering where a suit like him acquired a body like that, I knew it was only the daydreams of the deluded. I could smell straight a mile away. Actually I could smell *him* a mile away, and not because his cologne was overpowering. A light whiff of something clean and refreshing, like Irish Spring or fresh soap.

"Mackenzie Williams," I offered, without being asked.

"I've seen you," he said, his eyes going squinty. "Somewhere… I'm sure of it." Then his expression cleared. "Do you know Trevor Smith?"

I held back my groan, but barely. Would the roach never die? "Yes, I know Trevor."

"We work at the same law firm," he said. "I think I've seen you in his office a few times. I think he said you were his brother, right?"

"Maybe," I said, noncommittal.

That hurt, but I wouldn't let it get to me. Trevor hadn't been the first man I'd dated who was firmly stuck in the closet, but hopefully, he would be the last. In my card catalogue, the Dewey Decimal System had placed him firmly under Ancient History.

"So if you're not looking for Blake, who *are* you looking for?"

His expression closed, and I felt silly feeling a loss. "What makes you think I'm looking for someone? I could live in the area."

"You could, but this car lives somewhere else," I said. "Try again."

"I don't have to tell you anything."

He didn't. And really, I'd gotten what I wanted. I knew he wasn't there for Blake, and that should be enough. But my curiosity was begging me to dig, like a dog wagging its tail. If not for Blake, then why was he here? My incessant curiosity and attention to detail made me an excellent PI. It was also what was going to get me stuffed in a garbage can with duct tape around my mouth one day.

I leaned on his car. "You know, I bet one of the neighbors in the area would know who you are. Maybe I should just go door to door and ask." I widened my eyes. "You think one of them would recognize you?"

He leaned his head back on the seat and let out a sigh. "You really are an annoying cuss, aren't you?"

I beamed. "I haven't been called a cuss since my days on the Ponderosa, Hoss."

"*Bonanza* references? Really?"

The sound of a diesel engine drowned out my next *Bonanza* impression, and I watched the UPS truck pull up in front of the house two doors down. A man in brown shorts hopped down and started rooting around in the back of his truck.

I looked down at Jordan, surprised to see his face look pinched. "Get in," he said, knuckling the door unlock button.

"Why?" I asked, my brow furrowing.

"I don't want to be seen, that's why," he said through gritted teeth. "Will you get in the car?"

"You're a stranger," I said disdainfully, doing my best Kevin McCallister impression because well, that *Home Alone* movie still rocked.

Really, I had few qualms about getting into the car with him, but my radar had always been a little off. He seemed respectable enough, and he'd certainly had plenty of time to grab me and demand what pitiful little money I had on me. He also knew Trevor (not a ringing endorsement, but whatever), and Drew was literally eight feet away. And I liked a little danger with my Cheetos.

"Can I see your ID?" I asked, and I wasn't kidding.

"Are you serious?"

"Do you *want* to be seen?"

He huffed and stretched up, reaching in his back pocket. Within moments, I was palming his ID, noting that even *he* could look like a stoned late night gas station clerk in a DMV photo.

"All right, you've seen it. Now get in!"

I took pity on him and opened the door. As I slid in, I knew Drew was probably having kittens watching this go down.

"Thank you." Jordan sighed and looked over at me, tapping on my iPhone. "What are you doing?"

"Googling you, stranger," I said, pulling up his law firm's website. And there he was, smiling under an associate photo under the "who we are" tab.

"Why don't you just ask me what you want to know?" He sounded annoyed.

"This is more fun," I said, scrolling down. "So you're a Pisces."

"It doesn't say that," he said, hitting the door lock.

Ah, vintage kidnapper's move. I might get to use my judo after all. Actually, it was more like high-cardio Tae Bo, but beggars couldn't be choosers.

"It also says you prefer boxers over briefs."

He looked at me for a moment before sighing. "I don't know you, but suffice to say that sarcasm is your deal?"

I smiled a little. "You'd be right, Channing." I hit the sleep button on my phone and turned slightly in the buttery leather seat. "So. What's going on with either the peach house or the UPS man?"

"It's a long story," he said after a pause.

"Fortunately for you, I have plenty of time."

"Are you always this nosy?"

"When I'm on my job?" I pretended to think. "Yes."

"And what is work for you, exactly?"

"Private investigator," I said.

His eyebrows went high. "Should I be nervous?"

"Do you have something to hide?" I bantered back and then paused, confused. What was I doing exactly? I cleared my throat. "Don't worry. Your secrets are safe unless you hire me."

"Are you any good?"

I narrowed my eyes. "Good enough."

"Better than your people skills, I hope."

"Cute. That's a thirty percent markup for you."

Suddenly he was very interested in the mahogany and leather steering wheel. "Maybe I do have a job for you."

"What kind of job?" I asked curiously.

"Do you follow people? Looking for certain information?"

"I'm surprised the firm doesn't have someone on retainer."

"This wouldn't be for work," he said, tracing the silver logo with his fingers. They were long and ended in neatly trimmed, clean fingernails. "It would be... more personal."

"You're going to have to be a little more specific than that."

He was silent, clearly in some sort of debate with himself. Then, "How long have you been doing investigations?"

I shrugged. "Ten years or so."

"Are you licensed?"

"Of course I'm licensed." My response was a little terse, but I understood his caution. They were good questions to ask a PI before you allowed him to dig into your life.

"Well, what kind of things would you do in your investigation?"

"What would I be investigating?"

He let out a brief puff of air that sent his hair flying.

"Are you planning on telling me anytime soon?" I demanded.

"I think I changed my mind," he said.

I squinted and cocked my head to one side. "Let me guess, an insurance scam. Or a lost pet. No, no, a cheating spouse."

He gave me a level look, and the smile slipped off my face. "I'm not married," was all he said.

But a cheating girlfriend/fiancée/something, then. As if to buttress his silence, the door opened and a woman greeted the UPS man. She was pretty even from a distance, with a high ponytail and fitted yoga pants. She signed for her package and shut the door.

"Sorry," I murmured, hating the fact that I'd destroyed our easy banter. *Well hell, he's the one who brought up the private investigating business.*

"You get a lot of those?" he asked, a self-deprecating smile on his face.

"What's that?"

"Cheating spouses."

"You've just described the majority of my day," I said with a shrug.

He sighed and looked at me. "You feel up for coffee?"

I pointed at the Starbucks cup in his silver-rimmed cup holder, wondering how severe his brain injury was. "Are you aware that you *are* drinking coffee?"

He picked it up and shook the Grande cup side to side. "I'm due a refill." He turned the cup up to his mouth, and I did *not* watch the strong muscles in his throat working as he finished what was surely cold by now. "Ready?"

I looked around for a moment, pondering, as if I wasn't going to go with him. "I have to let Drew know. Then I'm ready."

"Drew?"

"My partner," I specified, winding down the passenger window and waving an arm briefly.

"Partner?" Was it just my imagination or did he look slightly disappointed?

"He owns half the business," I specified. I didn't care to examine why it was important that Mr. Unattainable was clear on the fact that Drew and I were platonic. "And he's pulling up next to you, so unwind your window."

Drew's car pulled up next to Jordan's car, and his window went down again. "Are you about finished?" he asked, ignoring my companion completely. Drew wasn't exactly known for his people skills.

"Actually, I'm going to go have coffee with Mr. Channing, here."

"Go?" Drew repeated it as if it was a dirty word. "You're going to go with this man? In his car?"

"I think his flying carpet is in the shop," I said, being an ass as usual. Jordan appreciated my humor, though, snorting lightly.

"Mac, a word?" Drew said, his eyebrows snapping together in a way that boded ill. He waved me over to his side of the car, his expression saying *don't give me any crap.*

I got out and sidled over to his window.

"I'm cooking spaghetti tonight. Are you in?"

An unexpected opening that I took cautiously. Unexpected but pleasant. I'd expected him to blast me for potentially riding off with a perfect stranger. I shook my head with real regret. A couple of forkfuls of Drew's delicious spaghetti with homemade sauce would go a long way toward redeeming this day. He'd learned how to cook in the military and rubbed it in my face when he didn't invite me to dinner.

"I'm bushed. After this meeting, I'm probably just going to head home and gnaw on a Lean Cuisine or something."

"Oh, okay," he said, nodding. "Well, now that that's out of the way, are you out of your fucking mind?"

Well, here we go, then. "What do you mean?"

"What do you mean, he says." Oh, it was never good when Drew started repeating you and talking to himself. "You're actually going to get in his car and let him drive you someplace? Why, because he's a hot piece of ass? Has all that blond streaking finally seeped into your skull?"

So he *had* noticed.

"He works with Trevor, and he's straight, by the way," I said, irritated. "And for the last time, I got these streaks surfing." It was true. Not that there was anything wrong with L'Oreal, but a little time in the sun had burnished my brown hair with some golden highlights that I adored. And so what if a man sprayed a little lemon juice on his hair before hitting the beach with his board?

He ignored my declaration about both Jordan's sexuality and the genuineness of my hair color. "And Trevor is so trustworthy."

"Trevor's a jackass—agreed. But he's not a murderer either. He's a lawyer at the firm. I saw his card... and his ID," I added. "He's legit."

"Did you at least call Trevor and see if he's heard of this Jordan Channing?"

"I did better than that. I googled him on my phone."

"Because the Internet never lies."

"For God's sakes, Drew. We're just going to a Starbucks. You can follow us if you wish. I have to schmooze a little."

"And it just so happens that you get to schmooze with a guy that looks like that? Where were you when the Bobbsey twins parked their respective rears in my office this morning?"

The "Bobbsey twins" were actually two sweet old ladies who thought their neighbor was... well, there's no easy way to say it... a murderer. And by sweet old ladies I mean harridans that argued with strangers, argued with us, argued with each other, argued with themselves... I shuddered to think of it. Really, I did owe Drew for that one, especially since I had been surfing with Asher and not doing anything remotely productive. The sisters swore the ax-murdering neighbor brought home a different woman every night, and she never left. The two bickering sisters also swore that he was stealing their TV Guide, and to be honest, I think that was the most important issue of all to them. Not the murdered women who were stacking up by the dozens, if their testimony (gathered from a pair of binoculars) was to be believed.

"Hey, if he happens to be good looking, well, that's just one of the perks of the job. Like stealing paper clips. Eating the extra french fries off someone's plate. Snacking on grapes in the produce section. That kind of thing."

Drew wrinkled his nose. "Good God, you don't do that, do you?"

"*Anyway*, I'll call you when we're finished, and you can pick me up from the coffeehouse."

"Because I have nothing better to do?"

"Exactly."

"This had better be worth it," he grumbled.

"Hey, this guy may be our newest client."

"He may also be a freaking serial killer."

"Ahem." Our gazes swung to see Jordan standing slightly past my left shoulder, dumping his coffee cup in a street receptacle. He did a nerdy move, using his index finger to push up his frameless glasses on his nose. It *should* have been nerdy. Of course it made him even more attractive, and I almost stuck my tongue out at Drew. "I'm actually not a serial killer," he continued, a slight smile on his lips. "But if I were, I would have definitely rerolled my duct tape and cancelled my plans by now."

Even Drew's mouth lifted a little at that one.

"Coffee?" Jordan asked with a lifted eyebrow.

"Coffee," I said in confirmation.

Drew pointed a finger in my direction. "If you don't call me in an hour, I'll assume you're dead."

"And then call the police," I said in a way that let everyone know I'd heard it all before.

"No, then I'll just assume you're dead and move into your office. You've got a better view."

I blew him a kiss. "I love you too," I said sarcastically.

As he peeled away, I got back in the car with Jordan, feeling strangely excited. I quickly banked the feeling. He was a potential client. Nothing else. I looked down at my cargo pants, glad they were loose fitting. Tell that to my dick, apparently. I sighed and buckled my seat belt, annoyed as Jordan took the gearshift in hand. He even looked sexy driving. Glad to know my gaydar was still on the fritz.

2

I'd forgotten how far the Starbucks at Riverwalk was from the parking lot. Not that I wasn't enjoying walking with the best-looking man I'd seen in a long time. We ambled down the red-bricked street, passing little shops and corner cafés and saying very little—I had taken the proverbial class of small talk and failed miserably. By the fifth block, my teeth were gritted miserably as my leg began to voice its complaints, and I knew I didn't have long before I'd have to sit down. The damn thing had been a pain in my ass since the accident, and I'd never quite forgiven it for making me quit the force. Although I suppose it could have been amputated, and that would certainly suck. As is, I'd had four months of rehabilitative therapy, and the right thigh was still numb in places and tingly. Of course, by tingly I meant that sometimes I'd get sudden pains like someone had shoved an electric poker up my ass.

I cast a side look at Jordan. "Hey, where is this Starbucks, exactly?"

"Not sure," he said.

Helpful lad, he was.

We turned a curve, passing another café, and I swore silently. Soon I'd be limping like a three-legged dog, and I didn't want to ponder why that bothered me. There were no possibilities here with Jordan—hell, I wasn't even looking. We were just guys, two guys getting coffee while we discussed business. If one guy noticed how they were the exact perfect height to complement each other, then that was all right.

I'd never been gladder to see the green awning of the Starbucks and even managed a smile at Jordan as he let me go in front of him. Soon we were at the sugar and cream station, a caramel latte in my hand as I watched Jordan open sugar packets efficiently and dump them into his cup. Grande again.

"Maybe you'd like some coffee with all that sugar," I suggested.

He grinned. "At least I didn't order that froufrou caramel latte." After another handful of yellow sugar packets disappeared into his cup, he took a sip and nodded. "Good."

"Hey," I protested, "compared to other Starbucks patrons, my order was relatively simple."

"Double skim milk, a shot of French vanilla, and oh, do you happen to have any Truvia? No? All right, then three Sweet'N Lows." He copied my mannerisms and tone exactly, making me blush. If he'd been my brother, I would have socked him in the arm or at least cuffed his ear.

"Funny."

I pressed my fist into my upper thigh and couldn't avoid the wince.

"You all right?" His eyebrow raised in query.

"Fine."

"I noticed you favoring that leg on our way down here." He paused. "There are chairs right here."

Though the Starbucks was overflowing with business, most of the customers were getting cups to go. Only two of the tables were occupied. The contrary part of me wanted to remain standing in case he pitied me. My leg made the deciding choice, as well as his matter-of-fact tone, and I sank into one of the chairs gratefully. Now I really needed a smoke.

"When did you get injured?"

"You ask a lot of questions, Channing." Questions I didn't feel compelled to answer. I took a sip of my latte.

"You answer very little, Williams," he said in a way that made me laugh.

I dug deep and forced myself to exercise little-used conversational skills. "You from around here?"

"In the Boca area, actually. Originally from Dearborn. Michigan. You?"

"Fort Lauderdale born and bred," I said. "Went to school in Miami, so I lived in Coral Gables for about five years, but then right back here."

"University of Miami?"

"Where else? You?"

"Duke."

"Well, la-di-dah," I said with a grin, and he laughed. "What made you come down here?"

"I was offered a job straight out of law school down here, with the contingency that I pass the Florida bar. The firm made me an amazing offer, and I have no ties anywhere else. I would have been crazy to pass it up."

"No family back in Dearborn?"

"I have two sisters that both live in Philly, and my parents are retired. They spend all their days traveling now, so there is no home base. Last I heard they were touring vineyards in Tuscany."

"Must be nice."

"That's what I said." He grinned.

God, his grin should be illegal. I blinked away the sight of Jordan's amazing smile and spent a moment people watching through the Starbucks window. It was silly, really, but I didn't want to know any more about him. I didn't want to know any more about his life or his family, his interesting parents or his success at his job. I already liked him way too much. Besides, who was I kidding? I didn't want to get to know him. I wanted to *do* him. Or be done by him. It didn't matter what order.

"The only thing I regret about the move is the weather," he said. "But the benefits are good."

"If that Benz is a sign of how much they're paying you, they must be pleased with you indeed."

"I don't know about that. I was supposed to be in court today and sent a junior associate instead," he said, smiling that ridiculous smile. "So they're going to pitch a shit fit."

"Ah, the benefits of working for myself." I pulled out my phone and thumbed through the applications until I brought up the word processing app. I typed Jordan in all caps at the top of the page before giving him a frank look. "Which brings us to the crux of the matter, I suppose. Tell me, Jordan," I said in my usual blunt manner, "who the hell would cheat on you?"

He went red a little, which should have made him look like a tomato. It didn't. "I suppose there's a way to snatch a compliment out of that."

I shrugged. "Take it how you will." I leaned back in my chair. "Let me guess. Some girl you want to marry, but you think she's after your money?"

"Rachel has her own money," he said. "I just feel like we're not clicking like we used to. All of a sudden, there's like this wall between us."

"And you thought, *ding*, I need a private eye?"

"No, I thought I should follow her. See what she's up to. Who she's into. Then a private eye caught me," he said, making me laugh. "And now I think you might be a little better at surveillance than me."

"Give me some details," I said, rubbing my hands together.

He shrugged helplessly. "I don't know what would help you. What are you looking for?"

"Something salacious, honey. I don't give a damn about helpful."

He looked startled before laughing. "You're a bit crazy, no?"

"And don't think I don't know it. Where'd you meet? What's she look like? What are her routines?"

He spent the next fifteen minutes giving me the rundown on who, exactly, Ms. Rachel Graven was. A Stanford graduate with a high IQ.

An only child whose stepsister gave Jordan the willies with her excessive flirting. An associate at a firm in the same building, but foreclosures and asset seizure as opposed to his tax law. Worked eighty-hour weeks and was back for more on Monday. Dark hair, dark eyes, and an affinity for blood-red lipstick. *Oh no, girlfriend.* She sounded like one cold, smart bitch. If she wasn't cheating on him, she could be my new drinking partner.

"I don't know." His deep sigh tugged on my heartstrings a little. "Maybe she's just not that into me," he said with a self-deprecating smile.

I didn't deny it. "Maybe she's just a ho."

"Aren't you supposed to be neutral?"

"That's Switzerland, dear. This is America, and we take sides."

He smiled. "So you're on my side, then?"

And your back, and your front. I forced my dirty mind back to reality. "I'm on whoever's side is paying me."

"Well, that would be me," he said, holding out his hand for a handshake.

I mock squealed like a Miss America pageant winner instead. "So I've got the job?"

He laughed and shook his head. "Against my better judgment." He checked his watch and did a double take. "Damn, it's been an hour. I've got to get going, and your friend is probably filling out a missing persons report."

"Drew?" I shrugged. "Bastard is probably so into his homemade sauce, he doesn't even realize I'm gone."

"You want me to give you a lift?"

"I'm good," I said, not wanting to be in his gorgeous proximity a moment longer. "I'm pretty sure biting a client's neck is a horrible way to begin a working relationship." *Oh shit.* "Good Lord, did I just say that out loud?"

From the looks of his red, stunned face, I did.

"You want to bite my neck?" he repeated slowly.

I want you to fuck my ass, actually. Long and slow. Bent over a coun-

tertop somewhere. I told my raging hormones to calm down before I lost a potential job. "Kidding, Jordan. Kidding."

"Right. The sarcasm thing, right?"

I nodded, a sanguine look on my face.

"Are you going to be all right?" He paused at the door, giving me an unreadable look.

"Perfect," I said and then winced. *Asinine.* I had a bad habit of using the word "perfect" when things were anything but. I waved him off. I felt a pang that I probably wouldn't see him for a while, and that was ridiculous.

After he disappeared, I left a message for Drew that went a little something like this: "Hey, you bitch, I know you went home without me. How the hell am I supposed to get home? See you tomorrow." I added one more bitch for good measure and hung up.

The older woman at the table next to mine was using all the peripheral vision she could muster to spy on me, and I sipped my coffee with an innocent look. "What?" I asked, facing her full on. "He knows he's a bitch."

She glared.

After I had prolonged my coffee as long as I could, I began the long walk back through Riverwalk, determined to call Drew until he answered. On second thought, because I knew him very well, I decided to head to the bus stop just in case. I walked to the bus stop, feeling the stretch and pull of the muscles of my knee. Oh, I was going to pay for this tomorrow. Hell, I was paying for it now. I sank down on the bus stop bench gratefully, wondering if it was lazy to call a taxi to pick you up from a bus.

I dug out my pack of cigs and a lighter from my pocket and finally lit my one of the day. My so-called family and friends had whittled my one pleasure in life down to a single moment of a twenty-four-hour day, one single moment to fill my damaged lungs with delicious cloudy air and let it out on a single breath. I did so immediately, almost feeling close to orgasm for waiting so fucking long. It was just as well that I was close to quitting. God knows you can't smoke anywhere anymore.

I eyed the police cruiser that slowed down next to my bench before the window lowered.

"Put that goddamn cancer stick out," the officer said.

I shook my head, letting it hang out of the side of my mouth as I gave him the one-finger salute. "Fuck you, five-O."

"You're not getting in my car with that thing," he insisted. "Disgusting, filthy habit. Put it out."

Lord, I'd heard it all before. "I just lit the freaking thing."

"You want a ride? You put it out now."

"It's my one of the day," I whined. The no-nonsense expression on his usually joking face finally made me stub it out on the curb. "Fucker."

"Now you're littering," he grumbled.

"Robby!"

"Been circling every hour or so," my brother said, waving me over. "Finally caught you. Drew said your sorry ass was in the area. Destitute. Homeless. As usual."

"For once I'm glad to see your face. What's up, Tao?"

"Is that the gratitude I get for coming to pick your ass up?" he groused, even as Tao, his partner, gave me a fist bump. "Get in. We're in a fire lane."

"Shouldn't I be wearing cuffs or something?" I asked as I clambered into the backseat. My leg was too tired to entertain them with my version of a perp walk.

"In your dreams, perv."

"Settle it, you two," Tao said mildly.

As Robert peeled away, I spotted the bus lumbering up to the stop and sighed with relief. He was an annoying little twerp, but today my brother was a lifesaver.

My apartment was dark, and I left it that way, making my way by the filtering light of the bathroom to my bed. I sat on the edge of the bed, glad I'd bothered to spend the extra money on a pillow-top mattress. I had to thank the South Carolina Doubletree, actually, where I'd once rented a room next to Cheating Spouse number forty-two. *Ching!* Fake register noise. Doubletree had to have the softest bed on earth, and I'd done my best to replicate it. The comforter was thick and dark brown, and I felt comfort for the first time all day.

I rummaged through the bottom drawer of my nightstand until I had an orange prescription bottle in hand. *Meloxicam.* After I'd explained the exact nature of my leg problem to my doctor, the unconcerned bitch had rattled off a prescription that did absolutely nothing for me, but I persevered anyway, taking it doggedly every day. I'd been tempted to hit CVS, sweep a mass of OTC products into my basket, and go all mad scientist on my leg. But for now, I sighed and downed another Meloxicam, dry.

Take with food, the bottle screamed at me.

Now that I was within two feet of a pillow? Highly unlikely. I fell back onto bed, pulling the covers over my head. It wasn't until I was half asleep that I realized I was now down to a half a cig a day.

"Fuckers," I muttered, before drifting off.

I knew nothing else until morning broke through my blackout curtains.

3

His eyes were wicked, stormy pools as he leaned over me, and I kept my eyes open as long as possible to watch his slow descent. I let them drift shut as his hot mouth fastened on the soft skin of my neck, and moaned a little.

"You're killing me," I managed, threading my hands through the silk of his hair.

"I'm trying," he teased, working a hot trail with his tongue down my neck and around the muscles of my chest.

My stomach contracted hard and bottomed out as he traced his way around my abs. His hand drifted down to my cock, which jutted upward for his attention. His hand instead palmed my balls gently and tugged a little as his tongue darted into the indentation of my belly button. His tongue went upward instead of down, and he used the broad side of it to surround one of my stiff nipples.

"You've got to be kidding me," I groaned, working my waist like a freaking belly dancer to try to get my dick closer to his hand, his skin, his mouth, his anything.

Soft laughter ensued before his hand finally took control of my leaking cock. "This what you wanted?"

"You're such an ass."

He worked his hand up and down, the precum dribbling from the mushroomed head slicking his way. God, I'd never been so turned on or hard. I even heard ringing in my ears. He leaned in, his voice whisper soft as he neared my ultrasensitive ear. "Maybe you should get that."

"Get what?" I shook my head in response, and feeling his hand draw away from my cock, I grabbed for his wrist. "Don't stop."

"Pick up. Pick up." God, even his breath wafting across my face was delicious. He smelled like mint and strawberry gum.

"Jordan," I murmured.

"Pickuppickuppickuppickup!"

My befuddled eyes snapped open, and I heard my specially programmed ringtone clearly. I slammed my head back down on the pillow.

"Fuck!"

I glared at my phone, having a vibrating seizure on my nightstand. It had better be good. I looked down at my raging hard-on and groaned, then buried my head in the softness of my pillow. It had better be damn good. I waited silently for the message prompt, enjoying the warmth of the morning drawing sunlit lines on my back.

God, why would I be dreaming about Jordan? He was off limits. Practically married. I pressed the unknown message and listened for a moment before groaning. Trevor.

"I want to talk to you about Finnegan," he said, enunciating his words precisely in a way that was now uniquely his. He hadn't spoken that way when we'd first met. He'd drawled, slow and long vowels, and skipped some consonants altogether. I'd thought it ridiculously sexy. Soon he'd eradicated it to the point that it only appeared when he was angry. Or passionate. Even now, I could hear the way he put six extra *a's* in *baby* when we were in bed. "As soon as you can, I want you to come over to my place." He paused and then added, "Laura gets home at six thirty, so sometime before then."

I grimaced, sitting up and pushing off the bed with a groan. I stretched, wishing I hadn't checked the message at all. I wanted to ignore him altogether, but he had my dog. He'd also taken off with the good television, the good linens, and most of the dishes. While I was fine eating Captain Crunch out of a jelly jar, he wasn't going anywhere with my dog.

I had walked Finn when he had to work late, trying to establish himself as a new associate instead of grunt number twelve at the law firm. *I'd* fed Finn, bought his food, taken him to the vet, and taught him the dumbest tricks known to man. There was a reason he barely responded to "sit," "stay," and "down." I found it more to my liking to spoil him, and if you said "gimme sugar," he was on you like white on rice.

High on my soapbox, it took me a moment to hear my phone buzzing, even though it was in my hand. I checked the flat face and groaned. Drew. Work.

"What's up?"

"I ought to ask you the same thing." Drew's voice was annoyance personified. "I rescheduled the meeting for this morning. Where the hell are you?"

"I'm trying to remember the last call I got from you that didn't begin that way." I found the remote amongst the disarray of the covers and pointed it at the TV. I immediately pressed mute so Drew wouldn't bitch.

"I'm trying to remember the last time you bombed so many appointments."

I halted in front of my dresser and opened the box of Nicorette one-handed, tearing the box a bit in the process. With friends and family like this, I didn't need cigarettes, I needed fucking cocaine.

"Do you know where I can get some good blow?" I asked, only halfway kidding.

"Mackenzie, will you get serious? Are you coming in to work or not?"

I slapped the patch on my upper arm and lit up a cigarette at the same time. "I'm sorry, you bitch, didn't you desert me yesterday?"

"Didn't I call your brother to give you a ride?"

"Yet another offense I've yet to collect for."

"Will you put that fucking cigarette out?" Drew sounded exasperated.

"I'm not smoking," I lied.

"I heard the lighter, you fruit."

Damn, but the surf forecast looked good. I turned the volume up a pinch, just enough to hear over Drew's monotone report about our morning meetings. I rummaged through the nightstand drawer and unearthed my leg brace that I only used when it got bad, and flopped back down on the bed when I found it. I eased it over my foot and up my leg as I listened to the report and not Drew.

"More typical July conditions this week, with a nice southwest swell. Bad news is we may be expecting a low-grade storm in the next two to three days. Good news is that the swell will increase slightly, making a good weekend for all you surfers out there."

I shrugged. Sooo... we may get creamed by a storm, but before Mother Nature hurls a tree through your window, by God, there will be surfing! The weather forecaster sent a toothpaste-ad smile to all of us at home, and I almost covered my eyes from the glare. Someone needed to ease up on the Crest Whitestrips.

"We have two consultations and an appointment with Randolph Kelly this morning," Drew informed me.

God. Randolph Kelly was an irate husband, a sixty-something-year-old who'd acquired a twentysomething girlfriend and *us* to monitor her, apparently. The grizzled bastard had hired us no less than six times, and this time was no different from any of the last. It was a good news/bad news situation—she wasn't cheating, but he owed me one hell of a bill for sitting next to her curb for two weeks.

"So what's your excuse for skipping out?"

"My leg is still hurting from yesterday, you know. It was a long walk."

"And you're still not feeling well?"

I shrugged even though he couldn't see me, not feeling the least bit guilty. Damn, but the report of the water conditions had me wanting to rearrange my whole morning. I blew a ring of smoke over my head, sad that the cigarette was damned close to my fingers. It was always gone too fast.

"Are you forgetting I went off with a murderer? I was almost killed, after all."

"That can be rectified." At my continued silence, he stressed, "This is important. By the way, did you seal the deal?"

"Yeah," I said, jamming the phone between my ear and my shoulder. "He hired us."

"That wasn't exactly what I was talking about." I could hear the smile in his voice.

"Oh, for God's sakes, Drew." I didn't need to see my face to know it was flushed. "It wasn't like that."

"Is our resident queen losing his pristine charms?"

"Shut it, bitch." I'd show him pristine. Sure, I was in a bit of a rut, but I enjoyed sex no more or less than the next person. Trevor and I had had a very active sex life. It was the only thing that bastard hadn't been deficient in. "Don't be jealous because I have standards."

"And Mr. Perfect didn't meet those standards?" Drew suddenly sounded quite sympathetic. "Is this because of Trevor?"

Hell, Jordan met standards I didn't know existed. My skin felt suddenly shivery, remembering my interrupted dream and his calloused, sure hands on my malleable flesh. I could still see his expressive eyes behind those glasses focused on me, only me, and it made me want to do crazy things to his person. God, to steal the words right out of Akon's mouth, he was a sexy bitch. He addled my senses and made me want to say "Trevor who?"

"Water temperature is in the mid sixties," Whitestrips continued. "Should be a glorious, sunshiny day for all you beach lovers."

"All right, all right, you twisted my arm," I murmured. I clicked off the TV and tossed the remote on the bedspread. "Reschedule one last time," I told Drew above his protests. "I'll be available tomorrow. I promise."

"Mac, you boy-bitch, I know you're going to the beach—"

I hit the End button on my phone, and it followed the remote. I mean, this isn't Hawaii—they get waves like this all the time. Hell, it's not even Daytona Beach. Not using a good surf day like this would be darn near un-Floridian.

It wasn't long before I was attaching my soft rack for my board on my old pickup. The door creaked as I opened it, and I slid onto the cracked vinyl seat. As the truck stuttered to life, I remembered my mechanic's last unsolicited advice, dire as usual, as he'd swiped my Visa card—"Those struts are about ready to be replaced."

I had just dropped a little over a grand for a new starter, a water pump, four tires, and numerous other repairs on my dilapidated old truck. Old Bessie had been good to me since college, but she had gotten tired of being put on the back burner.

Say what you will; Bessie was reliable as hell. I fiddled with the A/C a moment, waiting patiently for the hot air scorching my face to turn cool, but it never did. "Fuck." Add the A/C to that long list of repairs.

I slid behind the wheel and tossed the phone on the dash. I crammed on a pair of aviators and headed for A1A, waiting to merge into traffic with the rest of the morning maniacs. From the looks of their driving, people were either one of two extremes—late on their way to the office or early for bingo at the nursing home. Even gridlock couldn't quell my excitement.

I lived in a small apartment that was nothing special—one bedroom, one bathroom, open living area, and one assigned parking space. But the main draw was the location. According to the nearest green road sign, I lived only 3.8 miles from the beach, and it usually took a mere ten minutes in traffic to get there. It was rare that we had waves good enough to bother with, but when the conditions were right, being able to pick up a wave or two within ten minutes was ridiculously convenient.

I actually had Trevor to thank for finally breaking down and trying to ride the waves. His fascination with the beach had inspired me to take advantage of something I'd been ignoring my whole life. After the accident, he had spurred me on to live again. Love again, or so I'd thought. And then he'd taken it all away.

Before he'd gone to UM, Trevor had never seen the beach before in real life. Iowa born and bred, he'd confessed. As if his wheat-colored sheaf of hair and a big bucktoothed corn-fed smile wasn't my first clue. His accent alone told me he was from some flat state where farming was more than a vague thing that happened to our food before it appeared on the shelves at Publix.

I'd never contemplated such an existence—the beach was such a part of south Florida living that it was almost synonymous. Trevor had seen a lake, a reservoir, and fished on a couple of streams and ponds, but that was as close as he'd gotten to big water. A brief memory of him telling me that, and then surprising him with our first date on the beach filtered through my mind. His smile had seemed to cover his entire face as he'd kicked off his shoes and run down the beach like a maniac.

His smile didn't look like that anymore. He had polished, capped veneers. I knew it was ridiculous and an opinion that only I had, but I thought he'd looked better before. As I pulled into a vacated spot, small but prime in location, I realized it was the first time in a long time that I'd thought anything positive about Trevor. Just Trevor. Trevor, my buddy, who had dragged me to South Beach after class and laughed through Jell-O shots on Coconut Grove. My roommate, eventually more, and now, finally, less. I felt a brief spurt of anger that just the thought of facing what he was had been enough to send him running into the arms of the nearest woman he could find. No, that wasn't quite fair to Laura. She wasn't the bottom of the barrel—was actually an attractive woman if you went for that kind of thing. Trevor didn't. No one could suck dick like that and still be attracted to women. Trust me.

I shook off my doldrums and grabbed my board out of the truck, not bothering to wind up the windows in the sticky heat. I grinned at the sight of a familiar figure on the water, cutting through the waves so confidently it was obvious he'd made some sort of Devil's pact with Poseidon. Asher could surf like a professional and was the happiest beach bum I'd ever met. I stood and watched him for a moment, not wanting to interrupt his ride, letting the warm, salty surf lap at my ankles.

With the experience I had now, I realized that on my first time out, I'd looked absolutely ridiculous. I'd researched to my heart's content and let some sloe-eyed clerk at Ron Jon (cute, in an I-just-hit-a-joint way) sell me the best of the wax, best of the boards, and best of gear. I spent a small fortune on a board I was in no way qualified to ride and trotted out there determined to make it work. On my way past the parking lot, I'd passed a guy sitting on the back of his car—some kind of American muscle deal—laughing at me openly. I'd goggled for a minute—black, white, and orange striped board shorts riding low on his lean hips, skin burnished dark honey from the sun, damp hair curling on his shoulders—he was yet another reason to learn to surf. I spent most of my first time out pearling while I tried to find my balance, eventually losing that board on the rocks. Black/white/orange board shorts, I found out later named Asher, had been waiting for me on the shore.

"You givin' up?" he'd asked, a small smile curling on his lips.

"Does it look like I have a board anymore?" I'd snapped, annoyed beyond belief that I'd just lost a month's rent to the rocks and the ocean. The first time in months that I'd stepped out of my comfort zone, and I'd wound up looking like a wet rat, battered, beaten, and laughed at by the ocean.

"Wrong board anyway. Come out tomorrow. Waves are shit now anyway. I'll show you what you need."

He had. My board now was a quad fish, certainly nothing as high performance as Asher's gun board, but I couldn't do those kind of fancy tricks anyway.

Asher finally saw me and waved, managing to even make wiping out look cool. I paddled out to him and gave him a fist bump. (Really, one day, I had to stop doing that.)

"Nice wipeout."

"Shut up." He grinned, straddling his board with ease. "Waves are good today. I think even you could catch one."

"Fuck off, Asher."

We waited out two other hot doggers out there—God knows I would tank their wave.

"What's with the leg brace?" he asked, nodding at the black stretch bandage around my thigh.

I held it aloft briefly, shaking my head. "Strained it."

"You okay?"

"Don't I look okay?"

"You look better than okay, sugar," he said with a leer. It was fairly harmless. We'd already gone there. Done it a million times. Had the T-shirts. Ripped the T-shirts off. Did it again.

"You see the posters for the next competition? They're going up to Big Key in three weeks," I said, already knowing what his response would be. Or lack thereof.

For some odd reason, Asher seemed determined to hide his talent. He lived in a small bungalow near the beach and taught surf classes for the curious tourists that landed on our beach every now and again. As far as I knew, he lived in bare feet and board shorts.

He cut me a sideways look that made his already exotically shaped eyes even more pronounced. "Is that a hint or a question?"

"It's whatever you want it to be. Entry fee is a couple hundred. Although you could probably get BoardWay to sponsor you."

The surf shack on the beach would definitely sponsor him. He was practically a legend out here.

"You come out here to lecture me or surf? And you're corking again."

I resettled my center of gravity, grumbling about ungrateful people who hid their light. I took the next wave that broke, not waiting for Asher's advice, irritated with his stubbornness. I wiped out summarily, but not before getting a few seconds of air.

"Better," I sputtered, clinging to my board like a lifeline.

"Certainly can't get worse," Asher agreed cheerfully.

I grinned. We floated a moment before I pointed out a beauty of a wave and said, "Wait, wait, this is going to be my *Blue Crush* moment."

Asher laughed, managing to utter, "Go for it, dude."

As the wave came closer, he pointed, voice raised above the beating surf. "This is it. Cut right!"

I paddled like mad before rising up smoothly on my board like I'd been doing it all my life—actually I'd been practicing on my bed. I gripped the center with my toes and cut through the wave like a professional. Okay, maybe not, but I'd like to think I looked good out there. I rode the wave, feeling amazed instead of scared as the height of the wave rose to form a bluish-green water wall behind and around me. I put out my hand, dragging it through the frothy water wall before topping out and going under.

I broke through the surface, water pelting down on my hair and back like rain as I gasped and rubbed my eyes. My board bobbed to the surface, tethered securely by the leash, and I grabbed it. I spotted Asher giving me a huge thumbs-up and began a leisurely stroke toward him lying flat on his gun board.

"I'm getting better," I said, treading water beside his board.

"You still stink," he said, swiping the hair out of his eyes. The usually auburn locks were dark with water, almost black, and curled around his neck in waves.

Suddenly I felt this crazy fondness for him. He was probably as messed up as I was, but he was true and real. Something in my eyes must have changed, because he leaned in, pressing wet, cold lips to mine.

When he pulled away, his eyes were dark and serious. "You want to?"

"Still romantic as ever." I grinned.

He blushed, and if my answer hadn't been yes before, it was now. "Why not?"

4

There was nothing slow and gentle about the way we came together. He backed me into his door, hands in my shorts, secure on my behind.

"God, you must have the greatest ass," he groaned somewhere near my ear. Must be, since his hands hadn't left it in over five minutes. "So soft and round—the most fucking perfect bubble butt I've ever fucked."

All right, so I guess we know who's going to bottom, then.

"Shut it, Romeo. I'm not here for poetry," I deadpanned before claiming his mouth with mine.

Our mouths were open and hot as they meshed against each other and his tongue dueled with mine. He pushed me back against the wall hard enough to make me wince, and I bit into his shoulder as he shoved my shorts down to my feet and began jacking me off. There was no other word for it, because Asher was no romantic. He knew what he wanted, and he went straight for it. There was no buildup. No foreplay. Sometimes I wanted to tell him that there was something in between my dick and my lips, but not today. Remnants of my dream still lingered in my mind. Today I wanted it just as hard and dirty as he could give it. And if I was thinking of Jordan fucking me while he did it, well, so what of it?

He pointed to the shorts pooled around my ankles. "Off," he demanded, always the wordsmith, and I stepped out of them.

I allowed him to push me over the arm of the couch and rolled my eyes at his groan at the sight of me, face down on the soft leather, bubble butt high in the air. I don't know where he got the lube, but I felt a squirt somewhere in the region of my backside and ground my teeth at his lack of consideration. I had to try hard not to let annoyance ruin my mood, but apparently my erection had no hard feelings. This was nothing new. He was a good person, but Asher looked out for Asher. Always. I held out my hand for the lube, and he slapped it in my palm.

I know it was popular with some, but there was no way he was getting inside me without any prep, even if I had to do it myself.

"Condom," I reminded him, ignoring his groan as he began digging through the side table.

I squirted the cool lube over my fingertips and circled my rimmed entrance leisurely before easing a finger past the grasping muscle. Just that little bit and my head was suddenly hanging down between my shoulders as I lost myself in the sensation. I'd always been a sucker for anal play, and from the way the sound of rummaging ceased, I realized Asher was too.

"Let me," he said hoarsely, palming one of the globes of my butt, watching my fingers disappear inside my hole. I pushed his hand off.

"Condom," I said huskily, not wanting to get too far gone. Anal play was all well and good, but sometimes a guy needed a dick up his ass.

"I can't find one," he whined.

I added another finger, my breathing gone quite shallow as I pretended Jordan was behind me, fucking me for all he was worth. "If you don't hurry, you're not going to need one."

He cursed and stomped off for the bedroom, and I ignored him. By the time I added a third finger, he was back, and my dick was stiff as a brick. I removed my fingers slowly, wiping sticky digits on his couch cushion.

"Ass," he said, smacking mine, and I smirked. "Goddamn, Mac," was all the raspy warning I got before I got an ass full of dick.

There was a certain familiarity in the way he entered me, the way he could never resist pulling my hair back. There was no finesse, no fake declarations, no exchange of dirty talk, the kind that made you blush after coming. It was just a hard, fast fuck, and I buried my head in the crevasse of the couch cushion and resigned myself to not sitting for a week. *Worth it,* my inner slut acknowledged.

"You close?" His voice came near my ear.

"Ugnh," was all I could manage as I stroked myself so fast, my hand was a blur. A moment later, an orgasm was wrenched out of me, and I yelled, the muscles of my ass clamping down hard on his dick. He suddenly pulled out, and I heard the distinct snap of rubber as he disposed of the condom. His shout was hoarse as the warmth of ejaculate splattered on the small of my back.

We lay there for a second—me with my face buried in the cushions, him slumped over my back, panting like we were seventy.

"Out of shape," I managed to huff.

"I hope you're talking about yourself," came his amused voice in my ear. "Smokey Joe."

"Get off me, you oaf."

I heaved him off my body with what little energy I had left and lay back on the couch. "Ugh," I said, realizing his cum was all over my freaking back as I slid a little. "You know, Ash, that's what the fucking condom is for."

He grinned, wiping hair out of his eyes. "It's not acid."

I smiled sweetly. "Remember that when you're cleaning your couch."

I got up and stumbled to the shower, wrenching the levers of both hot and cold. I should have felt better, I thought, standing under the punishingly hot spray. Not only had I gotten laid, but I'd proven Drew wrong that I was the Wicked Ice Queen of South Florida. Bet you he'd never taken off a work day and gotten lucky. No, there was no postcoital bliss. No cuddling and no sense of well-being. It was relief of release and nothing more. When had that become not enough?

He had migrated to the bed by the time I came out, face half buried in the covers.

"I'm leaving my board," I said, toweling my hair, naked as a jaybird. "I'll pick it up next time I come down."

"This isn't a storage facility," he said from under a pillow.

"Better be in one piece," I threatened.

"No worries. I have no other pupils inexperienced enough to make use of that board."

I smacked him on the ass hard enough to make him yelp. The sight of his muscled cheeks upturned on the bed was enough to make me kneel over him, one knee on each side of his hips.

"Mmm, round two?" he murmured, not opening his eyes.

I kissed him between the shoulder blades, letting my semi-hard dick slide leisurely between his firm butt cheeks. "Just enjoying the view."

I'd just started to dry hump him in earnest when my phone buzzed beside the bed.

I groaned. "Did you bring that in here?"

"Yea," he answered, lifting his hips encouragingly when I stopped. "Your stupid alarm went off."

"Ergh." I pressed Talk and jammed it under my ear. "What's up?"

"Mackenzie."

I sighed and wished I had listened to my first instinct and let it go to voice mail. "I think I hear from you more now than when we were dating."

"What are you up to?"

"Fucking Asher," I said bluntly.

He laughed, probably thinking I was kidding. I began moving again, short strokes between his welcoming channel, and Asher let out a soft groan as he began pumping his own flesh. "Well, then I won't interrupt. Are you at work?"

"Sure." Why not. Asher tightened his butt muscles, and suddenly leisurely stroking became serious pumping. I avoided looking down at the rosy hole my dick was passing on each stroke, knowing I wouldn't be able to stop myself from plunging in if I did. And I didn't bareback. Ever.

"Am I disturbing you?"

"Sort of."

"Well, I won't hold you long." He paused as if waiting for me to contradict him and then continued with a huff. "I just wanted to speak to you for a moment."

"Are you calling to tell me you've come to your senses?"

His voice was hesitant. "About Laura?"

"About Finn," I said crossly. "I couldn't care less about you and the new missus. Maybe we should talk about this in person."

I sighed, irritated and exhausted both. My rapid movements stopped, and Asher let out a sound of protest. Damn that Trevor. Stealing orgasms now? Now that was just dirty.

"I just want my dog back."

I was tired of being snarky. I was tired of being sarcastic. In truth, Trevor had made his decision, and I had to live with it. At least that's what I said to myself in my more mature days. There weren't many of those.

Realizing I wasn't going to continue, Asher pushed me off and flipped onto his back. He began right where he left off. I felt more depressed. Even watching a hot piece of ass like Asher jacking himself wasn't enough to recapture the mood.

"I'd like to talk about this face to face." He paused, as if expecting me to interrupt. When I didn't, he continued. "Finnegan is my dog too."

He was right. Disgustingly right. I smacked my forehead with the palm of my hand. I wasn't about to create a custody agreement for a dog, but if he wanted a few minutes of my time, it wouldn't kill me. After all, what was I afraid of? Was I still in love with him or something?

"I'll meet you at your office," I blurted, scared of my own thoughts. "For five minutes, Trevor, not a minute more."

I hung up the phone and stood there watching Asher finish

himself off, groaning loudly. I smiled. He sounded like he was in the final throes of death. When he finally opened his eyes, he took in my expression and began to laugh, setting me off too. When we finally calmed down, he offered, in a very un-Asher-like moment of selflessness, "You want me to suck you off?"

I shook my head with real regret. "I have to meet Trevor at his office."

He made a noncommittal noise and a face before leaning over the edge of the bed, searching for something.

"What?" I demanded.

He found the sock he was apparently looking for and casually wiped the spunk off his chest and hand. He threw it back on the carpet when he was done, and I pulled a face.

He sent me a knowing look from light brown eyes. "Just wondering why an otherwise sane, relatively intelligent, good-looking guy would give that asswipe the time of day."

I gritted my teeth at the relatively intelligent but gave him a pass because of the good looking. "I just want to get Finn back."

"And suddenly he brings Finn to his office?" He ran a hand over his face and sighed. "Just be careful, Mac."

"Oh, play me a song on a tiny violin."

"Just admit it." He picked up the spunk sock and threatened me with it. "You still have feelings for him."

"I admit no such thing, Oprah."

"Never mind. No need for you to admit what we all already know."

"You're a lousy lay, by the way," I called, shutting the door just in time as he threw the sock at my face.

I searched the living room for a good five minutes before finding my shorts under a coffee table. As I pulled them on, the still damp fabric fought me like a living thing, souring my mood even further.

Fucking Asher. Since when did he become Madame Fortune Teller of Doom? Despite my irritation, I still turned the lock on his front door before slamming it behind me. I didn't want him to get shanked by a random beach bum. Yet.

5

Damn that Asher, I thought, on the drive over. It's not like I was going bungee jumping off the Swiss Alps (okay, erhm, so no one ever did that). I was just seeing my ex. At his office. Because no one ever had sex in an office.

I took a left turn viciously, causing a silver Altima to honk. I honked right back.

I had no delusions that Trevor might still want me. Because they *weren't* delusions. He did. And he knew that *I* knew he did. He might be bisexual or whatever, but you didn't turn gay off like it was a faucet. So we were back to damn that Asher, then. And damn Trevor too. And my weakness for inexperienced blond farm boys.

I was over him. I was over it.

But when his secretary directed me to the conference room, where he was in the middle of a meeting, I realized I was a bit of a liar. Looking at his serious expression, looking down at the glossy screen of his iPad, tapping an unnecessary stylus on the table, I felt something. He was keeping himself focused by jiggling his foot back and forth, and I knew his iPad was open to some sort of word processing document. Quickoffice, probably. Trevor loved Quickoffice. Trevor would *never* play an app on the job (I still don't feel guilty), and I knew without even a whiff that he was wearing Artemis cologne. I felt my throat getting ridiculously tight. What was I so upset for? We were over. He was just so damned familiar.

Sans the four-hundred-dollar suit and the preppy haircut, he could be my buddy in class again, peering over at my notes because he was too stubborn to go get glasses. And when I'd finally shamed him into going ("How can instant vision *not* be on your to-do list, Trev?"), I'd had to convince him that he was still super sexy in them. I blinked back sudden moisture in my eyes. Ridiculous. The creative ways I contrived to do that would just have to remain firmly entrenched in my memory.

The loft-style conference room was beautiful—arching high ceilings with track lighting that looked like it belonged in an artist's study. A long mahogany table dominated the room, flanked by at least twenty opulently appointed black leather chairs. The whole room opened into an arched window that spanned the entire back wall and gave them an unspoiled view of downtown Fort Lauderdale. From the two times he'd permitted me to visit him at his office, I knew it was equally as impressive. I was caught between a smile and... well, another smile—one sad, one pleased. I was happy for him. Proud of him. He'd done well. Angry at him. He wasn't mine anymore. Yes, I was the one who broke up with him, but I had only accelerated the inevitable.

Everyone leaves sometime.

It was hard to stalk someone sitting in a conference room made mostly of transparent material. As if I'd spoken aloud, he lifted his eyes to mine, and I was caught between the crosshairs of a cornflower-blue gaze. We stared at each other for a moment before I began backing away from the glass door. He held up a finger for me to wait, and I pretended not to see, turning on my heel and speeding down the hall. I didn't care how it looked. If I saw him right now, it would be embarrassing and awkward for only one person—me.

"Mackenzie!" I heard his hissed shout, still loud in the echoing halls of the cookie-cutter Brooks Brothers firm.

Someone grabbed my arm, and I yelped, too startled to resist being pulled into an office and relieved, even before I saw my captor, when the door closed softly behind us.

"Jordan," I said with a huff of surprise. "What the hell are you doing here?"

"I could ask you the same thing. I work here… remember?"

"You had two seconds before I busted out some judo on your ass."

He grinned. "Yeah, I'd like to see that." He walked around his desk, picking up a cup. "You want coffee?"

"Wow, you should really join some sort of support group."

"Jeez, Mackenzie, why don't you tell me how you really feel?" He sat in his plush office chair and cocked his head in my direction. "You never answered my question. What are you doing here? Is it about my case?"

I flushed, embarrassed for some reason. "I came to see… speak to, actually," I stuttered, finishing with a weak, "Trevor."

He was kind enough not to comment, but his eyes spoke volumes. He offered me a seat. "So where are we on the java?"

"I need more of it, you need less of it. That pretty much sums it up." I looked around his office for the first time. "You have nice digs here."

"I like it," he said modestly, dismissing the stylishly decorated office with a wave.

The office was roughly the size of my living room, with a seating area and the same ridiculous views as the conference room. Jordan's desk sat prominently, three ells long, sheer glass, covered with what appeared to be a million papers and manila folders and one flat-screen Mac.

Suddenly a buzz went off on the intercom, and a carefully modulated female voice said, "Mr. Channing, Mr. Smith is here to see you. Shall I show him in?"

Jordan's eyes met mine in a questioning manner, and suddenly I didn't care how it made me look. I jerked my head no.

"No, I'm currently in the middle of a meeting with a potential client," he lied smoothly to the faceless voice. "I'll have to meet with him later."

Thank goodness for strong-armed assistants. Had this been my rinky-dink operation, the only thing to stop Trevor would have been an army of dusty plants. Oh, and Miss Edith, the nosy octogenarian that practically lived in the window above my office space. She was in that window so often, I don't know why she bothered with renting the rest of the apartment. What was charming and helpful in a neighborhood-watch leader was detrimental to a business whose customers demanded secrecy. My last client, clad in Jackie-O glasses and a gigantic straw hat that had to have been straight from the border, had not found Miss Edith's nosy advice amusing at all. *Honey, the art of disguise is in blending in.* Although, that was what she got for wearing a hat the size of a straw UFO.

"Would you like me to cancel your lunch plans?" the voice continued, efficient as ever.

"No, tell Rachel I'll be there in a half hour."

"Rachel," I repeated once the voice clicked off. "My prey."

His look said he didn't appreciate my levity. "Yes. She works upstairs. Eighteenth floor." He continued in a flawlessly polite manner that I knew instinctively was vintage Jordan Channing. "You can join us if you want. There's always room for one more."

"No, that's all right. I don't make it a habit of horning in on a lunchtime tête-à-tête."

"Tête-à-tête?" He raised an eyebrow. "Really?"

I shrugged. "I'm colorful."

We sat there for a moment, staring at anything but one another, and I wondered why this moment was so awkward. Oh, that's right, because he'd rescued me running from my ex like a little girl from the boogeyman.

I tried to refocus my energy on something he might be interested in. "I did a little research on your fiancée last night. Ran her address through Google Earth too. Found another vantage point other than that spot on the street. I don't know when she'd possibly have time to cheat on you, though. Her work hours are—"

He interrupted me by lifting his hand. "Mackenzie, you don't have to talk about the case. You just started. I know that's not why you came." He shrugged. "If you want to just sit here and talk or be in silence, we can just do that."

"You don't have to entertain me," I said, going over to the window and that magnificent view. "I just need... a moment."

"Take as much time as you need," he said softly.

I listened to the soothing sounds of his typing as I watched the busy street below. People were so tiny they looked like dolls as they rushed past, dodging one-way traffic against the tricky streetlight at the corner.

He'd chosen to express his doubts about our relationship in an e-mail. Five years of friendship and four years of a relationship, and I'd deserved a fucking e-mail. My lips tightened. It didn't matter that I knew Trevor had trouble presenting himself. That he was the type of person to type a message before he called someone so he didn't mess up or forget what he wanted to say. He'd never wanted to sound stupid, like that boy who grew up in the flat states and ran barefoot through the corn. I'd felt privileged, like I was one of the few people who knew him. The *real* Trevor who didn't have to write things down to speak to me. The Trevor who didn't have to be perfect. That he'd reduced me to a long, rambling e-mail about finding himself and his true person made me want to smash something. It had certainly made me bleach a dozen of his fine Italian suits. It wasn't enough. Not nearly enough.

I had left him then, left him and his doubts both. His friends had supported his cowardly decision, and his sister had reduced my five-year presence in his life to a "phase." I was a fucking phase.

I had proof that I wasn't some experiment. We'd been saving for a house, dammit. A house. You don't save for a house with someone and then bail. What kind of monster was he? Especially knowing what had happened with Nick.

"He's not my brother," I said out of the blue, before I went absolutely crazy.

A look passed between us that I couldn't quite define before it was gone. "I know."

"You know now, or you knew then?"

"Both." He shook his head. "I thought I had you pegged. Maybe you were both just discreet, private people. But then I realized it wasn't about your relationship and downplaying PDAs. It was about being gay."

"What can I say? You've got me all figured out," I said glibly.

"Hardly. And now that I know you—"

"You don't know me," I said sharply. "You don't know anything about me."

He gave me a measured look in the ensuing silence, looking a bit taken aback by my vehemence. "All right," he said slowly. "Then my impression of you, after actually speaking to you, is that you don't seem to be the type to make any bones about who you are. I'm surprised you let him push you back into the closet when it was so hard to come out."

I was sorry I'd snapped at him. God, he understood being gay better than Trevor ever did.

"I understand him." I shrugged helplessly. "I understood him, anyway. It was hard to come out to my parents. My dad, anyway. My mom passed without ever knowing. I don't think he ever felt the same about me." God, why did just saying that make me feel a little choked up? "You don't want someone you love to go through that."

My phone buzzed on his desk, and he finally asked, "Are you going to get that?"

"Not really."

He looked at the screen and then laughed aloud. "Well, according to this log, someone named Asswipe called four times."

I grinned cheekily, glad for the distraction. "I changed a few things around in my address book." His amusement gave me the courage to answer the next time it buzzed.

"What?" I answered, as Jordan busied himself on his computer.

"What kind of game are you playing?" Trevor sounded a little pissed. "You said you'd give me five minutes, and then you run off with Channing. What could you possibly have to speak about with him?"

"Business, Mr. Smith, nothing for you to worry about."

"The firm has its own PI agency on retainer," he snapped. "What business could you possibly have with Channing?"

"Business," I repeated. "Did I stutter?"

"What kind of business? Business with his dick and your ass?"

My face went red hot. For God's sakes, I wasn't some sort of office ho, hopping from associate to associate, I ranted silently, forgetting that I had just had convenient buddy sex with Asher. Okay, fine. But that *still* didn't make me an office ho. Asher was clearly not an associate of the firm.

I wouldn't expect Trevor to understand the difference. I settled for, "I don't have to explain anything to you." *So there.*

He was silent for a moment before continuing. "You know he has a girlfriend, right? Fiancée, actually."

"Get bent, Trevor."

"Real mature." His voice went lower. "I'm only looking out for you."

I snorted. "Great job so far." I hoped my tone was sarcastic. Hoped I managed to minimize the hurt. His murmur said I didn't succeed.

"You looked good."

"Oh for heaven's sakes—"

"Come and talk to me. You know where my office is."

I knew that tone. Knew what it meant. After two years of wheedling, I knew exactly what that tone led to.

"You've got to be kidding me," I hissed. "Does Laura know about this?" Jordan had stopped pretending to work and was looking at me with his brow furrowed, fingers steepled.

"Know about what, exactly?" Trevor's tone went cold. Hard. And I suddenly knew what it was like to see him across the courtroom. It was what made him such a great lawyer. Such a great liar.

"Should I be more specific?"

"Do it and it's going to take more than Channing's secretary to stop me from coming in there."

"Don't tell me what to do!"

"Stop being such a brat."

"You wanted to talk? Let's talk. About the *one* thing that I care to talk to you about. I want Finn back," I snapped. "He's my dog."

"Dream on," he shot back. "I'd rather give him back to the pound."

"God, you're such a fucking—"

"Call me when you grow up, Mackenzie. You know where to find me. And tell that fucker Jordan where to find me after he's done playing Sir Lancelot. I can give him some tips on how you like to be—"

I hit the end button so hard I'm surprised I didn't crack the screen, then growled. It wasn't enough. Man, I missed the days of slamming home an actual receiver. I glared at the window, my fist threatening to clench the phone into dust.

Jordan tsked, looking at the thundercloud of my face. "Don't do it. This glass is so thick you'd only wind up needing a new phone."

"I can't believe I ever loved that moron." I began to pace, treading a path through Jordan's thick carpet. "He's being completely unreasonable and won't give me back my dog."

"So what are you going to do?"

"I know *exactly* what I'm going to do," I said, my face a mask of determination.

Jordan sat back in his chair. "Wow, I can practically smell the lock-picking equipment."

I made a face. "You heard him," I said, forgetting the fact that he, in fact, did not. "He's going to give him back to the pound."

"He's just being a dick," Jordan said, shaking his head. "He won't do that. Give him some time to cool down. We did, after all, just slam the door in his face."

"I don't have time for that idiot to cool down. He's determined to make sure I don't get my dog back. I may be a PI, but if he wants to hide Finn good enough, even *I* won't be able to find him."

"You need to go through legal channels," Jordan insisted, and really, what else did you expect a lawyer to say? "And will you please sit down? You're giving me a migraine."

I gave him a derisive look and flopped down in my original chair. "See where that's gotten me."

"Not in jail?" He pushed out of his chair with a smooth motion and rounded the desk.

He leaned back on the edge, folding his arms. I wondered briefly, off topic, if he knew how crazy sexy he looked. If he realized how ridiculously inappropriate our positions were—him at the perfect height to unbuckle his pants and me at the perfect height to.... Damn that Trevor for putting such ideas in my head (like they weren't there before). I *was* an office ho.

"Look," he said, raising his coffee cup to his lips and pausing to take a drink, "I think this thing with your dog could be moot anyway."

"Finn is *not* moot."

"The point is moot. Not your dog."

"Can we stop using the word moot?"

His laugh was tinged with frustration. "Will you listen to me?"

I shut up for a moment.

"The point would be... a nonfactor if you guys got back together."

"Apparently the rumor that straight guys don't listen is true," I said, rolling my eyes. "Let me refresh your memory. Me gay. Trevor straight. Me like boy. Boy like girl."

He rolled his eyes at my caveman impression. "Yeah, I heard what he said. I also heard what he didn't. You ever notice that people say the most when they're not talking at all?"

"Glad I was present the exact moment that you turned into Confucius."

"Fine, Mackenzie, use your sarcasm to keep me at arm's length. But you know I'm right. It doesn't sound like he's done with you. And you certainly don't look like you're done with him," he added.

I didn't debate the point because really, I was realizing something new and scary myself. I was *mad* at Trevor. Frustrated with him, certainly. He'd owed me more as his friend and boyfriend both. But he wasn't the one I desired right now. He wasn't the one who'd been on my mind all night. And he certainly wasn't the one I'd imagined fucking me at Asher's. Nor the one whose package I was covertly staring at, conveniently at eye level.

Suddenly his hand appeared in my line of vision as he laid it on mine and squeezed. My eyes shot up to his, and we looked at one another, his expression surely as confused as mine, before he yanked his hand away.

"Give him some time. Maybe he'll come around. I'll bet he's confused."

I gave him an eyebrow. My gaydar had the occasional fritz, but I knew I'd felt a vibe. "Seems to be going around."

He didn't pretend to misunderstand me and flushed adorably.

"Mr. Channing?" The voice was back.

Jordan answered the intercom, looking absolutely relieved to not have to field that one. "Yes, Susan?"

"Rachel just arrived in the lobby. Should I ask her to come up?"

"No," he said quickly. "I'm on my way down."

Feeling dismissed, I stood. I didn't offer my hand. It was just as well that I wouldn't be feeling the sparks from Jordan Channing's hand in mine again. What the hell was with me and straight guys lately?

"Want to walk with me to the lobby?" he asked, and I declined.

"I know my way down."

"Sure," he said, nodding. After a moment, he cocked his head and asked, "You're not going to listen to me, are you?"

Not a chance. The one guy *I* wanted to come running didn't even play for my team. I didn't say that, though. I waved instead on my way out. "Thanks for the save, Jordan."

6

I slammed the door of my pickup with certain force, and it threatened me back, nearly falling off. I was still pissed at Trevor but not pissed enough to miss lunch. I'd planned to be at my desk today, and to avoid Drew's evil eye when I usually sauntered out for lunch break, I'd brought my lunch with me.

Or at least that's what I called my sad sandwich and apple this morning. I shook out the paper sack, disbelieving I'd packed so light. Lunch always seemed less important in the morning, and you'd think I would've learned my lesson by now. Usually I was stuck staring at Drew's expertly packed meal—leftovers from the night before—complete with side dishes and silverware. I dug up an old bottle of apple juice from the cab and took a swig.

"Ugh!" Apparently old apple juice tasted a bit like urine.

I listened to random stations in my car, tapping my fingers on the steering wheel. At this rate, lunch wouldn't last long at all. I looked at my clock. I probably even had time to get in a little surveillance on the lovely Blakes. Suddenly the door of my cab opened, and Jordan stood there, holding my phone in his left hand.

"You forgot this."

"Thanks." I took it and tossed it on the dash.

His lips twisted wryly. "Glad to know it's so important to you. That I saved your very life."

My responding grin died as Jordan heaved himself up into my dusty cab. He shut the door behind him, squeaking on its rusted hinges, and settled down on the cracked vinyl.

"So what's up?"

I looked at him in confusion. "What *is* up? What happened to Rachel? Do you no longer need my services? A lot of my clients *do* just choose the put-her-feet-in-concrete-and-dump-her-in-a-lake option, but I never get used to it."

"Cute. Rachel came to tell me she has a meeting and can't meet for lunch."

I raised an eyebrow. "Should I be punching the clock, or what?"

"Nah, she really has a meeting. I think." He looked around, eyeing my cracked dash. "I came to find out what makes this so preferable to going to lunch with me. So far, I've got nothing."

I stared at him, nonplussed. I wasn't prepared to answer why, exactly, eating with him was such a horrible idea.

"I'm even paying," he said, his fingers resting lightly on the door handle. Which promptly fell off. "My God," he said, raising disbelieving eyes from the slain door handle to my defensive gaze. "Surely the PI business can't be that bad. Even in this economy."

"Is there something wrong with saving?" I demanded, taking a bite out of my PB and J sandwich. "And this is PB and J by *choice*. Not necessity."

He grinned.

"Besides, I was saving... we were saving. For a house." The sandwich suddenly tasted like dust in my mouth.

He looked sympathetic for like a millisecond before he was on my case again. "I hate to tell you, but Trevor makes more than enough for any kind of house you have in mind."

"I wanted us to be equals," I said defensively. "Especially in our own home. I have more than enough for the kind of house *I* had in mind, but Trevor.... Trevor has different tastes."

"You should teach a class in euphemisms. That your way of saying he's a stuck-up, social climbing snob?"

Even after all he'd done to me, I felt disloyal nodding.

He laughed softly, almost to himself. "And this is the person you're still pining for?"

"Pining may be too strong."

"Pining seems just about right," he said, almost affectionately. I thought if he was my brother, he might have ruffled my hair.

"It's so odd how he's just... moved on, you know? It's like some crazy part of me is waiting for him to come to his senses."

His smile was gentle. "And his senses would be loving you?"

I flushed. "I know I'm no prize, but... yes."

"I guess it depends on what the game is."

I think I almost gave myself whiplash turning to look at him that fast. I found him staring out at the passing traffic, expression closed, and I turned back to the front. Did he just say I was a prize? I couldn't take it anymore, and I figured there was only one solution, really, a novel idea. I had to ask. "Jordan, I don't like to assume anything, so I need to be frank."

"Shoot."

I could feel his eyes on me, measuring, assessing, but now I couldn't look in his direction. Otherwise, I would never believe I was about to ask Jordan, unbelievably gorgeous and put together Jordan, *straight* Jordan, if he was hitting on me.

"I'd like to think I'm a pretty good judge of character. And I don't think you're the kind of guy who would play with someone's feelings."

He nodded. "Yeah?"

"Nor do I think you're particularly oblivious, which leads me to believe you're well aware of all those signals you've been sending me." I waited for some sort of denial, but there was nothing. My heart started to trip a little off beat. Was I right, then?

He blushed, and suddenly *I* was embarrassed. What was wrong with me? Why did I put him on the spot like that?

"I have a fiancée."

"I know."

"I'm not gay."

I covered my eyes. "I *know*."

"Maybe I just like you. Maybe you should stop analyzing everything to death." The sunlight hit his eyes, making them impossibly beautiful.

"Do you wear contacts?" I blurted, almost mesmerized. It didn't really matter if he did, but as usual, I had to say the first thing that came to mind.

He reached through the open window and opened his door from the outside. As he exited my truck, he looked amused, as if he wanted to laugh. "I'll see you later, Mac."

"Am I fired?"

This time he did laugh. "Do you have no filter at all?" He walked two steps before turning back to my truck. "I may not be gay, but I think Trevor is absolutely crazy for walking away from you."

I went red as fire. "Thank you."

"I also think you can't put your whole life on hold for someone who may never come to his senses. I hate to tell you this, Mackenzie, but life is happening with or without you."

I went home in a sour mood. Jordan had a lot of nerve telling me how to live my life. Or worse yet, that I wasn't living my life. And pining for Trevor? Hah! I slammed my truck into park, and the transmission slipped a little, sending me into the parking stone with a little bump. Bessie was grousing again, and it brought Jordan's words into stark focus. So what if I could afford a better car? Didn't mean I wasn't living.

For the first time in a long while, I didn't enjoy the cool, dark interior of my apartment. Yeah, I could probably decorate a little. Clean a little.

Trevor had been the cleanbot in our relationship, often chasing after me with a dust rag and broom in order to keep my place presentable. I'd told him to relax, that it wasn't important to me, but try telling that to a guy who alphabetized his cereal. I winced, rubbing my neck. I could see four pizza boxes next to the garbage can —the overfilled garbage can. When was the last time I'd cooked a meal? Or eaten more than the limp, frozen vegetables that Lean Cuisine deemed a serving?

I couldn't hold Trevor responsible for the disaster that was my apartment and my diet. Or lack thereof. I rubbed a hand over my still-flat stomach. No definition anymore, but still not pouchy. Yet.

I stuffed a Pop-Tarts pastry in my mouth as I gathered my gloves and bleach. Oh well. Good-bye, abs. Three bags of trash, twelve soda cans, eighteen beer bottles and an hour later, I could see wood surfaces. Nice wood surfaces. I eyed my dining room table with a can of lemon Pledge but decided enough was enough.

My phone chirped out "Who Let the Dogs Out," interrupting the music Bluetooth technology had magically been piping through my speakers. I was a bit outraged that someone would dare interrupt my old-school Madonna marathon, and my greeting was a bit gruff.

"What?"

"'Bout time you answered my call. God knows you never call me back."

"Hello to you too, Dad."

"I've been trying to reach you for two days," he groused. "You never call me."

Good Lord, sometimes it pays to let your phone go to voice mail. I could be listening to "Material Girl" right now. "What are you up to?"

"Fixing that TV in the den."

"What's wrong with it?"

My dad has never found an appliance he can't fix. Only now that he's retired, his attention span is ridiculously short, and he never finishes any of the projects he starts. We have a strange pseudo Lowe's going on in his backyard—any appliance you need, halfway repaired.

"It's runs for about an hour before going out completely. You know what that sounds like?"

"Sounds like the picture tube to me." Couldn't believe he still had a TV with a picture tube, but that's what it sounded like.

"Exactly." His voice sounded muffled, like he was behind it this very minute. "I'm thinking about getting rid of the whole thing."

"You've had it for a long time. Since I was like fifteen."

"Longer than that, probably. Been thinking about one of those flat screen deals. You have to have a specific type of TV for that HD business, don't you?"

"Yes, Dad. You need a TV with HD capability." I decided to go ahead and attack the table and sprayed a fine film of Pledge across the top.

"I don't know how I'd get it out of here, though," he continued. "This thing is huge."

"I think they'll take the TV out for you if you have another delivered."

"Would you go with Best Buy or Walmart?"

I was silent for a moment, uncharacteristically frustrated. There was no reason to get brand new. This was it between my dad and I. Meaningless conversation and talk of repairing things. When I retired from the force, that had been even one less thing for us to converse about. Sometimes I wished we could have a conversation about something that really mattered. But that just wouldn't be Joe Williams's style. He had a simple name for a plain, straightforward guy. And even though he hadn't exactly enjoyed my "coming out," he'd still accepted me the best he could.

I humored him. "You know I love Wally World. You going this weekend? I could give you a hand."

Please say no, I prayed.

"Nah, I'm going fishing with Robby. We're going down to the 'glades and make a day of it. You should come," he added, almost like an afterthought.

"I'm good," I said wryly. The only thing more painful than hanging out with my dad was hanging out with my dad and Robert. Fishing used to be fun before my dad learned I was gay and Robert became a dick. Besides the fact that he insisted on calling me Apple because of my nickname, "Mac." When my mother had done it, it had been endearing. But my little brother? Oh, man, the annoyance. Pair that nickname with the fruit cracks, and I was just about done.

"Do you know how long it's been since all of us got together on the water?"

"Dear God, not the boat."

Dad had gotten the boat from Uncle Brennan, a collector of everything and anything with an engine. Uncle Brennan had lived about an hour away all my life, giving Robert and I plenty of time to hang out in his yard and play with things we shouldn't. We'd driven the un-drivable, everything from forklifts to ATVs, and had nearly given our mother fits worrying over us. If I had a nickel for every bone that Robert and I had broken, I'd be able to retire for real. Uncle Brennan had also been a mechanic, which made hanging out at his garage the ultimate thrill. There was nothing cooler to two little boys than hanging out with an uncle who collected and built racecars. He would be horrified if he could see Bessie.

"I gave your Uncle Brennan back the boat. You would know that if you called me more often."

"You loved that boat."

"It was a water hazard. It was rusting straight through. Not the kind of boat you want to take to Alligator Alley."

I laughed. "You finally afraid of those alligators, old man?"

"It'll take a lot more than a gator to get rid of me, boy."

"I don't doubt it."

"So, you busy or what? It would do an old man good to see his boys doing something together." He paused to let it sink in and then pushed harder. "You know I'm getting on up in age."

He may be getting older, but he had still obviously completed the mandatory requirements for Wielding Guilt for Parents 101. I grunted my agreement, and he finally let me off the phone. I swiped at the forgotten Pledge in hard concentric circles, in a better mood but dreading the weekend. God knew I loved my family, but the thought of spending my hard-earned weekend with them was enough to make me scrub the wood off that table.

7

I pushed my aviators on top of my head and set the tiny pair of binoculars to my eyes. Even though I was sitting there making money (my favorite type of sitting), I was irritated. And as I squinted at the closed door of her house, I realized the reason was a combination of three things: it was the crack of dawn (to me), I was working, and Jordan was inside with this Rachel person doing God knows what. Why the last should bother me, I didn't care to explore. Why images of them would torture me, I had not a cl—all right, I knew why. I wanted him for myself.

Not for a relationship, and not for long. Love could keep all her hearts and flowers and fake crap to herself. No, I wasn't looking for someone to share my breakfast table with. I wanted him in my bed, all long legs and soft, inviting eyes. He would look at me with that slightly amused expression and a raised brow and ask, "What are you waiting for?" The fact that my dream was impossible didn't dampen my spirits or my erection, and Drew's voice startled me out of my very pleasant musings.

"So what's the deal with this chick?" Drew's voice sounded close in my ear, and I adjusted the volume of my phone.

"Top of the morning to you too," I said. "She's Jordan's fiancée. A real business type, legal shark." Right now, Legal Shark's yard was quiet and empty, and I grabbed a video shot of the scene. "It's 8:40 a.m.," I murmured into the device.

"I can't believe you're up this early."

"*You* can't believe it? If I had to come in to the office, I would be setting up a hologram of myself right now."

He laughed. "And it would probably do more work than you usually do."

"Shut it, Rodriguez."

A woman in a short black dress elbowed open the front door, her hands full with two briefcase-type bags and a purse. I realized I was looking at her with a critical eye, almost as one would a rival, but I couldn't help myself. She was flawless from the top of her layered haircut to the perfectly manicured claws that hit her key remote. I watched the red bottoms of her black stilettos disappear into her car and threw my car in gear.

"She's on the move," I said. "And so am I."

"Don't forget we have to meet with McGarrett at one o'clock." When I didn't say anything, he continued. "Don't flake on me again," he warned, and I groaned.

My phone buzzed again, and Jordan's name flashed on the screen. "Gotta go," I said even as Drew was complaining, and clicked over. "Shit," I said as the white Beemer flew past me.

"Is that the way you answer the phone?" Jordan's amused voice filled my truck as I put him on speaker and pulled out into the street. I was going to need both hands for this.

"Yeah, pretty much."

"She just left," he informed me.

"Was that the white blur I saw?"

The Beemer made a high-speed turn and flew around the corner.

"Shit!" I exclaimed again.

If they'd ever seen any sort of TV at all, everyone knew the rules for following another car. Not close enough to get noticed, but not far enough to lose your prey. Actually doing it was another story. This

Rachel character was in one hell of a hurry. My beat-up truck cried as I sped after her.

"Did I mention she drives like a bat out of hell?"

"No, you didn't. Where is she supposed to be heading? Bank robbery?"

"She's supposed to be going to work." I heard the clatter of dishes on his end and had a vision of him puttering around in the kitchen on his day off. I was less interested in what I was supposed to focus on (my prey) and more interested in what he was wearing. I tried to concentrate. "Where does she work?"

He rattled off an address that gave me a vague idea of where I was supposed to be going. "You need me to repeat?"

"I'm good."

"I hope you're not writing this down while you're driving."

"You worried about me?"

"Hardly."

His dry tone made me smile, and I realized it was the first time I'd done that today. I couldn't hold back my curiosity a second longer. "So what are you doing?"

He paused but answered gamely. "Putting my coffee mug in the sink. Exciting stuff, huh?"

"It's no high-speed car chase, but whatever."

The sound of his laughter made my girly insides quiver a little. I could think of no further reason to hold him on the phone, and I concluded the conversation reluctantly. "I'll be able to e-mail you the uploaded video and a report of what I found. Or I can deliver it if you don't want the information electronically."

"I'd rather you deliver it," he said quickly.

My eyebrows shot up, and I smiled. He was probably blushing at how that sounded. I wanted to bang my head on the steering wheel. I'd found the perfect guy—smart, funny, adorable, and on a side note, good looking—and he didn't play for my team. God, I wanted to know what could happen if Jordan would relax and let things happen. But I couldn't begrudge him his preference. How would I feel if someone told me to relax and let things happen with a woman? *Uh-uh, girlfriend.*

"I probably don't even have anything to worry about." He stopped short and started again. "Everything's still okay, right?"

I gunned it onto the main road, tires squealing a little. The Beemer made a quick U-turn, and I groaned. U-turns were never good. U-turns meant a change in pattern, a change from the normal routine. Excepting poorly designed roads, no one scheduled regular U-turns into her daily routine. She was coming toward me, but all I could see through her tinted windows was a pair of huge dark shades perched on what I assumed was her pale face.

"Perfect," I said and winced. "I gotta run." I didn't wait for a response, but tossed the phone in the cup holder and made a sharp U-turn.

Bessie groaned.

I made it around the next bend just in time to see the tail end of the BMW fishtail onto I-95. I kept my eye fixed on her car while trying to navigate traffic, sliding neatly into her lane behind two smaller cars. They were big enough for a distraction between us but not too tall for me to lose her. She suddenly whipped into the HOV lane, and I glanced at my watch. The lane was restricted for another two hours, and I shook my head as she surged ahead. The highway crested into a high curve, and I watched her pull away with regret.

I wasn't the police anymore, and I wasn't looking to be stopped by them either. Nor was I going to get killed trying to see where this woman was headed. But it damn sure wasn't to work. Coral Gables was the other way. It didn't look good for Jordan, and I felt horrible that my first thought was pleasure. He would be devastated. *And then you'll move in for the kill.*

"For God's sakes," I snapped at my wreckage of a conscience. But no matter how much I scolded myself, I couldn't deny that I wanted Rachel to be a fucking dirty cheater.

I pulled off the next exit and coasted to a stop in a gas stationBP parking lot. I bought a Coke Zero and a bag of Fritos and wrote my report in my truck, muttering under my breath the entire time. I was a professional, and I didn't like to lose my prey. But the woman drove like a fucking stunt driver. Not to mention all the illegal turns and breaking the speed limit on every street and interstate she'd been on. I'd hand off the next shift to Drew—the Mazda would do a better job keeping up with her than my poor old girl.

I started up Bessie to coughing and sputtering. "No, no, no." I groaned as I tried to crank it up again. "Don't do this now."

In response, she coughed and died.

8

"You want to tell me again why we're going to a pub again?" I groused, shoving my hands deeper into the pockets of my stonewashed Rocco jeans. The heat was out full force even though the sun had gone down long ago. "Or why you parked on the moon?"

My brother was one of those freaks who parked in the last spot on the lot to get every crumb of exercise possible. His flat stomach and fit physique really put a cramp in my cop and donut cracks.

"We're going to the pub because Darcy is Irish. Don't give me crap, Apple. Today was the second time I had to pick you up this week."

"Can I help it that Bessie needed a break?"

"Don't even get me started on that stupid heap. I'm still not sure why I invited you," he grumbled.

To be honest, I wasn't either. I wasn't even sure why I accepted. Robert and I were typical siblings—we loved hard, teased mercilessly, and kicked the shit out of anyone who messed with the other. Even given all that, we rarely hung out. For starters, he was a pesky little brother and thusly should go where *all* pesky little brothers should go —*Deep Space Nine*. I'd settle for a black hole, a big one, one with no phone service or Internet to contact me. Growing up, he'd always been two years younger and light-years more talented. He'd seemed determined to do everything I did, only he did it better.

When I played football, my butt warmed the bench more than the heat of the sun. When my little brother finally hit ninth grade, what sport did he try out for? The little punk was the first freshman in our high school's history to make varsity. I'd been ridiculously proud of him and annoyed at the same time. I'd doggedly kept after it, playing my hardest and running my fastest, because at least when my dad came to Robert's football games, he saw me too. I'd given it up after I fumbled the winning catch in our homecoming game. At least they'd called it a fumble on the ride home with an ice pack pressed to my nose. I'd called it getting hit in the face with four seconds left on the clock.

For another, our groups of friends are different. Well, he has a group of friends, anyway. I think counting Asher and Drew as a group is taking liberties. Besides, that would mean I've slept with exactly fifty percent of my friends, and I don't like those odds. Robert's group of friends was younger, wilder, and rowdier. And no, I don't remember the moment I turned eighty. A good time to his crew usually involved football, yelling, fighting, and a lot of alcohol.

Simply put, we just had nothing in common. Other than his lifetime supply of Xerox on my life, that is. The only thing worse than someone copying you is someone doing it better. I graduated fourth in my class from the Academy—he finished second. By the time I'd retired with three commendations, he'd just hit his tenth year with four. I retired because of a bullshit injury and Robert was still out there saving the world. He'd given our father his first (and only) grandchild, and I'd announced I was gay. Maybe it sounds like I resent my brother. I don't. But if he comes home with the perfect man and announces he's gay, I'm going to kill him. That's after my dad does, of course.

No, going to a pub with a group of Robert's friends was not my idea of a good time. But he'd sworn to me up and down that it would just be Tao and Darcy, his old buddy from high school. Not John, Michael, Bobby, or Trace. Not Steve, who'd never met a chick he didn't like, or Travis, who'd never met a drink he didn't like. Even a hermit like me could handle four or five people.

The pub was a hub of activity, even on such a busy street. A pennant-shaped sign with old scripted writing declared it "Dubhlainn's," an Irish pub established since 1934. I tried to mouth the Gaelic words underneath, but the symbols and slashes finally got the best of me and I shrugged. The interior of the pub was much as I'd expected—tables and chairs in various shades of dark green with a green tartan plaid floor. The bar was the focal point of the room, with high-backed chairs all around. I looked at the various pieces of Irish paraphernalia littering the walls and beams while Robert scanned the crowd.

"There." He suddenly pointed and waved before wading through the crowd.

I had no choice but to follow or be left by the chalkboard sign declaring it three dollar Guinness night. I hurried so I wouldn't lose sight of him in the dark atmosphere, and we headed toward the high tables in the back.

I waved at Drew, Tao, and Asher before shaking the hand of the red-haired guy sitting next to them. His grip was strong, but then again so was he. He had to be at least six foot two and looked like he could bench press me. He held my hand too long, and I pretended not to notice, sliding into a seat next to Drew. I scanned my brain quickly to see if Robert had mentioned this being a setup of some kind. God knew I didn't always listen when he was rambling on.

"Hey, lover," Asher said flippantly, giving me a flirty wave.

I ignored him, but the flush on my face apparently spoke volumes. "Hey, Tao. Drew."

Drew narrowed his eyes at us both before rolling them. "Good God. Not again."

"Not again, what?" my brother asked, sitting on the chair with it facing backward. He looked at my face and then scrunched his own. "Could we not talk about you and your sex at the table?"

"I didn't bring it up," I pointed out, wishing my face would cool off.

"What can I say?" Asher shrugged. "I can't get enough of Mac's sweet—"

"*Jay-sus*!" Robert exclaimed, plugging his ears.

Drew pointed a finger at me. "Mac, I still have some flea dip from last time."

Asher threatened to dip his pinky in Drew's drink, which earned him a good hand twisting that I watched with a smirk. Good, I thought as he grabbed his hand and glared at Drew. The fool had to take out a billboard every time we had casual sex.

"God, I almost hesitate to introduce you to the zoo," Robert said to Big Red, who chuckled.

"I've seen worse."

"Everyone, this is Darcy." He pointed at the other side of the table. "This is Drew and my partner, Tao." They both nodded as Robert glared at the two of us. "Ho number one here is Asher. And ho number two over here is my brother, Mackenzie."

"Tao?" I asked sweetly. "Can I borrow your service revolver?"

Tao continued to sip his beer calmly, the sanguine look never leaving his face. He always got that look when his wife let him out of the house. Usually his nights involved baby diaper/feeding/bathing/rocking duty with their newborn. That is unless he and my brother worked the night shift, in which case his mornings were consumed with the same. Suffice to say, his wife was a woman who fully believed in an equal partnership. In layman's terms, a lot of diaper duty. At this point, Tao wouldn't mind if we did the electric slide on his squad car. He was *going* to enjoy his night off.

"Rounds are on me," Darcy offered. "We're having Guinness, but I can get something else if you like."

It was odd, but it seemed like he was talking only to me.

"Guinness is fine," I answered for both of us, and he grinned.

When he disappeared toward the bar, I hit my brother in the arm. "What the hell?"

"What?" he asked defensively. "You're gay. He's gay. I figured—"

"That we should start a club? Jeez, Robby, I'm not looking for a setup. I told you that."

"I thought it would help. I'm tired of seeing you mope over this Trevor asshole." He glanced around as if looking out for Darcy's return and continued in a lowered voice. "It's not like I set you up with a bum. He's a firefighter down at firehouse 144. He's the resident cook, and I hear he makes a mean lasagna."

I looked at him with an open mouth even as that asshole Asher started laughing. "Who are you, freaking Chuck Woollery?"

"Who the hell is that?"

"That host on *Love Connection*," Asher managed.

"Mac, I don't have time for your obscure game-show trivia. He'll be coming back in a minute," Robert hissed. "Now look, their boys and our boys went out for drinks after the PD/FD baseball tournament, and he might have mentioned he just got out of a relationship. Someone mentioned how he likes pretty boys, and your name came up." He eyeballed me critically. "I don't see it, but whatever."

I wanted to sock him good. "Glad to know a lot of thought went into this. But you can tell Big Red that I'm not interested." Someone with his face and build ought to spend the whole night working that one out. I pictured him looking dumbly in the mirror. *Someone's not attracted to... me? What*?

"God, you're such a prick."

I ignored this and tacked on, "And I don't mope," for good measure.

"That's all you do! Moping and moaning over someone who got over you as easily as wiping shit off his shoe. It's pathetic."

"You're pathetic," I shot back. "Why don't you get your own life? God, I'm just lucky you're not gay. You'd probably steal my boyfriend!"

"First you'd have to get one," he snapped.

"That's harsh."

"What you said wasn't?"

"You can't rush me out of my feelings," I snapped. "I'm sorry that you're tired of me being sad. Maybe we should see less of each other."

"Is that even possible?" he muttered, and I looked at him sharply.

"What is that supposed to mean?"

"You're a smart guy, Mac," he said. "You figure it out."

A brief silence descended upon the table. I folded my arms and let the awkward moment extend. I saw no reason to break it.

"This is why guys don't talk," Drew sighed.

I took a deep breath and tried to calm myself. In his own iron-fisted, heavy-handed way, he was trying to help. "Robby. I'm trying my best to get over Trevor in my own way. I'm sorry if that doesn't align with your master plan."

He shrugged. "You call sleeping with Asher exorcising your demons?"

"That's none of your business. I don't ask you about any of the hoes that walk in and out your revolving fucking door." It was on my tongue to say *that's why Case is so messed up*, but even *I* found that appalling and unforgiveable. My nephew's issues were his own to work out, not something to be used to win an argument.

"You're such a selfish jerk. Always have been. Probably why Trevor never—"

I slammed my hands against the table. "Don't you say it. Don't you dare lay the blame for that piece-of-shit relationship at my door."

"Why not?" Robert shrugged. "You left him, didn't you? Just like everyone else. I'm just surprised it lasted as long as it did."

"Enough!" Tao snapped. "You two are ruining my buzz."

"For real," Asher piped in. Unhelpful as usual. "Mac, you damn sure dish it, so you'd better be prepared to take it. Rob, you shouldn't have set him up, and you know it. And blaming him for Trevor's shit? Low blow, dude."

"Apologize," Tao said. When we didn't leap to his bidding, he snapped, "Now."

So we did.

Darcy came back to a table of absolute silence, but luckily he was the type of guy who would need OnStar to find a clue. He sat down, passing out drinks and limes, and told us a joke the shockingly Irish bartender had told him. Even when it met with halfhearted laughter, he followed it up with a hilarious story from high school. I glared at Robert even more, if possible. He was funny, cute, and available? *And gay*, I added to my fertile mind. Although that didn't seem to be too important to me lately.

Before long, Darcy's warm stories and funny nature had us all laughing. They kept the beer flowing, and before long, I realized that, damn, I'd had a good time. Damn that Robert.

Tao was the first to break up the party. "It's getting late, guys, and I'm not twenty-five anymore."

"Buzzkill," I said, inciting the rest of the table to boo him. But he was right, as I glanced down at my phone. It was close to 2:00 a.m. It was all well and good to party like a rock star as long as one remembered that rock stars didn't have jobs.

"I'm Audi too," Drew said, pushing back the bowl of nuts he'd refused to share. I didn't know how many times he would say that as his exit line before he believed me that it wasn't cool.

"Me too, meesh too," Asher slurred. "Gots to go. Gimme keys, Tao."

Tao gave him a look. "You gotta be kidding me."

"I'll take back rudds. Rudds." He swallowed twice and tried again. "Rudds!"

"Well, then that's settled." Tao clapped his hands. "Now. Who's going to warn all the people on the back roads?"

"*And* I'll drive slooowsh." He looked lost for a minute. "Slooowsh. Such an odd word."

"Fool. That's because it's not a word." I slapped the back of his head fondly. "You went out drinking with two cops and a fireman. If you try to drive that car, you won't be just DUI, you'll be D-U-M-B."

"Gimmee," he said, lunging for his keys and grabbing them from Tao.

"Nice try," Drew said, plucking the keys out of his hand. "Come on, lush, I already called a cab for both of us. Mac, meeting at ten?"

"I'm going to be working on my truck. For now, our morning appointments are on you."

Drew glowered at me.

"I know cars," Darcy offered, and I gave him a blank look. "And trucks. Well, I suppose trucks are cars, but...."

"Thank you for your offer," I said before the poor man stuttered himself into the next century. "But I'm pretty handy myself."

I wasn't. But I always thought I was up for DIY before I actually started the task. Besides, the last thing I needed was six foot four of fireman working in my driveway, shirtless... sweaty.... The image that materialized in my mind didn't have red hair. Fantasy Jordan wielded the wrench like a pro, the musculature in his back working under tanned, satiny skin. I tracked a droplet down his back, snaking down the hard plane and disappearing into his shorts.

"Grrr," I growled audibly, frustrated. I didn't know what his rear looked like. But it was *my* fantasy, after all.

To oblige me, he hooked his thumbs in the waistband and eased them down, down far enough to see the muscled globes, perfectly shaped and toned, with enough plumpness to warrant a good slap. I sighed. All this time I'd imagined Jordan fucking me. How small minded. What narrow vision. This was an ass to fuck. To *bite*—

"Mac?"

I looked up to find most of the table staring at me. The delicious taste of suntanned, dewy skin disappeared, and I tasted a bitter tang. My teeth were sunk clear into one of the limes, peel and all.

I cleared my throat. "Sorry about that."

"Okay, this blind date is officially over," my brother grumbled. "Growling and biting limes... goddamn, I'm good, but I'm not a magician."

I sent him a glare that should have had him sizzling like a skillet meal at Applebee's and scooted off my stool. "Bathroom," I announced to no one in particular.

The line outside of the bathroom was long enough to make me gnash my teeth, but I'd never been keen on pissing on a bush like a shepherd if I could help it. So I waited, jiggling foot to foot every now and again and trying not to gawk at the couple in front of me, making use of their wait time by exploring each other's jean pockets. For change, probably. I turned slightly to the side to avoid the show, and some dude behind me with spiky hair decided the back of my head looked friendly enough.

"Wassup, dude?" was all he managed before I turned back to the Spice channel in front of me.

"They're going at it, huh?" Spiky Hair whispered close to my ear, leaving a trace of booze-scented air behind.

I pulled out my phone and tried to look industrious. I scrolled through my contacts, adding details I could have lived without. When I came to Jordan's name, I paused. Pressed the arrow for call. Pressed End quickly.

"What the hell are you doing?" I shook my head at my own audacity. "Calling a client at a bar? Randomly?"

At—" I checked my watch "—2:00 a.m.?"

We're not friends. There's not even the possibility of more. I lectured myself sternly as the line moved by three people. Spiky Hair took advantage of the line shift to brush against my ass, and I gave him a narrowed eye. He held up his hands innocently, blinking rapidly.

One call and I'd banish him from my mind. *You can even make it about business*, I rationalized. I still hadn't told him about Rachel's strange behavior this morning. I beamed at my own ingenuity and pressed his name on the screen.

After a few rings, he answered, his voice husky and low. "Channing."

Oh jeez, I was in trouble. I ignored the tight clench of my stomach and tried to answer the phone like a functioning human being. "It's Mackenzie," I offered and then smacked myself in the forehead. *Lame.* Unless his phone was from the Stone Age, it had caller ID.

"I know who it is," he said, and this time I could hear the amusement in his voice. "Do you know what time it is?"

"It's only two o'clock, grandpop."

He made a sound halfway between a groan and a laugh. "Talk to me when *you* have a six thirty hearing."

I was ridiculously glad I had something to tell him so I could keep him on the phone. "I figured I'd give you an update about today."

"Right now?" His voice sounded smothered by the pillow, and I knew I was being rude. But I didn't want to let him go.

"I'll be quick."

"Hmmmph." Resigned sigh. Then silence.

"Jordan. Jordan!"

"What?" he croaked.

"You fell asleep."

"All right, all right," he groused. "Go ahead. Give your bloody update."

"I don't know where she went, but she wasn't going to work."

"What happened?"

"I lost her somewhere on the freeway."

His reaction was unexpected. He burst out laughing. "Please tell me you weren't following her in that hunk of junk you call a truck."

"Don't laugh at me, Jordan." Despite my words, I could feel a smile tugging at my lips. "I couldn't have caught that woman on the back of a silver bullet."

"You couldn't catch a cold in that truck."

"You haven't even ridden in it," I protested. "She's been good to me."

"She must be nearby," he deadpanned. "Think she's listening?"

"Actually, she's not working right now," I said archly. "She's resting in my driveway."

His guffaw made the annoyance of Bessie almost bearable. I'd try to remember this feeling when I tried to jump-start her in the morning.

Another line shift had Spiky Hair, aka Handsy, bumping into my butt again, hands outstretched.

"Hands off," I barked in my best cop voice, and suddenly I had a wide berth. I knew that he'd felt my gun—the asshole had gotten a real good feel this time. "And no, I'm not just happy to see you."

"Sorry," he said, holding up his hands placatingly.

"Where *are* you?" Jordan asked curiously, bringing me back to my conversation.

"A pub," I said, turning back to the front. "My brother helped tow my truck home, so I owed him. When he invited me out, I felt too guilty not to go."

"I hear you. Guilt is the only reason I'm using a week of vacation time for the annual family ski trip this year."

"Oh, the hardship, Channing."

"I'm from Dearborn, not Vail."

That made me smile. "Still. Skiing sounds so glam to me. Probably because I've only seen snow one time."

"Yeah?"

"Yeah. I spent Christmas with my grandmother one year in Ohio. She woke Robby and I up at three in the morning and said, 'It's snowin' boys. First snow of the season, just for my two angels."

"She sounds wonderful."

"She was." It seemed like everything soft and wonderful and miraculous came from my mother's side of the family. My grandmother from my father's side, still alive and kickin', that old bat used to take a switch to my hide regularly. Before I got too melancholy, I finished the story. "I went outside and said, 'so this is snow.' And then I dashed back inside to burrow under the covers for the rest of my visit."

He laughed. "Pansy Florida boys."

"You're next," Spiky Hair said helpfully, still maintaining his distance, and I growled.

"Damn. I gotta go, my turn in the john."

"Okay. Have... fun?"

"Cute, Channing."

I was surprised to realize I didn't want to hang up. Didn't want to end the connection. It suddenly struck me that I'd rather be sitting at his kitchen table, talking more about the snow and our families, than go back out in the pub with the boys. I didn't want to be anywhere else right now, or be talking to anyone else. It was sobering.

"I'll call you with more news," I said, my tone businesslike.

"You know, we're having a barbecue on Saturday. Sort of a welcome to the firm kind of thing for a new associate. You should come."

"Why?"

"Why not?"

I stared at the phone for a minute, letting all the reasons tick by in my head. I could come up with ten so far, the least of which being that I couldn't be around Jordan for three seconds without my body responding to all that eye candy. I also found lawyers rather dry. Stuffy. And the only thing that would be worse than listening to an evening of stuffy conversation would be doing it sporting a hard-on. Besides, Trevor might show up, and then I'd have to push him into the barbecue pit. I'd imagine the penalty would be high for doing something like that.

"Thanks for the invite, but I'm going to have to decline."

"It would certainly be a good opportunity for you to observe Rachel. She'll be there."

"So this would be a work thing?" I asked, my eyebrows arched even though he couldn't see me.

"No. Not exactly." He sounded adorably flustered. "Just think on it, all right?"

I thought on it all right. I thought about it as I reentered the smoky pub and parked my butt on a stool at the bar. I thought about it clear into my third Guinness and my long walk to the car, where I leaned on the bumper of Robert's Charger, smoking my one cigarette of the day. *One*, I reminded myself as I almost gave my fingertips second degree burns trying to make it last.

The neighborhood wasn't the best, but I couldn't rouse myself to be suspicious. I felt smooth inside. Liquid. Relaxed. It was a good night to fuck. I shook my head quickly to clear it. No, since I wasn't getting laid, I supposed it would be better to think of something benign. Hmmm, it was a good night to sleep in a hammock with a hat over your face. There.

I saw Robert approaching from the corner of my eye and waved lazily. "Over here."

"I see you." He stopped in front of me, neon lights from the corner store drawing crazy patterns on his face. "You should have waited inside. It's dangerous out here."

"Nobody told you to park on the corner of Murder and Rapeville. Besides—" I patted my back hip. "—I'm carrying."

"Still."

"Thank you, Officer Busybody, but I was a cop too. I'm good."

He made no mention of my leg or why I might not be as good as I was. "I said good-bye to Darcy."

"He *is* your friend." I blew a smoke ring out of the corner of my mouth by twitching my lips, not turning my head. I knew he got some in his face, but he didn't flinch.

"He's a nice guy, Mac. Someone who wouldn't break your heart like that... that—"

"Jackass? Dumbass? Loser?"

His lips quirked. "No lack of nouns, huh?"

"You got it."

"I got his card for you. Just in case."

"Since when do firemen have cards?" I grinned a little. "Does it have a little cartoon dancing fire? Call us at 9-1-1 when you smell something burning? Visit us online at whyareyoustillinthehouse dot com?"

"He fixes computers on the side." He held up a card between two fingertips, and I glared a little.

He stared back at me, his hazel eyes so much like my own it was scary. I knew that look too. Steady and determined. I sighed and then smiled a little. He was a bonehead, but he was still my brother. Still cared about me, even when I'd told him I was gay. "Accepted me" would be a mild term for it. Hell, he set me up on a date, my objections aside. I didn't know whether it was the Guinness or the earlier nostalgia from reminiscing about Grandma, but I was all out of fight. I took it from his fingertips and slid it into my hip pocket.

He smiled. "Ready?"

"You sure you're green lighted to drive, Chief?"

And that's as long as our truce lasted.

He held out a finger. "A, stop calling me Chief. You always do that when you're buzzed." Another finger shot up to join the first. "B, I had one beer. And three, put that damned thing out before you burn your fingers."

"It's C. Not three," I murmured, sliding into the car. I tossed what was basically smoldering ash by this point onto the pavement, and the wind blew it apart gently.

"What?"

"Nothing." I slammed the car door.

"You know that stuff is pure poison," he said, tuning the radio to something low and country. Someone murmuring something about a dirt country road, with smoke blowing out the windows and cold beer in the console. *Memory lane up in the headlights....*

I closed my eyes a little and then a lot, molding my body into the leather.

"I don't know why you do hurtful things to yourself." I felt his hands buckle my seat belt with a *click*.

Losing Nicholas. Loving Trevor for all that wasted time. Letting myself fall in like with Jordan. Setting myself up for heartbreak.

"Who knows why we do the things we do," I murmured. I was no longer talking about just the smoking.

My brother isn't always the lunkhead I make him out to be. He left it alone.

9

"Go around!" I shouted at the impatient car behind me, and as if that was the signal the idiot driver was waiting for, he zoomed around my truck. I don't know how much more of a sign he needed—the flat tire and me standing outside with my hair on end really ought to have done it.

"Hello, this is Lorna with AAA. How can I help you?"

You can stop being so damn perky. "Yeah, I need a tow."

"I'd be happy to help you with that, sir. Are you in a safe place?"

I snorted. "Not really."

"Would you like me to send the police to your location?"

My luck, it'd be Robert. "No!" I practically shouted and then added a saner "No, thank you."

I heard the cheerful clatter of the keyboard as she keyed in something. "And how are you doing this fine day?"

I pulled the phone out from my damp neck and looked at it. "Seriously? I'm stuck in an intersection in the middle of buttcrack and who knows where, and the only good thing is that I'll probably be killed from the idiot drivers waiting two seconds before they're about to smash into my bumper before swerving over. There! Another just did it!" I shook my fist at the offender even as I heard silence in my ear.

Then clickety-clickety-clack typing began again. *Customer has a bad attitude. Like a junkyard dog,* I imagined her typing. To her credit, Lorna was just as pleasant, if hesitant, as she got the rest of my required information. I was as polite as possible to make up for my outburst, but it was too late. I'd let up the window shade to my crazy for just a second, and once you see the crazy, you can't go back. She promised me a ninety-minute window that had me grinding my teeth, and we disconnected, each equally relieved to be done with the other.

I checked my phone battery before dialing another number quickly. It took me three tries, but I finally got through to Drew.

"How long do you think you'll be?"

"Couple hours, maybe? I don't have a spare. Probably have her towed."

"You need a ride?" I heard the *bing, bing, bing* of his car as he stuck the key in the ignition and slammed the door.

"No, I'm not too far. You take care of the Blakes."

"Will do. I'm on my way to Mrs. Blake's yoga class. They should be out in twenty minutes."

"No downward dog jokes right now, Drew. I'm not in the mood."

He laughed. "Poor baby. Call me if you need me."

"You know I will."

I made three more calls while I sat in the stuffy cab of my truck waiting on AAA. Two were return calls and a message for Jordan cancelling our two o'clock. By the time I'd cleaned up my cab and locked all my valuables in my silver cargo box, I was calmer. I heard a smooth engine pull up behind me and honk. Miserable cur.

I didn't look up until the car honked again, and I swallowed the curse working its way out of my mouth. "Go arou—"

The hot sun reflected off the silver car's gleaming paint, slick and shimmery, and I had to shade my eyes briefly before I could see the driver. Even though I fixed my face in a frown, waiting for his approach, I couldn't deny my heart gave an eager thump. He looked, quite simply put, delicious—his black and charcoal gray argyle shirt a perfect complement to flawlessly tailored black slacks. He looked like he'd just left court—probably had—and come straight to help me out.

I gave him the universal greeting of gratitude. "What are you doing here?"

Jordan gave me a look that said I wasn't too bright. "I figured, despite your pointed, *numerous* protests on my voice mail, that you might need a ride."

All right, so I had a hard time asking for help. So what?

"I'm getting it towed. No big.""

The look remained. "You don't have a spare?"

"If I had a spare, would I be...." I took a deep, cleansing breath. "No."

He didn't say a word about how irresponsible that was. And he didn't know the half of it. I didn't even have my jack. I wasn't about to volunteer that little bit of information. Not that he appeared to be waiting for my excuses. He had already squatted down by the tire, and was currently flicking a finger across the flayed tred..

I let the heavy cargo lid fall and joined him in the front. "You know something about tires?"

"No." He smiled, and I was briefly entranced by his movie-star teeth. "But I can lean in and stare with the best of 'em."

A startled laugh burst free, and I swiped a hand over my face. Embarrassed.

"You want me to wait with you?" he asked, raking back hair that fell forward over his mirrored aviators.

I shrugged. "Up to you."

"Oh my. That didn't sound like a thank you at all."

His sarcasm made me laugh, and I groaned, scrubbing a hand down my face. "Sorry. It's been one hell of a day."

"Tell me," he said simply, and boy was I tempted.

I was tempted to tell him how much today had sucked and how much I wanted to smoke. How I was messing up at work and falling for this totally inappropriate guy that smelled like sunshine and looked like sin.

I shook my head. "It's getting better now." And that was part of the problem.

It should have been miserable waiting there, especially when AAA trumped their own record for lateness. In truth, it seemed like no time at all. I was almost annoyed when the tow truck finally arrived. Glad when I found out the nearest auto store was within my free tow miles. Jazzed when Jordan offered to give me a ride. The proper thing to do would have been to turn him down, and thank him graciously for the offer. Which didn't explain how we wound up cooling our heels in the auto store waiting room, waiting for my tire change. I also requested an alignment and rotation. Because I needed one. I swear. Not because it would give me extra time to hang out with Jordan. Hell, if they needed to take the entire truck apart, they should go right ahead.

I "If you're late for something, you don't have to wait," I finally said.

"Nah," he said, "I finished my hearing this morning. I have a teleconference at four, but that's about it. Hearing was supposed to take all day and maybe tomorrow, but we settled before 10:00 a.m. Almost got everything we asked for, which was more than I expected. And I don't have to write a brief, which my client doesn't care about but is a huge time saver for me."

"Sounds like you really enjoy your job."

"Don't you?"

"It has its moments." Like this. "There are moments when I miss being on the force."

"I'd think it has some of the same elements."

"Not really. We rarely work with governmental agencies."

The last time I had, Robert had volunteered my services for a witness gone underground, like I was some glorified *Dog the Bounty Hunter*. I can still picture one of Robby's cop buddies giving me a slightly patronizing look. *I'm glad you've found something to do*, he'd said. As if when you hand in your badge, you're supposed to do the world a favor, shrivel up and die.

"You must get some interesting work."

"We do. Child custody. Alimony. Marital property disputes. Surveillance. Skip traces. It's a lot less glamorous than people think."

"No disguises? Funny hats and noses?"

"I actually do have disguises," I admitted. "A bag of them in my truck. Just uniforms and props, really. Drew says I just have a flare for the dramatic, but I think they're necessary."

He laughed. "Maybe a little of both."

"Maybe."

"Here. This will help your headache." His arm was propped up on the chair close to mine, and I almost had a girly swooning moment when his hand dropped down to my neck.

"How'd you know?" I managed.

"Your eyes were all squinty. And you had major attitude. Even for you," he teased, and I growled.

I wasn't sure if he was aware that his arm was pretty much across the back of my chair now. The guy sitting a few chairs down managed to shoot us a dirty look before going back to his magazine. I was unmoved. He could wave a rebel flag and threaten to burn my truck, but if he interrupted Jordan playing with my hair and digging strong thumbs into my neck, I'd pull out my Sig Sauer and neutralize him.

As if he'd realized what he was doing, suddenly the massage stopped. I growled. "Jordan, what's your damage?"

His gaze dropped to the floor, and a blush crept across his cheeks. "I don't know," he managed.

"Ugh." I wanted to scream. I wanted to yell. I wanted to make him admit he was feeling some of the same things I was. "Well, don't come near me until you've figured it out. I've already been there, done that."

"Mackenzie...." His phone went off, super loud in my sensitive ears, and suddenly my headache was back full force. I moved one chair over and snapped open a three-month-old *National Geographic*.

I could feel the heat of his gaze on my neck, and it took all I had in me to remain still.

"Hello," he finally snapped into the phone.

"Jordie!" I could hear Rachel even one chair over. "Where *are* you? We've been waiting an hour. We're going to be late for the meeting. Greeves and Wales both want an explanation for the settlement this morning."

"Rache, I'm kind of busy," he murmured into the phone, trying to be discreet.

As she began going on about the traffic on the highway and why he had to leave *right now*, I moseyed on over to the soda machine. The neon Coke sign made my eyeballs shrink in my head a little more, and I hoped caffeine would help. It didn't appear that I'd be getting any more of Jordan's massages. I stuck in a dollar, and the thing ate it whole.

"Damn it," I groused. I barely refrained from giving it a swift kick.

"Here." An arm went by my nose and stuffed some quarters in the slot. "Which one?"

"Diet Coke," I said. "But I can push the buttons all by myself, Pa." *Wow, you are feeling bitchy.*

The smiling mechanic—Joey, according to his name patch—didn't seem to mind as he tossed me the cola. "On me."

"Least you can do," I said archly. "Your tires cost an arm and a leg."

He grinned, and I smiled back. See? This was easy. The way it was supposed to be. Good to know my flirting was back on track with everyone except Jordan.

"If you follow me, I can show you how to change your own tire."

"I'm sure Mac knows how to change a tire," Jordan said, somewhere close by, and I jumped. I hadn't heard him get off the phone. He rolled his eyes at the guy's blatant come-on.

I did know how to change a tire. But wasn't this part of being healthy? Moving on to someone *available*, who might actually be a good match for me? The old me would have agreed with Jordan, flirted with him a little more, maybe even guilt him into another neck message. My eyebrows slashed down. If Jordan wanted to play, he was going to have to adjust his antennae. I wasn't into mixed signals.

"I'd love to learn," I announced.

"Come on back through here when you're ready," Joey said, giving me one last flippant grin before disappearing through a scarred gray door.

"You shouldn't wait," I said into the uncomfortable silence.

He looked at me, those blue eyes narrowed and still oh-so pretty. "Don't do anything I wouldn't do," he said lightly, but there was anger there too.

I decided to get him back for yo-yoing me around. "Oh, I plan to do a lot of things you wouldn't do."

I gave him a wave before starting through the door.

"Mackenzie."

I turned back briefly. God, if he just said the word, I would— "Yeah?"

He looked as if he might say something else, and then he sighed. "If you need a ride home, I want you to call."

My eyes held his for a moment too long, a moment I could only describe as strange. "Why?"

"Can't have my PI walking home in the dark," he said lightly.

I couldn't resist one last dig. "Thanks... Jordie."

He gave me a look that promised retribution.

What frustrated me the most was that no matter what I did that day with Joey, not the hand brushing as he "showed" me how to do it correctly, not the subtle sniffing my neck and hair as he stood behind me and I pretended to pay attention, not even the unsubtle grinding of his dick against my behind until I told him to back off... nothing matched that single look. Nothing. I had to admit the truth of it to myself. Whatever else was going on, I was clearly looking for more than a casual fuck. *Fuck*, my subconscious swore.

I nodded grimly. My thoughts exactly.

10

If anyone had told me I'd miss sweating through my clothes in Drew's car, I'd have called him a crazy loon. And yet here I was, baking in the relentless sun, patrolling a rectangular yard that had looked a lot smaller twenty minutes ago. My hat had a handy cam built neatly into the front visor, and I was free to push the ancient mower across stubborn grass.

Thanks to a group of mischievous young fools decorating the neighborhood yards with toilet paper (kids still did that?), neighborhood watch had been hypervigilant lately. And if you think cops are bad, you haven't seen a little old lady with a reflective vest and a flashlight the size of her own head. I'd been chased off by an octogenarian twice in the past week, so sitting in a random car was a nonstarter. My new ruse, if I did say so myself, was brilliant. On its surface. In reality, being hired as Mrs. Blake's next door neighbor's lawn man sucked *big* dick. Pro? I was able to get as close to the neighboring property line as I dared. I could *finally* catch an uninterrupted view of Blake's backyard. Con? I had to actually cut the fucking grass.

"Hey, stranger."

I cut the motor, choking and gasping as a cloud of dust and grass puttered out of the side of the machine and created nasty confetti. I glared at Drew, standing neat and stylish in Dockers and a white button-down shirt. He had the leash to a small, barking Pomeranian in one hand and an ice cream cone in the other. An actual ice cream cone.

"Are you just going to eat that in front of me?"

"Well, I would offer you a lick, but we're being watched right now."

I growled.

"Edith Brantworth, two doors down." He jerked his head in her direction. "She ran you off on Monday."

"Don't remind me. Isn't there an episode of *Price is Right* on?"

"Old folks don't watch that anymore. Not since Bob Barker left."

"How would you know?" I ran a hand through my sweaty hair, wishing I'd remembered a bandana.

He leaned down and gave the yappy dog a piece of waffle cone. "I know things."

"Where'd the dog come from?"

"Borrowed, my dear. Only borrowed. As long as I have her back in one piece by five, my sister will have no reason to end my life."

I gave the mower a slight kick. "Drew, if this doesn't make up for missing those meetings with the crotchety sisters, I don't know what does."

"I have to admit, this takes dedication. Nice touch with the truck, by the way. Nice and dusty, wooden crate on the back, couple dents in the side? Just like a lawn truck."

I scowled. "I didn't do anything to my truck."

He looked at me for a minute, slightly nonplussed. Then smiled brightly. "So, what's the plan?"

I had half a mind to swat his waffle cone right to the ground, but I had a feeling Edith Brantworth would have the cops here in five minutes flat. "I'm going to cut like a maniac and then lurk in his backyard. He has these incredible willows that are going to allow me to play 'I spy' for as long as I want."

"Good plan."

"We'll finally be able to figure out what the hell she's doing in the backyard so long every day."

"Smart money's on gardening."

"Well, today we'll know for sure." I ran a hand through my damp hair to push it back from my face and jammed a cap over it. "Now beat it. I have work to do."

Drew took himself and his yappy dog off with a wave, and I yanked the crank on the lawnmower viciously. With the help of some high octane tunes in my Skullcandy headphones, I was able to demolish the front yard in a half hour flat. Stopping briefly to shed my shirt and toss it on a porch railing, I looked back at the long neat rows with something akin to satisfaction. It actually looked pretty great. If I ever got tired of PI work... a fresh wave of heat prickled my back, and I shook my head. No, never. I'd bag groceries instead.

I dragged my mower over the driveway and through the side wooden gate, ready to tackle the backyard. I cut rows slowly, moving closer and closer to the fence. The trees would cover me peering into the Blakes' yard, but I couldn't quite figure out what to do about the person whose yard I was cutting. The back of the house had four windows, nice sized, facing my direction, and he'd been *very* clear about me not trimming his trees. I hemmed and hawed until, finally, he solved my problem for me.

"Son," he called from the gate over the roar of the motor, "I'm running out for a while."

I let go of the handle of the mower, and suddenly blessed silence reigned over the yard. "Okay," I said, probably smiling just a little too big. "I only have two more rows before I finish. I'll probably rake and trim that azalea too."

His arthritic hand trembled a bit as he struggled to pull money from his wallet, and I was suddenly glad I'd taken the job seriously. He stuffed a few crumpled bills into my sweaty palm. "You do darned fine work, Martin."

Now my smile was genuine. Mr. Nesbitt was actually a pretty nice guy. I stuffed his three twenties in my pocket. And sixty bucks would certainly look nice in my gas tank right now. I'd never worked so hard for sixty dollars in my life, but I shook his hand when he offered it. "Thank you, sir."

"I'll probably need you again in about a month. This grass grows like wildfire. Better not to let it get out of hand, you know."

"Yes, sir, you're right."

"If you just do a little at a time, you won't have such a big job when you finally get to it, you know?"

"I know."

"Now, don't trim those azaleas too close. They took a beating from the storm and haven't been the same since. This is the healthiest I've seen them since Hurricane Wilma." He ran two fingers over his quivering mustache, and I sighed inwardly. What the hell happened to his errand?

I heard a bang next door, like a back door slamming closed, and I cursed inwardly. This was my window!

"I like to go out to the Everglades and get my soil. Just a couple pots or two at a time, you understand, since I'm not really sure about the legality of it all. That soil is so rich and dark, Martin, you could probably grow an apple in Florida." He laughed, at the impossibility of that I assume, and continued. "I mix a little o' that with my yard dirt and a palm full of the Dynamite, and whoo-ee! You've got some real soil there!"

"Huh?" Was that giggling? "Yeah, sure. Good soil."

"For a while I did try makin' my own compost, but I could never quite get that mixture right. And damned if Beth didn't hate that smell. 'Stanley!' she would yell, 'Quit diggin' through my garbage and creatin' more garbage.'"

A rustle and a soft laugh filtered through the trees, and I swore under my breath. *No*. I did *not* cut this yard for nothing. I put a hand to my ear and looked off distractedly.

"Martin? Martin, are you all right?"

"Shhh!" I continued looking around wildly and then tiptoed toward the unsuspecting azalea bush. "You hear that?"

"Hear what?" He leaned in, even while proclaiming himself hard of hearing. "Damned timing of life, you know. Had perfect hearing for thirty years while my wife was alive. Perfect hearing through thirty years of 'Do you think your laundry walks *itself* to the laundry basket?' and other such, and now that I'm by myself, I can't hear a thing!" He gave a great belly laugh that totally ruined the drama of my moment.

I tried to recapture it by looking around wildly. "No, *listen*. You hear that?" He leaned in farther, casting a suspicious look at the bush.

After a moment, he nodded sagely. "You know, I think I do hear little something." He slanted squinty eyes at me. "What is it?"

"I'd know that sound anywhere. Last time I heard such hissing, I was in for the fight of me life." Okay, less Crocodile Dundee, more Steve Irwin, I scolded myself. "It's a snake. A big one, from the sound of it."

Mr. Nesbitt showed me that eighty was still young as he sprang away from the bush as if it was mired in quicksand. "What kind of snake?"

"Big one," I said, thinking quickly. "Erhm, optimal priminius. But don't worry, I'll kill 'er. You should probably go, though."

He nodded quickly, running a hand through his shock of white hair and then over his face. "Of course. Do what you can. Just get rid of that snake!"

When I heard his truck start in the drive, I dashed over to the fence. Hell, if he saw me near it now, I'd just claim that optimal priminius had slithered out of the bush and transformed into something real. My phone vibrated in my pocket, and I hit the Bluetooth button.

"Yeah?"

"You got what you need yet? I just saw Nesbitt take off as if his house was on fire."

"Just finished convincing him there was a big-ass snake in his yard."

Drew guffawed in my ear as I scaled the nearest tree with minimal effort. It was an old, sturdy tree with plenty of good footholds.

"What the hell did you do that for?" he managed through his laughter.

"He was gearing up for a nice long convo, and I heard something going on over here. Now I'm up in a big tree." I grunted, heaving myself up to the highest branch.

"With your eighty-year-old knee?"

"Shut it," I murmured with little to no heat, weaseling my way through some of the tougher limbs until I had a prime spot. As I parted the leaves, I felt that eager feeling settling in my stomach, the one where the culmination of all your hard work comes together. Mrs. Blake had been a little harder than most to catch, but look at her now, *shameless*, in her backyard where her children played, for God's sakes. Using the lawn furniture her family gathered on to… hold a Girl Scouts meeting?

I looked on in disbelief as a circle of ten or so girls, all clad in blue vests, sat on various pieces of lawn furniture, their attention held rapt by Mrs. Blake. She was holding up some sort of brochure and displaying the glossy, lard-laden pictures within.

"A Girl Scouts meeting?" I nearly shouted, and then stilled as a few girls nearest the gate looked around in the air. "A Girl Scouts meeting," I repeated in an angry whisper to Drew as he died laughing. Hopefully died, anyway.

"Okay, Mac. This mission will certainly go down in history. This is even better than if you'd found her with a rose bush and a sack of fertilizer in hand."

I sighed. "I can't believe I cut Nesbitt's yard for nothing."

"Not nothing. You got paid, didn't you?"

"Yes, it'll go toward my skin graft fund after spending three hours on the surface of the sun." The girl with brown pigtails tied with blue ribbons that matched her smock raised her hand quickly and then stood when she was acknowledged. I grinned. I knew a know-it-all from a mile away. She held up a box of Thin Mints that had come from God knows where, and my stomach rumbled.

"Drew, I've found the Keebler tree," I murmured. "I wonder if those cookies are for sale now."

"You know, now that you know she's not cheating, you're spying on a Girl Scouts meeting. Not a good look for a grown man. Hard to explain to cops," he added helpfully.

"All right. I'm coming, I'm coming."

"Harder to explain to cops," he quipped, and I snickered.

"Idiot."

"So what's our next move?"

I sighed. "Well, cookies obviously, but that's a no-brainer. Maybe we coax Blake to take a business trip. You know, a few days a whole city away?"

"He does actually have a job, you know. Not so simple."

"A weekend, then. Friday, Saturday, Sunday."

"Where to?"

"Who cares? Just tell him to get lost next weekend, and we see what Lolita does."

"She's not a Lolita yet," he said, and I caught a whiff of annoyance in his tone.

"She's cheating," I said, nibbling on my thumbnail. "I just haven't caught her yet."

"Not everyone's a cheater," Drew snapped, his tone making me start. "Sometimes people actually find the real thing. It *is* out there, you know."

"Chill, Cupid. I didn't say everyone cheats."

"Sometimes I feel like you're just waiting for it. And you're so damned satisfied when you're right."

"I'm just a firm believer that people shouldn't play with people's feelings."

"No, you're still just scarred from something that happened when you were like thirteen. Maybe it's time to stop reliving your parents' relationship over and over."

"Fourteen." I frowned at the weathered, bark-laden branch underneath my Cons. "And you're so annoying."

"When I'm right? I know."

"Besides, I *am* moving on. I don't tell you about every relationship in my life."

"Moving on to whom, the next straight guy you see? Like Jordan, who you don't think I know spent the entire day with you yesterday?"

"We staked out Rachel's mystery meeting. Turned out to be her real estate agent. She's seen him twice in as many days, and she ain't selling or buying. Property, that is."

"Since when do you stake out with a client? Or is Mr. Blake also in that tree?"

I sighed. "I'm coming down. You can bitch me out over food. Otherwise, it's just too depressing."

When I landed on the soft grass with an *oomph*, I stretched and straightened, glad the mission had at least been completed without a hitch. And then my gaze landed on the patch of unmowed grass. The unraked grass. The un-weed-wacked grass.

"Are you serious?" I rubbed my eyes tiredly.

"What?"

"Drew, get my cookies or suffer the consequences. Samoas. Not those damn Thin Mints. I'll see you in an hour."

11

After the morning I'd had, a swim in the community pool sounded like certain ambrosia. I dove into the deep end, slicing through the water cleanly, not taking the time to acclimate from the heat to the sudden embrace of cool water. The cold snatched my breath clean from my body, and I surfaced with a gasp, shoving hair out of my eyes. I expected a burn from salt water in my eyes that never came—I guess I was too used to wiping out in the salty ocean.

I did a couple of freewheeling flips in the water, getting acclimated to the different buoyancy. It was only then that I realized how long it'd been since I'd swam in a pool. Swimming for recreation had never really been my thing. Nick had been the swimmer between us. He'd swum like a beautiful fish, the lean muscles of his swimmer's body flashing in and out of the water. If I concentrated hard enough, I could almost see him grinning at me, water sluicing off his defined pectorals, the very picture of health. God could never decide which should be more golden, his hair or his skin, and there he was, framed by sun, his goggles pushed up on his head. A grimace twisted my face as I reached for him and he disappeared. It had been a stupid vision anyway. Now Nick couldn't even walk.

My unfortunate vision and my steadily tiring leg ruined what was left of my impromptu swim, and I slowly floated to the ladder. I slogged upstairs for a nap, lying down in the cool dark that I associated with my own private haven. I could only keep my eyes open for a few minutes before they began to flutter uncontrollably and then dropped shut as if a lead weight lay upon each one. My muscles ached restlessly as I rolled in my covers, like a gigantic guinea pig, searching for the right spot.

My body was tired after the rigors of my day—the yard work, the tree climbing, the swim (wow, my days had gotten strange)—but my mind refused to shut down without a fight. I finally fell into a jerky sleep of restless dreams. Dreams of dark roads and flashing lights that played on an endless reel. Nicky looking at me, talking to me, laughing, teasing me about my choice of music.

As he cast a glance my way, I simply looked at him, framed by sudden headlights where there had been nothing but darkness. He was so damned beautiful, but something was wrong. Why the headlights were coming at me and framing Nicky's profile hadn't registered just yet. The window exploded upon impact, and my eyes slammed shut instinctively. And then the night was alive with sound—wrenching sounds of sirens and screams. Nicky screaming. Me. Screaming? No, my mouth was an empty, soundless scream as he flew out of the car, and the slick black ice took him farther from me. The sound of crushing metal and shattering glass was horrific, leaden and metallic in my ears.

I twisted to the side, but I felt trapped in the heavy blankets, sodden from my sweat.

Are you okay? Okay? Okay? *Annie, are you okay*?

My eyes flew open as I jackknifed up in bed. "Annie, are you okay? Are you okay, Annie?" Words from the song "Smooth Criminal" blared from the clock radio.

I slapped a hand over the snooze button and ran a shaky hand through my hair. My dreams were rare. But when they came... they were overwhelming.

I stripped the bed of my sweat-sodden blankets and padded to the washer, dragging the length of my comforter behind me. I dumped in an excessive amount of laundry detergent (because measuring is for squares), and dragged myself to the shower. The hot water drained me and gave me energy at the same time, as I lathered myself with my new soap, hoping the scent wasn't too fruity. I sniffed. Smelled damned decent, actually. By the time I'd thrown on a pair of cargo pants and a faded black tee, I felt almost human again. I cranked down the air mercilessly—I wanted an ice cube to feel nice and comfy. I dropped down on the couch and flipped through my DVR menu restlessly.

Junk. Junk. I deleted another episode of *The Closer* that kept popping up. Junk I would guard with my life if anyone got froggy with the delete button. I set an episode of *Burn Notice* to record and let an episode of *Law and Order* play while I checked e-mail on my HP. Before long, I found myself browsing car websites and scratching leisurely. Just as God intended.

I had just gotten an interior tour of a Chevy Avalanche—thank you QuickTime—when my cell phone went off. I listened to the ring-tone until it was almost too late before picking up.

"'Lo?" Ah, four years of college education at work.

"Mackenzie, this is Jordan."

I sat up a little straighter, almost toppling my laptop. I was so ridiculously pleased to hear his voice it was embarrassing.

"Yeah?"

"You left your iTouch in my car. Didn't want you to go crazy looking for it."

"Damn. I thought I'd lost that. I'd actually kind of given up hope on finding it. Even cleaned my apartment looking for it, horror of all horrors."

I was aware that I was babbling like a fool, but he didn't seem to mind.

"I mean really," I continued, blabbermouth central, "do you know how many places something that small can hide?"

He snorted. "Somewhat. You should try keeping up with my Nano. It's precisely the size of a freaking matchbook."

"I'd never get something that small. It wouldn't last two days."

"It's good for jogging." I heard the murmur of voices and knew he spoke to someone else. "What? No, it's on the table."

Ah. Of course someone like Jordan wouldn't be sitting at home alone on a Saturday night. "Well, I don't want to hold you," I said before he could.

"Hm?" He sounded distracted as music began to filter over the phone.

"I don't want to hold you," I said louder.

"Oh no, you're not. We're having that welcoming party I told you about. It's also an excuse for me to christen the new barbeque pit. Really, it's just a glorified gas grill on the patio. Management is finally allowing us to have grills again."

I laughed. "Good for you. I'm still suffering with my Foreman grill over here."

He paused, and even though I could feel it coming, I knew I'd tell him no. "You really should come down," he said.

"With you and your friends? I'm sure I'd fit right in." I yawned widely, letting my eyes drift closed a bit. I would almost be up for another nap except I was sure the nightmares would follow.

"What's that supposed to mean?"

"That's supposed to mean I've gone to enough of those firm dinners and gatherings to know exactly what I'd be in for."

Trevor's associates gave highbrow a new, unpleasant meaning. Besides, I'd spent the better part of my morning in a tree. I wanted to spend my evening pleasantly, not eating hors d'oeuvres with people who thought your worth was valued by the series of your BMW.

"Not everyone at the firm is like that."

"I'm sure."

"Am I?"

My eyes snapped open. Well, damn, he had me there. "No. Is that your Perry Mason moment?"

He sounded smug. "A little bit, yeah."

"All right fine, let me know when the rest of them are gone, and I'll come hang out with you." I almost groaned, realizing how that had sounded. Instead I bit the fleshy part of my hand between the thumb and forefinger and continued on quickly. "You know, as friends. Watching the game or something."

He sounded amused. "Something butch, you mean?"

"Urgh," I said eloquently.

"Hang on." The noise in the background suddenly ceased, and I heard a door close. "I'd like it if you came tonight," he said, his words polite enough but the demand clear.

That kind of complete focus both thrilled and scared me. I couldn't imagine what he could do with that kind of single-minded focus in the bedroom. Hands under my thighs, spreading me wide, giving me exactly what I'd asked for. Begged for. He had strong legs. Fucked like a machine, I'd bet. *Good God*. My face went scarlet, and no one was even there to see.

"I don't think—"

"You think way too much. Now get in your raggedy-ass truck and bring your ass to the party."

"Raggedy?" My eyebrows shot up. "Bessie still has plenty good years left in her."

"If Bessie is that old, dilapidated heap I helped you charge, she should be shot and put down."

I was so busy snickering that I almost didn't catch his sneaky, "So I'll see you in ten?"

"Ten?" I squawked. "I live thirty minutes away."

"Thirty minutes, then." *Click*.

"No, time is not the issue," I growled to empty air. Talking to myself, of course.

I didn't know why I was fighting it quite so hard. I wanted to see Jordan more than I probably should. Now I had a perfect excuse. Maybe that was part of the problem. I argued myself into going, but I wouldn't change. That was my compromise. I thought about cologne and decided the Dove smelled just fine. He had invited me. If they didn't like me as I came, then oh well. I started Bessie up with crossed fingers, hoping she hadn't heard about me surfing the net for the Avalanche yet.

12

The small get-together wound up being about thirty people milling around Jordan's newly landscaped backyard. His choice of location denied me the opportunity to see the inside of his monstrosity of a townhome. It only appeared to qualify being a townhome by the fact that it shared one wall and driveway space with another such monstrosity. I made my way around the side yard, keeping to the flagstones and following the beams that bathed the backyard in soft yellow light like a forest fairy tale. I stood there for a moment, surveying the crowd and noting the faces.

It seemed like a different type of crowd than Trevor usually introduced me to. Jeans and tees seemed to be the sponsored outfit of choice, and I wasn't out of place at all. And was that beer? Before I could rudely migrate directly to the beer, skipping the hello to my gracious host, I spotted him laughing with some burly guy near the grill who looked less like a lawyer and more like a client. His eyes met mine. My breath stuttered in my chest for a moment, and I was grateful he had a bit of a walk before he reached me as, when he handed the guy the silver tongs, he'd waved. He headed my way, looking effortlessly amazing as usual, in white cargo pants, a white tee with "Save Japan" across the front in tiny black letters, and white flip-flops that slapped against the tile as he approached. I swallowed hard. Turns out I really dug guys who wore old relief-effort T-shirts.

"I'm glad you could make it."

"You make it impossible to say no."

His eyes widened a little, and I suddenly realized how sensuous that sounded. I didn't take it back.

I almost expected him to greet me and disappear back into the crowd of his friends, but he lightly touched my elbow to guide me around, introducing me to people. After the second group, I snatched my elbow away, not caring if he took it the wrong way or not. There were only so many tingles that could shoot up my damn spine.

Rachel gave me a curious wave from her perch on the balustrade, and even I, who had no attraction for the fairer sex, could appreciate a thing of beauty. Her dark hair set off her completely white palazzo pants and blouse to perfection, and as she brought a delicate wine-glass to shockingly red lips, she looked like a magazine ad. The girl wasn't classically beautiful, but she had damned lovely bones.

When he introduced me to her, it became clear just how little either one of us had thought this through. It would be kind of hard to follow someone who had met and spent time with you. I had no sooner complimented her Tory Burch sandals than I met someone else, and then someone after that. Somewhere between the time burly grill guy passed me a steak heavy enough to make my plate creak and groan dangerously and cute possibly gay guy (let's face it, frosted tips?) winked and offered me a chair next to his, I realized I was having a damned fine time.

I debated for a moment on where to sit, conducting a quick surveillance of the layout. There were several low glass tables set up with big cushioned chairs that no one was taking advantage of. There were also plenty of those same plush patio chairs set up in semicircles around the flagstone patio, where people seemed to be doing a balancing act with their food and talking a whole lot more than eating. There were several small bonfire circles set in white circular pillars that flickered off animated faces, and I was suddenly inspired to give being social a shot. I headed for the chair Frosted Tips was gesturing toward to put him out of his flirty misery. If he didn't stop giving me hand signals, a plane was going to take off somewhere.

It wasn't like it was a hardship. He was ridiculously good looking, even though his butterscotch hair had been razor cut into some sort of style that *could* indicate he had a severe case of Beiber Fever. He flashed particularly pearly whites at me.

"Doug makes a mean steak, doesn't he?"

"If Doug is that biker guy manhandling that grill, then I'd have to agree."

He chuckled, holding out his hand in the region of my face as I balanced my paper plate on my knees. I juggled my beer and my plate for a dicey moment to free up my hand and then shook his heartily. His hands were strong. Firm.

"Kelly Markey."

"Mackenzie Williams."

"I haven't seen you around the building."

"I don't work in the building," I answered smoothly. "That would be strange if you had."

"So are you with someone here?"

"Jordan, actually." I took a taste of the rosemary and garlic potatoes, enjoying them so much that I almost missed his raised eyebrow.

"Channing? You and...."

"What? No. *No.*" Oh, jeez, this was a new type of blunder. Outing someone who wasn't even gay? "He invited me as a friend. Just a friend."

He smiled. "I was going to say Jordan just doesn't give off that vibe."

"And I do?"

"I was right, wasn't I? Besides, you have way too many highlights not to be."

"Cute, Beiber." He actually was. *See, Mac,* I congratulated myself. *This isn't hard at all.* "So do you guys have many of these events? These welcome the new associate things?"

"I wouldn't know. I would be the new associate." He grinned. "Family law. Fourth floor. You should come see me sometime."

"As much as my family irritates me, I'm not quite ready to legally separate from any of them."

"So if you're not one of the attorneys, what *do* you do?"

"I'm a...." I thought better of revealing my actual profession just in time, but my thought left me with an awkward pause. *Think.* And then I smiled a little. "I'm in the landscaping business."

"Oh really? That so?" Kelly injected so much enthusiasm into his query you'd have thought I'd announced I was a lion tamer with Barnum & Bailey. "You know, I've been looking for a good landscaper to create a pond in my backyard."

Oh hells, no. "I'm kind of booked for a while. But I'll let you know if I have an opening."

"You must be good," he said, finally tucking back into his food.

I shrugged modestly. "I do all right." Hell, Mr. Nesbitt's yard had probably never looked better.

"So what's your professional opinion of Channing's yard, here?"

Lord above. He was going to pretend interest in my profession to be polite. And I was going to have to feign interest as well as expertise. I should have gone with the lion tamer thing.

"It looks good. Healthy. Well watered, but not too much," I guessed. Why not assume Jordan did yard work as competently as he did everything else?

We yammered on about our jobs for a little while longer. Then sports. Then weather. Then back to sports. It was around the time we started going on about the latest Heat game that I realized Kelly was actually pretty cool. And available. *You don't turn him down if he offers to get together again,* I lectured myself. *You forget Jordan. And Trevor. And Nick.*

"We're going to the Heat game next Saturday. You should come. The firm has a box and everything."

"Wow, you just got hired, and you're already all up in the firm's VIP box?"

"Hey, perks are perks." He shrugged. "So. You interested?"

And there it was, out in the open. *You say yes.*

I grinned. "In D. Wade? Of course." *That's not yes*, I silently screamed.

He laughed. "The game, Mackenzie. The game."

"As lovely as a box sounds, I like to watch my basketball games like real folk. In the cheap plastic seats with sticky armrests."

Kelly wasn't slow on the uptake, and he shrugged with a half-smile. "Maybe another time, then."

"Maybe."

We continued to talk and razz each other for another ten minutes before Jordan came to introduce him around to some of their coworkers. I meandered over to the table laden with food, swearing up and down that I would only get one more thing. Okay, two more things. A beer and then I'd git while the gettin' was good. And then the God of Pushed Luck appeared, and there Trevor was, right there between the seven-layer bean dip and a curiously spicy salsa. I munched down hard on my bacon-wrapped shrimp, hoping against hope that he'd keep moving.

"Mac. What are you doing here?"

"I was invited," I said shortly. I doubted he could say the same. There was no way Jordan would invite him without at least telling me he would be there. "Does Jordan know you're here?"

"Last time I checked, I was an associate at the firm. I didn't know I needed a written invitation."

"Is that Trevor-speak for no?"

He flushed a bit and hit back the only way he knew how. "Nice of you to dress up for the occasion. You look very... comfortable."

I narrowed my eyes. More Trevor-speak. Comfortable meant messy all day long. "I look like the majority of people here, actually. Last time *I* checked, an Armani suit is inappropriate for a backyard barbecue."

"I just left the office and didn't have time to change. And this is Hugo Boss, actually. I don't know *why* they haven't snatched your gay card yet." He brushed some invisible lint off said suit and continued, "Besides, you bleached all my Armani suits. I never thanked you for that."

"Welcome," I said in a singsong manner.

I dropped my empty buffet plate in the trash and migrated toward the beer cooler. Trevor followed like a bad rash.

"I was under the impression that this wasn't your type of event. I had to drag you to the last event we had for the firm. From what I recall, you insulted a partner by calling his wife his daughter, hid your mushroom caps in the potted plant because they contained pâté, and put 'Like a G6' on the radio."

I didn't know which of those to even address first, so I went with the most offensive. "It was *duck liver*, Trev. Did you know that?"

His mouth couldn't seem to decide whether it wanted to smile or frown. The half grin he settled for was far too familiar for my peace of mind, and I looked away. That half grin was usually followed by him saying "I don't know what I'd do without you." I knew without speaking that he remembered too. Sometimes the breakup seemed too recent for words.

"I also remember you demanding that we leave a mere hour after we arrived."

"I seem to remember you being satisfied with how I made up for it," I said shortly.

I bit down on my tongue, hard, and looked away swiftly. I could feel him looking at me and went for another bacon-wrapped shrimp. Laura waved at us from across the patio, where she was standing with Jordan. It didn't take my PI skills to see that her eyes didn't quite meet up with her open expression. They were like chips of blue ice glittering in our direction, and, judging from the way Trevor shuffled away a few steps, those eyes meant business.

"Time to greet the host, I suppose," I murmured.

"She doesn't give a damn about pleasantries," he said. "She doesn't want me standing with you. Or near you. Or in the same—"

"I get it." My laugh was bitter. "Tell her she has nothing to worry about. I've moved on."

"To what? Mr. Perfectly Unavailable?"

"Don't be ridiculous."

"Please. You've been watching him since you got here."

My mouth opened for instinctive denial and then snapped shut. Maybe I had. As I looked at him laughing in the firelight, rocking back on his heels, I realized I didn't have to defend admiring a person of such abject beauty. In the end, I just shrugged. "So what?"

His eyes went narrow. "You're barking up the wrong tree."

"Anything's better than the last rotted tree I fell out of," I murmured. I reached around the aforementioned Rotted Tree and snagged a beer out of a cooler stacked with ice. "But thanks for your concern."

I made my way down the whiteboard steps that led to the beach. Everything was so perfectly manicured elsewhere on the property that the third squeaky board was almost endearing. I left my sandals by the last step and trekked across the sand, letting the scents and sounds of the beach at night overwhelm my senses. The seawater smelled like salt and fresh linen, and it was cooler down where the ocean met the sand. I dragged a beach chair into the very edge of the surf and dropped into it, letting the water swirl around my ankles in a frothy white lather. I took a sip of my beer and let the bottle dangle from my fingertips, then dug my toes deep into the sand. I would probably track sand into my truck (and apartment), but I couldn't scrounge up enough energy to care. If the tide came in much farther, the water would wet the bottoms of my cargos, but I couldn't care much about that either.

The sound of a chair being dragged across the sand made me squeeze my eyes together tightly. God, if Trevor had followed me out here, I would—

"Party's up there," Jordan said, dropping into the chair now a few scant inches from mine.

I sighed in relief. "I know."

"I didn't know he was going to be here."

I waved a hand. "It's fine. Considering the lengthy list of bad names I have for him, Party Crasher seems mild."

His eyebrows went high, and he took a swig of my beer before sitting it on the arm of his chair. "That's a very mature attitude. Very unlike you."

I grinned and pointed at the longneck. "Three beers. I guess I'm a lightweight."

"You should stay here tonight, then. I have a few guest rooms."

"That would be weird."

"Weird how?"

"Let's see. You've squired me around, introduced me to your friends, and now you're offering me a place to stay? Weird."

"I squired you, huh?" I could hear the grin in his voice, even as he hid it behind the bottle.

"You did," I confirmed.

"We're friends. Friends, Mackenzie." He ruffled my hair. "Don't you have friends?"

Somehow I didn't think Robby and Drew counted, but I gave him a snooty look anyway. "'Course I do. But *we* are not friends."

He shrugged. "We're not enemies."

My peripheral vision was on overdrive as I drank him in like I was dying of thirst. Even his bare feet, digging into the sand, made my stomach clench. They had high arches. And clean, neatly clipped nails. Fuck, was I admiring his *feet*? I needed to get laid worse than I thought.

I don't know whether the beer made me loose or my conversation with Trevor made me bold. I had no excuse for the words that came out of my mouth next. "What I want from you, Jordan, friends don't do."

I expected him to be offended. Or stalk off and leave me and my perverted thoughts on the darkened beach. Or order me off his property. The last thing I expected him to say, his voice gone quiet, was, "I know."

When he added nothing, I narrowed my eyes. "What do you mean, 'I know'? You know and you don't care or you know and you're thinking about it? Or you know and you—"

"I don't know, okay? Sheesh. I just... *know*. We have this weird chemistry thing, right? And I would know what to do about it if... well, if you weren't...."

"A guy?" I pushed out of my chair and began stomping off. "You are so—"

He grabbed my arm as I passed and forced me to stop in my tracks. "Wait a damn minute. You can't get mad at me every time I'm honest with you. Or go off with another guy."

I flushed. "The mechanic."

"And Kelly. And Trevor."

"You've been watching me!" I accused.

"You've been watching *me*," he snapped right back. He sighed, letting go of my arm and leaning back in his chair. "Hell, this is just getting too weird."

"Well, it was a picnic at the park for me."

"It would help if you would stop dropping bombs on me and stalking off. For God's sakes, just... *sit*."

I sat. "So?"

"So... let's just talk, okay?" He dragged a hand through his hair and then down his face. "Can we do that?"

"Fine."

"Okay."

I leaned back in my chair and folded my arms. "Okay."

"Fine."

When I glanced over, he was shaking his head. "What?"

"I can't help but wonder what psychobabble my mother would come up with to describe all of this."

"Your mom's a psychiatrist?"

"Yeah. My father too. I'm sure they'd be up all night sinking their teeth into this one."

"Oh, you poor child."

He snorted. "And your parents?"

"My dad was a police officer, as well as my brother, Robert. So was I," I added as an afterthought. "Family business, I guess. And my mom is... gone."

"Gone?"

I shrugged. "Not around. I don't know what she does nowadays."

He gave me an unreadable look. "I don't know what to do with that," he said.

"Well, you could say you're sorry, which would be stupid because you didn't know her and you don't *really* know me. Or you could keep asking me questions about that trifling bitch, and I'd have to make one of those beautiful eyes quite black. So we should probably just sit and listen to the damn beach."

After a moment's pause, he said, "You think my eyes are beautiful?"

I turned to face him. "That's what you got out of all that?"

"My other options didn't appeal to me."

I laughed. God, it seemed like when I was with him I laughed a lot. Smiled a lot. I reached over and took his face in my hands and dropped a kiss on his cheek. "That may have been the best response I've ever had to telling someone about the most painful event in my life."

It was time to let his face go, but my fingers weren't budging for some reason. "Do you trust me enough to try something?"

"Like what?"

I exhaled on a cross between a strangled breath and a laugh. "Now, is that trust?"

He flushed. "I guess I'll try anything once."

"That's the reasoning you use for trying sushi, J, not a kiss."

His eyes went wide. Normally that amazing shade of blue, they were nearly black. "Oh, is that what you're going to do to me?"

"No, it's what we're going to do. To each other."

My thumbs, still resting on either side of his jaw, stroked the area there compulsively, the area where soft skin met rough stubble. He reached up, not to push me away but to lock his hands around my wrists. He let out a laugh that could only be described as nervous.

"You should have just done it. Now I'm all anxious about when we'll do it. How will it go? Will you take the lead or should I—"

I pressed my mouth to his, gently. His breath (which he'd apparently been holding) misted across my lips, soft and warm and slightly minty.

"Your mouth is just as soft as it looks," I murmured against his lips before kissing him again. Deeper this time. I pulled away and caught my breath.

"You didn't like it?" He sounded surprised, and I didn't blame him. His technique was perfect—just the right amount of pressure, just the right amount of tongue, but it was just that... technique.

"You're overthinking it."

He ran a hand over his face. "We need to try again. I keep thinking *I'm kissing a guy, I'm kissing a guy*. Makes it sort of hard to concentrate."

I laughed. "You're not kissing some guy, Jordan." I lowered my mouth over his again, almost touching. "You're kissing me."

I had time to see the determined glint in his eyes before his mouth covered mine, and all of a sudden I was falling, falling, falling, and I didn't want to stop. All the sensitive nerves that apparently lived on my lips and face and ears were sounding off like crazy as time slowed down to nothing at all. He changed the incline and slope of the kiss, sucking my bottom lip into his mouth with little ado, and I felt something wild and primitive building deep inside, trying to get out. I resisted the urge to reach for his zipper, resisted the urge to feel him pulsing and throbbing in my hands, helpless to my will. I didn't think he was quite ready for that. I was more than ready for that, as my dick wrote a proclamation and demanded to be heard. I was ready for a hand job, a blow job, a fuck-me-in-that-beach-chair-right-now job, and it was time to take a step back before I ruined everything.

We tore apart at the very last minute, when it was either breathe or die, and sat back in our respective chairs, not looking at one another.

"I should go," I said unnecessarily.

"Yes," he said, eyes trained on the water. "You should."

13

"I don't think I've ever seen someone sell so many cookies." I scowled at Drew, who didn't seem to understand that Girl Scout cookies were seasonal. "By the time I got back with cash, they were completely out of everything."

Drew grinned, tilting my chair back dangerously. "For God's sakes, Mac, did you at least get some useful footage?"

"If you mean three hours of Mrs. Blake manning a Girl Scout cookie booth with the worst inventory in the history of man, then yes. If you mean anything pointing toward any actual cheating, then no."

"Why don't you just accept that you were wrong? Move on with your life."

"If nothing else, these are going to be invaluable in their family album." I shrugged. "I got a great pic of the two youngest at the face-painting booth."

Drew stared.

"What? There was a face painter in the park today."

"Certainly explains the paw print," he said, rolling his eyes.

I turned my head to give him a better view of the glittery small paw print, painted on my left cheek. "It was *necessary*, Drew. For cover."

He grinned and motioned me forward. When I was close enough, he took my jaw in his hand, turning my head a bit more to examine the art. "Isn't the glitter additional?"

"Are you two ever planning to do any real work or stand there groping each other all day?"

Jennie, our long-suffering office manager, sailed past us both, her spindly, pale arms laden with a thick stack of folders. She unceremoniously dumped the stack on the already cluttered surface of my desk. The pile landed with an impressive whoosh on the flat surface, and a few papers fluttered in the air. She pushed thick framed glasses up on her pert nose with a careless finger, and gave me an expectant look. When you combined that expression with a bun so tight it could make a ballerina jealous, Jennie was *this* close to reminding me of my elementary school librarian.I grimaced. "I think you meant to put those on the desk one office over."

"You mean mine?" Drew grinned. "Dream on, pretty boy." He waggled his fingers, demonstrating no papers, I presume. "This is what coming to work every day looks like."

"Jennie?" I asked hopefully.

"This watch?" She pretended to glance at the slender timepiece. "Says five."

"And not a minute after? Jennie, is there some spell someone put upon you that will reverse if you're here a second past five?"

"You'll never know." She grinned and slapped a manila folder in my hand. "You'll need this."

I could actually differentiate each individual coil in that bun. Visions of liberating her chestnut hair danced briefly in my head. By any means necessary, I think Malcom X had said. I cut my eyes away from the scissors on my desk.

"Remind me again why I don't fire you?" I asked.

"I'm positively brilliant at my job." I would have loved nothing more than to disagree, but she couldn't have been more right. She continued at my silence, "And no one else can live on birdseed... which is all I can afford on my paycheck."

Also correct. Both the birdseed and paycheck part. She certainly was scrawny enough. Jennie had worked for us for the past five years, and I had yet to catch her eating something without a Yoplait label.

"Well, the both of you can leave," I said sourly.

"You don't have to tell me twice." A faint whiff of Chanel No. 5 was all that was left of Jennie. Expensive Chanel No. 5.

"Birdseed, my ass!" I shouted.

Drew set my chair back on all fours but made no move to vacate. "So you ready to call it quits with the Blakes?"

"This Sunday should be the end. At this point, it's just painful to watch. My last stakeout, the woman took the kids to a matinee at the Discovery Museum. That's the day after the cookies and face painting. My camera is so full of dedicated wife and mother, I could barf."

He smirked. "What'd I tell you?"

I shrugged. "If it didn't ever happen, we wouldn't almost own this illustrious, tiny-ass building."

"Here's to three more years of people not trusting each other as far as they can throw one another?"

"Let it be said, let it be done." I grinned. "Now get your ass out of my chair."

I felt a sudden prickling sensation between my shoulder blades, and before Drew even drawled, "Well, look who's here?" in greeting, I knew he was there. When I turned, Jordan was standing in my doorway, face impassive, looking damn near edible. Faded whitewashed jeans clung to his long legs like a second skin, and a faded pale blue Abercrombie and Fitch T-shirt clung to the rest. Jordan in a suit and tie was impressive, but he did casual *very, very* well.

"Jordan," I said.

He seemed to ignore my greeting completely as he said icily to Drew, "Rodriguez."

"Channing."

Cold voice met colder voice, and my head whipped back and forth between the two of them. Confusion didn't begin to describe it. Drew didn't seem perplexed at all, which led me to wonder if they'd had some sort of confrontation I didn't know about.

I made big, scary eyes at Drew. *Get out*, they said. He ignored me.

"You come for an update on your case?" he asked, leaning back in my chair again.

"Which I can handle," I said, making menacing eyes again.

"Mac, weren't you going to finish that report for the Blakes?" Drew asked innocently. "I'd be more than happy—"

I gave up on subtle. "Get lost."

I closed the door on his laughter after he finally ambled his way out. I gestured toward one of the chairs in front of my desk. "Have a seat."

Jordan nodded and passed in front of me to take the chair I indicated. My eyes shot to his perfectly formed ass in those faded jeans like a googly-eyed yo-yo on a string, and I warned myself to be professional. The man shouldn't be allowed to wear jeans. Before he could catch me ogling him like a horny teenager, I looked down at the manila folder Jennie had thrust at me earlier and unclenched my sweaty palm enough to read the label. Channing, Jordan.

Damn. She *was* good.

"What can I help you with?" I asked, taking a seat in my chair.

"What's up with you and Drew?"

"What?"

"You and Drew. Your business partner."

"I know who Drew is," I said, confused. "I'm just not sure what you're asking me."

"Forget it." He leaned forward, bracing his elbows on his knees. "I'm not here about the case."

My breathing was doing this strange herky-jerky dance in my ears. "Why are you here, then?"

"I've thought about what happened between us. A lot. Shit, listen to me going on, and I don't know if it's even crossed your mind."

Only every time I close my eyes. "A bit," I said noncommittally.

"Well, it's crossed my mind a lot more than that." He let out a huff of self-deprecating laughter that made my stomach flip. "And I've come to a conclusion."

"Yeah?" My voice was huskier than usual, and there was nothing I could do to stop it. If his conclusion involved anything about a repeat performance, the only question in my mind would be who could lock the door faster.

"Yeah." When he looked back up, his voice seemed different somehow. Different than he'd ever used with me. Unsure. Sorry? Piteous? I knew then that I wasn't going to like what he was going to say. "There can be no relationship between us, Mac. It just wouldn't... work."

My ears questioned me. *You're the ones who aren't working properly*, I argued with my ears. *No, that's what he said*, they insisted. I sat there for a moment, sorting through the feelings coursing through my body. Disappointment. Anger, yeah. But not a drop of surprise. That fact made my shoulders slump briefly in acceptance. I was not, in fact, surprised at all.

The proper thing to do would be to discuss how he wanted to close out the investigation. Thank him for his honesty and encourage him to call me if he needed anything. I was considering beaning him with the folder. I've never been overly mature.

"Let me get this straight. No pun intended, of course. You came here to tell me that kissing me was a mistake? Is that about the whole of it?"

He flushed. "Not a flattering depiction, to be sure."

"Not as unflattering as I wanted to be, Channing."

"We just don't make sense, you and I. I can't wrap my mind around changing something that's been so completely unquestionable my whole life. I've thought about it, and obsessed over it, and it's a bridge I just can't cross. I just... can't." When he looked up at me through his lashes, those half-moon eyes filled with misery and something else I couldn't define. I wanted to hate him. No, I wanted to *despise* him. Unfortunately, I wasn't quite up to the task. *God*. I *told* you relationships were a shit-fest.

I folded my arms across my chest and leaned back in my chair. "I understand," I finally said.

He snorted. "No, you don't. Your mouth is saying 'I understand' while your body language is saying 'fuck off.'"

"I meant English. I understand English, Jordan. You don't have to keep repeating yourself. It was one kiss. It meant nothing."

He looked a bit taken aback. "So you're... cool?"

No. "Perfect," I said coolly. "As for your case, I should be prepared to give you my final report within the week. I'll be able to deliver the report via mail."

"All right. Okay." He wiped his hands on his jeans, betraying his confusion. "Well, I suppose I should just go."

"Yes." When I met his eyes, I knew he would remember. "You should."

He flushed and stood. "You're angry."

"Bingo. Give that man a prize."

He stood there, watching me work in silence. I wouldn't give him the satisfaction of looking up. He had done his dirty deed. Now he could go. Was I supposed to assuage his conscience as well?

He came around the desk, next to my chair. I looked up, mouth agape at his brazenness as he propped himself up on my desk, hoisting himself onto the edge. Clearly Jordan wanted to hash this out. *Dig up that dead horse and bring your stick so we can beat him to death again.*

"It's not like you just know these things." He shook his head. "I guess I'm just not as sure as you were. Newsflash: I'm not like you."

"That's certainly what you seem to be telling yourself daily," I murmured, shuffling through several of my files.

He slammed a hand on my desk and made my eyes go wide. Apparently he wasn't kidding about worrying over the decision. I let the manila folder drift to the desk in silence.

"All right, you have my attention."

"Please stop treating this as a joke," he said through gritted teeth. "I'm trying to sort through something here, and whether you and I get together or not, you should be helping me with it. As my friend."

I *was* his friend, damn him. In the beginning, I had lusted after his hot body, yeah. Who wouldn't? But somewhere along the line, I had grown to like him as something else.

I sighed. "There's no crime in being bi, Jordan. You've known there was something between us for a while now. If you had devoted as much energy towards it as you did fighting it, we'd be in bed right now."

"This weird chemistry thing? Yes. Yes, I did!" he exploded. "But what am I supposed to do with that? I've never—"

"It's not weird chemistry," I said hotly. "*I* am not weird, and neither is being attracted to men."

"Could you stop twisting my words for like two seconds? I mean, how would I know?" We sat there for a moment, silent, before he probed further. "How did *you* know?"

I sighed. "I just knew. I knew that, even though I could appreciate the beauty of both male and female, there was something extra there for the male. It wasn't just an appreciation of beauty; it was like my sexuality came alive. Being with a man awakened my senses, made me feel differently. I never questioned it. It just *was*. I *was*. All hard, flat lines and musculature, long legs and broad shoulders...." I trailed off as my eyes traveled up Jordan's body. "Flat, toned stomach and thick, muscled thighs. Like a work of art come to life," I finished weakly, looking away.

I felt very animalistic all of a sudden, heated from the inside out. I could smell his arousal and mine, comingling in the air, and I was suddenly exhausted, fighting the most intense attraction of my life. If he wasn't going to be gay, then the least he could do was go away.

"Jordan, why are you still here?"

"Maybe you could help me. Help me know if this is real or not. You know." His gaze slid from mine. "We could try some things."

I smiled even though I was feeling far from perky. "Ah. And there's the rub."

"Yeah, maybe some of that too." He gave a half smile.

"Cute. That's real cute, J. So you want me to be your dirty little sample, then. Something to test the waters."

"That's nice, Mackenzie," he said, his tone sharp. "You know it's not like that."

"What's it like, then?"

"You act as if I'm supposed to just know exactly what to do. It's like I woke up one day and everything I knew was different. *I'm* different."

I *did* know what that was like. At least I hadn't had to change everything I knew about my own sexuality—I'd had no sexual identity to speak of. And one day, I suddenly knew why. It wasn't a flash-bang grenade or fireworks on the beach, just an organic, quiet knowledge of who I was and *what* I was. I didn't have anyone saying it was wrong or I was evil. I'd revealed the information to those closest to me and begun living my life as I knew I was born to.

Oblivious to my internal struggle, Jordan continued. "I'd like to know if this is real. If I'm really... something other than what I thought. Something tangible to hold on to before I turn my entire life upside down."

My undersexed brain could not comprehend why this was a bad idea. Jordan had made it clear that he wasn't interested in pursuing a relationship with me. The only way this *would* happen was right here. Right now. My hand went to his belt buckle, and I don't know why.

"Like a hand job."

He went red as fire. "If that's what you wanted to do."

It is. I continued on, casually, as if I hadn't been dreaming about tasting him since I'd first met him. "So what, you just plan on asking all your gay friends if they'll introduce you to your own sexuality?"

"I wouldn't trust anyone else to ask this of them," he said honestly, and I wanted to punch him in the stomach. If he continued to make this about more than sex, I would kill him. Well, first I'd fuck him, and then I'd kill him.

I flicked the belt through the loop and let the heavy buckle fall to the side. He wouldn't be here long enough to take it off. "Let's get a few things straight, Channing."

I don't think he was even breathing as I slid his zipper down the track slowly, maintaining eye contact. "There are a few rules you need to acknowledge."

"Yeah?"

"Yeah. First, I'm no experiment. I'm doing this because I've wanted to do this since I first laid eyes on you."

His eyes flickered over my face, but I paid no attention to his soft "Okay." My fingers traced his erection, tenting blue silk boxers, and he let out a hiss.

"This is about one thing. Getting you off. Yeah?"

"Yeah."

"Second, this isn't about friendship. I don't do this for my friends." I grinned a little. "Despite what Asher says. This is about getting you off."

He opened his mouth in what I can only imagine was a protest, until I rubbed his erection through his boxers. He subsided with a weak "Sounds real good right about now."

"Lastly, this isn't about trust. We are not going to hold hands and sing *Kumbaya*. This is about what again?"

"Getting me off," he groaned as my hand went up and down, teasing his rigid cock through the soft fabric.

"My pleasure," I said.

I pulled his shirt free of his pants and pushed the fabric up far enough to ghost my mouth across his well-toned stomach. I was aware that this went beyond the scope of what we'd agreed upon. This went beyond proving a point.

You can still leave him wound up, I consoled myself. *Get him just far enough. Then walk away.*

"I love the way you respond to me," I murmured, running my hands over the silken skin of his stomach and up to his flat nipples. He hissed as I circled one with the tip of my finger and then the tip of my tongue. "But how far, exactly, do you want this to go? Hand job? Blow job? A finger in your ass? More than that?"

His face was absolutely scarlet, but he pulled my face up to his and gave me a thorough kiss that made my smart mouth a little less smart. "Whatever feels good," he responded. His hand made the journey from my face to my neck, where he held me still enough to look into my eyes. "And right now, you feel fucking amazing."

He smelled good. He felt good. Hell, I felt good, and he hadn't done anything to me yet. I frowned and pulled back. I was in control. And it was about time he realized it.

I dropped back down in my chair and leaned back, easing my erection but not unzipping my pants. If I took my pants off, I wouldn't be able to think at all.

"Show me what you got," I said lazily, enjoying the fresh bloom of color in his cheeks. I wasn't going to make this easy. He wasn't going to pretend this just happened so fast. He wasn't going to close his eyes and pretend it was someone else, either.

To his credit, he didn't drop eye contact with me as he pushed his jeans farther down his thighs. I stared at the outline of his thick cock through his boxers and hoped I was as strong as I thought I was. Dropping to your knees is a poor way to show someone you're in control. But arousal seemed to be sucking the air clear from the room. I felt hazy and overheated as I wormed a finger in between my shirt collar and my neck, pulling the shirt from the heat of my skin.

"Keep going," I snapped.

His eyes narrowed at my tone, but that didn't stop him from pulling down his briefs. His cock sprang free from his neatly trimmed thatch of dark fuzz, thick and long, eight inches of sculpted perfection. Smooth, silky looking balls hung low behind, dusted with fine hair. *Move over, David,* I silently told Michelangelo.

"You manscape?" I asked dubiously. Another straight guy myth right out the door.

"Sometimes. It's cleaner," he said defensively. "Anything wrong with being clean?"

My hands drifted over his balls, those perfectly round spheres, my fingers teasing, probing. "I'll get back to you on that."

He jerked a little and then let out a shaky breath as I continued my exploration.

"Please don't stop," he managed, knuckles turning white as he gripped the desk.

He gave me far too much credit. I didn't think I could.

"Touch yourself," I managed.

"I thought that's what you were here for," he said smartly.

I thumped a finger against his balls, and he yelped a bit. I continued rubbing them in the palm of my hand with a smirk at his glare. "In due time. Show me how much you want it first."

Seriously, would he go up in flames with all that blushing? It couldn't be healthy. Combined with the flush of his arousal, I don't think he had any more blood left for important bodily functions. He was far too aroused to deny me anything. If I'd asked him to lift his legs and finger his own asshole, I thought he just might. Just the thought sent a frisson of lust through my body, and I had to quickly think of something else, anything else. Baseball. Hockey. *No, not the man-on-man action*! I scolded my panicked brain. Scores and stats.

His hand drifted down to his cock, and I was lost. He worked his hand up and down his length with a sure grip. He slid a finger through the leaking slit, maintaining eye contact, and a groan slipped past my lips. He had picked up quite a rhythm by this time, and suddenly I looked past the beautiful sight unfolding in front of me and recognized the signs. His eyes had drifted shut, the tendons in his neck stood out stark underneath satin skin, and his balls were tight as a drum. He was closer than I'd realized. I didn't know what the result of our little experiment would be, but there was no way he was coming anywhere but my mouth.

"Put your hands on the desk," I said, my voice thick and husky with arousal.

He pumped his cock through his tight fist twice more before groaning and letting his hands drift to the desk. He flopped back flat on the desk, his erection an impressive monument to my powers of seduction. "Mac, I asked you to help me, not give me a coronary."

I pulled my chair directly in front of his jerking cock. "No reason you can't have both," I said, smartass to the end, and engulfed him fully in my mouth.

"Jesus!" He popped back up like a jack-in-the-box.

I bobbed up and down on his hard cock like he was candy because, well, he was. Every time I pulled back, his hips jerked upward to reclaim every inch of space in my mouth.

"Damn it," he swore, his breathing fast and heavy. "You're... really fucking talented, you know that?"

"I do," I confirmed, pulling back just enough so the tip remained in my mouth. I tongued the spongy head gently before digging in the salty slit with my tongue. He nearly came off the desk, and I braced my forearms on his thighs, continuing my journey, seeking more of the salty fluid. At this point, he was leaking so much I could hardly keep up.

"God, I've never felt anything like this," he said fervently.

I was too busy to respond, of course, but my licking turned smug. Of course he hadn't. Not only did I love cock, but turns out I *really* loved his cock. And I had one thing on Rachel when it came to sucking cock. I had one. And I knew what I liked.

I took my time exploring his length, running my teeth along his satiny length and then sucking him down to the root. I'd never been so glad my gag reflex was weak.

When I pulled back, he let out a bereft sound, and I met his eyes. He was watching me, eyes half-closed, stormy blue orbs demanding that I finish what I'd started. My nostrils flared, filled with the scent of his arousal and mine. His cock towered in front of my face, precum making the purplish head shiny and slick. It was time to mock him, time to throw his own desire in his face.

I hesitated just a second too long, and his impatient fingers tunneled through my hair, not pushing, not tugging, but caging my head in front of his dripping cock.

"Suck me," he demanded, and my cock leaped in response.

If anyone else had said that, I would have been irritated. Angry. But the contrast between patient, unfailingly polite Jordan who wasn't sure if he was gay and authoritative, turned-on Jordan instructing me to suck him right-the-fuck now pretty much emptied my head of ninety percent of my thinking capability. The burst of flavor on my tongue when I finally took him in my mouth blew out the rest. Suddenly I was an empty-headed sex doll who wanted nothing more than to be face-fucked.

I groaned as the hot flesh slid through the suction of my mouth.

"God!" He clenched his fingers in my hair as I made my way up and down his cock—up, and then down again, losing myself in the rhythm. "Fuck!"

I had a moment of satisfaction that I'd reduced the professional wordsmith to grunts and monosyllabic words before tightening my fingers on his hips. I concentrated on taking as much of his length into my mouth as I could while stroking the rest with a firm hand.

He knocked my hand away and gripped my head on both sides. My eyes went wide, and my mouth parted in surprise. That apparently was the only opening he needed, as he surged between my lips again. My eyes fluttered shut, and I reminded myself to keep them open so I wouldn't miss a minute. When he started pumping his hips to meet the rhythm of my bobbing head, I realized he was going to fulfill my wish. I let him face-fuck me roughly, his balls slapping against my chin with every thrust of his cock down my throat. My voice was going to sound fucked out, but I didn't care as I tightened the tunnel of my throat.

He made a strangled sound like he was trying to hold back, and then a shout followed when he failed. He exploded in my mouth, hot blasts of cum shooting down my throat in unbelievable volume.

I only had a second's notice before my sac went tight and my throbbing cock shot off, sending white cream shooting God knows where. I groaned as my body shook, a little shell-shocked. I didn't think I'd ever come without even touching myself.

I licked every drop from his cock, pulling back when the head became sensitive. I closed my eyes for a minute, enjoying the moment, that satisfaction that comes after bone-rattling sex.

"Goddamn, Mackenzie. I don't think I'm going to be able to move for a month." When I opened my eyes, Jordan was surveying me with a lazy expression I knew mirrored my own. And that was wrong.

"Even though it's a case of when the wrong one loves you the right way?" My eyebrows climbed my forehead like Mount Kilimanjaro.

He flushed. "Come on. You're so good at making me out to be a villain."

"You don't get hurt feelings, Jordan. I'm the one who just got face-fucked before you came down my throat."

The words made his eyes drop to my mouth, and suddenly the room was very quiet. Yeah, I could see a round two. And a three and a four, until we were both sweaty, sticky messes, exhausted husks of our former selves.

My hands clenched on the arms of my chair. What had I proven? That he liked getting a blow job? That he loved sex? Who didn't? I was no closer to making him *mine*, and I wasn't clueless enough to pretend I didn't want him. But I wanted *all* of him, not just to be his... goddamned booty call.

My gaze shot up to his, and he sat up straighter at the fury in my expression. Yeah, I'll admit, I changed gears pretty quickly. But the fact that he was so hot he'd distracted me from my leaving-him-high-and-dry plan just served to make me madder.

I ignored his "Oh boy, here it comes" mutter as well as I stood. He busied himself, pushing off my desk and then tucking back into his pants.

"Good enough, then? Better than Rachel?" I gave him a push, and he stumbled back a bit. "I'm not an experiment. You come find me when it's more than a curiosity, Jordan."

He frowned. "What about you?" Of course he would be the kind of guy that cared whether I came or not. Which made me even angrier. I didn't bother to tell him that he'd been so hot coming that I'd shot off in my pants like a fucking teenager.

"You sure you're ready for that, Jordan? Ready to take me in your mouth? Feel me, taste every bit of me? Have me hitting the back of your throat with my dick until you don't know where I start and you end? Taste me coming in your mouth and swallow it all down like a good little cocksucker?" Despite his denials, his eyes were still dilated and his nostrils flared in arousal. I certainly knew what it was doing to me. "Because that's really, really *gay*, Jordan. All of those things."

He stared at me for a minute, the expression in his eyes completely unreadable. And then he jammed his hands into my hair. "Damn it, Mackenzie, you drive me absolutely crazy."

He pushed me up against the wall, even as I pushed back ineffectually. He ground against my suddenly hard cock. Hard. Again. His hands weren't gentle as his mouth slanted over mine. Hungry. Seeking. Tongues and teeth and everything else as we rubbed against each other like two cats in heat. I pushed at his shoulders, and he didn't move at all. He was so much stronger than me, in fact, that I realized suddenly that he'd always been in control.

I finally managed to push him off, ignoring the fact that I really wanted to pull him closer. Near me. On me. Inside me.

"What do you think you're doing?"

He sighed, shoving a hand through his hair in mute frustration. After a moment, he said "Should be fairly obvious."

"You got what you wanted," I said hollowly, unsure of why, exactly, I felt so angry. "Now go." I couldn't say why tears had sprung to my eyes, but I'd be damned if he'd see me shed them. "*Go.*"

So he went.

I sank down in my chair, fumbling in my drawer for the one thing I needed more than air. I found the crinkled pack and my lighter easy enough, and lit one with shaking hands. I really didn't need a cigarette. I needed a fucking exorcist, because every cell of my body was crying out for someone I couldn't have. I let it burn to ash between my two fingers without taking a single puff, staring at the gleaming end.

14

"You should come up and see the bed-and-breakfast. It's everything I ever dreamed of. And I know Peyton is practically dying to meet you." There was a long pause. "I'm not going to stop calling until you answer. You really should know me better than that by now."

"End of message," the automated voice taunted me, as I stared zombielike into the fridge, drinking my orange juice slowly.

I pressed the play button again and listened to his voice on speakerphone as I tried to make a decision for breakfast. Nick sounded like himself. He sounded normal. It was hard to picture.

"I'm not going to stop calling until you answer. You really should know me better than that by now."

I did. I let the fridge door slam shut as I dropped the handle, and rinsed out my juice glass. I pressed a button on my phone. "Message deleted." Well, that was done. If only I could erase my mind that easily.

My foot landed on one of Finn's squeaky toys, and I winced. After checking my toes for permanent injury from the *Daily Growl*, aka we're-so-clever dog toy newspaper, I stared down at the offender, lying silent on the linoleum. I missed that dog like a front tooth, and I still had no ideas for getting him back. I picked up the worn, abused toy, touching the tooth marks with my finger. After a moment, I tossed it in his dog toy bin with new resolve. We wouldn't be separated too much longer if I had anything to say about it.

I suddenly remembered that I'd promised to bring the food and drinks to our fishing trip, and groaned, scratching my bare belly above flannel bottoms. I had a lot to do for it being only 5:00 a.m.

I pulled the cooler out from under the sink and washed it out slowly, rinsing away the months of nonuse under the soapy spray. I mean, really, what did Nick think we had to talk about? How I had walked away from the accident and he hadn't? How he had, ironically enough, walked away from me and our relationship? *Just like everyone else*. I didn't care what Nick said, I wouldn't be going up to Vermont to meet his partner, Peyton. Nor would I be staying at their quaint B and B.

I began emptying ice trays from my freezer into the cooler, building up a nice mountain of ice, and left them on the counter for refilling later. Then I went back to one of my favorite activities, staring into the fridge, as I debated what to bring. I was really the worst kind of host, and I didn't know what they'd been thinking, asking me to contribute in this manner. I had plenty of leftovers, but I didn't think anyone wanted the rest of my Kung Pao chicken or my Chicken Masala in the middle of the Everglades. In the end, I packed away the remainder of some KFC in a Ziploc container, and lunch meat and cheese in another. I tossed in a few containers of precut fruit and began jamming longnecks into the ice mountain, wishing I'd sprung for a bigger cooler. I fit in as many as possible, tested the lid to make sure it'd close, and dusted my hands. There.

And then, because I'm not a healthy individual, I undeleted the message and played it one more time. My ringtone broke through my playing of the message for the third time, and I answered reluctantly. "Hello?"

"You ready?"

"Hello to you too, Robert."

"We'll be by in ten, so if you don't want the old man in your place, you'd better be outside and ready."

I looked up toward the ceiling with a quick prayer of thanks. "Sometimes you're a good brother."

"See you, twerp."

I growled as we disconnected. After a long glance at the cooler, I thought about my irritating brother and removed the fruit. Then I crammed another half a case of beer into the container. We would need it to make it through the day with one another.

I sped through my living room and dove into my closet, digging through my abundant Florida wardrobe for anything weather appropriate to wear. As I sifted through at least three dozen tees with mostly foul sayings, beer slogans, and *No Fear* mantras plastered on them, I kept an eye out for anything long-sleeved. While the weather made you want short sleeves and short pants, I had no intention of being bitten a million times over—the Everglades' Mosquito Posse rode deep and took no prisoners. I finally decided on a pair of faded jeans and a long-sleeved Nike shirt warning me in white letters about being a first-place loser.

I jammed on my Hurricanes baseball cap on my way out and hurried to grab the cooler. Just as I lifted the handles, my dad started in on the horn, and I gritted my teeth.

"A pause between honks would be nice," I yelled.

I thought better of my earlier decision and removed the lunch meat and cheese and stuffed them back in the fridge. Then I crammed the other half of the case of beer into the cooler. It was going to be a long day.

My dad's black Dodge Ram was a bit of a monster truck, with a quad cab and dual tires in the back. The headlights cut through the early morning gloom like spotlights, and I waved as I locked my door.

I slung the cooler in the backseat, barely avoiding Robert's lunge (to give me a noogie, no doubt), and closed the door on his irritating face. Robert's son, Case, slept peacefully on the other side. Thank God. I don't think the little shit said anything that didn't begin with "epic fail" or (an oldie but a goodie) "your face" nowadays. I slid in the front after levering myself up and shut the door.

"Dad."

"Mac. You like the new fog lights?"

I was proud of myself. I didn't say *one* snarky word about him not needing fog lights. "They're nice."

"Grill guard is new too."

I grunted.

"You going to be this talkative the whole way, boy?"

"*Dad*. It's early."

"Can't fish at noon, son."

When I was a kid, my dad had had a small stick-shift Isuzu that jerked like the very devil. I remember sitting in the back of that truck, clinging to the silver toolbox on the bed, ears laid back in the wind. I guess sitting comfortable in the cab is one of the perks of being almost thirty. The conversation? Not so much.

A stop at McDonald's for coffee and Egg McMuffins all around had me two steps closer to feeling human again. By the time we pulled into a tackle shop, it was nearing six fifteen, and my dad didn't even wait for us to all clamber out of the truck before disappearing inside the shop. Case finally woke and joined us, dragging at least ten feet behind.

One foot inside the tackle shop, he sniffed the air and announced, "I'm going to the car. It stinks in here."

"It's a bait shop," I managed to get in before the teenager plugged his ears with whatever MP3 player he had in his pocket. Disturbed's "Criminal" blared out briefly before he slammed the Ram's cab door.

I wandered around the shop, seeing what was new in bait and tackle since the last time I'd been fishing. In a word? Nothing. I could hear laughter on the other side of the shop, and I peered through a bucket of rods and reels to see my dad introducing Robert to another guy in tall fishing boots. A manly man from the looks of it. No one would wear all that flannel unless he was okay crushing beer cans on his forehead. I rolled my eyes as Robert preened under the attention, and slunk off to the Pepsi machine.

I'd brought enough beer for a NASCAR race, but I'd forgotten about Case. As I fed the machine quarters and bought three cans of Pepsi, I wondered how someone as old school as my retired police officer father had ever accepted a gay son. I guess it helped that I still watched sports, built things with my hands, had no idea of how to decorate, cook, or keep house, and was basically, well, let's face it, a bit of a slob.

I'd actually told him over *Sports Center* blaring on one TV and C-SPAN on the other—how the man listened to two televisions at once, I'd never know. As my voice had warred for supremacy with Ted Koppel and Charles Barkley, I'd snatched the remote and muted both televisions in my version of a hissy fit. I'd repeated myself firmly and slowly. "I said, I'm gay."

"I have ears, boy."

"Then *say* something about what I just said."

"What do you want me to say? Nothing you don't already know."

"Say it anyway," I'd demanded, my eyes hot and dry.

"Oh for God's sakes. If I didn't know you were gay before, I'd know it now." He'd cut a glance my way, and something in my face had made him sigh. "All right, then. I ain't happy about it. I think you're making a mistake. I think you're a little touched in the head. But you're my son. And I love you." He'd gone as red as the plaid on his ratty old armchair. "Ain't nothin' gonna change that."

"That's... all you have to say?" I'd asked. Nothing about dishonoring the family? No f-word? No slinging my clothes out on the lawn?

"No. Turn back on my damn C-SPAN. *That's* all I have to say. Damned Republicans," he'd muttered for no reason at all. He'd always loved to blame everything on the damned Republicans.

I'd shrugged and done as he'd asked. If he wanted to blame my gayness on the damned Republicans, that was fine by me.

"Minnows or fly fishin'?"

I blinked to find my dad standing in front of me with a bucket and a questioning look. "Sir?"

"Minnows or fly fishin'?"

I don't know how long I'd been there clutching Case's sweating

Pepsi cans, stuck in the past, so I shrugged. I may have always tried to be manly for my pops, but there was no way I was touching live bait. He knew that by now. He just had a strange sense of humor.

"Up to you," I said gamely. "I'm not touching anything living."

Robert snorted, and I made a face in his direction. Yep, my father still baited my hook, and I wasn't ashamed to admit it.

As our dad made off to the minnows tank, I touched one of the ice-cold cans to Robert's neck. He yelped and swatted at me.

"You look stupider than usual," I said, pointing at the strange glasses he was wearing. He looked like the henchman in a steampunk film.

"They're high-power fishing goggles," he said, taking them off and turning them over in his hand. "They're supposed to tell the fisherman exactly where the fish are. Like x-ray vision for the water."

"Doesn't that defeat the purpose?" I asked, squinting at the package. They were two hundred dollars' worth of overpriced garbage.

Robert, despite the hemming and hawing, would eventually purchase them. The man loved his toys. The motorcycles, the ATVs, and the bumblebee Camaro in his garage were only second to the gigantic flat screen that he crowed about every single game day. And while I thought most of his toys were pretty damn cool, I didn't see the point of the fishing goggles. If I wanted to know where the fish were, I'd go to Publix.

In the end, we all left the store clutching our bounty—Robert and his stupid goggles and me with my soda. Our dad followed behind with a bucket full of swirling yellow minnows, darting back and forth as if they knew what was waiting for them. I crammed my reflective aviators over my nose, watching the steam rise off the hood of the truck. The sun was starting to peek over the horizon, and heat was starting to make my back prickle in the long clothing as I clambered into the A/C of the truck.

We passed a Miccosukee reservation and two wildlife reserves before my dad found a spot he liked. He didn't like the spots actually designated for fishing; he liked the small openings in the forestation that led down to the water. Less traveled and better fish, he always swore by them. Robby carried the cooler while I carried the minnows gingerly as we made our way behind our dad down the steep slope. My dad carried his machete, carving away misshapen bushes and grass like he was freaking Indiana Jones. The machete wasn't for show, in case we met something that thought *we* would taste delicious on some bread. Case carried himself and a blue Nintendo DS.

My bum leg started to burn as I strained to take the steep slope, but I wouldn't say a word. I didn't even have the pleasure of a grimace as my dad watched me with a gimlet eye, just waiting to take the bucket from me.

It wasn't long before we were set up on upturned buckets and a beach chair, each swearing by the spot we'd picked, and waiting for a bite. As I stared at my lure, willing it to go under, I was soothed by the soft chattering of my father and brother. They were talking about his job, and I tried to be happy for the two peas in a pod. So what if I was a carrot? Peas and carrots still went well together... sometimes in the same dish.

My lure bobbed under briefly, and I was excited before I realized I'd been picked clean. "Damn," I mumbled under my breath. "Sneaky little devils."

"Epic fail, Uncle Mac," Case announced in a way that made me want to bean him with my fishing rod. He was lucky I loved him like he was my own son. Whoever created epic fail should be tied and stuffed in a sack with whoever created work, discrete calculus, and "Where is this relationship going?" then drowned in a river.

Feeling quite snarky, I snapped, "What's the point of fishing if you're just going to have your nose buried in a DS all day?"

He shrugged, flipping a wave of overlong caramel brown hair out of his eye, and I felt like an ass. Maybe he just wanted to spend time with his dad. Or his grandpa. Or hell, judging from the distance of his bucket chair from mine, maybe even his Uncle Mac. I tugged the DS from his hands and stuffed it in my back pocket.

"Here." I handed him my line. "I'm going to show you how to cast."

The quiet murmur of my dad and Robert faded into the background as I showed Case the basics, and we cast and cast again. The kid had a good arm—probably would make a great ball player someday. Terrible fisherman. But a great ball player.

"Back over the shoulder," I instructed, and he slung it over his shoulder like a Louisville Slugger. The bait sailed into the trees, and the hook caught on a branch. When he pulled, the tree shook, as if it too were holding back laughter.

Three minnows and two hooks later, he was throwing a pretty good line. "You're in the reeds, Case." I mimed pulling the line back. "You need to cast again."

"Stuck again?" He frowned down at the dark water. "How can you tell?"

"See mine? It's bobbing and shifting a bit with the wind and current. Yours is—"

"Still as a rock." He scowled, yanking the line back into the trees. "Don't worry, Uncle Mac," he assured me as we tried to find his lure in the bushes. "By summer, I'll have the hang of it. We can come out here anytime then."

"Maybe."

Weren't children dragged off to summer school anymore? I had no intention of spending my summer on the fishing creek, but I was hesitant to ruin any of Case's non-teenager, I-hate-being-alive moments. We picked our way through the bushes to find his caught line, branches and hidden mangrove scraping at my jean-clad legs.

When we returned from our Search and Rescue operation, Robert had apparently tried on his new fishing goggles and was staring down into the water intently, brows furrowed.

"See anything, Rob? Fish? Spare tires? Loose change?"

He gave a noncommittal grunt to my ribbing, and I wondered what had put him in such a foul mood all of a sudden. I mean really, I groused to myself as I grabbed a beer out of the cooler, one moment he was talking to Dad, and the next.... Oh, man. A little too late, I saw my father's eyes narrowed in my direction, and I knew he was making the rounds. Rare it was when my father decided to get nosy, but unpleasant nonetheless.

"How about you, Mac? How're things going down at the firm?"

"Good." I bobbed my head, clutching my beer like a lifeline. Calling my tiny PI gig a firm was a bit ritzy, but why not? "Real good."

"Meet anyone nice lately? Anything new on the dating scene?"

Oh dear Lord. I couldn't meet my brother's eyes. Even if they were covered by those stupid goggles, that would set us both off. I would *not* laugh at my father when he was trying so hard to make conversation.

"No, but you'll be the first to know."

"I tried to set him up with this great guy I know, but he's got a crush on some straight guy," Robert tattled for reasons known only to him and the Lord above.

I sent him the darkest glare I could muster, which, as far as I could tell, bounced right off his thick head. "Thank you, Robert."

"Welcome," he sang.

"Chasing after someone who is straight." My dad nodded. "Sounds productive."

A snigger came from Robert's general direction, and I suddenly knew where I was going to wing my beer can when it was empty.

"It's more fun than you can possibly imagine." I sighed and dropped the sarcasm. "But even a hope that we could have been something more is gone."

"Oh?"

I had to give him props. Even though his face was beet red discussing his gay son's love life, he seemed to be determined to stay his course. I rewarded his effort with the truth, embarrassing as it was.

"He told me that he's uncomfortable with the idea of dating a man and can't see or talk to me again." He wasn't that specific about seeing or talking to me, but I was an expert at reading between the lines.

"Bastard." Robert scowled.

"He's really not. He's just... not gay. Which, to be fair, he told me in the beginning. He's actually a pretty cool guy, which makes it that much worse." I gave a half smile. "But don't you worry, my love life is going just fine, thank you very much."

"Is it?" My dad's next words made me regret sharing. "I heard from Nick."

I took a swig of my beer. "Did you now?"

"Don't give me that tone." My dad's cheeks had gone dull red. "He told me he can't get in touch with you. Wanted to know if he had the right number."

"Well, he does."

"Glad to hear it." I really should have known better than to hope the subject had passed as he continued. "He wants to see you. It's not really all that easy for him to travel."

"I don't want to talk about Nick."

"The accident was nearly six years ago," Robert said. "Right before you hooked up with that loser, Trevor."

"The only thing I want to talk about less than Nick is Trevor."

"We're just concerned," my father interjected. "Nick wouldn't want you to—"

"What part of I don't want to talk about Nick don't you understand?"

"Now wait just a minute—"

"God, you have no respect for—"

"I have plenty of respect!" he groused. "But I know something about missing someone you love."

I was silent for a moment, letting the anger slide and settle somewhere in my stomach region, where it burned like acid. But he had pulled the trump card. The mom card. My mother had run off fourteen years ago, but the old man still had us every time. She had left him and us for our neighbor, a man half her age. Our father had raised us without malice, never taught us to hate her for what she'd done. But just the pain in my father's voice when he spoke of her made me want to hit something. Or someone.

"You been pining ever since, and that Trevor was a poor substitute," he went on. "'Course that didn't work out. That boy is all about himself. Don't have one thought that isn't about Trevor. Never did like that boy."

He'd loved Trevor. Everyone had. Or maybe they'd just wanted me to move on.

"You can't use the mom card for at least another year," I said sourly.

He shrugged. "I want to meet this Jordan fellow."

"Why? It's not like we're dating or anything. He's not—"

"Gay, I know, I know. I can still hear just fine, boy. Just let him get to know you, and he'll like you just fine. Young people today are so determined to slap labels on everything."

I refused to explain why sitting Jordan and I down in a playpen like toddlers would not work. And us liking each other "just fine" was part of the problem. That day in my office, we'd nearly "liked" one another into a sexual coma.

"I got one!" Robert hollered suddenly.

"Not for long with all that noise," my father said as we both swiveled around.

I noted two things fairly quickly—one, Robert looked like a complete idiot with those bug-eyed goggles on, and two, if we made it out alive, we were getting a refund on those glasses.

"Let go of the pole!" I shouted.

I grabbed Case's collar and threw him toward the hill and then began scrabbling up behind him on my hands and knees, rocks scraping my legs even through the jeans. I hoped that was my father I heard behind me, scrabbling up the hill, and not the beast Robert had unleashed from the deep.

"For God's sakes, Robby, it's an alligator!"

15

Mud squelched in my shoes as I made my way up the drive, muttering dire threats against my brother. Between the yelling and cursing and one unidentified squeal that no one would cop to, we'd all managed to perch on a ledge—a rickety ledge, may I add. It had, however, given us the opportunity to observe the alligator raiding our mini-camp with feckless abandon.

"Stupid Robert. Stupid Robert and his stupid glasses."

I stopped short when I reached my door. Of course Jordan was sitting there—Murphy's Law was a real thing, after all. He was sitting on the narrow strip of my stoop, forearms perched on his stonewashed jean clad knees, taking in my appearance in a decidedly wide-eyed manner. My heart gave a little gallop that I was more than happy to ignore.

"What happened to you?" His nose wrinkled in a way I refused to identify as adorable. "You smell like a creek."

"I was attacked by an alligator." I stomped past him, enjoying the way he leaped up to give my mud-speckled appearance a wide berth.

"What?" A forgotten Starbucks cup dangled from his hand. "You were attacked by an alligator?"

"Well, the cooler was." I dropped my keys and baseball cap on the end table nearest the door, toeing off my filthy sneakers. "And he managed to drag my fishing pole and cooler back to the hell from whence he came."

I didn't want to go any farther than I had to, dripping Everglades on my carpet. Socks followed quickly after. I paused before stripping off my shirt, hands curled at the hem of the filthy garment. My eyes shot to Jordan, but he was already making his unsolicited presence comfortable in my living room. Frustrated that I'd even given him a second thought, I yanked the shirt over my head.

"I'm going to take a shower," I said. Waiting. Awkward.

"Oh yeah? Go ahead. I'll be here."

Thank you for giving me permission to shower in my own home.

He settled into the cushions of the couch, moving one of the throw pillows beside him. He looked comfortable there… here, in my living room. With me. *You come find me when it's more than a curiosity, Jordan.* Well, he'd found me. So what did that mean? Despite the chain of questions running through my head, I knew I should go for casual and breezy. Crazy, desperate people wound up with cats and afghans.

I settled on a terse, "Why are you here?"

He managed to look adorably flustered with very little effort. "I wanted to see you."

"And what does that mean? I thought I made myself perfectly clear—"

"God, Mackenzie, you think way too much. Just chill, okay? Go." He shooed me. "Take your shower."

Now I was tired, dirty, *and* huffy. I thought too much? Maybe if he wasn't so determined to keep me tied up in knots….

"Make yourself at home," I murmured, heading for the bathroom.

The hot water did a half-assed job of lightening my mood as I scrubbed every nook and cranny. I stood under the spray, letting the knotbetween my shoulder blades take a good pounding. The water sluiced over my shoulders for an obscenely long time as I stalled/bathed. I lathered the soap between my hands absently, not knowing why I was so unsettled. *You wanted him here. He's here. And you're hiding in the shower.*

I shut the water off with a wrench of the shower knob and tried to pretend I was a normal human being. I changed into a pair of threadbare jeans and a T-shirt that had seen better days before padding into the living room, rubbing a navy blue towel over my shock of hair. He was standing in a shaft of sunlight, examining the sparse DVD collection strewn about the entertainment center.

For a moment, I stood like a dope, clutching my towel like a lifeline, staring at the strangely delicate shell of his ear. He had tucked tendrils of his hair behind the ear, a study of soft peach and pink. It felt strangely intimate, studying the back of his ears. I wanted to touch them. Trace them with my fingers.

I marched over and stuck my hand past his nose to take the stack of DVDs from his unresisting grasp. "You're still here."

"Yes," he agreed.

"Why?"

For the first time, he looked a little unsure. His gaze slid from mine. "I-I don't know."

It was expectedly awkward. Maybe because I was expecting our... whatever this was, to turn into a relationship. I was tired of thinking about, over, and under it. I was tired, period. Maybe he was right. I did think too damn much. *Just let him get to know you, and he'll like you just fine*. Oh, goody. Now I had my dad's voice entrenched in my mind.

I set the DVDs on the coffee table and plunked down on the couch. I ignored him as he plopped down next to me, and clicked the TV and cable box on. "You like TV?"

"What am I, an animal?"

I took that to mean yes. "The Heat game is on."

"Whatever you want."

What I wanted was to finish what we'd started in my office. I tried not to think about the lube and condoms in my bedside drawer, hopeful sentinels that barely got used, waiting a scant few feet away.

We watched the game in companionable silence, punctuated by my attempts to couch-coach the team and Jordan's attempts to shush me. They didn't need my help. By halftime, they were up sixty-three to forty-four, and LeBron was showboating with an easy layup that fluttered on the rim for three seconds before dropping into the net.

"Do you have anything to drink around here?"

"Bring your own beer, princess."

"What kind of host are you?"

"The lazy kind."

Remembering my visits to his house and office and how hospitable he had been both times had me sighing. I levered myself off the couch and made my way to the refrigerator. I ignored Finn's empty, waiting bowls by the door and leaned in, enjoying the cool blast of air on my face.

"Let's see. I can offer you mustard or... pickles, looks like. Yeah, pickles." I scratched my head. "Maybe we can order some pizza."

"Or I can take you out somewhere for real food." His voice near my ear made me jump.

I hadn't heard him follow me into the kitchen, but now that he was so close, I don't know how I could have missed the heat radiating off his body. He looked a bit flushed, and I wondered if he had been checking out my ass. His eyes widened at my squinty-eyed stare, and I knew he had been.

It would be so easy to turn, just the slightest bit, and press my body into his. He was just the right height—my face would just meet the curve of his neck. What I would do when I was there? Well, that practically wrote itself.

"Mackenzie?"

"Yeah?"

"You want to eat out? Or stay here?"

"Out," I croaked. Anything was better than being so close to my bedroom. Maybe then I could get my mind out of the gutter and enjoy his company. I shut the fridge and turned to face him. "You have a place in mind?"

"There's a little Japanese place downtown I've wanted to try. What do you think?"

I thought I was courting trouble. But I said only, "Perfect."

A guy's gotta eat, after all.

I couldn't shake the feeling that this was a date. The atmosphere of Peking Tokyo was jovial and fun, your typical Benihana experience. The lights were a little low, but the music was some kind of peppy Gangnam Style deal. Yet our table had a warm feel, a small, intimate space for two. The small round tables were perfect for their tiny-ass plates of food. Delicious. But small. The chef had long since deserted our table after we made him do the onion volcano trick like four times.

I gave the remnants of my stir-fry a poke. I usually didn't eat bean sprouts, but as hungry as I was, I was willing to give it a go.

"How was it?" Jordan asked.

"Perfect."

He chuckled softly. "You only say that when something is wrong, you know."

A flush climbed my neck, and I couldn't help it. I sent him a glare over the candlelit setting. "Okay, it's small."

I only needed to eat light when I was planning on some heavy aerobic activity after. Preferably in the bedroom. And suddenly, I had to ask.

"Jordan, why does this feel so much like a date?"

It was hard to tell under the dim lighting, but I thought he might have blushed. "Does it?"

I narrowed my gaze. "Are you trying me out again?" He reddened further, and I sighed. "Oh, for fuck's sake—"

"I'm not *trying* out anything, okay? Calm down. I just wanted to take you out for a nice dinner."

"Because...."

"Because you're funny. And smart. Hot," he admitted, and I was pretty much close to full forgiveness. "I like being around you and talking to you... and I'm trying to figure out if I'm bi or if I just like you."

"Forgive me if I've misunderstood, but why do I feel like I win either way?"

He smiled a smile of relief and put his hand over mine. His hand was warm. Big. Comforting and arousing at the same time. "So this is okay?"

"This is very okay."

We sat, grinning at one other like fools until the waiter placed the check between us. I glared. Moment killer.

I busied myself by shrugging into my jacket. Even though our forecast was usually one word—hot—sometimes the ocean breeze kicked us a little somethin' at night, and we gleefully pulled out those jackets we'd been saving for the slightest hint of cool weather. Every native Floridian had a winter wardrobe that rivaled that of any snowbird, which my Northern friends usually found quite amusing. When the thermometer inched below seventy, it was jackets and UGG boots *on*. His voice cut through my wardrobe musings.

"So what are we going to do now?"

A million things raced through my mind, all of them too dirty to even speak of. He wasn't ready for any of that. The next time we got physical needed to be his call—I had led the horse to water and all but pushed his face into the trough.

I clenched my jaw with resolve. "Maybe a movie. Dessert? I know this café downtown that serves a mean cheesecake. Maybe coffee? You like coffee," I babbled.

"And after that?" His tone was quiet.

"What do you normally do after that?"

His eyes went wide, and my heart began fluttering a million miles a minute. God, he was just so damned cute. "And not that either. Coffee. Talking. Then that's what we'll do."

The waiter came by, and Jordan tucked his Visa and the check back into the black portfolio before handing it to him. He turned to me as the waiter disappeared, a frown creasing his brow. "Until when?"

"Until," I answered vaguely.

"When?" he prodded.

Damn, but that waiter was fast. He brought back the portfolio and slid it across the table before disappearing again. Jordan pocketed his card and signed for the tip and receipt.

"Until you ask for something more," I said, thoroughly exasperated.

His eyes glinted devilishly, and suddenly his face was very close to mine. "I'm asking for more."

"Like what?"

"Kiss me."

I swallowed hard. "That works too."

Apparently, when Jordan made a decision, he was all in. I was suddenly glad the restaurant had such dim lighting—I had a monster hard-on, and I hadn't even touched my lips to his yet.

I couldn't turn my brain off, even as I relished the thought of getting his silky soft lips against mine again. After all of my badgering him to make a decision, he had, and now I was the one filled with doubt. I had gone through this before with Trevor. I didn't know if I could go through that again. My catch and release program was hell on the nerves.

I stopped, close enough for our noses to touch, close enough to see the black limbal ring around his iris. "Are you sure?"

He closed the distance between our mouths with no hesitation, and suddenly I couldn't think at all. His mouth worked mine over so thoroughly that I barely participated, only took what he had to give. He worked his tongue into my mouth so seamlessly I wasn't even aware he'd done it until I was dueling his tongue with my own, sliding against his in a way that made my stomach clench violently. When he sucked on my tongue, I whimpered into his mouth, embarrassed that the sound had even come from me but unable to care enough to stop.

When he tore his mouth away, we were both breathing heavily. He rested his forehead against mine until we regained normal breathing ability.

"I want it," he said hoarsely. "All of it."

"All of what?"

"All of those things you said. Tasting you. Feeling you. Making you come. I haven't been able to think about anything else without your voice running through my head. Thanks for that, by the way," he said with a glare.

"I didn't know that," I said stupidly. Of course I hadn't. If I had, he would have been flat on his back in my bed the moment I saw him on my stoop.

"And now that you do?"

Images flew through my head so quickly I couldn't even sort through them, but I knew we were naked in the majority of them. Good enough. I grabbed his hand in response. "Let's get out of here."

"But what about the movies?" he said innocently as I dragged him along.

"If you have a video camera, I'm feeling a little creative."

16

We're lucky we didn't get arrested for public indecency for making out in the car. Or the street, Jordan's hands firmly cupping my ass and lifting me against his rigid cock. Or fumbling our way back into my apartment before finally slamming me against the door. I'd never been quite so glad to get a door between me and prying eyes before as I sank to my knees and mouthed his cock through his jeans.

He hissed. "God, the way you get me going should be a crime."

"I haven't even started yet," I said, managing to undo his zipper and boxer flap one handed. I couldn't be bothered with buckles and buttons as I slid his erection through the space. My nostrils flared at the sharp smell of his arousal, and my mouth watered at the sight of precum already leaking around the head of his cock. God, he was so beautiful. And for now, he was all mine.

I couldn't wait to taste him. I wanted to bite him, to lick his skin like the salt on the rim of a glass right before the smooth slide of margarita. And for once, there was nothing stopping me.

I didn't bother with the preliminaries. I sucked him down to the root without hesitation, without a drop of resistance. He groaned like he was dying of some terrible malaise, his head slamming back against the wall so hard I feared permanent damage.

"You okay?" I managed around his dick.

"Better. Than. Okay." Another groan escaped, and his flat stomach expanded under my palm as he struggled to get his breathing under control. "Please don't stop."

"You give me too much credit," I said, swirling my tongue in the pool of cum at the tip of his cock. "I don't think anything short of a hurricane could stop me now."

"Best news I've heard all day." He ran his hands through my hair, but his fingers didn't push or pull. They seemed to just be digging into my hair, massaging and luxuriating there.

He bucked up to meet my increased suction, and my hands shot up to still his hips. If he started face-fucking me, I was done, and this time, I wanted something a little more. We seemed to be of one accord as he pulled me to my feet and took my mouth in a mind-melting kiss.

I pushed him back. "The couch," I demanded.

On my way there, I could hear him behind me shucking his clothes—the belt buckle hitting the floor, the rustle of jeans. I followed suit, leaving a trail of clothing wherever they fell. We came together naked at the couch, and I pulled him down on top of me. I buried my face in his neck as we ground against each other, spreading my legs wider to increase the friction. I would be embarrassed later, but for now I just wanted as much skin-to-skin contact as I could possibly have.

After a moment, he wrenched my wrists together. "Tell me what do to before it's too late."

Crap. The supplies. "I need a minute."

I tried to get up, but he forced me back down, running his hands down the strong lines of my thighs, currently spread like a wanton slut. When his finger slipped into my hole, I lost the power of speech and the will to make rational decisions. I'd forgotten what a butt slut I could be, but his finger sliding into the tight heat brought my predilections screaming back. My eyes slammed shut, and my heels dug into the couch cushions.

"Yessss," was all I could manage, as that insistent digit played me like a master pianist.

"You go nowhere. I've been dreaming of having you here, just like this."

"We need lube. Condoms," I gasped out.

His tongue swathed a path from my balls and in between my cheeks, and a shiver rippled down my spine. I felt his hands underneath my hips suddenly, spreading me farther apart, holding me immobile. Bossy fucking top. I'd known he would be. He hesitated at my sensitive opening, his breath misting across my skin. I waited breathlessly, knowing what he *wanted* to do. I just wasn't sure if he *could*, despite what he'd said to the contrary.

His jaw tightened, and suddenly his tongue was sliding into my hole, warm, wet, and demanding.

"Holy fucking shit," I blurted.

His tongue twisted and unfurled in my ass, teasing me, exploring me, until he was tongue fucking me relentlessly. I couldn't stay still. Couldn't breathe. Restlessly shifting as I made noises I'd never heard another human make before. I twisted my fingers in his hair, pulling him up. Thought I'd wind up with tufts in my hands when I was done.

"Need you," I demanded. "Now."

"You've got me," he muttered as he teased my entrance with the head of his cock.

"Might be easier if I turn over," I suggested as his mouth trailed down my pecs. My breath stuttered in my chest as he began teasing my swollen nipples.

"I want to see you. See your face."

I bit back my refusal, wondering why it left me so rattled. It was just so intimate, so immediate. I wasn't ready for that. But I was more than ready for his cock. My slutty side won out, and I ran my hands down the definitions of muscle in his tanned stomach.

He hung long and thick between my cheeks, creating friction as he tunneled there. He took my mouth, and I knew at that moment that it would never be like this with anyone else, never be better than this at all.

"Where?" he ground out, and I didn't have to ask what he meant.

"Bedroom. Side drawer."

He was back before I could get a good rhythm going stroking my cock, and he rolled the condom on with little ado. He struggled with the cap of the lube for a moment, looking adorably flustered, before spreading way too much on the rim of my hole.

"Holy K-Y, Batman," I grumbled, but I had to admit I enjoyed the glide of his finger as he worked the lube around and in my hole. And from the looks of his swollen cock—the thick head leaking, the strong column jerking and jumping against his stomach, I was going to need it. Even a seasoned pro like myself (no cracks, dammit) appreciated a little prep work. I whimpered and canted my hips up a bit, ignoring the bastard's cheeky grin.

"I must be doing something right."

"Add a finger," I said, bearing down on the one I had.

He did, and I moaned like the good butt slut I was. He finger-fucked me, working the fingers in past the knuckle and swiping that little walnut-sized bundle of nerves that I love oh so much.

"Yessss," I hissed, my hand circling his wrist. I didn't know whether it was to stop him or clock him if he actually did.

When he finally removed his fingers from my prepped channel, I groaned with regret. There really *wasn't* anything he didn't do well, and finger-fucking was no exception. He pressed his lips to mine, hard, while positioning himself at my entrance. He eased the engorged head past the ring of muscle, gripping my hands in his. I wanted to pull away, look away, move away, but he just gripped my hands tighter where they were pinned, next to my head. And then he entered me in one swift plunge that left us both gasping.

My back went ramrod straight as I adjusted to his girth, his length. Goddamn, did he have to have so much of both? I slipped my hands from his and put them firmly on his flanks, holding him immobile, gratified to feel the shaking there. It didn't look like he was holding on to his control by very much.

"Sorry, sorry," he whispered, dropping kisses on my cheeks and lips in apology. "I should've gone slower."

His mouth on my neck and his hand on my dick had me going in less than a minute. Every one of my senses seemed enhanced, my skin sensitive to the slightest of touches. His breath rasped in my ear. I could feel him pulsing inside my inner walls, my hole deliciously stretched and quivering around his cock.

"Shit," he swore. "You feel like a goddamned vise."

"Move," I said hoarsely. I needed to be fucked. Now.

His hands locked around my hips, he began a slow rhythm, pulling almost all the way out and then pushing back in. He seemed mesmerized by the sight of our joining, the sight of his thick cock stretching me impossibly, deliciously. I was equally mesmerized by the wonder on his face, the satisfaction that I'd put that look there. I worked my muscles around his cock in a way that had his face contorting, the muscles in his shoulders tensing.

"You keep that up and I'll only last a minute," he warned me.

"That's all you have?" I taunted, working my ass like a separate entity. (Good Lord, was I twerking?)

He gave a pained laugh and pressed his forehead to mine. "Shut up, Mackenzie."

He began thrusting into me in a way that made talking (if I'd been so inclined) impossible. Suddenly he was pounding me into the couch, and I was taking it and loving it. I slammed my ass back against him, meeting him stroke for stroke. When the curve of his dick met my prostate, I nearly shot off the couch.

"Fuck!"

He looked shocked and pleased as he hit that spot again, damn him. Or bless him. Or whatever as he began ramming that spot for all he was worth. I began pulling at my dick with a shaking hand, jerking myself with no rhythm whatsoever. Stars began twinkling in the edges of my blackened vision, and a stream of cursing, swearing, and nonsense filled the air as he fucked me into the couch.

My limbs felt cold and heavy as my climax ripped through my body, and a scream (manly yell, I mean) erupted from somewhere in my throat region. My body shook uncontrollably even as I registered somewhere in my fogginess his groan and the warm feel as the condom filled in my ass.

He was heavy, his face buried in my neck. He mumbled something in my ear about smothering me, but I wasn't ready to move him just yet. I ran my hands down the sweat-slick muscles in his back and up to the strong column of his neck, pressing him farther down on me.

"You good?" he murmured.

"Mhmm."

"I guess that's good." He sounded ridiculously pleased with himself.

"Yeah," I said when I could manage real words again. "I guess it is."

17

A strange buzzing sound jarred me out of sleep and into the land of the living. I opened my eye a crack, trying to examine the room with just one rolling retina until a shaft of sunlight stabbed me clean in the eye. I groaned and rolled to a sitting position, swinging my feet off the couch. I could feel all the muscles I'd abused that night coming alive and protesting as I groped the floor for Jordan's pants. When I encountered the jeans, I shook out his phone and pressed snooze, then tossed it on the couch. I was alone and... naked, but he was still here, somewhere, which was either reassuring or irritating, I couldn't decide which. Reassuring that he hadn't taken off, but irritating if I'd just caught him making his escape.

I rubbed a hand over my rooster hair and stumbled to the bathroom. I drew up short next to the bathroom door, hearing the shower going. I thought about knocking for a scant moment before shrugging. He'd had his tongue in my ass—I assumed we were past shyness. I opened the door to a cloud of steam and made my way to the toilet, taking care of business with little ado.

"Do you ever knock?"

I grinned a grin that ended in a yawn, even though my eyes were closed. "It's my place."

He laughed, and after a flush, I turned to leer at him through the glass. His body was a study of beautiful definition, rivulets of water cascading down his shoulders and back. His hair was dark with water and slicked in a thousand different directions with gel shampoo.

"You look good enough to eat," I managed.

"You should talk."

"We should have gone to the bed last night." I stretched, scratching my stomach. "I think I have a crick in my neck."

"I think I could help you with that."

"Oh yeah?" My brows went high. "You could have helped me with that in, oh, say three hours too."

"I have work. Some of us aren't self-employed." He grinned. "But you're welcome to join me."

Try and stop me. "You make it worth my while?"

"I'll see what I can do."

"Promises, promises."

He pulled the shower door open, eyes locked on mine. I gulped. Apparently, Jordan kept his promises. When his hands fisted my cock, I wasn't feeling quite so mouthy. They traced my length slowly, leisurely, as if he had all the time in the world. My focus narrowed to the mesmerizing sight of him stroking me, swirling a thumb in the pearly liquid gathering on the top and lubricating his path to the base.

His hand wrapped around my cock, wet, deliciously suctioning, and he pulled me forward gently. I entered the shower without being aware that I'd done so, but suddenly there was water beating my back, so I guess I did. I would have gone anywhere that he led me, as long as he didn't let go of my cock. When he dropped to his knees, I hesitated, putting a stilling hand on his shoulder.

I couldn't seem to form the words, but I wanted him to be sure. We could fool around without him doing that, even if I wanted his mouth on me more than I wanted air in that moment. "You don't have to...."

"I want to." His hand worked up and down, rubbing me into a

frictioned frenzy. My good intentions disappeared like smoke, and I twisted my hands in his wet hair.

"Then do it," I demanded.

He didn't hesitate, letting my cock slide through the hot wetness of his mouth, a slow glide that made my eyes roll back in my head. His tongue teased me, tasted me, bringing me to the brink and then easing back, kissing my thighs and stomach until I was ready to go again. I couldn't look away from his lips, swollen and stretched around me as he tried again and again to fit me deeper into his mouth. I felt the pressure building in my balls, but I didn't want to miss a single second of the best wake-up call I'd had in my life. My thumbs massaged the hard line of his jaw and up through the ends of his hair as he constricted his throat around my cock.

"Guh," I muttered. "Gah."

I could see the amusement in his eyes, even through the fringe of thick, dark lashes. The bastard was *amused* at my inability to form words, and I was determined to score a victory. So the fuck what he was a natural. He hadn't exactly been chatty during his blow job.

"Good," I managed. "So good." *So there.*

His fingers were suddenly behind me and then in me, and I came hard, exploding down his throat. He started for a moment and then relaxed his jaw again, finger-fucking me slowly, milking every drop.

"Fuuuuuck," I wheezed, patting his face, his hair nonsensically. I was lucky my knees hadn't buckled.

He came to his feet and opened the shower door. He rubbed his feet on the rug quickly, exiting the shower like it was now a burning inferno. He looked back at me expectantly.

I returned his look hesitantly. Coming in a guy's mouth was a big deal, especially without asking, and I was pretty sure it had been his first time giving head. I winced. Boy, when you told me you were bi, you'd better have meant it. "Look, I'm sorry. You're just… really fucking incredible at that. Took me by surprise—"

"Where?" he gritted out.

My eyebrows shot up in surprise. "Where what?"

"Condoms. You have them in here, yeah?"

I grinned, relieved. "Nah. I normally don't get lucky in the shower. Or at all, really."

He groaned and was streaking through the apartment in no time. When he came back, he had two packets in his hand and was ripping another with his teeth.

My eyes widened. "That's… optimistic."

He grinned. "We'll leave a few in here."

My heart stuttered a bit. That certainly implied more encounters, more time with him… more everything.

Turns out we didn't leave any. Not one. He'd done me in the hot, steamy water, hands secure around my bottom as I braced myself on the slippery tile wall. Then the lukewarm. Then the ice cold. My water bill was going to be sky high, but I didn't give a shit. Every time we were so… fucking… close, he slowed down, long and slow strokes that drove me insane. I'd been right; he fucked like a machine. I could hear the slow-motion suction as he left my ass completely and the slow rasp of skin on skin as he entered me again. I threatened. I swore. I threatened to swear.

"Please," I managed. "Please."

But then he was back, his fat cock tunneling its way into my ass like a screw head on a drill. I felt light-headed and dizzy.

"If I pass out, you're going to have a hell of a time carrying me to bed."

"Shut up, Mac, and enjoy," he whispered, nipping the soft skin around my nipple before sucking it into his mouth.

I felt the tremors start way down deep in my thighs before I came hard, yelling my fool head off as ropes of cum shot out of my cock, coating the flexing muscles of his stomach as he groaned and plunged deep one more time. I felt him swell and the gush of his seed into the forgiving latex, my quivering, still clenching inner walls grasping at nirvana.

He lowered me slowly, and I was glad when my knees decided to work and I stood. Wobbly. Wrecked.

"That's one hell of a good morning," I sighed, resting my head on the wall. I peered at him through partially cracked lids. "You do realize that you still have shampoo in your hair."

His eyes sparkled. "Something came up."

I swatted him. "Let me wash it out for you."

He turned his back to me, and for a moment I was breathless from the sight of his broad, muscled back, all golden skin tapering down to his waist and a high, sculpted butt. I wondered again where such a desk jockey got so many long, lean muscles.

"Kickboxing," he answered out of the blue, and I realized I'd spoken aloud.

"I didn't know you kickboxed."

"You would if you did more than use me for sex." He grinned, and I swatted him again.

And then pressed my face against his back, my arms sliding around his waist. Oh, it was bad to be this far gone with someone who was barely in. We didn't say a word, and we didn't move.

"Lean down a little," I instructed quietly. He had me by an inch or two. Or three. Okay, like four, really. He bent down a bit, and I began washing the shampoo out of his hair, focusing on the simple task like it was nuclear science.

I wanted to ask if he was going to break my heart. But I couldn't speak words so patently obvious. So I cleared my throat and skated to neutral territory.

"You never took me to that movie."

He huffed a laugh. "You didn't let me."

"Don't cheap out on me, J."

"Didn't I pay for dinner?"

"If you want to call that tiny meal dinner, that's between you and your conscience. Close your eyes," I said, using the sprayer to wash the last of the shampoo from his hair. "You should stay here next weekend. We can grab that movie and come back here. Then grab some other stuff."

"I'd have to bring a few things," he said, swiping wet hair out of his eyes, which I promptly sprayed back over his face.

"Hold still. Yeah, you should pick up a few things. We're close in size, but, Stretch, I don't feel like seeing high waters on you all weekend."

"Close in size my ass. You don't have nearly as much bulk."

I swatted his muscled behind. "It's not polite to say so."

His hands slid to my ass and squeezed. "Trust me. I like everything on you just the way it is."

I tried not to get giddy, but it was hard. A lot of guys like a bubble butt, I scolded myself. You didn't just land the cover on People's Most Beautiful issue.

"All done, princess," I said, sticking the sprayer back in the holder.

He scowled at my nickname and ran questing hands through the freshly washed strands. "You got it all?"

I put on my best Vidal Sassoon voice. "If yoo don' look good, vee don' look good."

He snickered and kissed the end of my nose. "You're so fucking cute."

We stared at each other for a moment, one timeless moment that said more than we could have managed on our own.

Dark, waterlogged lashes swept down to hide something in those eyes, big sky-country blue, and I tilted up his chin. "What?" I asked softly.

He shook his head, dislodging my hand, and kissed my palm. He leaned past me and shut off the ice-cold spray. "I need to get to work."

Which was basically code for "I need to be somewhere you're not."

It was the most substantial thing he would say from the time he pulled on his clothes, gathered his belongings, declined my hesitant offer of coffee, and kissed me hard on the lips. Oh, that and "I'll see you."

I do see you. I see everything about you. I lay down on the bed and threw a hand over my eyes. "I guess our weekend's off," I sighed.

The apartment seemed too quiet after his departure. I had another moment's regret that we never made it to my bed—at least I could have rolled around in the sheets and smelled him… you know, to complete the essence of weirdo. I sighed.

He was weirded out by our chemistry, drawn to our spontaneous combustion. I scowled. Yeah, well. So was I.

18

I lowered the camera from my eye slowly—I wanted to see this with my own eyes. The car that pulled up in Rachel's driveway was not the one I was expecting. The realtor she was fooling around with had a blue midsized sedan. No, I knew exactly whose car was pulling smoothly into the drive. He got out and made his way up to the front door. Rang the bell. Disappeared inside. Never glanced back.

My teeth started to ache, and I made a herculean effort to loosen my jaw and relax. Breathe. He had to know I might be here—he'd *hired* me to spy on her. He had to know that I would see him with her after he hadn't bothered to call me.

I tossed my camera on the dash, resisting the urge to bash it into a million pieces. I would need that camera later, and it had been expensive. I drummed my fingers on the steering wheel a bit. Pulled out a yogurt from my mini cooler even though I wasn't particularly hungry.

I expected this, didn't I? Isn't this what I always harped on to anyone who would listen? *Everyone leaves*. My eyes felt strangely dry. I don't know when I'd begun to hope for something different, but I knew why. Jordan was... special. He was different. I guess it was just hard to believe that someone who had felt the passion, the spark, the *rightness* of the way we fit together would make such a stupid decision to leave it all. Didn't he know how rare that was?

My mouth quirked. Obviously not. Tuesday made three weeks since we'd spoken to or seen one another. Three weeks since he'd kissed me, three weeks since we'd hugged or touched. Three weeks since we'd fucked. Three long weeks to wonder if I'd had enough Jordan to last me a lifetime. I had pole vaulted over sad and gone straight to annoyed. I mean, if he was going to blow me off, the least he could do was use me for endless sex beforehand.

I actually wasn't sure *what* to do. My options ran the gamut from nothing at all to rending my clothing and yelling *whyyyyy* to the heavens. I could try to run into him somewhere. Be casual and flirty and show him that he wasn't the only one who could play it cool. I could think Jordan thoughts telepathically and hope they got through. Or I could be an adult and call, of course. But let's not get ridiculous.

Besides, he'd already made himself perfectly clear. Going on an intimate date with his girlfriend while he knew I'd be watching? Put a stamp on my ass and mark me "return to sender."

I stuck a spoon in the yogurt—blueberry—and swirled the fruit around. Robert was right—I *was* pathetic. I still wanted him, and not just on a physical level either. I wanted to see him. Talk to him. Smell his scent. Taste his skin. Learn more about him from his own mouth, not from behind the camera's viewfinder. Hear his voice.

I sighed and tossed my empty yogurt container and plastic spoon into the depleted cooler. I didn't remember eating it during my musings, but I guessed I had. There was no need for me to stay and rub my nose in it. She clearly wasn't meeting with the realtor tonight. I glanced at the bedroom window again, trying to convince myself to leave. I didn't care if that light came on. I didn't care if they moved their date to the bedroom. *Just leave*, I coached myself. *Now. Before you see something you can't forget. Leave*!

All the lights went off, and I groaned. Oh, I hadn't thought about that. Yeah, that was worse. I started my car and gave my own face a slap. *When I tell you to leave, you leave*, my subconscious threatened me. *Like in a horror movie*.

My phone buzzed as I drove away, and I clicked the Bluetooth. "Yeah."

"You got something?"

"Hello to you too, Drew."

"Hello. You got something?"

Something that's going to haunt my dreams tonight? *Sure*. "No. I'm wrapping it up for the night. I think I've seen all there is to see here."

"You coming back to the office?"

"No, I'll e-mail you my findings."

I couldn't quite tell Drew that Jordan had been at Rachel's house. He knew me well, and despite my denials, he knew that Jordan and I had been seeing one another on more than a business level. I saw it in his face when we talked about the case. I heard it in his voice even when we were talking about something else. And I knew I would hear about it when he got my e-mail. For now, I really couldn't take his smugness.

"I might stop by Asher's," I said absently. "See if we can see a movie or something."

There was silence on his end. And then a sigh. "You're doing it again."

"Watching movies? I know, every time I say this is *the* last one, but they just keep coming out with sequels."

"He's not the right one. Just like Jordan. You're just attracted to the unavailable. The unattainable."

"That's not true." My protest was automatic.

I didn't bother to tell him that I'd *attained* Jordan already. Three times. Because then I'd have to explain how he hadn't called in as many weeks. Drew steamrolled on, oblivious to my inner argument with him. Just as well. In our inner argument, I had just called him something rather unforgiveable.

"Just look at Trevor," he said.

"Oh, jeez." I sighed heavily.

I patted my left pocket before remembering I'd left my smoky crutches at home. I didn't know then that Jordan would be with Rachel tonight. Or that Drew was going to exercise his spooky timing again and harangue me about my love life.

"He was emotionally unavailable to you, and you knew that from the beginning. You pursue dead-end relationships like the proverbial rabbit after the carrot. Then when they fail, *and they will fail*, you can step back and say 'Told you so. Love doesn't exist.'"

"What a lovely portrait you've painted of me. I should hang it on the refrigerator."

The red fluorescent sign of a Walgreens caught my eye, triggering an apparently deeply rooted, long forgotten memory that I needed batteries. Triple A. I whipped in and parked as Drew scolded me some more. Clearly he was determined to have his say, whether I cared to hear it or not.

"Go ahead. Do your sarcasm thing. But you know I'm right. Look at Nick."

"You can't penalize me for Nick. That was a viable relationship. And not just in the good times either. I took care of him, Drew. I took him to rehab and helped him with his exercises. I cooked for him and did laundry and—"

"No one is saying you weren't a great friend to him. But that's all it was. Friendship. And maybe a little guilt mixed in."

"He was driving, Drew. Not me," I said sharply.

"And you never let him forget it either."

I closed my eyes briefly, swallowing. It was a moment before I spoke again. "I knew it wasn't rational to blame him. I'm not saying it wasn't rough. You know I wasn't happy about leaving my job. But I *stayed*. I was willing to work it out."

"Yeah, you felt guilty because you never loved him the way he loved you. But before that accident, you were on your way out. After you knew the extent of his injury, you weren't going anywhere. You were going to be his rock and his friend... but you would never love him like he needed to be loved. So he left instead."

"I was crushed when he left. *He* left. Not me."

"You practically forced him out the door. He knew you weren't all in from the beginning."

"I was too!" I squawked, ignoring the fact that a grown adult (me) had just uttered "Was too!" in a non-playground setting. "How much more in can you get? We met each other's families—"

"You met *his* family. You never introduced him to your dad or Robert."

"I...." I faltered.

Well, yes, that was true. But it didn't seem like the right time. My dad was still coming to grips with me being gay. I mean, I'd spent thirty minutes alone debating on how to introduce him. "My boyfriend" seemed so high school. "My partner" felt somehow wrong and something I wasn't quite ready for. And "my *lovah*"? Well... come on, you can't say that to your father with a straight face. If I didn't even know how to introduce him, I knew it was the wrong time. Seemed as good an excuse as any. And looking back upon it with fresh eyes, it had been just that. An excuse.

Try explaining that to Drew, who had clearly picked up speed. "You never even got rid of your apartment when you were 'living' together. A nice 1500-square-foot safety net."

I sighed. "What do you want from me?"

"Stop putting yourself through this. Try going out with someone who is emotionally and physically available to you. Try for something real. What was that guy's name at the pub? Darcy?"

"Big Red? No way!"

"And when you speak to him, don't call him that either. It takes people a while to warm up to your... er, ways."

I narrowed my eyes at the phone on the dash. Hopefully, he would begin the process of burning to a crisp. My humor was delightful.

Drew moved on, clearly uncharred by my glare. "He was interested. Available. *Gay*. Gainfully employed, handsome, funny...."

"Maybe you should date him," I murmured.

"I heard that, bitch. Do yourself a favor, Mac. Take him out on this date instead." I mulled this over in silence before he spoke again. "I called him, you know."

"Who, Nick?" I sighed. "Why am I not surprised? He seems to be in contact with everyone I know lately."

"No, doof. Jordan. I called him and explained to him some of the finer points of dating a friend of mine."

"Certainly explains the chilliness between you two."

"Yeah, he wasn't pleased. He seemed rather concerned about our relationship."

"And you of course told him there's nothing between us." Silence. "Drew."

He chuckled. "It'll do the golden boy good to worry a little. Just... just be careful, okay?"

"I thought you wanted me to call Darcy."

"I do, but since when have you ever done anything I've asked you to do?"

I cocked my head, considering. "True."

"Besides, I have a feeling you're not going to stop thinking about it until you've taken a ride to Jordan town."

Already took the scenic route. I filled the silence with an offhand laugh. "You know me."

Gasp. Silence. Then, "I *do* know you," Drew said accusingly. "You *ho.*"

"Gotta go."

"Mac! I knew—"

I clicked off my headset on something that sounded suspiciously like "slutty boy bitch," but I couldn't be sure.

I looked at the phone for a minute, wondering if Drew was right. Was I as disillusioned as all that? Seeking out relationships that were doomed from the start for the sheer sake of watching them fail? I bit my lip. Maybe I'd known that Trevor wasn't the right person for me. He'd been a good friend, a best friend, and it was easy to segue into lovers. I couldn't really say I'd ever loved him that way. And though I missed our friendship, the end of our relationship brought some sense of relief. Relief that it was over. Relief that I didn't have to pretend to look for houses anymore for our "future." Relief that I didn't have to keep finding things wrong with the listings he sent to my e-mail. To be perfectly honest, I missed Nick in the same way. He had been a friend that I turned into a lover.

"Huh." I frowned.

So apparently, I was determined to say no to love until sexual urges forced me to hit on and create faux relationships with my friends. Wow. That was kind of lazy. Not to mention destructive.

I *did* believe in love, despite what Drew thought. I knew it existed. But the end result just hurt too much to participate. My father had experienced that kind of love, clearly love my mother hadn't shared. Even now, on the rare occasions he let us actually meet someone he was dating, I felt Mom... Ellen's shadow there. She was there in the way he sometimes forgot and spoke about her. His downcast eyes when he realized he'd done it too much and fucked the date up good. My eyes burned a little, thinking of my gruff, tough father and his one-sided bond with a woman long gone. I guess watching that for half my life had affected me more than I cared to admit. Not to mention what I did every day. It made it so easy to forget. I had a whole eight gigabyte memory card full of "love."

A car horn beeped, and I jerked a little. Looked around. Hmm. Once again clueless as to what I needed at Walgreens, I grabbed my phone.

I'd never felt this way before. I'd never wanted to spend day and night wrapped up in and with someone. Never wanted to call him out of the blue, just to hear his voice. Never sniffed the couch cushions for a whiff of his cologne. Sure, I had more than my share of screwups. But didn't that make me an authority in what it *wasn't* supposed to feel like? Didn't I owe it to him to make sure?

I started the car and reached for the A/C before realizing I still had none. "Hey."

"Mackenzie?"

"Yeah."

There was a pause. And surprise. "Hey."

Not the most stellar reception I'd ever had, for sure.

"You free for a movie or something?"

"Yeah, of course. I'd love to see you. I thought you'd lost my number."

"No, I've just been... busy lately. Maybe we can try the new iPic? It's a little far, but it might be fun."

His laugh was deep. Nice. "I'd meet you pretty much anywhere. I think you know that."

Despite the fact he couldn't see me, I went beet red. He was a charmer, for sure. "You want me to pick you up?"

There was a pause. "In that heap you call a truck?"

I couldn't help the snicker. "Is that a yes or no?"

There was a windy sigh. "That's a yes. But I'm expecting some kind of payment for that kind of sacrifice."

"Popcorn?" I suggested innocently.

He laughed again. I really liked that laugh. "We'll see."

19

I picked him up in my rust bucket in the lot of the firehouse, determined to leave the ghost of Relationships Past behind and have some fun.

He whistled as I opened the truck's squeaky door for him. "I see you went all out."

"Spit polished and shined, Darcy. Just for you," I teased. "All the discarded bottles are in the flatbed."

He grinned, and then his face turned serious. "You look. Amazing."

Aw, shucks. I tried not to do my Gomer Pyle impression, but I could feel a sheepish half smile pulling at my mouth anyway. I did clean up pretty well, I guess, and I would just accept the compliment. My wine-colored oxford hadn't ironed itself, after all. I'd actually managed to stuff both handfuls of my rear in some skinny jeans, and really, wasn't that a cause for celebration?

He hadn't turned out too badly himself. I won't insult his muscles by just calling them muscles. His muscles had muscles, and they were displayed to perfection in a form-fitting white Hollister tee. I loved the fact that his jeans looked like they'd seen better days, and worn boots completed the fuckable picture. I could actually smell him from here, and It. Was. Good.

Hollister. Huh. I'd always thought of them as a teenybopper kind of brand. Oh Lord, I'd turned into my grandfather. Was I now using teenybopper in regular conversation? *And who cares what kind of shirt he's wearing*? I scolded myself. He looks hot. Even though I really could smell him from over here. Cologne was good, but kind of strong. I mean, there was no need to take a bath in Jean Nate for my benefit. *You know it's not Jean Nate, you freak. Stop being so picky. Your mind is so full of Jordan you can't recognize a good thing when you see it.*

I gestured. "Your carriage awaits."

He groaned and vaulted up into the cab. I fiddled with the A/C for a moment before remembering again. I turned to speak, but he'd already guessed and groaned comically.

I grinned. "Carriages don't have air."

"You're so cute," he said, and I froze.

I'd last heard that in a steamy shower, cocooned from reality, my hands on either side of Jordan's face. I didn't expect the swift kick to the gut that came along, free of charge, with that memory. I blinked and shook myself visibly. Didn't matter what I thought I'd seen in his eyes. I'd been wrong.

I put the car in drive, determined not to pick out anything wrong with Darcy for the entire ride. By the stoplight, I had five things. Five. Okay, taking away the Hollister tee, then I had four. But the cologne wasn't dissipating. I mean, I have no A/C, you know. People do need to *breathe*.

We made it to the iPic theater in record time, blowing past the rabble (yes, rabble. Teenaged rabble with purple hair and lots of obnoxious friends) with my prepurchased tickets. I enjoyed my James Bond moment as I flashed my iPhone screen at the counter guy, and soon we were ensconced in our plush orange recliners, munching on free popcorn.

"Thanks for treating, by the way." Darcy stuck his iPic pillow behind his neck like we were on an intercontinental Delta flight. "I like a sugar daddy."

"Cute." I gave him a poke in his flat stomach. "Dinner's on you. Besides, you put out, right?"

He laughed that great belly laugh that I was really starting to like. Then he startled me by dropping a kiss on the curve of my neck. "I sure do, beautiful."

He put a piece of popcorn in my astonished mouth, forcing me to close it or choke. I chewed on the buttered piece, pondering my two pressing concerns: one, how did movie theaters get their popcorn like that, and two, was Darcy a top or a bottom?

"So what are we watching, anyway?"

"Fast six." I realized the polite thing to do would have been to ask if he liked the *Fast & Furious* series, but if he didn't, I couldn't date him anyway.

"And if I haven't seen one through five?"

"Then you're basically un-American. Besides, what's there to know? Fast cars, pretty girls, hot guys, stealin' stuff in ways that could never happen... aaand you're all caught up."

His beautifully chocolate brown eyes went skyward. "Let me guess, you're a Rock fan?"

"And Paul Walker, and Tyrese... the Asian guy, and a little Vin Diesel action doesn't go amiss either. Any way you look, you win."

"I haven't liked the Rock since SmackDown."

I pretended to clasp my hands in prayer and closed my eyes. "Let him keep his gay card, Lord, for he knows not what he says."

He grinned. "You're lucky you're fine."

"Am I?" I lifted my brows. A queen did need his compliments, after all.

His hand on the back of my neck should have alarmed me, especially since it was fairly bear sized. But he was gentle, and the callused pads of his fingers rasped gently on the sensitive skin of my neck. When he pressed his mouth to mine, my eyes fluttered shut and my hands went to the collar of his Hollister shirt. His mouth was clean. Firm. Minty breath misted over my face briefly as he pulled away, and I smiled.

"What are you smiling about, beautiful?"

"I'm glad we decided to do this."

"Been waiting on you, darlin'."

My eye went from blissful to slightly squinty. I could do without all the nicknames. I mean, my parents had given me a perfectly serviceable name. Sometimes they'd told conflicting stories about how they'd decided to give it to me, but still. I *had* one.

"Mackenzie."

Exactly. See, Jordan knew my name. Wait, that hadn't just been in my head.

My head whipped around to see Jordan standing in the aisle next to our seats, giving me a decidedly unpleasant look. I felt guilty. Caught. As if I was doing something wrong. And then I remembered. Oh, yeaaaah. I let him fuck me and then he didn't call. What did *I* have to feel guilty about? What, should I have been pining at home with my phone clutched in my cold, lonely fingers? I was *glad*. Glad he saw me out with a hunky, cute guy living my life.

"Jordan," I said neutrally.

He looked good. He *always* looked so damn good.

Rachel stood a scant two inches behind him, as if they were attached by Velcro, looking effortlessly fabulous, as usual.

"Didn't expect to see you here," he said.

My eyes cut to Rachel, and I smiled sweetly. "Obviously. Hey, Rachel. Good to see you again."

Hopefully, Jordan would know what I really meant, which was *I'd cut a bitch if I could.*

She smiled politely, clearly unsure of why we warranted anything other than a brief wave and a hello. "Nice to see you too. You were at Jordan's party, right?"

"Good memory."

Jordan was ignoring both of us and was squinting, laser-like, at my redheaded companion. "This a friend of yours?" He pointed to Darcy.

I shrugged. "I tried going to movies with my enemies, but it just wasn't the same."

Darcy grinned. "Is he always like this?"

Jordan sighed. "Unfortunately. My name is Jordan, by the way." Pointedly. He all but said, "And you are?"

Luckily, my date was just as clueless to the presence of tension as he was handsome. "Darcy. Good to meet you."

There was an awkward silence that settled between us.

"I talked to Drew," Jordan said. "He told me you were on the job tonight."

"I finished early," I said sanguinely. "So I called a friend."

He flashed a smile that wasn't a bit genuine. "Good to know your phone is still working."

I smiled. "It is."

The cartoon popcorn and its goofy looking soda companion danced across the screen, and Rachel tugged at Jordan's arm. "Honey, we should get to our seats."

"Good to meet you, Jordan. Rachel." Darcy gave them a friendly wave and resettled his pillow behind his head.

Jordan's jaw went tight, and I wondered if the cool, always collected Jordan would cause a scene. God knows I wanted to. It took everything in me to remain detached and aloof, when all I wanted to do was get closer to him. Put my hands on his face and kiss all the objections out of that gorgeous head. And I knew then that my date was over. Getting over Jordan wasn't really an option right now, and Darcy was far too good to be used. Too bad he wasn't an asshole. Crap. That made me even more annoyed than usual.

I looked pointedly at the crowd building behind him. "You're blocking the aisle."

He narrowed his eyes at me before Rachel ushered him on, and I pretended absolute ignorance as the chairs behind us squeaked. The little shit was sitting right behind us. I could hear their whispers, probably as she questioned his bizarre behavior and he made up something to spin it away. I could smell him, even over Darcy's atomic cologne cloud. I could even feel his eyes making the back of my chair rather prickly. I was glad the chairs were so big he couldn't see my head, because my ears were definitely turning pink.

Darcy leaned close after the first preview finished. "We should see that," he whispered somewhere near my ear.

"We should," I nodded. We wouldn't. Not unless he understood that we could only be friends.

His tongue took advantage of the closeness by traversing down the shell of my ear, and I shivered a bit. *No*, I told myself sternly as his teeth sank into my lobe. No to whatever my asshole, which had decided that involuntarily clenching was an acceptable activity, was thinking. After a quick glance at his lap, I bit my lip. No to whatever his dick, clearly visible through his worn jeans, was thinking. That wasn't fair to either one of us. When I turned my face to tell him so, his mouth landed on mine, and I wasn't capable of speech for a minute or more. I blinked as he pulled away, feeling a little confused.

"Don't bullshit me."

"I'm not," I said, avoiding his eyes.

He took my chin in his hand, and suddenly I was forced to meet those velvety brown eyes. They were warm but perceptive. Hmph. I guess Darcy understood a little more than he let on. "So he's the reason you took so long to call me?"

"Maybe," I whispered.

His lips misted over mine again. His tongue dipped into my mouth this time, briefly, before he ended the kiss. "When you're done playing in the closet, we'll go out again."

I flushed. "That's fair."

He groaned, letting go of my face and scrubbing hands down his own. "Nothing is fair about me not getting to tap that sweet ass." He peeked through his fingers. "Unless...."

I grinned. "Dream on. Thanks for the hard-on before a two-hour movie, by the way."

He flashed a white grin my way. "Just reminding you of what you're taking a pass on. And why I'd be worth it."

Damn. I snorted. I shouldn't be surprised. I knew Jordan would be a cock blocker the first day I met him.

I munched on popcorn as the lights went low. Damn me not calling him before I fused my brain to that closet case. Damn me for not meeting him first. My questing fingers reached the non-buttery part of the popcorn too soon. Damn the teenaged Kirk Cameron lookalike working the butter dispenser. Someone who thought eighties teen idol was a good look shouldn't be trusted to dispense buttery goodness. And I *needed* butter if I was going to die alone, wrapped in an afghan. Anything else was just inhumane.

20

The A/C unit shut off, sighing like a great beast, and almost on automatic, my legs did the Russian Cossack dance. The covers went flying. I wasn't hot. Or cold. I was... restless. Waiting for... something. Nothing?

In lieu of my old nighttime ritual—that smoky, delicious, lung-killing bitch, nicotine—I'd decided to give tossing and turning a try. I wouldn't break, no matter how much I wanted to. It had been a month since my last, and I was making good on this promise. But sometimes late at night, when the mood was right and the silence was good, I wondered if my fingers would always itch for her papery touch and her smoky kiss.

I wondered if Nick still smoked. What he was doing. Feeling. Wondered what he'd think of this Jordan situation, certainly. And if he agreed that Drew's bitchy observations about my patterns were correct. That was certainly the bad thing about dating friends. When you broke up, you lost in more ways than one.

Before I knew what I was about, I was putting in my iPhone code and pressing an old number. I listened as it rang with bated breath, half hoping to get his answering machine and not his actual—

"Hello?"

"Hey. Nick. It's...."

Oh, jeez, did you say "it's me" after so long? Or it's Mackenzie. He knows who it is; he has caller ID. For Pete's sake, say something before—

"Mac? Are you still there?" The warmth in his voice made my legs go a little weak. "Where the hell have you been?"

"Nick. I've been... busy."

"Uh-huh. Busy." His tone made me grin. "Too busy to return my damned calls? Why're you ducking me?"

"I... I don't know." I really didn't. I guess playing the injured prima donna suited me better than facing our past relationship like a mature adult. But I wasn't going to *say* that.

"Well, at least you're here now. I have a ton of crap to tell you. I don't know how we're going to catch up," he lamented.

I laughed. "We should start at the beginning, I guess."

And it was just that easy. He told me stories of meeting Peyton and tsked when I told him about Trevor. We laughed over the hilarious trials and tribulations of running the bed-and-breakfast and were nearly reduced to tears over my telling of spying on that Girl Scouts meeting. And as always, he made me retell my first day on the job hijinks, which he laughed at as if it was the first time.

His laughter finally reduced to chuckles. "Jeez, Mac, no one can make me snort with laughter like you do. I mean, what's it been, like four years?"

"Five." My throat felt tight. Too freaking long. That was the problem with disposing of old friends—leaving pieces of yourself behind with each one. You could make new friends, but there were only a few who knew what you looked like back in college. Less who remembered what your first day on the force was like, when you locked a perp, your badge, and your gun inside your running patrol car. Less still who'd held you late at night after your mother ran off on your family, letting you cry until you felt like an emptied out husk of your former self.

I snapped my fingers for Finn to jump up on the bed—he was horrible at fetch, tricks, and Frisbee, but he was a champion at snuggling, especially for the difficult times. Then my forgetful mind remembered anew that Finn wasn't there.

Only when Nick snorted did I realize I'd spoken aloud. "I remember when you got that mutt from the shelter. I can't believe you let that prick have your dog."

"I didn't *let* him do anything," I said, annoyed. "One day I came home and Finn was gone."

"Jeez. You can pick 'em, can't you?"

"I picked you, didn't I?"

"I picked *you*, dear. Man, that Alzheimer's is a bitch, isn't it?"

I had to admit—he was right. He *had* done the picking up, on a three hour flight to Los Angeles, talking my ear clean off while I tried to sleep and ignore the chatty blond. Somewhere over the Sierra Mountains, I'd slammed my mouth over his—I maintain, just to shut him up. We'd spent the weekend in Santa Monica, holed up in his aunt's cottage, making fun of her California cooking (bean sprouts and sushi mostly) and getting to know each other. We hadn't been apart much after that.

"You picked me in that you were a chatty fucking monkey, yes. But I made the first move."

"Well, you *were* sluttier, dear. But if I hadn't pushed, you would have spent that whole flight scrunching your neck pillow into a ball against the window."

"In peace."

"Peace, schmeace. There was no way I was getting off that plane without your number, graduation or no."

"My mom was so pissed, especially since I gave them the lamest excuses ever for disappearing that entire weekend." I grinned, remembering how I'd made excuses why I couldn't *possibly* stay another minute at Robert's graduation celebration before blowing off the after-party. Hey, no one told him to go all the way to USC.

"It was worth it. I knew from the moment I spilled that Coke on your tray table and you said—"

"Watch it, you freaking klutz."

"Exactly. And I knew then," he continued dramatically, "that we were meant to be."

I chuckled. "You're a fool, you know that?"

"It didn't hurt that you had those dreamy hazel eyes and ridiculously long lashes. And an ass to shoot dice off of."

My face was a little red. "Does Peyton know you talk to strangers like this?"

He laughed. "Peyton's right here. He can admire a work of art like your ass. And he's very secure."

As if on its own, my hand migrated to the nightstand drawer. I glanced over, seeing all manner of items I wouldn't need tonight—my Meloxicam, a pack of gum, my safety pack of Newports, a lighter... condoms. Lube. *Certainly* wouldn't need those tonight. I grimaced, releasing the silver knob, and the drawer slid shut. Habit was all it was. Talking to Nick brought me back to a damned good place, a place where we could talk for hours and smoke one or five.

That was then. Listening to Nick wax on about Peyton reminded me, more than anything else, that this was now. I reached back in and tossed my Newports in the bedside trash can.

"We never thought we'd be B and B owners. It's a lot of work but totally worth it. It's really amazing in the wintertime, and you should see the deer...." He trailed off and then laughed self-consciously. "I'm talking too much, aren't I?"

"No," I said, meaning it. "I haven't heard your voice in forever. I missed this. I missed... you."

"Well, why didn't you call? I left the relationship, Mac. I didn't leave you."

I sighed. "I know that. Now. There was so much anger between us... from me," I corrected at his automatic protest. "I was pissed because of the accident, pissed that I couldn't be a cop anymore... scared at the new changes in our life. Mine. Yours. Especially yours." I was silent for a moment before forging on. "Do you think I don't believe in love? Drew said I pick relationships that are destined to fail, as if to prove that love is a joke. Doesn't exist."

I flopped onto my stomach, burying my face between the pillows.

All I needed to complete the picture was to swing my legs back and forth while twirling a long phone cord. (Sorry, I'm old.) My ramblings nearly blinded me to the fact that Nick hadn't answered my question for several minutes.

"Do you think that's true?" I prodded.

I could almost see his shrug. "Probably."

"Gee, thanks."

"Well, do you want me to lie?"

Yes. "No," I said, begrudgingly. "Why do you think that is?"

"Jesus, Mackenzie, should I pull out the psychiatric couch?"

"If you need one to answer a simple question," I shot back.

"Like this is a simple question." He sighed. Gustily. "Probably because of what your mom did. I know I would be hurt. Pissed. Down on love. So even though you say you are looking for love in your many... *many* relationships—"

"Watch it."

"You feel like it will never happen for you. And then you seek out people to prove you're right."

"Like you?"

"We weren't right for each other. But I wanted you so much I couldn't see that for a while. And once I did, I was so in love with you I didn't care. And there was the accident."

We'd been driving home from a baseball game, laughing and talking and being silly. Then there were headlights coming at Nick from the wrong side. A truck ran a red and plowed into his door. Then there was nothingness.

"It was quiet after the accident. You asked if I was okay. And I said—"

"I've been better."

I remembered. It had been dark and rainy, droplets spattering up from the pavement and into the truck as we hung, wedged in the upside down cabin. My emotions vaulted from relief that we were okay, to wanting to know exactly how *okay* we were.

"When I found out about your injuries, you know what I was

thinking? I thought, he's going to dump me now. This is just the reason he's been looking for."

"*Christ*, Nick."

"Just… just listen, okay?"

I nodded, and even though he couldn't see me, he went on anyway.

"I realized then that our stories were twined together, for better or worse, because of the magnitude of what we'd gone through. That you would stay with me until the end, if that's what I wanted. But you'd never love me the way I loved you."

Hearing it again, this time from the horse's mouth, made my head bow under the strain. "I'm sorry."

"Mac, I'm good. We're… good. I love Peyton, and he loves me the way I deserve. If it hadn't been for our relationship, I would never have met him." He tried to lighten the mood. "You would know that if you'd come to visit me sometime."

"I will." My hand tightened on the phone. I needed to see for myself that he was okay. "You've been a good friend to me."

"Oh Lord, he's gone and got melancholy on me."

"Shut up. I love you, you asshole."

He laughed. "I love you too. But then you already knew that. So when are you coming up?"

"I have two weeks of vacation coming up pretty soon. Spending it at a bed-and-breakfast sounds much better than bumming around the house."

"You should. And don't feel weird about bringing this Jordan person you're seeing either."

My mouth fell open. I hadn't told him about…. *Drew.* Urgh.

Nick took my silence to mean I wasn't sure. "Seriously. All of us will have a really good time. Besides, the bed-and-breakfast is good for any weary traveler, but the suite I'm putting you in is made for lovers. Trust me, when you see that fireplace and Jacuzzi tub, you'll wish you had someone to share it with."

I grimaced. *Yeaaaah, about that….* I just couldn't tell him that

Jordan and I were already done. Especially after the conversation we'd just had.

"I'll ask," I promised. "But I haven't even decided yet."

"Come on," Nick groaned. "You'll love it. Besides, didn't you say you wanted to see if I was okay?"

My protest was for token's sake and because I was born ornery. "I don't really need to see you and Peyton feeding each other little bites at the dinner table to know you're okay."

"Stupid," he said, his tone warm with amusement. "We save that for the breakfast show. We like to start the day off right."

"Now that you mention it, I do seem to remember you liking to start the day eating sausage." I grinned at his groan. *Man, I forgot how fun it was to torture Nick.* "Long, hard saus—"

"Okay, enough!" He groaned. "For Pete's sake—"

"What, Peyton doesn't know you like sausage? What *do* you do up there in Vermont?"

I was so busy chortling from Nick's fake death sounds, I almost didn't hear the knock at my door. Polite and light at first and then a little more insistent. I scowled. "Nick, I gotta go. Someone at the door."

"Okay," he said obligingly. "Call me later."

I hung up on him singing "booty call" in my ear and pushed off the bed, tossing my phone on the dresser as I passed.

"Yeah," I said loudly to hopefully staunch the knocking. "I'm coming."

I padded to the door, uncaring of my dishabille. You come to my door at one in the morning, you get what you get. Sweatpants and no shirt was too good for the likes of—

"Jordan." I whispered his name to the peep hole like he could answer me back. Then louder, "Jordan?"

"Yeah." The morphed Jordan figure looked directly at the peep hole. The convex glass made his blue eyes look huge and alien as he peered at the hole. "Are you going to let me in?"

"Y-yeah. Of course," I shook off my reservations and undid the bolt and the locks in a series of *click, click, clickety-clicks* that made me seem a little psycho about security. I swung the door open, and the object of my unrest suddenly filled my doorway. I squinted up at him, haloed in the light of my mini porch. I hadn't realized until then how tall he was. Or how gorgeous. Okay, that was a lie. I'd always noticed that part.

"Hey."

"Hey."

He used a finger to adjust his glasses, and I smiled a little. "You're wearing your glasses."

"My contacts were getting scratchy. I strained my eyes a bit at the movie." His voice faltered, and suddenly the elephant in the room had sat his big butt down. The movies. His date. My date.

"Can I come in?"

I shook my head slowly. "I don't think that's a good idea." No, I *knew* it wasn't a good idea. "Why are you here?" My voice gained strength and sharpness. "And how the hell am I supposed to get over you if you won't *go away*?"

His throat worked. "Maybe I don't want you to get over me."

"That's pretty selfish," I snapped. "All things considered."

"What's that supposed to mean?"

"It means I didn't particularly enjoy seeing you at Rachel's house the other night. Or the night after that."

"I didn't sleep with Rachel. I slept on her couch," he admitted. "I had an early hearing, and she lives closer to the office. Besides, I knew… I knew you would probably be watching."

Well, if he'd wanted me to be just jealous, he'd failed. Devastated? Questioning all my relationships since the beginning of time? Check and check.

I sneered. "Nice."

Those pretty eyes narrowed at me, and I knew he was getting mad. "You didn't exactly call me, Mac."

"Was I supposed to? Don't phones work both ways nowadays?"

"So what, was this date—punishment? To make me watch you and your boyfriend give each other mouth to mouth?" His voice was raw. "Because I don't think I deserved that."

I felt guilty enough, and I winced. Guilt made my acerbic tongue even saltier. "Yes, Jordan, we waited around the iPic theater, forty-five minutes away from my house, making out until you eventually showed up. Three weeks was a long time, but with Chapstick and a Gatorade IV, we made it through. That was the *master* plan. You got us."

He stared at me for a moment before shaking his head. "You're a real piece of work, you know that?" He spun on his heel. "I made a mistake coming here."

Watching him walk away made my chest feel funny. Tight. Dizzy. Like I was the one making a huge mistake. I knew what it had taken for him to come here. Did I really want to let him walk away?

I had a feeling if he walked away, he wouldn't be coming back again. *Good*, my inner lonely girl said. *We don't need him. By the by, where's your afghan?*

"I didn't exactly enjoy seeing you with Rachel," I blurted.

What are you doing? The inner voice was angry. *He's slowing down. Dammit, he's coming back!*

"Shut up," I hissed, and the inner voice flounced away.

I hope you can find your dog for comfort before he dumps your ass, bitch, she snapped. *You're on your own.*

He stopped closer this time. Close enough to touch. "You didn't look like it bothered you at all."

"Well, it did. I wanted to claw her eyes out," I admitted.

He rewarded my hypothetical violence with a half-smile. "That was just... just...." His shoulders slumped. "That wasn't real. That was me doing something I used to do because I thought I wanted to be that guy again."

"Before you met me," I said evenly.

"Yes. No! Before things were confusing. Before I couldn't stop thinking about you. Obsessing about you."

Go on.

"Hell, I don't even care about the investigation anymore. It doesn't really matter if she's into someone else. I know that anything I thought I felt for her is nothing compared... compared."

I didn't make him finish the comparison. "I'm glad you don't care about the investigation, at least. Because, well, let's just say it's a good thing."

He shrugged and then cocked his head. "Wait. What?"

"I thought you didn't care."

"I don't, but a guy has his pride. Sheesh." He looked flummoxed for a minute and then shook his head. "Just as well. I guess I can't exactly throw stones."

"Yeaaah, there's a lot of glass in this proverbial house." I shrugged. "But you're still paying me, yeah?"

"Opportunist."

I shrugged. "Hey, this is just business. Do you know how many gaskets I blew tailing that woman?"

"Was it 'just business' when you were giving me head on your desk?"

And just like that I was half hard, an instantaneous rerouting of blood to my southern regions. "Darlin', that was pure pleasure."

Great, Darcy's use of darlin' had officially rubbed off on me.

He chuckled and shook his head. "God, I missed you."

And that was enough. Talking to Nick had only enforced that he and Peyton were right for each other. He practically glowed over the phone when talking about the guy. There was nothing there. I was tired of being the "if-it-wasn't-for-our-fucked-up-relationship-I-wouldn't-have-met-so-and-so" guy. If it hadn't been for me, he wouldn't have Peyton. And Trevor wouldn't have Laura. I kind of liked being the "God-I-missed-you" guy.

I opened the door wider and sighed. "Get in here."

We attacked each other right there in the doorway, our mouths, tongues, and teeth meeting with urgency—nipping, soothing, stroking, merging. A moan vibrated against my lips as his tongue surged into my mouth, and suddenly it was like the first damned time again. Every time. Every time was like the first damned time.

"What the hell took you so long?" I muttered against his ear as his mouth slid down my neck, nipping and licking a path that made me shiver deliciously.

"I was afraid you might not be alone. Thought you might be still on your date with tall, red, and handsome."

"He's not you."

"So I stack up against the muscle-bound stud?" He sounded ridiculously pleased. "Awesome."

"I didn't say all that. You're going to have to prove yourself."

"You do owe me a weekend," he reminded me.

I did. And I didn't welsh on an offer. Especially when that offer might have Jordan balls deep inside my ass, being pounded within an inch of my life into my mattress. I pushed him away a bit, making a show of inspecting his person. "I don't see any bag, but you're welcome to go naked. We at Chez Mackenzie don't mind. We encourage it, in fact."

He smiled a little. "I really didn't bring any clothes or essentials." He looked a little embarrassed. "I didn't think you'd let me in. Besides, you have no food."

"You're really thinking about food right now? I must have lost my touch."

"I will be after," he said, raising an eyebrow. "And I don't plan on eating olives and mustard."

"The olives are gone, darlin'." Och, damn that Darcy. "Just mustard from now on."

"Urgh. Your accommodations are decidedly second rate."

"Maybe you should go get a few things. Come back," I suggested with a shrug. "Whatever you need for the rest of the weekend."

I ignored his hesitation and looked at him expectantly. I wasn't going to chain him to the bed and make him stay. Either he wanted to be here or he didn't.

I worked my apartment key off the ring and handed it to him. "Let yourself in." I held it out with a raised brow, hoping my casualness covered the fact that I hadn't breathed in over a minute.

He narrowed his eyes at me and plucked the key from my fingers. "I'll be back," he said darkly.

I waggled my fingers and turned to close the door.

"Oh, and, Mac?"

I let out an involuntary squeak as he circled my wrist with his hand and turned me back around. He pressed me to the door and took my mouth roughly, his mouth slanting over mine in a hungry, possessive manner that was exciting and confusing all at once. I slid my hands into his hair, gripping his face in place as if he would dissolve if I let go. His touch was exploratory as his hands roved down the curvature of my spine to grip my ass. And then he smacked it, ending the kiss regretfully.

"I never back away from a challenge."

I swallowed, looking after him bemusedly as he disappeared in the darkness. I was counting on it.

Hands on my skin brought me to life, cold on my warm, sleep-scented skin. I didn't even mind when the hands removed the covers to expose the rest of my skin to the cool air. I had chucked my sweat-pants before climbing into bed, and feeling those hands run from my feet to my calves and grip my behind, I knew it had been a good decision.

The hands made their way over my shoulders as I pressed my face into the pillow, unwilling to open my eyes wide enough to identify my dream lover. As long as he didn't stop, he could be a burglar at this point. Hell, a massage this good certainly deserved a TV on his way out. Long, deft fingers worked their way into my muscles, and I betrayed myself with a groan.

"Good God, you have magic fingers, J."

"I'm glad you think so. As long as you do, I can keep touching this body."

"You took a while." I suddenly understood why Finn extended his body like that when I rubbed his back, and arched into his touch. *Shameless hussy*. I had fully expected him not to come back. I'd never been so glad to be wrong as he pressed warm kisses down the curve of my spine.

"I had to get my stuff. And I brought groceries," he said against my skin. When he ended with a kiss in the dip of my spine and pulled away, I growled in frustration. "They're in the trunk."

"Why are you telling me?"

He slapped my behind. "So you can help, lazybones. Didn't think you'd go to sleep on me and actually be in bed while I braved the elements."

I snorted. "What elements? This is Florida. The closest to elements you're going to get is iron and metal."

"What about the heat? You could melt a s'more on my dash, and it's still dark out."

"Well, since you're already overheated, you should go ahead and finish the job." I yawned. "You can't succeed if you quit, J."

He chuckled. "You're full of it." This time the slap was gentler. Not followed by words.

Without looking, I knew exactly where his gaze was centered, and I planned to take full advantage. "I'll make you a deal. I stay here, cool and cozy. You get the groceries."

He made a clicking sound with his teeth. "And in return?"

I wiggled I bit, making sure he got the full picture of my wanton behavior. "Your boon is up to you." When I looked back, the doorway was empty, and I chuckled. "I'll take that as a yes."

He caught me just on the delicious cusp of falling back into dreamland, and I swatted away his soft kisses this time, fully intending to welsh on the deal.

"Go away," I groused.

It was his turn to chuckle. "We had a deal."

"I said that because I was sleepy," I said crossly. "I'll say anything when I'm sleepy."

"Let's see if you'll *do* anything when you're sleepy."

I had to admit, the liquid feeling of lube drizzling down the crack of my ass did a lot to recapture the mood. His questing finger certainly did the rest. I hissed and arched as he slid slowly inside me. His slow stroking turned rather quickly into pile driving, and I soon found myself rising to my knees to meet his thrusts with shameful eagerness.

"Every time I get inside you, I swear I can't think," he managed. "Can't seem to slow down."

"I don't want you to."

"I'm a consummate lover, you know," he informed me. "I swear I usually have more finesse than this. I've had good reviews."

"We'll make sure to post you on Amazon dot com," I reassured him. "Now move."

He groaned as I backed up against him, and then again as I took him in slowly. When I slammed against him and he sank into me to the hilt, his fingers flexed against my hips hard enough to leave marks.

"Stop. Moving. Please," he managed through gritted teeth.

I could feel his face buried in the curve of my neck, whispering something. When I glanced back, his eyes were tightly closed, as if in prayer.

"Mother Mary, full of grace," I whispered, helping him along so he'd move.

He laughed painfully. "I really hate you."

I worked my inner muscles around him, determined to have my way. Who needed to sit, anyway? "Prove it."

21

I woke to a strong aroma, delicious trails of java that invaded the covers over my head. Good enough to get up? I wasn't quite sure yet. My nose caught something else, and I stuck the tip out of the covers, sniffing strongly. Bacon? Maybe eggs?

One slit of an eye joined the tip of nose, and I peered at the alarm clock. Six thirty on a Saturday. *Sweet baby Jesus.* Some sadist was whipping up a feast in my kitchen at an ungodly hour, and now I was so hungry I had to join him and his religion.

I stumbled out of bed and into my sweatpants before making my way to the kitchen. I peered at a bright-eyed Jordan, bustling about my kitchen with nothing on but a pair of low-riding jeans and a dish towel slung over his shoulder. I ogled him for a minute, silently thanking God for his damn fine creation. Even at this ungodly hour. The way he filled out a pair of jeans made the bacon sizzling and popping in the pan the *second* hottest thing in my kitchen. The Celtic knot on his bicep flexed as he whipped eggs expertly. *Mother may I*? I asked while trying to stop the drool. *You already did*, my inner voice answered me tartly. *Quite a bit, actually*. Bitch never did want me to be happy.

"You had me at bacon." I said blearily, shuffling to one of the island chairs and dropping into it dramatically.

He grinned. "Thought I might. Here," he said, pushing a glass of juice my way.

My sleep-dulled reflexes almost watched it sail off the counter before clumsily catching the sweating glass. I sipped, wincing at his whistling, which he did while pouring the eggs into the pan. They screamed from the heat and began to cook immediately, and he scrambled them as they sizzled.

"Are you always this chipper in the morning?"

"Only when I got laid. Three times." He gave me a lopsided smile before turning back to his eggs. "You know anything about that?"

"I just might."

My ass sure did. The ache was a good ache, but we probably wouldn't be using that particular part of my anatomy for a little bit. If I could control myself, that is. So the proper thing to say would probably be we *shouldn't* be using that particular part of my anatomy for a little bit. But we probably would. I eyed him working in the kitchen, handling the frying pan with a deft surety that he used with everything else. Being the singular object of his abject focus was a remarkable experience. Yes, I confirmed with a nod. We definitely would.

He dropped off a plate in front of me with toast, eggs, and bacon neatly arranged in a dainty circle. I blinked. "You can cook?"

"Does that make you want me more?"

I tilted my head, considering. "Yeah. Actually, it does."

"Then I cook," he confirmed, dropping a kiss on my brow before going back to make his own plate.

Ill-mannered beast that I was, I took a bite of my toast while I was waiting, watching him move in my kitchen like he did this every single day. I didn't know why it was making me a little grumpy. Except now I had another memory with Jordan I didn't know what to do with. Hell, by Monday, I was going to have a whole weekend full of them. I took another grumpy bite of toast. He had no right moving in here like this, playing house with me like this. Fucking me into the mattress was one thing, but this? This was something different entirely.

He slid into the chair in front of me with his own plate, and while I got my hand swatted for stealing a square of his toast, he did let me make off with it.

"What do you want to do today?" I asked, feeling a bit perkier. Toast was more delicious when you stole it.

"You're looking at it," he said. "I want to eat, sleep, fuck, and be with you. Sometimes together and not necessarily in that order."

Heat blazed up inside of me, and I forced myself to keep eating. I'd need my strength, apparently. "Sounds good. Add to the list dropping off cupcakes for Case's soccer team, and I'm in for every single one of those things." I paused, watching him pour sugar and cream into his coffee like it was an ancient art, and stir carefully. "You should really lay off the coffee."

He took a sip, managing to flip me off at the same time. "I'm glad you agree, who is Case, and fuck you."

I grinned. "Case is my brother's kid. His mom is pretty much in and out of his life, so he's stuck with my brother. Which is probably why he will eventually tack the word 'mental' onto the beginning of his name."

"I'm surprised the soccer team is requesting cupcakes. Shouldn't they have something a little healthier?"

"They don't win a lot," I said, and Jordan choked a little on his coffee. "I don't think it matters."

"You're an ass."

"I try. Besides, one cupcake per kid won't kill them."

"Mac, I hate to point this out, but you don't *have* any cupcakes."

"I was going to bake them last night," I said indignantly. "But someone had to get his rocks off. I hope you're happy, J. I mean really, what about the kids?"

He grinned. "You're going to buy them, aren't you?"

I pointed a piece of bacon at him before stuffing it in my mouth. "From your lips to God's ears," I mumbled around salty, fatty deliciousness. "Two dozen from a lovely little woman named Ona at the Cuban deli."

"Sounds tasty. How'd you find this Ona person?"

"I did a little work for her in the past. Located her daughter in Omaha, Nebraska, of all places, two years after she'd run away. She was 'waitressing' at a seedy strip club, which everyone knows is a half step away from shakin' that ass for cash. Not that there's anything wrong with that, but she really didn't have to do that. She *had* a home to go back to, parents who were willing to help her out. Not like some of those girls I saw in there."

I cut myself off, embarrassed at how simple breakfast convo had gotten so deep so fast. *This* is why I wasn't allowed in polite company. But Jordan had pushed back his cleaned plate and tucked into his coffee, and he still seemed interested. Very interested, as if my little PI stories were worth telling.

"How'd you get her to go home?" he prodded.

"At first I couldn't. I mean, the job was technically over. Ona had paid me to find her, and I did. She didn't have money to spend on me to stay there for however long it took to convince her daughter to come home. But I stayed anyway." I shook my head. "Drew certainly gave me an earful about that. I was in Omaha for three weeks after I found her, trying to convince her, drinking overpriced, questionable drinks at the bar and watching overpriced, questionable tail shake their asses in my face."

Jordan snorted, and I shrugged. "I convinced her that her mom still loved her and that she'd never stopped looking and that, whether she stripped in Omaha or stripped in Miami, she had a family that loved her and wanted her back. However she decided to come, they wanted her back. We took turns driving back because she didn't want to fly. I still wasn't sure she was going to go through with it, and I took the time on those dark, quiet roads to tell her about my mom. What I would do to get one chance to talk to her again. See her again. Tried to open her eyes that she still had that chance."

I bit my lip. I hadn't meant to say that. I liked to say I hated her, but that wasn't entirely true. I hated what she'd done. How easily she'd left. But if she hadn't been a good mother in the first place, it wouldn't hurt this bad.

My mother had found all my stories interesting. She had really cared about the small things I had to tell her and the on-dits about my boring day. I was her Mac, and that made my stories important by the sheer fact that they were coming out of my mouth. I swallowed, the greasy bacon in my stomach settling solidly. The bond between you and the woman who gave you life should be infinite. Unshakeable. It was jarring to walk through life knowing that it wasn't.

When I looked at his face, he was smiling a little. "That's a little bit awesome."

I gave an embarrassed laugh. "Not really. But I get free cupcakes from Ona for life, which has really come in handy for my pooch."

"You have no pooch," he said, shaking his head at my silliness.

"I will, darlin'." I leered. "Especially after I get the two dozen cupcakes for them and two extra on the side for me."

"Mac," he said, laughing helplessly. "*Two* extra? Of huge specialty cupcakes?"

"One of them is for you," I said indignantly. "Hey, I fit into my skinny jeans last night. Didn't even have to roll on the couch to get 'em on. That means I'm in the clear until that zipper stops moving."

"Your form looks damn fine to me." He took my chin in his hand and kissed me. "But I'll help you work it off."

"Promises, promises."

He grinned, and I shook my head ruefully. "I forgot you keep your promises."

"All of them, baby. Every single one of them."

We didn't see the light of day until four, when we finally ventured from the apartment. A quick stop at Ona's bakery—and by quick, I mean the forty-five minutes she'd spent catching me up on every particle of her life, harassing Jordan for details about our relationship, and pinching my arm for not coming sooner—and the car smelled like sugary-sweet goodness.

By the time Jordan pulled into a gas station, I was more than ready for some food of some sort. I zipped inside and bought two waters, two Slim Jims, and a granola bar. I risked life and limb to rip open the slippery Slim Jim package with my teeth while crossing the busy thoroughfare (totally worth it), before gnawing on the end.

Jordan shook his head, watching me with no small amount of amusement, his arms crossed as he leaned against his car. "I thought you said you were going to get food," he said as I got closer.

"These aren't for you," I said haughtily, sticking the other Slim Jim in my pocket and tossing him the granola bar.

"You eat like a goat," he said. "All that's missing are the tin cans and an old muddy boot."

He tore the package neatly, following the recommended "tear here" path on the wrapper with eerie precision. Sucker. Who does that? Better to rip it and then try to scramble and catch all the broken pieces of granola as they tumble out haphazardly.

"You love it," I said, pointing my half eaten Slim Jim at him. "Besides, if you didn't, why would you let me drive your precious car?"

He grinned. "Is that what I'm doing? Because I don't remember that being *anywhere* in the plan."

"Indeed. Gimme the keys."

"Shows what you know." He pulled out one honey-oat granola square and bit into it. "I'm not letting someone drive who doesn't know there are no keys."

"Come on," I wheedled. "The things I let you do to me last night... I mean, I can't even *speak* of them. The least you could do...."

He laughed. "You asked me to do those things," he accused. "But fine. Go ahead."

I held my gloating inside for a later time and slid behind the wheel, sighing as the fine genuine leather gripped my behind.

"Come on, come on," I hassled Jordan out the window. "You're taking forever."

He grumbled but stuffed the receipt from the machine into his wallet instead of filing it away neatly like I knew he wanted to do.

He kept his car pristine, and the burl wood dashboard gleamed like some kind of glass. I doubted a leaky cup had ever violated that cup holder. The silver Mercedes emblem winked at me, and I winked back.

Wanna have some fun? It asked flirtatiously.

Darlin', you have no idea.

"Man, I hate cheating on Bessie, but this CLS is a smooth-talking bitch."

"Mac, be careful."

"Yeah, yeah."

"It doesn't look like there's enough space to—"

I whipped into Robert's driveway with the expertise of someone who's been there a million times. I knew every crack, corner, and crevice, and managed the impossible, squeezing in next to his cruiser.

I exited the vehicle with a grin that the shaky Jordan did not share and bounced over to him. "Can I drive home? Huh? Can I, can I—"

He put a hand over my mouth but nodded weakly. "This time, try to keep it under a hundred, yeah?"

"What's the fun in that?" *Oh, Bessie my love, your days are numbered.*

I reached in the backseat and rescued the cupcakes from the floorboards. "Oops. They still look good, though. Ona packages them pretty well."

"Apple, I didn't hear your heap pull in—oh, hello."

Robert came toward us from somewhere in the open garage. He was barefoot and bare-chested with a pair of scruffy shorts on, and his eyes went wide as they went from Jordan to me. Back to Jordan. Then me. Okay, so I didn't bring people home often, but this was ridiculous. His next words reinforced why, exactly, I didn't bring people home often.

"Who's your friend?" he asked.

"Oh Lord," I groaned. "Don't do this."

His hazel eyes glittered wickedly as he continued. "You bring a boy home, and I want to know who he is. Who his folks are. Do you have a job, son?"

I elbowed him in the gut as Jordan burst into laughter.

"I do, sir," he managed to answer. "Thank you for letting me date your brother."

"Oh, you *really* shouldn't be thanking me for that." He grinned and offered a hand. "Robert Williams. My friends call me Robby."

"Which means everyone calls him Robert," I confirmed, only grunting when he elbowed me back. "Where's Case?"

"Inside. Xbox 360 is his lord and master."

I held the cupcakes up in explanation. "I brought him these."

"That's all he needs." Robert rolled his eyes. "Why don't you give them to him? I'll keep your friend here company."

I turned to Jordan. "I'm sorry in advance for anything this troll might say. Please don't stop dating me."

He and Robert laughed simultaneously, and the sound was scary enough to send me scurrying into the house to the sound of Robert's warning yell, "And don't touch my sauce!"

The smell of garlic, tomatoes, and spice wafted to my nose like a beacon as I let the side door bang behind me. "Mmmm," I mumbled, stumbling toward the kitchen like Frankenstein. "Smell good."

Of course I had a taste or two. Or three as I licked the spoon clean and wondered how a dunderhead bachelor like Robert could cook so well. I washed the spoon and placed it in the drying rack—he was obsessive about keeping things neat. Not because of an inherent need to clean but a lack of one. You didn't have to clean if it never got dirty, and to hell with the dust on the lampshades and under the dressers.

Another burst of rapid machine gun fire reminded me of why I was there in the first place. I grabbed the cupcake box and migrated toward the noise.

"Case!" I called over what seemed to be World War Z going on in the den. "Case!"

"Got 'em! Yessss!"

I peered inside the den to see a Zombie Apocalypse going down on the sixty-five inch plasma. My nephew was sitting on the edge of a V-rocker chair, working the controls furiously.

"Case, you're going to go deaf and blind from this game."

"Worth it, Uncle Mac. Totally worth it."

I grinned and set the cupcakes on the coffee table. "I brought your cupcakes. I only had one. Swear."

"Thanks." He paused the game briefly, and the option screen popped up. "You wanna play?"

"No way," I scoffed. "This game is stupid. For kids."

He grinned. "I'll let you have the shotgun this time."

I eyeballed him. "You know, in this political climate it's not exactly PC to use any manner of oversized weaponry to blow someone's head off."

"They're not people, Uncle Mac." He rolled his eyes as if adults were just too stupid to live. "They're zombies."

Well, I guess that *did* make a world of difference. After a pause, I snagged the second controller and the pump-action shotgun on screen.

"I'll play for a minute or two," I said as he pressed the Play button. "But this game is really stupid. *Christ*!" I unloaded my twelve gauge in a creepy zombie's face as he darted out from under an abandoned car. "Eat that, freak."

I hadn't realized how much time had gone by before I felt my brother's presence in the doorway. I couldn't turn from the abandoned town in front of me, but I could hear enough irritated sucking of his teeth to know it was him.

"Where's J?" I asked worriedly. Not worried enough to miss throwing a pipe bomb into a mass of angry zombies, but worried still.

"Had to make a call. I was showing off my toys. Especially Bumblebee."

I groaned. "You didn't." Of course he did. Jordan wasn't the first person my brother had roped into a tour of his garage, and he wouldn't be the last.

Robert shrugged. “He seemed interested. He’s a really cool guy, you know.”

I happened to agree, and not just because he apparently knew how to feign interest really, really well.

“You want in?” I offered. “We could use some support in the next level. We’re going through the sewer, and we could really use someone who knows how to use a damn sniper rifle.”

Case and I glared at one another.

“Someone tried to breach the cabin too early,” Case said. “I told you not to scare the witch.”

“You had your flashlight on, and it spooked her,” I squawked. “I said ‘lights off,’ did I not?”

He propped a hand on his nonexistent hip. “Well maybe if you didn’t use the pipe bombs the moment you get them, we could have blown her up.”

I narrowed my eyes at him. “You know, this zombie apocalypse has really changed you.”

Robert snickered. “You two sound positively ridiculous. No, I’m not going to join you.”

We shrugged, and Case pressed Play again.

Robert continued, determined to have his parental say. “I’m going to finish making dinner so we can eat on time. You know, like adults? Besides, this game is stupid.”

Despite his protests, he stood in silence, watching us creep down a shadowed hill. A zombie howl sounded nearby, and I used my scope to scan the area.

“You see the hunter?” I asked Case.

“Not yet.” He snapped his flashlight on and panned around screen. “I hear him, though.”

“He’s over there,” Robert pointed.

“Over where?”

“In that corner,” he instructed me and then clicked his teeth when I darted into the empty corner. “No, not that one. Sheesh.” He grabbed a controller and plugged in. Then wasted that zombie ass with a rifle butt to the skull.

"Nice one."

"Mmhmm."

A wave of zombies came scattering down the hill, sending the hairs on the back of my neck on end. Damn, these games looked ridiculously real nowadays. No matter. I knew how to shoot zombies, pixilated or in liquid plasma deliciousness.

"Jordan!" I yelled. "Get in here. We need someone to man the tanks!"

He stuck his head in the doorway with his cell up to his ear, one hand clasped over the bottom speaker. "I'm on the phone in here—"

"For God's sakes, we're dying, man!" I hammed it up enough to make him grin and shake his head.

"I gotta go. No, I gotta go. I'll call you later, Rache."

Rache. As in Rachel? As Robert tossed him a controller and signed in a fourth player, I gritted my teeth so hard I feared a fine powder would tumble out when I finally opened my mouth.

"I'm in," Jordan said, and his character appeared on screen next to mine.

I let off a round into his shoulder that had his character scowling at me. Blue eyes slid to mine, and I shrugged. "Sorry. Friendly fire."

He narrowed his eyes, and I smiled. "After you."

The road home was quiet, and we were comfortably silent. I loved this time of night, when the roads were empty and all the lights smiled green smiles as we sailed on through. Jordan's hand absently massaged my neck as I drove, the other hand drumming on his thigh.

We'd wound up staying for over four hours. We'd managed to wipe out the entire zombie force and the majority of Robert's special spaghetti as well. He'd sent us home with the rest in a Tupperware container, which made me beam at him and say, "Thanks, Mrs. Cleaver." He'd tried to take it back and almost paid with a thumb.

Jordan's voice in the silence made me start. "Your family is nice."

I smiled. "They're all right."

"You're going to love mine." He yawned widely, keeping those magical fingers moving on my neck, tangling in the shaggy ends of my hair. "They're going to be here this Thanksgiving."

We came to a lone red light that hadn't got the memo—we *own* the night—and I slowed to a stop. As his clever fingers paused, I realized I hadn't said anything to his comment and met questing eyes.

"You like turkey?" he asked with the gravity you would ask "Do you need medical assistance?" and I smiled a little.

"Mmhmm."

My smile faded. *Would* I meet them? Would we even be together then? Hell, were we together now? His call from Rachel had jump started my reality solenoids. I pressed my lips together, refusing to let the questions tumble out that neither one of us could plausibly have an answer to.

"What are you thinking?"

I started, then rubbed a hand over my eyes. "Just tired, I guess."

I was tired. Tired of waiting for the other shoe to drop. I looked at him apologetically, pasting a slight smile on my mouth. It felt twisted, and I knew from the concern in his eyes I didn't succeed very well.

"I was just wondering why we're the only people on the road and we're stopped at a red light. Kind of ridiculous if you ask me."

His eyes were pensive as he took my chin in his hand. "No, you weren't."

I blinked rapidly. No, I wasn't, but he wasn't supposed to know me this well yet. I wasn't supposed to miss him like this, before he was even gone. "Kiss me."

He leaned over the console, his mouth landing on mine tentatively, soft as butterflies' wings.

"Again," I whispered when he was through.

"Light's green," he said, smiling a little.

"Again," I demanded.

He wasn't gentle this time. His lips, tongue, and teeth were demanding, demanding something I didn't even know if I could give. He pinned my head against the headrest, working my mouth over with his, our kisses getting sloppier and more desperate. We pulled away when it was either die or breathe and sat for a moment. My breathing rang harsh in my ears as I tried to refocus my attention on driving.

"Fuck me," I demanded, my body taking over my mind. That didn't help.

"Drive," he said hoarsely.

I did.

22

I had suspected coming home after work on Monday afternoon would be different, but I hadn't been prepared for how empty the apartment would feel. Even when Trev had moved out, leaving me a neatly printed note on the one nightstand he left, it hadn't felt this empty. That had been more of a relief, and this was just... silence.

I shook off the doldrums (or tried to). It wasn't anything bigger than a few dates. We'd had a weekend. A weekend to have sex, and that was it—a sex-a-thon, and now it was over. You weren't supposed to wonder what your fellow sex-a-thon partner was doing for dinner or if he was going to watch the game tonight. Or if he was missing you as much as you were missing him.

I scowled. We shouldn't have gotten out of bed. See, that was the problem. Then I wouldn't know that he hated all of my television shows and delighted in making fun of my favorite characters. Which I pretended to hate but secretly found amusing. I wouldn't know that he was good with my nephew and polite to nosy old bakers who served their cupcakes with a side of intrusive questioning. I wouldn't know how he smiled at me indulgently when I tried on his glasses and how he let me make it worth his while to blow off work on Sunday night. Man, I had it bad.

I toed off my shoes and skated to the kitchen in my socks. I forced myself to go about my usual after-work routine, opening mail and taking out the trash and fixing dinner and all those other little things that signal that the work day is truly over. I had just settled down in front of the TV with dinner when my phone rang.

I answered without looking, continuing to scroll down my DVR list. "Yeah."

"Hey. You busy?"

Just hearing his voice had a goofy smile spreading across my face, and I bit my lip to keep my face in check. "Hey. No, what's up?"

"What's up is I haven't seen you in like ten and a half hours. I'm going through withdrawal here."

I let the grin free, and suddenly the nagging feeling that had been bothering me was gone. There were no games, no need to play aloof. "I thought I was the only one. Has ten and a half hours ever seemed so long?"

"Not in recent memory, no. So. Are you busy or what?"

"Not really. Watching a bunch of overly tanned, overly blond social misfits scream and claw at each other and then call each other friends." I flicked off the TV and tossed the remote on the couch. "What do you have in mind?"

Say sex. Please say fucking me into the mattress.

"Dinner," he said, clearly unaware of my inner slut. "I'm fixing something right now. Are you hungry?"

I looked down at my chicken pot pie with apple crumble that had looked so appetizing just moments before. A home cooked meal was sounding better and better.

"Starving."

Sorry, Marie Callender. I trotted my dinner tray right back to the kitchen and began wrapping it in foil.

"What are you making?"

"Something buttery and garlicky, and that's all you need to know."

"My siren song," I sighed dramatically. "I'll be there in thirty."

"I'm using salt too," he teased.

My arteries gave a little shiver. "Make that twenty."

. . .

I woke slowly, lingering in my foggy subconscious much longer than I usually did. I was comfortable and replete but somewhere I'd never been before. I stretched, reveling in the delicious soreness in my muscles, especially the tender region of my backside, before finally opening my eyes. My breath hitched on a swift intake of air. Well, then.

You're not in Kansas anymore, Dorothy.

I silently agreed with my inner voice—Dorothy would have shat herself for a view like this. I wasn't in my own bedroom; that was for sure. I had many things, but a complete glass wall that gave me a panoramic ocean view was not one of them. The ocean stretched before me like a painting in motion—midnight blue punctuated by dark shapes of rock, where the waves crashed and settled with white foam. The scene stretched as far as I could see, far into the distance, where the blackness of the sky melded into the dark rush of the ocean.

In a moment, it all came tumbling back. Jordan's delicious chicken fricassee, eating on the deck with the stars twinkling above and ocean rushing up to meet us. Then someone had mentioned something about dessert (him), and someone had gotten suggestive and slutty (I won't mention names), and we'd wound up tumbling into bed, tearing off clothes like they were made of paper. I couldn't deny, just the memory was sending interesting messages to my cock, which twitched and let me know it was awake already.

I shifted to my other side, only to see him propped up against a pillow, laptop on his lap, staring at the screen intently. The incandescent light was bright on his face, and while I watched, he adjusted his glasses with a quick finger to the center of the frame.

"You're looking sexy, professor."

He looked startled for a moment, the look of someone awakened from deep concentration, and gave me a half smile. "You sleep well?"

"As well as I could. Someone used my ass like a speedway."

He blushed, which made me laugh and made him hit my shoulder. "You loved it."

"Every minute of it," I said sincerely, catching him off guard.

His smile faded as he turned to put his computer on the nightstand. When he turned back, he leaned down to cup my chin. "You up for a round two?"

I pushed the covers down to my ankles, revealing my nakedness and already throbbing cock. "And a three and a four."

His eyes went dark, and then his hands were on me, running down my sides and caressing my thighs. He rolled onto me, catching his weight on his elbows, and for a moment we just looked at each other, enjoying the charged energy, my cock trapped between us, jerking against his belly. His mouth descended slowly, and I didn't close my eyes until the very last second, not until his mouth landed on mine and we began to devour each other. I had always thought kissing was a waste of time, just a prelude to the main event. I would never think that again.

A half whimper escaped my throat as I locked my hands in his hair. I thought maybe I could kiss Jordan forever, that maybe if the world was ending and fire was raining down all around us, I would reach up for just one more kiss like this.

But his kisses did other things to me and my insides, and all too soon, I had to move or die. I ground against him, my hands drifting down to cup and grip the perfectly muscled globes of his behind. "I need," I managed against his ear.

Instead of sliding inside me like I wanted, he took my hands in a powerful grip and pinned them above my head. "Leave them there," he growled, and I felt my cock jump in response. *Turns out, I really like growly, bossy Jordan.*

"But I'm ready now," I whined.

"You're always in such a goddamned rush," he said, his mouth quirking in amusement. He kissed my mouth, then my chin, then down the sloped column of my neck, one precise kiss after another. "This time, I want to take go slow."

"That's a great idea for next time," I wheedled, moving my hands just the slightest bit and then stilling as he glared.

"Move them, and I *will* spank you."

I groaned and snapped my hips against his a little, causing my cock to buck between us. That was so *not* the right thing to say if he wanted me to stop. The idea of lying on his lap, having him "discipline" me with his hand, smacking my ass until it was flushed and pink, flashed in my head. Then spearing my pink ass with that thick cock and pounding me... the mental imagery made me a little crazy.

His eyes went wide and then dark with understanding. And need. Raw need. "Hands still," he ground out and then went back to work on my neck.

He played with my nipples, pulling and rubbing the sensitive brown nubs until I growled.

"There's slow, and then there's torture," I informed him, a half second before he took a nipple between his teeth. I hissed as he nipped the bud and then sucked on it strongly.

When I looked up, his eyes sparkled with amusement. "Trust me, I know the difference."

It was clear from his teasing licking and sucking that he did indeed. By the time he moved down to my quivering stomach, I was just about a puddle of goo. He nosed the throbbing column of my cock aside, scraping his teeth against my bellybutton, just enough to make me jump and let my cock slap back in place. A drop of creamy liquid pearled on the engorged, purplish head, and his nostrils flared. I knew he could smell my arousal. I certainly could. He dipped the tip of his tongue in the liquid and swirled it around, tasting delicately. My stomach clenched the clench of a thousand crunches, anticipating that moment when he would finally take me in his warmth, and I could fuck that pretty mouth. But he kept journeying instead, down past my cock to my trembling, splayed-open thighs.

I looked at him, flabbergasted. And he winked. The bastard winked as he massaged my thighs and then the tense muscles of my calves.

"Argh," I grumbled. "Sadistic bastard."

He pretended not to hear. "What was that?"

"Nothing," I managed loudly, flinching when he nipped my calf with his teeth.

His magic fingers danced across my skin, sending me hurtling through stages of relaxing and tensing, as if my body couldn't decide which one it wanted to do. As his hands stroked the soft skin underneath my thighs, my body decided on tension, and every muscle felt bowstring tight as I waited.

He gently took my balls in his hand, and I melted into the mattress with a groan. Twisted the sheets in my hands. Fast was good, but this... this was something else entirely. Now that he had primed my body, wreaked havoc on my senses, every touch was like fire. Every touch threatened to set me off. When his tongue swept over my sensitive entrance, I skyrocketed.

"Jordan!"

When he speared the pink hole with the point of his tongue and tunneled into my entrance, I saw black spots, flickering across my vision.

God. A broken cry fell from my lips, and my eyes fluttered shut as I pulled my thighs tightly to my chest and locked my arms underneath. I felt torn apart by the sensation, incapable of speech. I didn't know if I was going to survive, but I wasn't going to miss a minute.

I writhed on the bed, moaning, wanting, needing more as he withdrew and penetrated me again, fucking me roughly with his tongue. I fought the explosion rising inside me, fought it with every fiber of my being, but it was useless. I could feel it coming as I mumbled nonsensically, tossing my head side to side. He replaced his tongue with one finger and then two, pushing slowly inside me to the knuckle, and I was done. My entire body shuddered as the orgasm ripped through me and hurtled through every nerve ending in my body from my fingertips to the tendons of my neck, stark against smooth skin.

"Fuck!" Air came surging back into my struggling lungs, and I lay there panting. "Fuck," I said again weakly, because I couldn't remember any other words yet. I didn't know that losing control could be so much fucking fun.

His soft laugh was damned sexy. "What year is it? Do you know who the president is?"

"You're a riot," I managed. "Should take that act... on the road."

My sarcasm would have had more impact if I hadn't spasmed just then, shaking like a leaf as the aftershock passed through my body.

His eyes went dark. "You're so crazy hot when you lose control like that."

It was only then that I realized his fingers were still moving inside of me, thick and deep. Rubbing against my prostate in a way that made me grunt and bear down. Probably why I was still hard as a brick even though I'd just come harder than I'd ever come in my life. *I didn't have stamina*, I groused. But somehow my body was made for this... made for him? All I knew was I'd never felt this before, never felt this *way* before, and I wasn't ready for it to end. Instinctively, I felt my hips working with his questing fingers as they pumped in and out of my hole.

"You ready for me?" His voice was husky as he settled on his knees between my splayed thighs.

I raised an eyebrow. "You have to ask?"

My attitude was ruined as he pulled his fingers out of my grasping hole, and I whimpered at the loss. He rolled on a condom in no time at all and braced on his elbow. He guided himself into my entrance, pushing past the tight ring of muscle, rubbing against every ridge and groove on the way in. Though I urged him on with my hands, he was still, his heavy balls snug against my ass.

"Is it weird... that I've never felt this way before?"

My gaze shot up from our joining to his, and there was an open honesty there that shook me to my core. The look on his face was tender and caring, and it took my breath clean away.

"No," I said thickly. "Not weird."

He looked as if he wanted to say more and then gasped as my muscles began fluttering and grasping around him. He started to move, pulling nearly all the way back out and moving slowly back in.

He sucked the skin of my neck, and I knew he was marking me. I didn't care. Our bodies worked together like they were born that way, like beautiful synchronized music. Somewhere in the back of my hazy mind, I realized with a start that we weren't having sex. We were making love.

Damn it. My eyes felt a little wet. We weren't supposed to make love. We were supposed to fuck. Have fun. What the hell were we doing? Before I could formulate an answer, his thrusting became more intense, angling across my prostate in a way that snatched the breath clean from my body. When he dragged back across it, I cried out, digging my fingers into his shoulders.

"Again," I demanded. "Just like that." I didn't care what we were doing. Just do it again.

His fingers gripped my hips as he slammed across that spot again and again, picking up speed and setting a punishing pace—I could only hold on for the ride. Muscles stood out in his arms in stark relief beneath the honey-colored skin as he braced himself above me. Sweat dripped from his forehead onto my chest, and I wanted to feel it, taste the salty drops bursting against my tongue. I slammed my eyes shut against the visual feast to stave off my orgasm, but it was no use. The sounds of our lovemaking echoed in my ears—the slap of our thighs, his balls thudding against the crack of my ass, and our harsh breathing meshing and melding together.

"I'm… I'm…." was all I managed as the most intense orgasm of my life shot through my spine and hurtled through my body. I tightened around Jordan's cock with the force of my orgasm, and suddenly he shuddered and convulsed against me as the storm hurtled through him too. I felt him expand and pulse inside me and wondered if I'd ever get to feel him coming inside of me without the latex barrier. For now, this was enough, more than I'd thought I'd have, certainly.

We lay there for a moment, breathing like collided trains—wrecked, steam whistling from our collapsed bodies. I ran my hands absently over his sweat-slicked skin, wishing he'd never move, that he'd never have to pull out. Eventually he did move, just long enough to take off the condom, and I was gratified when the always-neat

Jordan tossed it somewhere near the trash. He didn't seem at all concerned if it made it in or not as he flopped back down beside me, facedown in the pillow, and buried his head between folded arms.

"You're going to regret that in the morning," I predicted to a mop of silky black hair. "You *are* fussy, you know."

"I am not fussy." His voice was muffled in the pillow.

"If there's a drop of dirt or dust in this place, I haven't seen it."

"You haven't looked. You've been too busy keeping me within three feet of the bed."

"It wasn't that hard." I grinned.

When he unearthed half his face to turn to me, I could see the hint of a smile on his full lips. "Something sure was."

"Oh, is it bad pun time already? I should have seen it *coming*," I said, waggling my eyebrows.

He snorted into the pillow. "Your postcoital talk needs work."

"At least I don't use terms like postcoital."

"There are worse things. Like a bedmate that never quiets down and sleeps."

"I slept," I reminded him. "You were working, so you don't remember. What time is it anyway?"

He grunted in response, and I swatted his shoulder. I leaned over him, squashing him good (hopefully), and began groping the nightstand surface for my watch. Even as I almost knocked something off and pushed a water glass dangerously close to the edge, I continued to grope blindly—habit was so hard to break, and I'd been blind nightstand surfing my whole life.

"It's four thirty," he said with a yawn. "Go back to sleep."

"I should get back," I said, finally locating the leather band of my watch with an "Aha!" I peered at the quartz face for a moment, only to realize his guess was accurate. "I have work in the morning."

"Anything you can blow off? I have a meeting in the morning, but we could meet for lunch."

"You were the bad kid in class, weren't you? The one who would stage a walkout if the professor was three minutes late?"

"Five minutes, Mac. It's only polite. How can you mold young minds if you can't be on time?" He rolled to the side, facing me, and propped up on an elbow. "So? How about it?"

Faced with the sight of all that deliciousness, I almost forgot my own name, much less that I should say no. "I have to go in, but I can meet you for lunch. Somewhere near the beach."

He grinned. "You surfing or working? Don't make me call Drew."

"I'm meeting a prospect at their board shop. Call it a little of both," I said with a wink. "And don't you dare."

"Don't worry. I need you alive for dinner. And after."

"Oh, we're doing dinner too?" My eyebrows went up. "I have to keep my other men happy, darling. How's a guy supposed to retain his other relationships?"

"You're not." He leaned over and kissed me thoroughly, one hand anchored in my hair. "I think I could bear to have you here for a little while. What do you think?"

I thought I really liked his hand in my hair, massaging my scalp. I thought I really liked lying in his bed, talking in the dark. I thought I really liked waking up to him in bed beside me. I thought I really didn't want this to end.

Tell him. Tell him how he makes you feel.

"I... I...."

His piercing gaze halted the words before they made their final journey, and they huddled together in my mouth. The truth of the matter was I wasn't sure enough about us to confess something like that. I was a chicken. Even though part of me knew that love was never guaranteed, I needed to know Jordan was *all in* before I laid my cards on the table.

"You what?"

"I-I want food," I blurted. "All this work has made me hungry."

He stared at me for a moment, and I wondered if he would call me on the lie. His mouth quirked, and I knew he wouldn't press the issue. Sure enough, he swung his long legs over the side of the bed with a groan.

"What work?" He stretched, and I admired the pull and play of the muscles in his long limbs. "I was the one working up a sweat."

I squawked. "I'll have you know I'm a fantastic fuck, J."

He paused in the doorway and gave me a curious look. "You're more than that. I didn't think I had to tell you that by now."

That and a million other things. A million times over. I decided to remain mute on what, exactly, he was going to have to do to make me believe this was real and followed him to the granite and stainless steel mausoleum he called a kitchen.

We ate cereal in his bed, because that's what you do when sex is too new to bother with clothes or eat real food. I stirred my Cheerios gratefully, glad he had caved and put sugar in them at least. I had been dismayed to learn that Jordan's tastes only ran to Mueslix, Raisin Bran, or plain Cheerios when he felt festive. Plain. I slid my gaze to him sitting beside me, cross-legged, with his bowl of Cheerios, the light of the television flickering on his glasses. It made me concerned for his mental state, frankly. I mean, they had like five different flavors of Cheerios nowadays.

He looked over at me. "What?"

I pointed my spoon in his direction. "You should try these with sugar."

His nose scrunched adorably. "I tried your Pop-Tarts, but I have my limits."

"You don't know what you're missing."

His eyes twinkled. "Cavities, empty calories, and early death?"

"Sweet goodness. And it's my turn to choose a show."

He snatched the remote from the covers before I could reach it, squawking when I dived for him. He held his bowl aloft as I leaned and reached around him.

"We're going to need to reach an agreement before I acquiesce," he announced.

"What kind of agreement?"

"No housewives. Of any county. No Bridezilla. No..."

"Anything but crime shows?" I finished, giving him a poke in the ribs.

His mouth twitched. "I watch other things."

"Please. Name one of your shows that don't begin with a gruesome description of where they found the body."

"*Dateline ID*," he said triumphantly. "They work their way *up* to the body. And that's if they found it at all."

I stared at him. And pulled up an *On Demand* episode of a show on his impromptu no-no list. He groaned and fell back on the bed.

"Drama queen," I said, rescuing his empty bowl and putting it on the nightstand. "Compromise. By one party. Suffering through a show you hate is what relationships are all about. It means you care."

When I looked back over at him, he wasn't smiling like I'd intended. His expression was serious. Intent. "Is that what this is?" he asked. "A relationship?"

"Isn't it?" I asked casually.

It was probably only a second before he answered me, but it felt like four hours. His answer, when it came, was simpler than I expected.

"I guess it is." He rested his head on my thigh in order to get a better vantage point for the show he hated. "I guess it is."

23

JDizzle: I'm getting home early, so I'll start dinner. What sounds good?

McMoney: U starting and finishing dinner.

JDizzle: Cute. There's an apron waiting for you. I need a sous-chef.

McMoney: Fine. Then I want carbonara.

JDizzle: Oddball.

McMoney: U asked.

JDizzle: We need eggs for that.

McMoney: Then someone needs 2 go 2 the store.

JDizzle: I'm guessing you're talking about me.

McMoney: Well, u are off, JDizzle.

JDizzle: I've asked you not to call me that.

. . .

I snickered at Jordan's text. Wait until he saw how I'd programmed him in my phone. I had my fingers poised to respond when Drew elbowed me.

"Pay attention," he murmured out of the corner of his mouth.

I sighed, pocketing my phone. I didn't know why *I* had to pay attention. We were holding interviews for Jennie's assistant—this was her show, and if her business suit was anything to go by, she didn't mind letting them know it. Generally, we were a little more casual here. As long as she was happy with the candidate, what did I care?

Jordan was in the middle of a big case, and time with him, *not* working, was becoming rare. I could be home right now. I frowned. Home nowadays could be his place just as much as mine. I wasn't quite sure how that had happened. Just humans being human, I guessed. We started out meeting at a particular place for dinner, and then it just seemed silly to waste all that gas. All of a sudden, we were driving places together. After having sex, neither one of us wanted to get up and drive home at the crack of dawn, so suddenly I was staying the night. But then I had work in the morning, and going home to change was such a bother. So I started bringing a bag. But keeping up with that bag was like living out of a suitcase. Then I started leaving things at his place.

I sighed. *My, what a tangled web we weave... when you play house with your boyfriend.* That's what he was, wasn't he? I was hesitant to put labels on something still in its infancy—we'd only been seeing each other for two months. Two months to get to know each other's likes and dislikes, routines and patterns, thoughts... dreams, hopes....

I couldn't lie; I liked this getting-to-know-you stuff. I knew that he was a freaking morning person (which, frankly, had almost been a deal breaker), and had a serious problem with caffeine. He talked on the phone when driving *most of the time* (he wouldn't admit it) to "kill two birds with one stone." He worked too much and crashed on the weekends and only had a passing acquaintance with the word "relax." I wasn't even sure if he *knew* the word. And he liked me.

Cue schoolgirl blush. But he did. Sometimes I even caught him staring when we were supposed to be working at home. (Bad idea, we always wound up fucking.) And when I caught him looking at me with that *look*, I almost imagined this was real. That I wouldn't come home one day and he would be gone.

Shouldn't spending all the time with each other lessen the need to hear his voice? See his face? And there in the interview, right in the middle of Bella answering a question, it hit me smack dab in the face. I sat up straight. Breathed in sharply. I was in fucking love. *No*. Fuck love. Love was for suckers. *Jump in a wrapper, darlin', and call yourself a lollipop*. My mouth twisted bitterly. Fool. Even I couldn't muster up the level of denial I'd need to deny it. My arms weren't strong enough to shovel that much bullshit.

"Oh, man," I whispered.

This had so not been a part of the plan. I started to drop my head in my hands and remembered my audience just in time. Varying degrees of confusion and annoyance graced Drew and Jennie's faces. I smiled weakly at the only person smiling back at me—Bella, our hopeful candidate.

"Oh, man, are you qualified," I ad-libbed poorly.

Drew rolled his eyes so hard I'm surprised they didn't land on the table. "Go on, Bella," he encouraged. "You were talking about your organizational strengths and weaknesses?"

Bella beamed and continued talking about her unique filing system while I tried to breathe normally while thinking about… you know, love and crap. The stupid part of my heart ached to celebrate—my brain had finally received its messenger hawk and the note in his beak. I wanted to enjoy it and not be filled with this crazy, irrational fear that it would all end any minute. But it wasn't a crazy fear, was it? People left all the time, even when they claimed to love you.

My jaw firmed. I guessed I would just have to enjoy him while it lasted.

"Well, Bella, if you have any more questions, you should feel free to e-mail or call me." Jennie's voice filtered through my musings, and I sat up straight. *Finally*. "Do you have any questions for me?"

"No," Bella said, shaking her head obediently.

I sighed and half stood—but she wasn't quite done.

"I would like to say something more about my qualifications. I like to consider myself the full package, the A to Z in assistants." She smiled confidently as I eased back down in my chair. "I actually have qualifications to match that A to Z package. A is for my attitude, which is always helpful and team-oriented. B is for...."

Oh, jeez. I wriggled in my seat, hoping someone would stop her. But Jennie's crossed leg only twitched before settling back into a routine swinging back and forth, and Drew's fingers steepled. That was the only reaction from my fellow interviewers. I wanted to run screaming into the night. Or midafternoon. Surely it was midafternoon by now? Surely the apocalypse had come and gone? I prayed she would forget the rest of the alphabet.

After ten more minutes, I couldn't take it anymore. I excused myself as Drew shot me daggers, and I was in my car before Bella got to "F is for fidelity." *F is for fuck this shit.*

I owed him big for this. But I couldn't wait another second to... to what? *If you tell him you love him, you'll ruin it.* No, I wouldn't tell him. But I wanted to be with him, and that was enough.

By the time I finally kicked the front door shut with my foot, it was nearing six o'clock. Traffic had fried my patience thoroughly. People who had apparently received their license in the mail today had managed to turn a thirty minute drive into an hour plus. I dropped my keys in the bowl Jordan kept near the door and toed off my shoes. I was seriously debating sneaking a cigarette in the bathroom when the smell of garlic wafted by my nose. *Ah, my siren song.* I gave up the image of me crouched on a toilet lid, chain smoking with a hand fan and a can of Glade, and headed for the kitchen.

He was on his phone, tucked between his shoulder and his ear, stirring something on the stove. He seemed to be doing more listening than talking, I noted with amusement, punctuated by his stock "I'm not paying you any attention" responses. Mmhmm, uh-huh, and yeah are some of his all-time favorites.

"Uh-huh," he said, reaching for the pepper, and I had to grin.

I took a minute just to enjoy the sight of that damned fine man. He hadn't changed yet from his work clothes, had just discarded the dress shirt to reveal the undershirt beneath. His feet were bare as he padded across the hardwood floor, and I thought maybe I could watch him like this endlessly. But then he turned, and my free peep show was over. He smiled, cheeks flushed from the steam. His finger went up in the universal "give me a second" gesture, and I waved him on.

"Yeah, I completely understand, Mom. Mmhmm." He held the phone away. "How long have you been there?" he asked me in a whisper.

"Long enough."

I pushed off the doorjamb and decided to make myself useful. "What can I do?"

"Salad?" he suggested. "No, not you," he said into the phone, turning back to the stove. "I'm talking to Mackenzie. Just a friend, Ma, jeez."

I washed my hands with Dawn, spurning the hand soap in the fancy glass jar. I wished it could wash away discontent as easily as grease. His "just a friend" comment had sent my blood pressure into the stratosphere, but I gritted my teeth and resolved to just make the damn salad. I poked around the kitchen, gathering ingredients in a bowl. I set the bowl on the cutting board and whisked the cutting board to the center island. A crisp head of lettuce and juicy ripe tomatoes joined a sharp knife from the knife block.

Was he supposed to just tell his mother before dinner that he was gay? No, can't talk about you never having grandkids, Ma, I have to eat. These kinds of things take time. *Chop*. He already broke up with Rachel, didn't he? *Chop*. Just because he won't hold your hand in the grocery store doesn't mean he's changing his mind about you. *Chop, chop, chop*!

"Uhm, that's probably enough, huh?"

I blinked at Jordan's whisper, only to find myself before a mountain of lettuce. I had dispatched the whole head with serial killer efficiency. I smiled weakly and took out a Ziploc baggie from a side drawer. I guess I was less okay with this than I thought.

I bagged most of the lettuce, put a suitable amount in a bowl, and diced up a tomato to join it. Flicked my wrist and made the bowl jump to toss. I felt calmer as I rinsed off the knife—chopping was strangely soothing.

"No, I gotta go. I will. I will. Talk to you later. Love you too." He tossed the phone down on the counter. "*Gawd.* That woman could talk the ears off a truck full of corn."

"And you love her."

He grunted, head still shaking at his mother's remarkable talking ability.

"You're a good son," I teased.

"I do try."

I gave him a kiss that was meant to be short. Followed by another that wasn't. My tongue swept through his mouth and then settled in to play with his for a bit. I sighed into his mouth as his hands went for their all-time favorite place. I think someone, at some point, had put homing devices in his hands and calibrated them for my ass. I didn't mind a bit. The microwave beeping made us part reluctantly.

Jordan cleared his throat. "I should, ah, check…." He waved vaguely behind him at any number of appliances. "Something."

He turned back to his pot and gave it a vigorous stir, and I grinned. Good to know I wasn't the only one. I checked the microwave, only to pull out a bowl of broccoli. I waved it under his nose with a raised eyebrow before sitting it on the counter. Far away.

"I don't remember requesting this."

He threatened me with a wooden spoon. "You'll eat it and like it." The next time I saw the wooden spoon, it had a coating of cream sauce on the end. "Here, taste this. Try to forget the sight of the wicked broccoli."

He looked delicious. Fuck the sauce. But I took a taste obediently, and my eyes closed from the explosion of flavor on my tongue. I moaned, taking the spoon from his hand to lick more thoroughly.

"Good?"

The husky timbre of his voice made my eyes open slowly. So we were back to fuck the sauce. I maintained eye contact as I crowded his body against the sink, reaching around him to drop the spoon in the dishwater. I pressed against him and flicked my eyes down the length of his body.

"Good," I confirmed in the tense quiet.

More than the sauce was good. *This* was good, and the fact that he might not recognize it was driving me a little crazy. When had he ever had this connection, this unique sense of right with someone? When everything just *worked*. The need to possess him pressed the impulse-control center of my brain, and some part of me recognized it as foreign. Tried to reject it. I had never been against topping, enjoyed it sometimes, but I was a natural bottom. I loved that vulnerable feeling of physically taking him into that inner part of myself that no one else knew. I loved sharing that part of myself with Jordan. Wondered if he would ever offer me the same privilege.

I doubted it. Because while he had been remarkably free about doing all manners of taboo things *to* me, he hadn't been quite as comfortable on the receiving end. During one blow job, my thumb had caressed his hole, and he'd been taut and tense as a vibrating wire. He had always taken the dominant role there, and for what? Because pitching wasn't quite as gay as receiving? The thought of him holding back any part of himself from me was enough to make me almost angry. Desperate. A growl rumbled somewhere deep in my throat

"I want to fuck you," I gritted out. Then slid my hands to his ass to make sure he got the picture. Molded and stroked the muscled cheeks while pressed flush against the length of his front.

He looked at me. Just looked. Apprehensive. His cock, which normally would be thick and hard against me, seemed to be stalled at half mast. I ground into him, and he made a small, needy sound. So he wasn't entirely against the idea then.

"Are you good with that?" I asked.

I could tell from the way his jaw tightened that he wasn't

completely okay with it. But whatever he saw in my eyes made him say simply, "Okay."

My feverish gaze dropped. I didn't want him to be just "okay" with it. I knew trusting me to do this was a huge deal, but I already knew he trusted me. You don't lay your head down every night next to someone you don't trust. Now I wanted him to *want* me, want me to take him in this way. I wasn't sure he did, and guilty feelings crowded my arousal. Was I just pressing his boundaries to prove a point?

My hands made short work of his belt and slacks, and they fell to his thighs with very little convincing. Silky boxers joined them soon enough, revealing his semi-hard state.

"You okay?"

His voice was a little thin. "Why wouldn't I be?"

Why indeed. The stove timer going off saved me from a response, and I pushed the cancel button. Slid the pot off the stove. The control knob of the burner made loud clicks in the silence as I turned it off.

When I looked back at Jordan, he hadn't moved. His pants and boxers had gathered at his thighs, restricting his movement. His hands were braced behind him on the sink, gripping it like a lifeline, and my jaw clenched. I didn't have the strength to change my course—every time I saw the beauty of Jordan's perfectly sculpted body, my mind short circuited. Logic board—fried.

I helped him step out of both garments, touching every bit of skin on the way. Pushed his shirt up his firm, muscled torso and over his head. My fingers were drawn to his hardened nipples, and when I plucked at them, I heard his swift intake of breath.

"You're so fucking responsive. I love that." I couldn't help the words that tumbled out of my mouth, even when they made him blush.

Long dark lashes swept down over his eyes. "Can't seem to help it."

He moaned when I licked at them, nipped them. Took them in my mouth as my hand worked down his stomach to take him in my grip. I stroked him, building up a rhythm that had him moving his hips frantically. The fingers of my other hand tightened on his hip, pressuring his legs apart. His rhythm broke, and his hand landed on my wrist. My eyes shot to his face, but he wasn't looking at me. His eyes were trained on my chest, and I took the momentary breather to calm my racing heart.

I wished I had it in me to give him a respite. But I didn't have that kind of control. I *needed* to have him this way. Just not like this. I would make it good for him, and not just because his arousal always triggered my own. I loved him. I accepted this truth quietly as it rolled through my consciousness, and placed a hand on either side of his face. Kissed him softly.

I took his hand and led him to the bedroom. "Come with me."

He followed willingly enough. "What about dinner?"

"Later. It'll keep."

I disposed of my clothes on the way, tossing them haphazardly. By the time we reached the bed, we were both naked. The mussed bedcovers made me snicker a little. It had been hard, but I'd finally broken him of his habit of making the bed in the mornings. As he'd ungraciously put it, making a bed was bloody difficult with someone still lounging in it. I gestured toward the bed, and Jordan gave me a pitiful look.

I gave him a push and watched, amused, as he toppled on the mattress, face forward. He landed in the pile of bedcovers with an audible *ooof*. I poked him in the side to get him to flip, but after a small quiver, he just lay there. I straddled him and tried to roll his body, but he wouldn't budge. I finally gave up, laughing helplessly as his shoulders shook with mirth.

I took a moment to enjoy the sight of his lean, muscled form stretched out on the bed. *Mine*. From the tips of his silky black hair to the arches of his elegant feet. *Mine*. The thought came from nowhere, and my amusement fled. My hands trembled, tracing the rounded curves of his bottom. *Mine*.

I buried my face against the broad expanse of his back, rubbing my hands down his well-toned arms. Traced the Celtic tattoo. Licked the dark lines lovingly. A sigh floated up from his general direction as he let me explore all the hills and valleys of his body, the sweet line of his spine, the indent of his trim waist. The muscled masterpiece of his ass. My cock pulsed, hard and thick against his thigh. I had planned to just rim him a little and maybe use my finger, but, like most impromptu ideas, the plans had changed. I wanted *in*. I may have been a happy little bottom boy, but the sight and feel of Jordan's ass against my cock was too heady to ignore.

The soft exploration had gentled him to me and relaxed his tense shoulders, the rigidity of his thighs dissipating like soft rain. His next action spoke stronger than words as he spread his legs and lifted up on his knees. There was a small tremor under his skin when I placed my hand on the small of his back and moved between his thighs. I sucked one of his balls into my mouth. His back arched, but he didn't make a sound. I alternated between the two, sucking them and licking them until I thought I heard a whimper.

When I looked up, he was motionless, his face still buried in the pillows. But the sound of his harsh breathing was loud in my ears and was as good as a green light in my mind. I lowered my face to his tender crevice, seeking out his flushed hole. His unique scent, a little Irish Spring and sun and something strictly Jordan, filtered up through my nose. Made my nostrils flare. *Mine*.

My tongue plunging inside his tender region finally wrenched a groan from his throat. I lapped at him aggressively, unwilling to let up long enough for him to regain his equilibrium, and he pushed back against my tongue, increasing the depth of my penetration. Fucked himself with it as I slid one finger and then two under the smooth glide of my tongue. He gritted out my name. Moaned. Panted through some garbled sounds. I couldn't understand a word of it, but I understood the way he spread his legs wide. It was absolute, utter surrender, and I just stared at him for a minute, impaled on my two fingers. Trusting me to do what no one else had done. I snarled. What no one else would ever do.

A third finger went more smoothly than the first as I readied him, sliding my fingers in and out of his scorching channel. When my fingers finally slipped out completely, he let out a bereft moan that had me smiling crookedly. It was a bit caveman-like and something I'd never admit aloud, but I liked taking care of him this way.

I rolled on the condom with shaking fingers and touched myself as little as possible with a quick stroke of lube. I didn't know how much longer I could resist the pull down low in my stomach, that short, sucking pull that had me wanting to detonate all over his back. By the time I lined up my cock with his glistening hole, the tension was back.

"Relax," I whispered.

His shoulders went slack as he tried to visibly do so, but when I tried to enter him, he was locked up tight. I refused to hurt him.

"J, you have to relax," I said again.

"I'm trying," he said, his voice a little annoyed. "You telling me to relax isn't making it easier."

I huffed a breath of laughter. "You getting pissy just makes me want to fuck you more."

"Then do it."

"I'm not going to hurt you, and right now, that's exactly what I'd do." I slipped my finger back into his hole, and he hissed. "I'm a lot bigger than that finger."

"I can handle it," he said, but his voice was small.

I was briefly undone. If I hadn't loved him before, I did now. I was unbearably touched that this strong, accomplished man was willing to do this for me, just because I'd asked. Giving yourself to someone was a big deal. It made you intolerably exposed. Defenseless. I was momentarily tongue-tied, trying to express how much this meant to me, but then I gave up. It just wouldn't be my style.

I smacked his left cheek. "Come on, J. You're tighter than an old maid. I bet there are cobwebs in there."

He collapsed in laughter. "I prefer hot young coed," he said. "Virgin, cherry hole?"

But my ridiculous words relaxed him enough that I breached his tight ring of muscle as we both held our breath, then let it out as a slow hiss as I filled him, stretched him, all the way to the hilt.

God. I felt my eyes cross briefly as my cock adjusted to his heat.

Then his inner walls rippled around me, and I swore. I had to move. *Now*.

"You good?" I gritted out.

"Feels... different." He wriggled his ass experimentally, and I almost blacked out. "But good."

I pulled out slowly, just leaving the head in. And then pushed back in deeper. Harder. Repeated it. Felt my hands shaking on his hips as I stroked in and out of his core. I gripped the shreds of my tattered control with steel claws until I found his spot. He snapped his hips back at me, and I was lost. I felt outside of myself as I pounded into him repeatedly, realizing somewhere in my foggy subconscious that this is *not* how you treat... what did he call it again? Oh yeah, virgin, cherry ass. But he seemed to be right there with me, meeting me thrust for thrust, making coarse, primitive noises. Or maybe that was me. Or both of us.

"Dammit, right there," he panted.

"Touch yourself." My voice sounded different. Rough. Demanding.

His hand disappeared underneath his body, and from the moan that followed, I knew he was doing as he was told. I anchored one hand in his silky dark hair to pull his head back roughly and hurtled us both toward the finish. My back arched as I felt the orgasm building, my balls tingling, and I hoped he was close. And then he was coming, shooting on the bedsheets and tightening around me like a velvet fist. The orgasm ripped through my body like a hurricane as I jerked against him, crying out, letting it lift me up and scatter me to parts unknown.

I collapsed on top of him, unable to even lift my head. My eyes finally cracked open to the sight of our joined hands. At some point, we had locked our fingers together, joined our hands as we spent our passion in and on each other. Probably initiated by me. I winced as I pulled my hand out of his. *Way to keep sex light and breezy, Mac.*

To be fair, he didn't seem to mind. As he folded his arms underneath his head and pillowed his head there, he seemed rather peaceful, actually. Even with my dead weight on his back, my face buried in the crook of his neck.

"I should move," I eventually acknowledged.

"You're fine," he croaked.

But I wasn't fine. I was more in love than ever before. I was just lucky I hadn't blabbed yet. The thought gave me the strength to move, and I levered myself off him. Disposed of the condom. Used the bathroom and cleaned myself up. Brought him a warm, damp washcloth. When I returned, he was still lying there, splayed on his front with his ass up in the air. My cock jerked, and I looked down at it disbelievingly. *Calm the fuck down before you fall off*, I scolded it. *I'm not twenty-five anymore, and neither are you.*

"Here."

He opened one eye to find the rag dripping two inches from his face. He looked at my face and cocked his head, like he always did when he was puzzling something out.

I offered the towel again. "It's dripping."

He plucked it from my fingers, and I turned away. I could hear him getting up as I picked through the various items of my clothing we'd left on the floor. I pulled on my jeans.

"You feel like dinner now?" I asked.

"Sure." By the time I turned around, he was wearing my boxers. I flushed, remembering I'd divested him of his in the kitchen. He was still looking at me curiously. "You okay?"

I was in love with a man who was in his first gay relationship. I was the first man he'd ever been with. So what would happen when he decided to test his new fairy wings, find someone a little better? And he would. My own mother had decided to find something, *someone* a little better.

Everyone leaves.

Was I okay? I was in love with a man who had promised me nothing. *No.*

"Perfect," I said.

He groaned. "You only say that when things are very much not perfect. Why don't you just tell me what's wrong?"

"The only thing wrong with me right now is that I'm starving." I took his hand, pulling him toward the kitchen. "I want fooood."

His eyes twinkled as he shook his head at me. "I guess I'll have to feed you, then. And then fuck the answers out of you."

I grinned. Wouldn't happen, but I would certainly enjoy him trying.

24

It was turning out to be a hell of a day. My tip to find a bail jumper hadn't panned out, and now I was waiting two doors down from his mother's house in a questionable neighborhood, slouched down low with my hat over my face. A couple of youths walked by my truck again, giving me a side eye, and I wondered how long it would be before they tried something. I hated the heat, I hated skip traces, and I hated the fact that Drew had saddled me with this one. But leaving Bella's interview early had its price. I'd heard the sweet tune, and now that bitch the pied piper was here to collect. I picked at my thumbnail for the third time, trying to smooth the ragged edges I'd created on the second time. It wasn't like I had anything to do.

Jordan was going out of town to meet a client in NYC tonight and would be gone for a week. He had booked a red eye specifically so we would get a chance to see each other before he left, and here I was stuck in a hot car on a skip trace. My eyes flickered toward the clock in the dash—I only had an hour to wrap this up before he would have to leave. I still had hope. Just thinking about him lifted my mood, and I knew without consulting a mirror that my face had a big, goofy grin on it.

The connection to Nick's phone crackled a little, and I remembered that he had been talking my ear off before I'd drifted. While I was happy for Nick (happier now that I was getting some on the regular), listening to him blather on about Saint Peyton was giving me a headache.

"—and then I said Peyton shouldn't be embarrassed to go into a nail salon. I mean, men do go there nowadays. How can manscaping be wrong?"

Nick had volunteered to keep me company, but I was absolutely thinking of hanging up on him. My fingers itched for the End button. One little button. That's all it would take.

He prattled on, oblivious to my inner dilemma. "He planned this wonderful getaway for us, just so we can get away, you know? Reconnect."

"You live at a bed-and-breakfast. Where do you get away to? A regular house and a job?"

"Running a bed-and-breakfast is a full-time job, and it never stops. The guests always seem to need something, and they're looking to you to provide it. Like a hotel, only the concierge, cook, and maid service is you. I love it, but we do need time away."

"Time away to fuck like bunnies?" I teased.

"Tacky. Just tacky. I don't know why I'm surprised you know nothing of romance. You and your endless line of men. You're a serial dater."

He said that like it was serial killer, he really did.

"Shows what you know, Nick. I'm in a committed relationship now. The shop is closed."

"Committed?" He snorted.

"Yes, committed, thank you."

"How can you be committed with someone who's not even out yet? In fact, isn't he still engaged?"

Is it still wrong to push someone out of a wheelchair if said person is a real Mitch?

"No, he's *not* still engaged. He broke it off weeks ago. And I'm willing to give him time to come to terms with our relationship."

We were still finding our groove, was all. I bit my lip. We ironically had no problems with normal couple issues—he did the cooking; I did the dishes. We walked the beach sometimes after dinner and talked about how it would be when we could take Finn with us. I found out his secret to keeping his home so clean—a short, stout housekeeper named Meredith, which totally worked for me. It meant I could still leave my wet towels on the floor, and, three times a week, he could keep his house military clean. We just clicked. Only… it was like all the relationship issues had been replaced by one biggie—one party was altering his entire sexual identity.

He'd claimed to be all right with how things were changing, but little things he did let me know he was still getting used to it. He was unwilling to be affectionate in public and even more unwilling to admit he had a problem with it.

I tried to be supportive. Mostly by torturing him. Brushing up against him subtly in the checkout line. Offering to get his wallet for him when his hands were full and copping a feel. Hard to explain a hard-on in front of the tomatoes at the farmer's market. Licking the foam off my macchiato slowly in a way that made him forget his own coffee order. The barista had repeated himself three times, and J's face was red as fire as he'd finally ordered.

Sexually, we clicked, and I was thankful for that too. Sometimes we barely made it to the bedroom before we were doing unspeakable things to one another. We'd probably used my couch more for fucking than sitting at this point, to be perfectly honest. He was creative, fun, uninhibited, and always willing to go a second round. *Great.* I shifted in my seat uncomfortably. And just like that, I had wood hard enough to pound nails with.

"So are you two living together, or what?"

"It's too soon for that," I lied.

Yeah, we kind of were. I rustled around my console before finding a Diet Coke. It was warm, but I was too thirsty to be picky.

"I am staying at his place while he's out of town," I continued after popping the tab and taking a swig. "Keeping an eye on things."

"Snooping through his stuff?"

"How else can I keep an eye on things? Honestly, no wonder no one ever asks you to house-sit."

"Everyone knows house-sitting is bullshit," he said. I could picture the eye roll from years of experience. "A house sits by its damn self. Doesn't need you holding up the foundation. That's some bullshit move couples do to prove they're in a different, more committed stage."

"You've cracked the code, boy wonder. What would you have me do, throw his keys in his face? Catch him right in the teeth?"

I drummed my fingers on my thigh as I surveyed the goings-on of the neighborhood. Little kids playing some sort of tag game in the street, every now and again yelling at the cars that honked to get them out of the way. Two old men had parked themselves on a stoop and were smoking cigars and gesturing wildly. Somewhere in the midst of all this normalcy, I knew Dominic was hiding. I don't know what made me madder—someone who thought it was okay to commit identity fraud or someone who thought it was okay to make his mother lose the car she'd posted for his bond. When that person was all rolled up into one, he deserved a genuine ass kicking.

"Mac, are you even listening?" Nick's voice sounded annoyed. "You used to be a lot more attentive."

"I used to be banging you too," I informed him absently. "I found your opinions about my love life a lot more interesting."

Oh Lord, why did I say that? He launched into another speech that had me rubbing my temples.

I tuned Nick out and eyed the small teal house with the ramshackle fence and sagging drapes. All the windows were open, some with broken screens, and I could hear the sounds of a family's evening going on inside. The sounds were crystal clear, and even without a line of sight, I could tell exactly what they were. A pot clanging in the kitchen, a spatula against a frying pan. A sink turned on briefly—washing dishes? Water for a boiling pot? *Jeopardy* blaring from a set in the living room that tossed psychedelic light patterns on two of the droopy drapes. A dog, somewhere in the backyard, giving an occasional bark for the sheer joy of smelling food he wouldn't be getting any of. The mosaic of any American family. Oh, except for the fugitive they may or may not be harboring. God knew if *I* was the mother he'd skipped bail on, he'd have a bullet in his hide the moment he set foot on my porch. But I'd found that, when it came to family, love often defied logic.

"Since when are you a bounty hunter, anyway?"

"Not bounty hunting," I clarified. "This is strictly a consulting gig."

Nick seemed enthralled by the thought of my "bounty hunting," despite my protest. "You going to try to take him or call it in?" he asked.

"Depends."

"On what?"

"A lot of things."

Depends on how big he was, how fast he was, and if I saw him before he saw me. Frankly, I knew Drew wanted me to bring this one in, but this wasn't *Grand Theft Auto*. No reset button. If Drew wanted this guy so bad, he should have come himself.

This was a cleaner job, and the fee was huge. The bail bondsman had less than thirty days to bring this guy in and had hired numerous skip tracers and a bounty hunter that had come up with diddly-squat. We had done two weeks of research for this moron, and more than that in surveillance. After the tip from the disgruntled sister-in-law fell through, I couldn't just slink back to the office. I had to follow a hunch, even if it would truly be the irony of ironies if I found the big lug at his mother's house. The $10,000 finder's fee? Not half bad either.

If I could do it all in—I glanced at my phone again—twenty-five minutes, I'd have a hero's celebration. Of course that meant giving my beautiful boyfriend a quickie before he had to leave for New York. Maybe even letting him give me head on the way to the airport, which, I had to admit, the formerly straight man had a unique talent and desire for. Cocksuckers like that weren't taught. They were *born*.

Thirty minutes later, I was gnashing my teeth as the sun began its descent and shadows crept through the streets. Not only had I missed my baby, I was going to miss the jumper too. This wasn't a neighborhood you wanted to find yourself in at night, finder's fee or not. Just as I threw my cap on the dash, I saw a flash of red out of the corner of my eye. I groaned softly. The "kid," a baby-faced criminal from the neck-up shot we'd had, clearly enjoyed body-building as a hobby. His red tank showed off muscular forearms with matching pitchfork tats.

Maybe calling it in would be best.

Dominic nervously shuffled down the sidewalk, and I took a quick glimpse of his pic on my iPhone.

"Yep," I whispered.

"What's going on?" Nick whispered back, as if he was the one who had to tackle a body-building kid six years his junior.

I tucked my Sig in my waistband as he unhooked the ragged gate. No matter how big, how bad, how dysfunctional they might be, they always came home to momma. "Gotta go, Nick. I can't let him get inside."

Just the sound of my truck door closing had his brown-eyed gaze swinging my way, and I dropped all clever deception and sprinted for him. I had surprise on my side, but as I barreled through the gate, I realized he was far too close to the porch. He flew up the steps, but I pushed past the pain in my leg and gave a flying tackle. My hands closed on the thin material of his tank, and before I realized I even had him, we went down in a tumble of limbs. We rolled on the ground, kicking up dirt, brambles attacking my skin like claws. Somehow I wound up on top, and I struggled to pin him, wishing I had a third hand to cuff him. Or the strength to choke him out.

"Stop. Fighting," I gritted out, trying to be quiet. Right now it was one on one, but I knew from research he had plenty of family on the inside. I didn't know whose side they would be on, but I had a feeling it wouldn't be the one trying to arrest their little boy. At least that's what they'd called him in court, when they'd pled for reduced bail.

He bucked, and I was briefly unseated. *Little, my ass*. I scrambled back on and rolled him in the dirt. I huffed, slapping the cuffs on his wrists. I almost couldn't believe I'd subdued the Incredible Bulk, but I had the scratches and a fat lip to prove it. I thought I might have cut it with my teeth in the fray. I licked at the spot gingerly and tasted coppery blood in my mouth. I drew back my fist before remembering he was worth ten grand… although I couldn't remember whether the bail slip had specified dead or alive.

"Get… the… fuck off me!" he growled, and I mashed his face in the dirt for making me run. And busting up my face.

"Good to see you, Dom. Maybe this time the charges will stick? Don't think Mama will bail you out this time."

He roared with fury, and the door opened at my back. We both froze.

I swung around to see his mother silhouetted in the doorway, housecoat, pink rollers, and all. She had a frying pan in one hand that made my eyes go wide. Oh, *Christ on a crutch*, the last thing I needed was a frying pan upside the head.

"Ma'am, I'm just—"

"Get him off my lawn," she instructed.

"Mom!" Dominic shouted.

She flinched but shook the frying pan threateningly. "This is what was waiting for you on this side of the door. Dominic, you face your consequences. We all have to face our consequences, my baby." Her face crumpled a bit, and suddenly she was cradling the pan to her ample bosom. "And then you come back here."

Her words seemed to take all the fight out of him, and he allowed me to haul him to his feet. I led him away to my truck and knew she watched the entire time. He didn't speak as I opened the driver's door, but his grimace said it all. I wasn't going to give him the chance to run by putting him in the passenger seat and circling around the truck.

"After you." I gestured, and he rolled his eyes before scrambling in.

He got stuck on the gearshift, and I gave him a push, waiting as he wormed his way across the console. My phone rang, and I clicked the Bluetooth. "Yeah."

"Hey, baby."

"Hey yourself." Hearing Jordan's voice just reminded me what I was missing to pick up this lug, and I gave him another push. Not so gentle this time. He grunted and finally fell into the passenger's seat. I knuckled the lock and the child safety locks and clambered in. "Have you left yet, or do I still have a prayer in heaven of seeing you?"

"Already through security," he said and laughed as I groaned. "Trust me, this isn't what I wanted either. Did you get your guy?"

"Got him," I said, starting up the truck to get the hell out of Dodge before it got any darker. "I'm a little banged up, though."

"*You*?" Dominic gave me a surly look. "You gave me a black eye!"

"I don't remember doing that," I told him. "Oh yeah, and shut up. I wasn't talking to you."

Jordan was clearly trying to stifle amusement on the other end. "I wish I could tend to your wounds. And everything else."

"What would you do?" I asked, pulling into the busy traffic carefully.

"I would kiss them to make them feel better." His voice went low, almost whisper quiet. "Then I'd suck on you to make you feel great."

"*God*. How much to buy a ticket to New York again?"

He laughed. "Don't worry, I'm due two weeks' vacation after this, and I'm taking it. Maybe going someplace where clothing is optional? Maybe I'll see you there?"

"You mean our bedroom, dear?"

I was gratified to hear his laugh again. "Be careful. I left my car and took a taxi, so you can use it instead of the rust bucket queen. Water my plants, dammit. You always forget. They are *not* plastic. Don't erase my shows from the DVR—I *will* know and you *will* pay. And...I'm going to miss you."

"Yeah. Me too." My throat was *not* tight. "I'll see you in a week."

I clicked off and drove, silently. The joy of catching the elusive jumper was suddenly eclipsed by loneliness. *Get a grip, Mac. He's not even gone yet.* The depth of my feeling was scarier than I could express verbally. *But he will be. And not just to New York.*

"Dude, is that like your boyfriend or something?"

I forgot how loud my Bluetooth was sometimes. I gave Dominic a glare. "Yeah. So?"

"Gross. You don't fight like a queer."

"You don't look like you'd enjoy another black eye. And yet here we are."

He huddled next to his door sullenly, but I didn't care. This douchebag made me miss my last fucking for a week. He was lucky I didn't dropkick him to Chicago. I switched on the radio to something low and classical to distract myself. Reminded me of Jordan—he was so fucking classy sometimes, and I loved to tease him about it. Drinking wine and playing piano and all manner of things I'd previously laughed at but now found kind of sexy. Everything he did was kind of sexy. I shifted in my seat, remembering him on the bed, losing himself to the rhythm of my body. Man, a week was a long time.

25

I danced into Drew's office, ignoring both the fact that he was on the phone and the hand he put up to shoo me.

"Yeah, uh-huh. I'll tell him. No, he just came in."

I waved our check under his nose. Stuck out my tongue. Our finder's fee had finally come through, and I was beyond proud. After all, I'd risked life and limb (and wrenched my knee pretty good) bringing that goon down.

"Yeah, I'll talk to you later," he said, scowling at me. "He won't go away."

"Nope," I said in a singsong manner. Did the Roger Rabbit beside his desk. When he finally hung up, I stuck the check under his nose again. "And you thought I couldn't get him."

"If I didn't think you could get him, I wouldn't have sent you." He tried to take the check, and I held it back.

"This is worth a vacation, don't you think?"

He growled, grabbing for the check again. When I wouldn't relinquish my bounty, he sighed. "I guess."

I beamed and held out the check, which he snatched. "Two weeks, my friend."

He stuck the check in our bank drop envelope and tucked it back into his drawer. I watched as he locked the drawer and pocketed the keys.

"You think it's too soon for vacationing together?" I asked, plopping down in one of his guest chairs.

The look he sent me was unreadable. "Not for me to say."

"When has that ever stopped you?"

"True." He looked at me so long that I began to get nervous.

"What? What is it?"

"So if I knew something that you probably needed to know... but didn't *want* to know, you'd want me to tell you, right?"

Oh, jeez. When did anything that started that way end up good? My eyes felt fixed, staring at the spot slightly past his shoulder. I took a deep breath and let it out. Measured. Calm.

"Yes," I said. "I'd want to know."

He sighed. "That was my cousin. You know, Javier? He owns that fancy restaurant downtown."

"Yeah, I think I met him a few times," I said slowly. "Why?"

"You need to get down to his restaurant." He took out a pen and scribbled something on a Post-it.

"Now?"

"Right now," he confirmed.

"I-I don't even know where it is."

"I was debating on when to tell you. Or whether I should tell you at all. I wasn't sure you'd even want to know. But I love you, and I don't want you to get hurt. So... here."

I stared at the Post-it stuck to his outstretched thumb. I didn't want to take it. I had forgotten to finish that statement: I don't know where it is and I don't *want* to. Because there was only one reason he could be sending me there.

I wanted to squeeze my eyes shut against the sight of the offensive yellow note. Cheery little bitch. I was *not* one of my clients, and I trusted Jordan. More importantly, I knew what it meant when I started checking up on him. When I doubted he was exactly where he said he'd be. If I took that Post-it, our relationship was already over.

"This is typical of you, Drew," I said. "You're always after me about love—believe in love, everyone's not a cheater. The moment I actually give it a whirl, you're spying on him to prove me wrong!"

"I was *not* spying," he said, sniffing in a wounded manner. "My cousin called me and told me there was something there you should see. Actually, he snapped his fingers and said, 'Gurrrl, he'd better get down here right now and see what that fine boy is up to.'" He shook his head. "My cousin is a bit... a bit...."

"Flaming," I filled in. "The word you're looking for is flaming."

I sighed, running my hand through my hair, raking it into my eyes in the process. Pulled hard on the ends. They were more brown than blond again—I hadn't been surfing that much lately. No, I'd been holed up in my dream world pretending everything could be infinitely unspoiled and flawless.

"I trust him," I said, rubbing a hand across my eyes tiredly.

When I opened them, he was standing in front of me. He pressed the Post-it into my hand. "You know the old saying: Trust, but verify."

The red-checkered pattern of my father's sofa was as familiar as a treasured baby blanket, but it was unquestionably hideous. It was also obviously chosen by a man who didn't know how to color coordinate a damn thing. To be fair, I didn't either, but I knew where to find a Rooms To Go.

I ruffled the torn fabric on the armrest absently. I'd had juice on this couch, watched cartoons on Saturday morning, and spent one long summer as an indolent teen lying on it. Usually with one arm thrown across my face to ward off the sun, vampire-style. My dad would wander through every now and again and threaten my life if I didn't get up and do something. A small smile crossed my lips, and I smoothed the fabric down. It would be Case's turn soon, and he was well on his way to Disgruntled Teenville.

I could feel my dad giving me side glances every so often, but I didn't try to engage him in conversation. I crossed my legs, propping one sneakered foot on my left knee. I didn't know why I had even come, really. Maybe because somewhere deep inside I associated our childhood home as my safety net, home base in a hectic life of "tag, you're it." A place to come and reset. Reflect. At least I could if my dad would stop trying to make random conversation.

As if he could read my thoughts, he spoke on cue. "You like the new TV?"

"I do." I tapped my fingers on my Converse sneaker.

"They installed it, like you said. I put the old one in the backyard. I'm going to fix it one of these days, as soon as I get the picture tube."

"I hear you." *Tap.*

"Anything specific you want to watch?"

"No, I'm good."

"Wonder where your brother got to with our pizza?"

"No idea." *Tap, tap.*

He flicked through the channels again, and I sighed. I'd made a mistake coming here searching for peace of mind. Ever since Drew had decided to become a big Buttinsky, peace didn't exist. I'd wanted to turn on him. They always say don't shoot the messenger, but I think that's more of a suggestion than a rule. Like a "use by" date or a price tag at a flea market. So I would still be within my rights to cut off his ponytail with scissors for intruding on my rosy bubble.

He'd called me from the office, wanting to know if I'd made it to the restaurant. I had. He'd wanted to know if I'd seen them yet. I had.

Or to be more specific, "I'm not blind," I'd snapped. "I don't see what the big deal is."

"There is none so blind as he who will not see," he'd murmured.

Refusing to answer his little proverb or rise to the bait was my only action. That and hoping he'd have a big slice of shut-the-fuck-up pie. No such luck.

"I knew this would happen," he'd said.

I'd shrugged, forgetting that he was on the phone and had no visual on my dismissive action. "So he's meeting her for dinner. You and I have had dinner. We're not sleeping together."

"Where did he say he was again?"

"Out of town. New York. I guess he got back early.

"And hasn't been home. Because you're there."

"I get it, okay? But he doesn't have to account for every single second of his life to me." And I'd watched Jordan lift Rachel's hand to his lips and kiss it. I'd repeated softly, "I get it."

They'd laughed at something together, and they'd looked like a beautiful couple, a matched set—her gleaming cap of dark hair close to his. He didn't appear to be afraid to kiss her hand in public.

Drew's voice had been unusually hesitant. "You mad at me?"

"No. *No*. I'm mad at...." I'd taken one last look at the laughing couple. "I'm mad at myself."

Because despite all my protests to the contrary, I'd started feeling hopeful. Stupid and hopeful.

"—Blu-ray," my dad finished, and I looked at him blankly.

"Huh?"

"You know, that DVD player has been skipping lately. I'm probably going to replace it with a unit with Blu-ray."

I didn't know whether it was my frustration with Drew or my anger at Jordan that made me so cranky, but I snapped. "I don't want to talk about that damned TV anymore. Or any f... flipping appliances." I caught the *fuck* and aborted it just in time. I may be an adult, but there were just some things I couldn't say to my dad. Not without catching hell about it.

He blinked. "I didn't know you felt so strongly about it."

"I'm just... not in the mood, okay?"

"Okay." He peered at me for a moment and went back to his TV.

I felt like a jerk.

This was how Joe Williams communicated. This is what we talked about. Anything more in-depth was far and few between. I looked at him. *Really* looked. And I wondered if my mother had ever gotten tired of communicating through appliance repair. If she'd felt this unreachable gap, filled with all the unspoken things she wished she could say.

My jaw firmed. It was no excuse. Relationships were made to be fluid, constantly changing entities that twisted and twined, growing stronger. More solid. Capable of withstanding a category-five gale on

Florida's worst day. What was it that made people just *give up* on you?

It surprised me to see the crow's feet around his eyes. Wrinkles in places they hadn't been before. And when he flicked the button on the remote, his finger trembled. It was just a small tremor, something I was one hundred percent sure he wasn't aware he did. I gazed at his hands, fixated on that tremble. He was my dad, still larger than life, but he was a person. A man. And my mother had been a woman. She'd made her mistakes, and I didn't forgive her. But they weren't the end-all, be-all for how things worked in a relationship. Not my relationship. I wasn't ready to give up on Jordan just yet.

That finger trembled over the button again before pressing it, and suddenly I was filled with love for him. He may never love me like Robby, probably would never look at me the same again, but he was my dad. Whether we talked through appliances or not, I always knew he loved me. I stood and went over to his chair. Then hugged him tightly from behind, ignoring the way he instinctively went rigid as stone. It reminded me so much of Finnegan's duck-and-cover move that I chuckled against his thinning hair.

"What was that for?" he asked gruffly.

"Because you're my dad," I answered simply enough.

"Mac?" His voice was uncomfortable, begging me to end this atrocious display of affection.

"Now hug me back," I demanded. And he did.

I heard Robert groan as the front door slammed behind him. He'd slammed that door since he was a little kid, and he'd always gotten in trouble for it. The big lug never learned. He managed to smack me on the back of the head, even with his arms full.

"God, I thought you said you can't catch gay," Robert said, dropping the pizzas off on the kitchen counter.

This of course prompted me to chase him around the room as he screamed like a girl. And our dad to yell at us both before turning up the TV.

. . .

I sat on the top step of the back porch, arms around my knees, rolling a cigarette between my fingers. I wasn't planning on smoking it. I'd better not, not with my dad and brother within one hundred feet. No, I'd developed a new, stranger habit of keeping them tucked places on my person—in a pocket, in my sock... behind an ear like a character in the musical *Grease*. At the post office earlier, one of them even fell out of my wallet. Cigarettes were truly the devil.

My phone trilled in my pocket, and I looked at the time before answering. Two in the morning. My, my, don't we stay up late in "New York"?

"Hey, Jordan."

"Hey, sweetheart. I missed you earlier."

His voice was like a punch to my stomach and sent desire spiraling up my spine. I meant to be cool and breezy, but once again, I'd underestimated his undiluted effect on me. I'd have to cut him with premium vodka next time—Jordan on the rocks with a splash of Ketel One.

"I was a little caught up," I lied. "Couldn't answer the phone."

"Yeah?" I heard him yawn and pictured him stretching out on... on what? Where *was* he exactly?

His next question was eerily similar to what I wanted to ask him. "Where've you been?"

"At my dad's house." I rolled the cigarette some more. "We were watching the game."

"I didn't know anyone was playing."

"There's *always* someone playing at Joe's house."

His laughter almost made me smile.

"So where are you?" I asked.

His next laugh was a little uneasy. "That's an odd question."

"Is it?"

"Yes, it is. I'm still in New York. I'll be home tomorrow."

"Home," I repeated softly. Interesting concept.

I looked up at the sky. Millions of diamonds on God's rich, velvety cerulean backdrop. Glittering. Sparkling with expectation and promise. What the hell did they know? They were just interminably burning balls of gas, whiling away time in the sky.

"Everything okay?"

"Perfect," I said. Some part of me realized that he knew what that meant. I didn't try to clean it up. "Just perfect."

26

"You finished the paperwork for the skip trace."

"Yup."

"Left me all the details for the Hernandez case."

"Yep."

"You finished the report for Mr. Blake."

"Yup. Finished a full report with video and left it with Jennie." I was surprised to see my exit coming up so quickly. Driving just seemed quicker in Jordan's Mercedes—she responded to my every move smoothly. Almost intuitively.

Don't get used to her, I reminded myself with a happy flutter that couldn't quite be suppressed. *My boyfriend's back and you're gonna be in trouble....*

Yes, I'd have to give up the Mercedes, but I'd also get to see him. It was a fairly even trade. I had to admit, I felt pretty good. Jordan was back, and I was on vacation as of... five minutes ago.

Drew still wasn't satisfied, but I didn't care. I'd taken my two weeks, and that was that. He'd have to bitch at someone else in that time.

"Drew, I gotta go. See you when I see you."

"Better see you in two weeks," he warned, but I could tell he was amused.

"We'll see," was all I'd offer as reassurance and clicked my Bluetooth off. And tossed it on the dash. He's lucky I didn't toss it in the trash. When I was off, I was *off*. Sandals. Shorts. No shirt. Shades. Here I come.

A week had never seemed so long or so tedious. Surrounded by his things, sleeping in his bed alone, made the feeling worse. When I turned down his street and saw the garbage and recycling bins had been taken in, I felt eager as a freaking puppy. Embarrassing. I was so impatient to pull in, I almost missed the sleek white Beamer parked by my truck. I'd seen that car before. I'd followed that car before.

Rachel. I swore. She was like a bad fucking rash. Either that or Jordan was giving her the most mixed signals I'd ever seen. She just didn't seem like the clingy sort. If he'd given her walking papers, she would stick those tiny feet back in her stilettos and march on out.

Both spots were taken in front of the house, so I parked on the street, close to the curb. I turned off the engine. And sat there. Part of me wanted to drive off as if I hadn't seen her car, maybe even call and alert him I was on my way home. I knew that would be cowardly, but for a moment, it was deliciously tempting. I nibbled on my nail. They could be having a private conversation. *Another*?

My inner bitch was right. What was with all these damn private conversations? Coming back early and not telling me?

Staring at my truck in its usual space annoyed me. The smell of cooling pizza in the backseat didn't help. I'd had very definitive plans for how I wanted to spend tonight—it included pizza, fucking, and beer, and not necessarily in that order. None of my plans had included a visit—a private visit, from the looks of it—from Jordan's ex.

My annoyance grew as my mind flashed over their previous secret little meeting at the restaurant. What the fuck? Besides, if anyone had a right to be here between the two of us, it was me.

I got out of the car and pulled out the pizza box, stopping to grab the mail on my way up to the door. *I* was the one who had a key. I was the one whose stuff was strewn about inside. I was the one who was parked in the guest space.

I... was the one who hesitated briefly before using the key in the lock. But then I was entering the house as if nothing was wrong, with the mail and pizza in hand. I dropped the pizza box off on the kitchen counter and made my way to the living room. He would be happy to see me. We hadn't seen each other in a week. He would greet me warmly, and I'd realize I was being ridiculous.

There was nothing but silence as I entered. I was sure it hadn't been that way before.

When I entered the living room, she was sitting on the couch, legs crossed elegantly as one shoe swayed back and forth. She looked surprised to see me and gave me a little wave. My gaze swept over Jordan, perched on the coffee table in front of her. His expression was fairly neutral, and I decided that two could play that game.

"Hey," I said.

"Hey," he responded easily.

"I got the mail." I waggled it unnecessarily.

"Oh, thanks. Can you just leave it on the table?"

Leave it, he said. Leave it as in "leave it before you go do whatever you were going to do"? Or leave it as in "leave it before you let yourself back out"? I decided I wouldn't live my life by assumptions. If he wanted me to leave, he could ask. But that didn't mean I wasn't angry. I tossed the mail on the table.

"I brought pizza. Does anyone want any?"

They looked at one another and then me. "No, thanks," they said simultaneously, and I wanted to kill them both. But you can't kill someone for sharing private looks.

"Rache and I had an early dinner," Jordan explained. His ears looked flushed.

I stared at him, a muscle ticking in my jaw. A dinner, another dinner, and an after-dinner meeting at the house. Better and better. As I marched off to the kitchen, I heard her ask softly, "Does he have a key or something?"

Or something, sweetheart. I forced myself to keep walking, act naturally, and not bang dishes like I wanted to. I pulled out a plate and set it out on the counter next to a prescription bag. My eye caught the name on the bag, and I realized it was mine. He'd picked up my prescription. It made me more confused than ever.

I could hear the soft murmurs of their voices but not the words. I found myself shuffling closer to the door, trying to get close enough to muddle out what they were saying. I found my vantage point at the same time her voice broke, right in the middle of whatever she'd been saying.

"I'm pregnant," she said. And burst into tears.

27

The inside of Jordan's home may have been a showpiece, but it had nothing on the view from his deck. Usually getting this close to the beach in South Florida involved stalking someone for metered parking for at least twenty minutes. I sat on the bottom step, which allowed me to dig my feet in the sand without getting it in my jeans. I was pleased with the compromise. I picked at the faded, frayed denim of one ankle while watching the goings-on below.

A small gathering of Jordan's neighbors frolicked down on the dunes, a circle of hazy golden light in the darkness of the beach. The laid-back group, having some kind of barbecue around a pit, had invited me over several times. I declined. I wasn't exactly the best of company right now. It was one of the main reasons I was out here, letting the sound of the wind and lapping of the waves soothe my nerves. Oh, that and a kiss from my nicotine mistress of course. The waves crashed eagerly on the sand, farther up than before, sending the frolicking neighbors shrieking and laughing to higher ground. My fingers itched for my surfboard.

I heard the screen door slide open but didn't turn around.

"Did she get to sleep all right?" I asked.

"Yeah." Jordan slid the screen door closed behind him. "She finally relaxed and fell right out."

She'd certainly been through enough. We'd taken turns comforting her on her emotional roller coaster as she'd gotten out the story through sniffles and tears. I'll save you the trip and give you the highlight reel: she is pregnant, she isn't sure if Jordan or her new beau is the father, and even though she is ecstatic, she doesn't know what she is going to do with a baby right now. *Now back to you in the newsroom, Bob.*

By the time she'd finished and calmed a bit, it had gotten late. I'd recommended that she stay in one of the guest rooms, to the surprise of everyone, including myself. She'd accepted and given me a hug. Then we'd all snacked on pizza in front of the TV—her choice of show had been one of the vapid housewives shows I loved. Damn. But for the fact she might be having my boyfriend's baby, I could actually like that girl.

When I glanced back, Jordan was mussing his perfect hair up into some sort of faux hawk. When he dropped his hands, the terrified strands fell back into place. "I tried to give her warm tea, but she has a sweet tooth to rival yours," he said. "I gave her some milk and a few of those cookies you've been hiding in the bread bin."

"You mean the ones you weren't supposed to know about?"

"I hope you don't mind." He sounded faintly amused.

I shrugged. What are a few cookies when your life is imploding?

He didn't say anything about my cigarette, which was worthy of at least some sort of nationwide treaty, and sat beside me on the squeaky clapboard step. "You okay?"

I took a long drag and let out a cloud of smoke. "Do I look okay?"

He drew his knees to his chest and looped his arms around them. "No," he said simply.

A baby. I knew it shouldn't change everything, but it just did. No, I was not okay.

"Talk to me," he said, nudging me with his shoulder.

I knew he was trying to give me time and space to process. Freedom to ask questions without getting anger or defensive answers in return. I was appreciative, but frankly, I just didn't know what to say. Or think.

"I'm not in the mood to pretty it up for you, J. I'm having a little trouble with this."

"So am I."

"I mean, this is just irresponsible. Like the Maury Povich show irresponsible," I blurted out. "Haven't you all ever heard of a tiny little thing called protection?"

He didn't seem to mind my rudeness.

"They were using double contraceptives. So were we," he said, shaking his head. "She's on the pill, and we used condoms. It's... it's unexpected to say the least. She's still in shock."

Though I'd spent most of the evening out on the deck, I knew she had to be. Conducting an investigation on Rachel had given me an unfair, intimate glimpse into her life. What made her tick. I knew that she was career driven and focused, and having a baby right now was nowhere in her master plan. I'd imagine the term "shock" was an understatement.

"Can you please put that out?" He looked at my cigarette with intense dislike.

I ignored him, taking another drag and letting out a smoky breath. A finger appeared in front of my face as he plucked the offending cigarette out of my mouth and stubbed it out on the steps. I shrugged and pulled out another. Flicked my lighter and lit the end. Took another puff. He grabbed that one too. I glared.

"They come in a pack, J. I guarantee you'll get tired of this before I do."

He stubbed it out and tossed it in my ashtray, sitting one step above us. He glared right back. "I thought you'd quit."

"Please. If I hadn't been a smoker before, today's turn of events would have made me start."

He was quiet a minute before he spoke. "I'm sorry. Sorry for all of it."

"What does sorry do?" I muttered, sticking another cigarette in my mouth. I tossed the crinkled, half empty pack on the top stair defiantly. He didn't get to tell me what to do anymore. I didn't even know if we were an "us" anymore.

"Sorry is how I feel for putting you through this. But not how I feel about the baby if it is mine. I didn't plan on having kids at all, much less right away. Even when we'd been engaged, we'd planned on five years down the road. Minimum. But now that we're here, I have to deal with what is."

I could feel his eyes on my face, but I couldn't manage to look at him. Not when he was making sense. Not when I was picturing a little Jordan and Rachel baby running around in our lives. Beautiful, smart, overachieving little thing with two corporate lawyers for parents and a strange "uncle" that kept Daddy company. Or a more depressing picture, when mother and father decided they should be a family. And that "Uncle" had been a phase.

He ran a hand through my hair. Anchored at my neck. Rubbed the muscles there in a way that made me lean toward him unconsciously, like a flower to the sun. His hand moved soothingly. Absently. He did it so often, I wasn't even sure if he knew he was doing it anymore. I didn't want him to ever stop. *God.* My eyes felt a little wet. Love is for chumps. And masochists.

I needed to get as far away from him as I could before I promised him anything. Anything he wanted, just don't leave me. I pulled away and jammed my fists in both eyes. Hard. Crying was also for chumps. I just needed to get... out of here.

"I don't want you to go." His voice was quiet.

My eyes shot to his, and I wondered briefly if I'd spoken aloud. But then I realized he just knew me. Knew what I did when things got rough.

"But I owe it to you to be honest," he said, looking a little miserable himself. "If it's my baby, I plan to take care of it. Rachel and I don't have to be together, but we'll be the best co-parents we can. Make the best of a situation turned... unique, if you will."

Unique? I lit up again, staring stonily at the ocean. Try miserable. Try horrible.

"She's going to talk to Donovan in the morning. Then you and I can have breakfast. Talk."

Donovan, aka possible baby daddy number two. I gave him a humorless smile. "I'm a little old and jaded for the 'tomorrow is a new day' philosophy." I took a drag of my cigarette, my last, and stubbed it out viciously. "Tomorrow is the same fucking day with a different name."

"I'm not asking you to be okay with everything. Just... we'll talk, okay?"

He took my hand and pulled me up from my refuge. I followed behind obediently as he led the way inside. I'm sure to someone observing us, it probably looked like we were a normal couple, going inside to start their nighttime routine. But nothing was normal about this day or night. After showering the sand from my body and changing into pajamas, I found myself curled on the couch, tucked in a blanket.

Jordan padded into the living room twenty minutes later, freshly showered, in pajama bottoms and an old college T-shirt, rubbing his hair into spikes with a towel. The soft, worn shirt read Duke U. on the front in faded print.

"It's getting late," he said. "I'm going to head to bed."

"Okay."

"You want the light on or off?"

"Off."

He flicked off the overhead light, and the room was plunged into darkness, saved from pitch only by the flickering of the TV.

"You're going to fall asleep out here."

"Then I fall asleep." I kept my eyes trained on the animated late-night host, even when I felt him staring at me in the doorway.

After a long, metered moment, I heard him sigh. He pressed a kiss into my hair. "G'nite, baby."

Our eyes met at the word "baby." He sighed again, and my eyes went back to the TV. I strained all kind of eye muscles watching him out of my peripheral vision as he disappeared into the bedroom. He didn't close the door like we usually did.

I stared at the gaping hole, now dark. It seemed… almost symbolic. He was leaving the door open for me to walk through, but at what cost? Was I just setting myself up for more heartbreak? How many signs did I have to pick up on before I accepted the answer? He wasn't ready for this… wasn't ready for me. I couldn't even say if he loved me or not. Sometimes I thought he might—just something in his eyes or the way he touched me that made me think he loved me the way I loved him. Maybe that was just wishful thinking on my behalf. And maybe I was checking the definition of the same word in eighteen different dictionaries, hoping for a different answer.

He wanted to talk, but I didn't really see anything to talk about. I was tired, and I could feel my baser nature taking over. I didn't want to fight for our relationship. I wanted to give in and take off. I bit my lip.

It wasn't his fault, but I had done this once before in the not-so-recent past. I knew the signs. I could remember being Trevor's "phase" and how he hemmed and hawed about us not working out. Worrying about being gay. Introducing me as his brother to coworkers. I'd chosen the pain of leaving when it'd begun to hurt just as much to stay. And I hadn't felt even *half* of the things for him that I felt for Jordan. I should be *grateful* to Jordan for showing me early on that this wasn't going to work. As my tired mind tried to work out the good in this situation, I flicked off the TV. Turns out, I wasn't as wired as I'd thought.

Besides, I needed my sleep. You had to get up pretty early to skip out on breakfast.

28

My new Audi was a color that Jett, the salesman, assured me was ibis white. Jett had been casually interested in the sale as only the seller of luxury cars can be—buy it or don't, I'll be over here. His pitch had rubbed me the wrong way until I'd seen Audi—hereafter known as Audi Darling—crammed in between two Quattros. Slightly under twenty-five thousand miles, fully loaded, and no more vinyl for this behind. Oh yeah, and she was smoking hot. My hands had shaken when signing the purchase agreement, but speeding down the highway helped my anxiety a bit. Now I was just glad she was mine. Or would be in five years, anyway.

Bessie had broken down on the highway for her last time... in my hands, at least. After Jett had laughed in my face at the idea of trade credit, I had Bessie towed and dumped on my Aunt Janet's driveway as a gift for my youngest cousin, Tripp. She did not appreciate this. At least that's what I gathered from the screeching message she'd left on my phone. *I'll call her back sometime around the time Bessie stops leaking oil on her driveway... so yeah, never*. Tripp had also been less than grateful. He'd deemed it barely an upgrade from his skateboard. Saucy brat. But he was good with cars and had too much time on his hands (the hallmark of most teenagers), so I knew he'd take care of her. When I left, he'd been saying something about painting flames on her that I pretended not to hear.

I cut the engine and stared up at Victoria Towers, a tungsten and steel high rise that soared up twenty-two stories high. The building looked cold and imposing, but I wasn't in the mood for second thoughts. No, I wasn't second-guessing my plan. I was pondering the code into Trevor's building, trying not to press my memory too hard. It seemed the harder I tried to remember, the more codes, passwords, and pin numbers just oozed into one meaningless jumble in my brain.

I still had nothing by the time I reached the well-hidden key pad. I stood by the entrance trying not to look suspicious, hemming and hawing over the right numbers. It was either his birthday forward or his birthday backward. The code wasn't rocket science, but I only had one shot at it. And that's if he hadn't changed it altogether. Maybe it was Laura's birthday now, backward or forward. Hell, maybe it was Finn's. Or his mother's. He'd always been too attached to her.

I sighed and set my fingers to the keys authoritatively. *Beeeep*!

The panel around the keys went luminescent green, and I forced myself to look unsurprised instead of doing the happy dance. As I pulled open the glass lobby door, I stopped short at the sight of the night doorman. From the look on his friendly, open face, he remembered me. I groaned inwardly. Way to get out unnoticed.

"Haven't seen you in a while," he said with a large smile, standing at his usual post by the elevator doors.

I smiled weakly. "Been working a lot."

Cheated on. Dumped for a woman. Again. You know, the usual.

It was clear he wasn't suspicious in the least. And why would he be? I'd been to Trevor's place more often than my own in the last two months of our relationship. The last two months when I'd felt him slipping away and hadn't known why.

"Mr. Smith is out at the moment," he informed me helpfully. "Are you here to walk Finn?"

Blessed, nosy man. You're damn right I am. "Of course," I said airily.

I let myself into the condo without turning on a single light—a feat I was proud and amazed I'd pulled it off—and closed the door behind me quietly. In the darkness, the living room opened up to a wide wall of windows with a breathtaking view of the city. The dark night sky was speckled with orbs of blurred orange and white—streetlights and headlights illuminating a city gone dark. I could see the blinking red lights of the airport in the distance, and I briefly wondered how close it actually was.

Ah, yes, the best part of a cat burglary. The part where you stand around in the person's apartment and enjoy the view. I hastened myself into action and began calling Finn softly.

I walked around, slightly stooped, my calling becoming less cajoling and more threatening. "Finn, if you don't bring your furry.... *Ouch*!" I banged my shin on the sofa and gritted my teeth.

Everything was placed differently. I couldn't navigate in the dark anymore. The couch hadn't been here, a rug was. I rubbed my shin absently. This just showed that Laura was an idiot. Who would put a couch there? That's how people got hurt.

I peeked into their bedroom, all red and gold overtones with a fluffy comforter and at least a million throw pillows on the oversized bed. Well, there was certainly one benefit to living with a woman. I'd never been that type of guy. I didn't know a duvet from a hole in the wall. Apparently all I'd gotten in my gay starter kit was a pink half tee, a glitter stick, my how-to-crush-your-father's-world guide, and a sudden affinity for dick.

Suddenly there was a snuffle and a wet sneeze, and Finn ambled out of a red dog bed in the corner, shaking his overlong golden fur wildly.

"Finn!"

He dove for me like a dog possessed, and we went down in a tumble of fur and limbs. I finally grabbed his furry muzzle and planted a kiss between his eyes, right above a giant doggy smile. "I missed you, mutt."

See, he loved me best. All right, I didn't know that. Maybe it was just because he hadn't seen me for so long. I'm sure he loved Trevor too. But no time for extended reunions. I fastened the harness around his torso and clipped his leash to the D ring.

"Let's roll, Finn."

I heard the key in the lock a split second before the door opened.

Please don't be both of them, I prayed. Laura and Trevor walked into the darkened room, each carrying a restaurant doggie bag in the shape of a swan.

Please don't turn on the light. Light flooded the room, and I blinked in the sudden brightness.

Please don't let them see me! I heard a gasp, and I sighed. Obviously the big guy upstairs wasn't a fan of breaking and entering.

"Mac?" Trevor laid his swan on the table in the entry and then closed the door behind him with an audible *wham*. "What the hell are you doing in here?"

I looked down at the dog and the leash and then back up at him. "Kind of obvious, Trev."

"I'm calling the police," Laura said, palming her smartphone so fast I wondered where she'd been hiding it.

"I am the police," I sneered in a snotty manner that wasn't quite true anymore. But *she* didn't know that. Besides, I'm sure if I wheedled enough, I could get Robby to throw me in the drunk tank instead of with hardened, angry criminals who would love the fact that I was an ex-cop.

"We'll see about that," she almost screeched. I had pushed the elegant Laura past her breaking point, and after she disappeared into the den, the door slammed shut behind her.

Trevor's eyes were full of understanding as they drifted over me, finally settling on my fingers clutched around Finn's leash. "I know this is hard for you," he said, soothing. "But you've got to let it go."

I followed him mistrustfully with my eyes as he circled around. "Finn is mine," I said, my voice flat.

"This isn't about Finn, baby." His voice puffed over the back of my neck, and I realized he was suddenly a *lot* closer than I'd thought.

"*Baby*?" I swatted my neck. "And just what the hell are you doing?"

"Laura's overwrought," he said, his breath misting my shoulder again. "I can probably calm her down, and you and I can settle this... man to man, you know."

I glared at him. "That's for court to decide."

"You want me to let her call the police?"

"Doesn't look like I have a choice," I snapped, my voice tight.

I thought I heard the first filtering wails of sirens and dug my fingers into my thigh. It was one thing to be big and bad in theory; it was quite another to wait at the scene of the crime while the police drew closer.

"So you're not willing to negotiate?"

"Negotiate what?"

"You and I," he blurted. "You and I working something out."

"Oh, for heaven's sakes." The slow, clumsy come-ons that I'd once found amusing almost made me hurl. I shook my head disgustedly. "I can't believe I ever loved you."

"Well, you did," he snapped, his face blooming bright red. "Still do, if you ask me."

"Keep dreaming."

"If you'd rather go to jail than do something you've already done a million times, then you're not quite as bright as I thought."

"I'm a PI, Trevor. Do you really think this is the first time I've gone down for a B and E?"

"Get out of my house," he yelled, close enough for spittle to fly onto my cheek.

I didn't flinch. The things Trevor and I had done made spittle a very little deal indeed.

"Police are here," Laura announced from somewhere in the den. She slammed the door again.

Oh, God. They're going to impound the Audi. Finn leaned into me as if he understood exactly what was going to happen to me and my precious new car.

When I heard Robby's voice, my heart started beating again. I didn't know how my brother had gotten the call and how he had gotten here before anyone else, but I was grateful. I didn't even know what he would do to me, but I knew it would go a hell of a lot better than if it had been a cop that didn't share my DNA.

He looked tired, irritated, and very official. "What the hell is going on, Mac?"

"Shouldn't you be asking me that?" Laura snapped. She slammed the door again.

"Stop that!" Trevor yelled.

Robert ignored them both. The radio on his shoulder crackled with sudden static, and Tao lifted his shoulder to respond into it, walking toward the kitchen area.

"He has my dog," I said, pointing at Finn, nestled on my feet, unnecessarily. Obviously that was the dog. There was no other dog in the room.

Robert rubbed his eyes with two fingers in a V shape. "Please tell me I didn't intercept this call to settle a domestic?" he pleaded with the ceiling.

"I want him prosecuted!" Laura. *Slam.*

"Trev, do you want to press charges?" Robert asked.

I crossed my fingers and hoped against all hope that this night wouldn't end with me huddled on a jail bench. Trevor looked at me hard. And then sighed. "No. I did… take the dog. I thought… I knew he would have to come to me for it."

"Finn's not an *it*," I snapped.

"I think he means 'Thank you, Trevor, for saving me from jail.'" My brother gave me a warning glare that I met stubbornly.

"Can we go?" Tao asked. "No one is reporting any crime, and I need some coffee."

"Well, what about the dog?" Trevor asked. "Who gets it… him?"

Tao shrugged. "It's a civil matter. Not really our job, guys."

I felt raw as I gripped the leash so hard I felt the imprint in my palm. I had already lost Jordan. I couldn't lose Finn too. Robert opened his mouth to agree, and then his gaze met mine. I don't know what he saw in them, but he sighed.

"Let the dog go and see who he comes to," Robert said authoritatively.

"That's not exactly unbiased," Trevor said, and rightly so.

I didn't care. I liked that idea a lot and bent quickly to unclip Finn's leash. I gave him a fond rub before I stood, and Trevor said, "I saw that."

We stood there, stiff as dummies, until Robby prodded us both. "Go on, get to it," he said, making a shooing motion.

Trevor reached down, crouching nice and low, calling to the retriever in his sweetest voice. Finn cocked his head, looking at Trevor oddly. After a moment, he began scratching his ear with his hind leg, never taking an eye off of Trevor. I didn't blame Finn at all. That tone was the same tone you would use to coo "here kitty, kitty," if you had a knife behind your back.

"Come here, baby," I said, clapping softly. "C'mere, Finn, boy."

He gave me a doggy smile but didn't move. His light-brown eyes danced, and I knew he was being vintage stubborn again. I hoped Robby had had dinner—this could take a while. I put my hands in my pockets and jiggled them a bit, hoping Finn would get the hint.

Finn did, trotting over quickly. I rubbed his head, covering up his sniffing motions as he tried to inspect me thoroughly.

I smiled a smile I hadn't smiled in a while, big, that made my cheeks crease with dimples. Most people didn't even know I *had* dimples—just didn't seem to be that much to smile about. "Mine," I said to a scowling Trevor.

Neither Robert nor Tao deigned to talk to me in the elevator (I was a criminal now, after all), but they did help me carry Finn's stuff. As I opened the trunk with the key fob, Robert whistled. "When did this happen, and how do I get to drive her?"

"Today, and as soon as I rewrite my will and die."

He tossed the bag of dog food in the open trunk and sent me a glare. "Ungrateful beast." He stomped off, followed closely by his partner.

Finn waited until I covered my passenger seat with an old sheet and then jumped in, sniffing suspiciously. "I know it's not the old truck, boy, but we're riding in style now."

Robby blew me a kiss as he drove by. “Wait till Dad hears about this,” he said with a grin.

I sent him a one fingered salute as he squealed out of the lot in his cruiser, and rubbed Finn’s head as he sniffed out the treat in my cargo pockets.

I’d had no doubt Finn would choose me over Trevor. But I was a big fan of insurance.

And it never hurt to carry bacon in your pockets.

29

Anyone who has ever driven from down south to way up north knows that the journey through Florida seems endless. I remember popping up in the backseat as a kid and asking the same question over and over again—"Where are we now?" And getting a variation of the same answer, depending on who bothered to answer.

"Still in Florida, sweetie," from my mom. "You want a snack?"

"Hush, boy. You ask that question every fifteen minutes." My dad, looking relaxed and enjoying the ride.

"Sit down, moron. Mom, Mac is out of his seat belt!" Robert. Always the tattletale and extremely noogie-worthy.

I grinned at the memory, one square of film on a reel of many, a reel that made me the man I was today. It was the first memory in a while that I'd entertained of my mom that made me want to smile, not smash something. I enjoyed the moment, just for a moment, and gave Finn a quick rub between the ears. Unlike when I was a kid in the backseat, I knew exactly where I was, and that was twenty miles outside of Fort Drum. I was making good time.

After my victory at Trevor's, the idea of going home held no appeal for me. After all, it was the start of my hard-earned vacation, which I would now be spending alone. So after a quick call to Nick and a stop home for a hastily packed bag, Finn, the new Audi and I had hit the road. I was not going to mope. I was going to enjoy my new car, an old friend, and have a good time.

My phone rang, and I looked down at the screen. It was him again. I made a face. At some point, I was going to have to answer. I pressed ignore. But that time wasn't now.

I drove until the sky darkened around me, dusky sunset pink fading to purple, trees and shrubs becoming undefined shapes that blurred as I flew past. In the encroaching darkness, I tried to turn on my headlights but couldn't find the controls that would switch the running day lamps to headlights. Well. There were some things Bessie just couldn't be beat on—simple operation was one of them. And she had come with a paper manual, not a link where I could download the pdf.

I decided now was a good a time as any to walk Finn and stop for gas, so I pulled off the next exit and into a Texaco. After filling up at the pump, I took Finn on a jaunt around the mostly concrete gas station for a whiff of the few patches of impeccably manicured grass. He sniffed each and every one before deciding on a good spot and lifted a leg shamelessly, plumed tail waving in the breeze. I made a quick trip inside for coffee and a muffin and tried to pull up the manual on my phone. It rang again just as the pdf was loading, and I growled.

"What?"

He didn't bother with the pleasantries either.

"Where the hell are you?"

I craned my neck to see the visitor's sign and had a secret moment of pleasure. I couldn't help it. Some remnants of my father inside me enjoyed making good time.

"Somewhere outside St. Augustine," I informed him.

He was silent for a moment. When he spoke, I could hear the barely restrained anger. "Why?"

"I'm on vacation, J. I've decided to enjoy it."

"Apparently without me," he said dryly.

"Is there something I can help you with?"

"You can stop being a little prima donna and bring your butt back home."

I shrugged, even though he couldn't see me. "I still have to make it to North Carolina tonight, stud, to keep on schedule. Going backward is not an option."

"Stud?" he repeated with a snarl.

I could picture his eyebrows scaling his forehead at my cavalier tone and resisted the urge to snicker. I did *so* enjoy getting under Jordan's skin sometimes.

"Do you realize how worried I've been?" he asked. "I must have called you fifteen times in the past five hours. I called Drew and went by your apartment. I even went by your brother's house. I didn't know what to think. We were supposed to have breakfast. And talk. I'm trying to remember where in the plan involved you driving off to parts unknown, but I seem to be drawing a blank."

"I needed... to go."

"Without telling me?"

"Well, I couldn't have been abducted," I rationalized. "I did leave the key."

"I saw." When he spoke again, his voice sounded funny. "Does that mean what I think it does?"

Yes. The simple answer was yes, but I couldn't quite get it out past my tight throat. Breaking up was easier to do without hearing his voice.

"So you're breaking up with me." He sighed. "Drew warned me about this."

"This isn't like the others," I defended. "I'm not the one who...." I took in a deep breath. No, this wasn't the way I wanted to end things. He hadn't done anything wrong. There was nothing to feel angry about. It just wouldn't work out. "Look. You have a baby now. A family. And it's not like you were okay with our relationship anyway."

"So you're thinking for the both of us now? What will I do with all my extra time?" he asked, voice laced with sarcasm.

"Take your kid to the park. The swing set. I hear they like that kind of thing."

"For heaven's sakes, we don't have to break up because Rachel's pregnant. You don't have to have a shotgun wedding anymore. We can co-parent." He suddenly paused, as if something had occurred to him. "Unless you're against kids? We never talked about it, but you're so good with your nephew I just assumed—"

"I'm not against kids," I said. "This is just... all too much, okay?"

His voice was quiet when he spoke again. "Not okay. How can I give you the assurance you need if you won't tell me what's wrong?"

What was wrong? There was nothing he could say to make me believe our relationship was built to last. But he wasn't quite done.

"As far as the gay thing goes, I think I've been doing pretty well. It's an adjustment, yeah. But it's still really new to me right now. This is a lot of change in a very short time. It's not going to be smooth sailing."

"You almost had a heart attack when I reached for your hand in the store. I'm not going to spend the next five years of my life resisting the urge to so much as brush lint off your shoulder if someone else can see."

"Some people aren't into PDA, Mac," he said hotly. "Have you ever thought of that?"

"You didn't seem to mind touching *her* hand at dinner." *Whoops*. I resisted the urge to whack myself in the head. Maybe he wouldn't catch that. I hurried on before that could sink in. "Besides, you got back in town a day before you were supposed to and you didn't even tell me. What's the deal?"

There was silence on his end. And mine.

"Problems dating a PI, 101," he sighed.

"I *am* observant," I agreed.

"She was having second thoughts about us breaking up. Now I know why. I owed it to her to talk about it."

I was skeptical. "You had to meet with her to accomplish that?"

"Well, should I have broken it off by e-mail? Fax? Carrier pigeon? I almost married the woman. I think she deserved a face to face breakup."

"It certainly didn't look like you were breaking it off," I accused.

This time, I didn't quite get away with it. Maybe inside I didn't want to.

"You were there?" The silence was charged. He wasn't happy. Well, neither was I.

"Yes."

"I'm not one of your goddamned clients, Mac. You have no right to spy on me."

"You lied to me!"

He sighed, and I could picture him driving fingers through his hair. I knew him well enough by now to know he was doing exactly that.

"Well, we certainly have some trust issues to work on," he said dryly.

"There's nothing to work on."

I started my *new* love, which would never leave me—Audi darling—and finally stumbled on the headlamp switch. The interior ignition sound pinged insistently as xenon headlights blazed into the darkness.

"So that's just it," he said.

"That's it."

He made a sound of disgust. "I'll call you when you cool off. You're clearly in no mood to be reasonable."

"Don't," I warned. "Don't call me. Whatever we had... well, we tried. And it was a mistake." I gritted out the word mistake, and my mouth felt like it was full of glass. Calling what we had shared a mistake felt like plunging a knife in my own chest.

After a beat of silence, he twisted that knife good. "Nothing lasts forever, I guess."

"Exactly," I managed. I didn't have enough verve left to respond to his casual "See you" before he disconnected.

I tossed the phone into the cup holder. Nothing lasted forever. That included heartache, right?

30

I took Nick's advice and sprang for the water taxi that would deliver me less than a mile from the B and B. It had hurt to leave Audi Darling in extended parking, but she and I had been soothed by me murmuring, "Papa will be back soon," as the parking attendant rolled his eyes at us both.

Standing at the railing like most of the other passengers, I tunneled into my windbreaker a little more as the wind bit into me. I didn't mind. It wasn't just a chilling wind. It was crisp, revitalizing. Refreshing. I breathed in deep. Perhaps this had been a good idea after all.

I scanned the shore to see if I could see Nick, and before long, my eyes landed on a familiar figure. We locked eyes for a moment—he was so damned familiar to me. The dark-haired man standing beside him, hands protectively curled on the handles of Nick's wheelchair? Not so much. My gaze darted between the two figures as the ferry groaned into port, and I was glad I would have at least until the slow-moving ferry docked to examine them at will (most likely ninety-eight days, the way the ship was moving). I wasn't surprised he was tall—so was I—but everything else about him seemed the antithesis of me.

His muscles seemed to come from cutting wood instead of a gym, and he wore his flannel so comfortably, I knew it was a usual look for him, if not a favorite. And he had a beard. My hand stroked over the smooth bottom half of my face. Hmph. Apparently Nick was now into the Paul Bunyan type. I couldn't help the half smile that crept over my face as I looked at Nick again. The tips of his blond hair curled at his ears and lay against his jacket—a heavy blue thing that looked like it could withstand a windstorm.

I pointed at my jacket and pantomimed a shiver. Then shook my fist. I saw his middle finger flip up, and suddenly we were both grinning. The second my boots hit the dock, we were hugging, Finn running in crazy circles around our feet. I pulled back after realizing our hug had lasted indecently long, but Peyton was only smiling at us indulgently.

I swatted Nick on the shoulder. "It's fucking freezing here!"

"Please. You're lucky you beat the frost."

"Lucky I brought my long johns."

He shook his head. "A Florida jacket isn't gonna do it, Mac. Between Peyton and I, I'm sure we can rustle you up some outerwear."

I looked Peyton up and down. "Hrmm, I think it's on you, Nick. Unless Peyton's coat comes with some muscle pads to fill it out."

Peyton's belly laugh was as burly as the rest of him. "Good to see you, Mackenzie. You're just like Nick said you'd be."

I raised my eyebrows, but Nick only smiled, scratching the wildly sniffing Finn's floppy ears.

"I couldn't wait for you to get to the inn," he said as Peyton tossed my duffle over his shoulder like it weighed nothing at all. "I connived and tricked him into letting me meet you at the dock."

The walk up to the van was long and hazardous, and I soon realized why it had taken conniving to get Peyton to push Nick all that way. I was having a hard enough time walking, much less pushing another person. Finn spent most of it running ahead and then back down with a confused look on his face, as if to ask "*What* is taking so long?" On the way up, Peyton and Nick entertained me with stories of the guests and the inn, interrupting and complimenting each other at the same time. And despite my initial balk at Peyton carrying my bag, by the time we crested the hill, I was beyond grateful.

When we reached the van, Peyton helped Nick into the vehicle with practiced ease. Nick curled his hand in Peyton's hair and kissed him before he shut the door, and I turned away. I wasn't jealous of the man, but that moment… that moment stole the wind from my lungs. Replaced it with water. It was that secret, special moment couples share that only takes a second—a shared dance that only they know the moves to. A sudden longing for Jordan was expected but still surprising for its strength. I hadn't known all the steps to our dance yet. But I'd wanted to. I didn't know why my eyes suddenly pricked with tears, but I swiped at them, hard. I would not spend this vacation thinking about Jordan.

The five-minute drive from the dock to the inn was uneventful, and despite myself I grew excited as the lush, green scenery flew by. When the Sugar Valley Inn finally broke free of the landscape, I goggled, feasting on the sight of the sprawling two-story house nestled in the mountains. Sugar Valley Inn was exactly what I thought it would be—gorgeous views, a home-style, natural stone covered house that blended into the landscape, an *actual* picket fence, and meticulously manicured lawns.

"God," I breathed, stepping out of the car. My boots crunched on the gravel drive. "Nick, this is beautiful."

"Surrounded by 200 acres of majestic mountains," he declared proudly. "Meadows. Ponds. It's like being part of nature."

"Amazing."

"I knew you'd like it," he said smugly. "So I done good?"

"You done spent a crap load of my money, paying for this trip," I said, giving him a halfhearted swat. "But yea. You done real good."

"I told you; you're not paying us," he said, wheeling into the beautifully decorated lobby. He waved to two of the guests exiting and pointed a finger at me. "You and Jordan are our guests." His brow crinkled. "Speaking of…."

"I *am* paying you," I said, not wanting him to start in on me about

Jordan. Somehow, I knew he would make it my fault. It was, but that was beyond the point. "I already arranged it with Peyton. Paid two days ago." I stuck out my tongue. "So there."

His incredulous gaze swung to Peyton. "You took his money? I *told* you—"

"Now, babe." Peyton's voice was neutral. "He wouldn't take no for an answer—"

"I told you how he is," he hissed as I poked around the lobby, snagging an apple and several brochures for activities I probably wouldn't do. "You can't give him the opportunity to negotiate. You just do it and tell him later."

"Funny. That's exactly what he said about you," Peyton said, and I could hear the laughter in his voice.

I plucked my duffle from his shoulder and decided to leave him to Nick's outrage.

"I'm going to see if the upstairs matches the beauty down here, or if there's flowered wallpaper and antiques to contend with," I said.

I waved at Peyton. I didn't know him yet, but I could recognize a how-could-you-desert-me look anywhere. Better him face Nick's wrath than me explain where Jordan was.

Upstairs didn't disappoint—big, comfy beds and crackling warm fireplaces, with the same spectacular view of the mountains. Immediately, I could tell that Peyton had put me in a room better than the one I paid for. The top floor of the home was split into two gigantic rooms, and my key fit one of the gigantic wooden doors.

There was a bowl of red apples, acorns, and nuts on the dresser that I passed before dumping my luggage next to the huge bed. The whole effect was comfy and cozy, and I hardly blamed Finn for snuggling down next to the fireplace. Well, first he shook his long, wet fur everywhere, spraying me, and *then* he snuggled down next to the fireplace.

I put my hand on the wall, feeling the rich wood paneling that went all the way to the pitched ceiling, which had three skylights that flooded the room with light. I prowled the room like any curious guest, and when I was done, I wasn't sure which impressed me more —the Victorian king-size or the deluxe whirlpool tub.

There was a perfunctory knock at my door, and I called out, "Come in."

Nick rolled in, balancing yet another goodie basket on his lap and a map in his teeth. I rescued the map and goodie basket and set them on the side table.

"What's all this?"

"Guest amenities," he said, smiling. "I want you to be comfortable."

"At this point, if I was any more comfortable, I'd be dead."

"We deliver breakfast in the morning," he informed me. "I would tell you all about our menu, with the finest of seasonal and locally sourced foods, but I know where your heart is. Peyton makes a killer blueberry cheesecake french toast."

I simply stared at him. "You had me at deliver."

He laughed and swatted me. "I guess your order is in."

"With bacon," I said slyly, testing my luck.

"With bacon," he parroted back.

"And coffee."

"Vermont-roasted, dark."

"Mmm." I shouldn't be this excited for breakfast. "That covers tomorrow, but what about today? I feel like I could eat a bear. Or at the very least an elk."

Nick looked amused. "Sorry, no big game served here. Only the occasional venison when Peyton gets his way. I did prepare some lunch, but I wanted you to get settled first."

I used my foot to move my duffle closer to the dresser. One inch. "Settled."

He grinned. "Come on. We can eat in the kitchen and catch up."

My evading lasted until we were ensconced in a comfy kitchen nook, our plates loaded up with heavy chicken salad sandwiches with crisp lettuce and plenty of juicy vine-ripe tomato. Peyton dropped off tall sweating glasses of iced tea and dropped a kiss on Nick's forehead. "I'll be out back."

"Don't be late for dinner."

"Where's he going?" I asked as he strode toward what I assumed was a door to the back.

"Out to chop wood. We're expecting more cold weather in the next few days. We're trying to be prepared." Nick followed Peyton's tall body all the way to the door with his eyes, and he didn't blink until the door swung shut. When Nick looked back my way, he colored at my amusement and shrugged. "What?"

"Don't worry. I love to watch my man walk away too."

He dug into his sandwich. "Speaking of which, where is this Jordan you've been going on and on about?"

"We didn't...." It was harder to say the words than I thought. "We didn't work out."

Nick's eyes went wide. "You *didn't*."

"Now, why does it always have to be *my* fault?" I asked, forgetting for a moment that this time it absolutely was.

"Well, was it?"

"Well. Yeah, I did dump him but—"

"I knew it!" Nick shook his head, mumbling around his food. "I knew you would screw it up before it had a chance to succeed."

"Very nice," I growled, biting into my own sandwich. "But this time, you don't know what you're talking about. Jordan and I didn't work out because he is having a little trouble letting go of his ex-fiancée, who is now pregnant. And being gay, even if he won't admit it."

"That's a lot of change at once," Nick said, nodding understandingly. I had a feeling his understanding was for Jordan and not me, which he soon confirmed. "Babies are a big deal. What a wonderful addition to your life, though."

"Well." My brow furrowed. I guess that was one way to look at it.

"And as for being gay, you and I both know it's hard enough to fall in love without it changing everything you believed about yourself, all at the same time."

"Well. Yeah, I'd imagine...."

"Not to mention the sexual changes at that. Looking at everyone differently, yourself differently, wondering if everything you ever knew was a lie or just half the truth of who you were. Are his parents very supportive?"

"I don't exactly know… if he told them," I trailed off, picking at my napkin.

"Well, at least he had you to confide in."

"Hmm." I thought back to all the times he tried to talk about this new "lifestyle," as he called it. How angry I would get and usually shut it down. It had just seemed like the more he analyzed the new things happening to him, the more I was afraid he would see that I was a mistake. That he didn't *like* where the new things were taking him. That he wanted things to go back to the way they were. "I didn't really—"

"Jesus." Nick shook his head. "You are truly determined to be alone forever."

"Not fair," I said angrily. "I may have not been the perfect confidant for him, but he did lie to me." And I explained in detail exactly how he had lied. Nick could not have been less sympathetic.

"Good to know you're judge, jury, and executioner."

"You don't understand."

"I understand, Mackenzie. I understand you better than your brother, better than your father ever did. I was there when your dad told you the truth about your mom, remember? And I saw you change into someone who was so afraid of losing everyone that you pushed them away first. The more Jordan analyzed the relationship, the more confident you became that he would find out what a mistake it was and leave you. So you left first."

I looked at him, feeling raw and exposed. My eyes burned a little, and I was glad no one else was there to see me like this. The faint *chop, chop, chop* was soothing, as Peyton chopped wood methodically.

When Nick spoke again, his voice was barely a whisper over the classical music piping in over the sound system. "And how do you feel now?"

"I… hurt."

I realized that my sentence-making ability had broken down

completely, but it described my insides perfectly. I hurt, and there was no fancying that up. Deep down to my chest, where it seemed to seep into the bone and settle there, cold and weary. I had thought I'd made a clean break before things got messy. But irrespective of how long we'd known each other, I was already in too deep. There was no clean break.

I buried my head in my hands. "I *hurt*."

He grabbed me into a hug, face in hands and all—really just wrapped his arms around me so tight I was afraid my bones would crack. "See, Mac, that's why getting out before anyone can hurt you doesn't work. You hurt anyway."

"Well, I was right, wasn't I?" I cried out. "He accepted it with little more than a 'see ya' in return."

"I'm sorry," Nick said, over and over into my hair. "I'm sorry."

I was too. Sorry I had ever loved. Sorry I had ever lost. Sorrier still when Finn made off with the rest of my chicken sandwich, plucked delicately off my plate while I cried in Nick's arms.

"Shoo!" Nick said, waving his hands, and Finn took off with his treasure to parts unknown. "I'll make you something else."

I shook my head.

"You want to take a nap?" He rubbed my hair soothingly. "Or are you up for a tour? Take your mind off things."

I nodded. "I'll take that tour."

31

"I'm not doing it." I glared up at Nick.

He just grinned and beckoned me forward. "We've almost reached the summit."

"I'm lame, dammit. Don't you have any sympathy at all?" I pointed to my bad leg, which actually felt limber from all the exercise and stretching.

He snickered. "Trotting out the old leg injury, Mac? Sad. Come on, the trip down will be cake."

My cooperation had reached its eventual limit. I had forgiven him the canoeing. The hiking. The kayaking and all manner of other activities that couch potatoes shouldn't attempt. But the biking up Mount Fuji was just *wrong*. All right, it wasn't Mount Fuji, but it was tall enough, dammit. Day four, and I was starting to wonder which of us needed Nick's wheelchair... or whatever that contraption was he was currently riding in. It looked like some sort of dune buggy for one person, and he used his strong arms to muscle up the trail with ease.

"There had better *be* cake waiting at the bottom," I muttered, cranking the pedals that seemed mired in mud.

I complained, but I had to admit—I was having a good time.

Vermont seemed as far away from Florida as Mars at this moment. We had pedaled through quiet roads and farmland, and a sleepy village with a tiny church. I'd seen more apple orchards and hayfields than I could count and snagged more maple candy than I cared to admit. I would admit, however, that I was a little in love with Vermont.

"Wow."

I coasted to a stop at the top of the pass. (Okay, okay, it wasn't a mountain at all. But it was steep. Sheesh.) River valleys surrounded by hills, flanked by abundant maple trees, stretched as far as the eye could see, a gorgeous clash of green, red, and orange, vibrant as only nature could provide.

"This is fairly incredible," I said.

"Isn't it?" He beckoned me closer. "Sit next to me. I want to watch the sun go down."

For sharing this with me, he could have whatever he wanted. I laid my bike down off the trail and sat in the soft grass next to him.

"I gotta admit, this is better than my plan for today."

"Which was?"

"Sleep. Followed by more sleep."

I looked his way as he laughed, and his laugh made me smile. Backlit by the sun, Nick's eyes appeared more golden than light brown, and we didn't look away.

"You look good," he said.

I ducked my head. "Thanks."

"Tan," he continued. "Been surfing again?"

"What else is there?"

"Such a fucking Florida stereotype."

I slugged him. "Look at those lily-white knees," I said. "You could use a little sun. Or daylight at the very least."

He grinned. "Keep it up. I make muffins for tomorrow's breakfast —yours can be bran or it can be blueberry like everyone else's."

"With crumble?" I asked hopefully.

"How else is there?"

I ruffled his hair. "You look happy."

"I am happy," he said softly.

"I'm glad to hear it." I was. Learning that Nick had lost the ability to walk was one of the lowest points of my life. God only knew what it had done to him. "I'm glad you found everything you were looking for."

"Looks like you found something you needed too."

I winced. "I thought I did."

He shook his head. "Same old Mac. Don't give up on him just yet." He knocked shoulders with me in a way that was so familiar, I almost went weak at the knees. "Look how much time we've missed. I don't want that for the two of you."

I looked at him thoughtfully, head cocked like Finnegan's. Truth was, baby or no baby, I didn't want that either.

We held hands as the sun finally disappeared, and as we made our way back downhill, I was full with the surprise and joy that closure was a very real thing.

Peyton was pacing the porch as we rounded the gravel drive, and Nick waved. "Aw, my honey was worried."

He did look worried as he hustled down the steps to meet us and gave Nick an absent kiss. "Can I talk to you for a sec?"

Nick and I exchanged looks and shrugs before I went off to turn in my bike to the sour-faced activities manager, Darren, in the back barn. Darren circled the bike like it was made of solid gold, and I whistled tunelessly, hoping he didn't notice the nicks I'd put in the metallic blue exterior.

"It looks damaged."

I shrugged. "I got it like that."

"My equipment is pristine," he said, raising his eyebrows.

"I don't know what to tell ya." I migrated over to the glass covered sugar cookie tray on his desk. "Are these maple?"

He scowled, and I took that to mean "Yes, take three."

"I'm going to need a voucher for a bike tomorrow."

"Very well." He ended the Vermont Inquisition and rounded the desk. "Are you going on the Ben & Jerry's factory tour?"

I stopped and stared. "I'm sorry, what?"

"Ben & Jerry's? The ice cream factory?" He went back to writing my voucher, and I slapped a hand over the paper.

"Hold on a damn minute. You're telling me there's a Ben & Jerry's factory to visit, and this fool has had me reenacting the damn Tour de France?"

The sour man grinned. I didn't know he had it in him. He held up the voucher. "Are you still going to need this bike?"

"Not at all, Darren," I proclaimed, snagging another sugar cookie. "I suddenly have other plans for tomorrow."

I made my way from the barn to the main house, which certainly took longer without my trusty bicycle. I soothed my nerves from walking about in the semidarkness by eating sugar cookies and licking the crumbs off my fingers. It had been fun traipsing around the countryside with Nick, but now it was time for some Mackenzie-approved fun. The kind that involved one of those fluffy Sugar Valley Inn robes, some hot chocolate in a mug, and a hefty dose of liquor of some kind.

As I approached the main house, I heard Peyton say, "I thought you said they broke up."

I popped up on the porch in time to make them both jump. "Who broke up? And whose van is that?"

Nick smiled weakly. "Airport van."

"Are you expecting…." My voice trailed off as a figure emerged from the van.

I had to blink a few times before I convinced myself that, yes, it was Jordan emerging from the van. I had plenty of time to think of something to say, recover the ability to speak. From the time he heaved a heavy bag onto his shoulder, spoke briefly to the driver, and walked up the drive to the porch, I should have been able to come up with something. Anything. But I couldn't think of a single thing to say as Jordan stood before me. He didn't look pleased as he stomped his boots, pink cheeked from the cold.

His black trench and gloves should have looked out of place next to our rugged wear, but he wore it so comfortably, it looked natural. I did my best not to sniff him, but my nostrils did flare a bit. He always smelled so good. I wanted to fling myself at him, go rolling down the porch steps. But when my eyes made it up to his face, his jaw was hard. Eyes flinty. He looked pissed.

Lucy, you got some splainin' to do.

I sighed. "Hey."

"Hey?" It didn't sound like a greeting. Which he immediately confirmed by raising an eyebrow. "That's all you have to say to me?"

"You must be Jordan," Nick said hastily. He held out a hand which Jordan shook automatically.

"I'm surprised he even told you my name," Jordan said, his gaze sliding to mine. "But thank you for your hospitality."

Nick's smile was a little too bright, and I could tell, from years of knowing him all too well, that he found my dressing-down hilarious. "Let's get inside, you guys. It's too cold out here."

Peyton fled inside, as if all the tension was just too much for the mountain man. Jordan followed, leaving Nick and I to bring up the rear.

"You failed to mention he looks like a GQ wet dream," Nick whispered, elbowing me. "You always were a forgetful little thing."

"Shut up," I hissed. I had a hard enough time not focusing on his looks as it was.

By the time we reached the coat area, Jordan was squatting down by Finn to scratch his ears.

"What is he doing here? Did Trevor change his mind?"

I paused in my methodical removal of my coat and other outerwear. "I, err, sort of broke into his house. Stole him."

"What?"

"Whoa," Nick said at the same time.

"He *is* my dog," I said defensively.

"I wondered where you had gone," Jordan said. "I stopped by your apartment. Your truck wasn't there. Please tell me you didn't drive that thing up here."

"I sold my truck." *Sold it, pawned it off on a young, desperate teenager, what's the difference*? "I bought a new car."

He stared at me, and I flushed. Yeah, when I finally decided to make a move, I was kind of like an avalanche that way.

"Jordan, you guys have about an hour to get settled in if you want hot chow," Nick said. "We're about to fix dinner for everyone."

I don't know who this "we" business referred to. If he was speaking of the ghost of Peyton present, he'd fled the room and all its tension long ago. Peyton was probably hugging a moose and cursing city people as we spoke.

"I assume Mackenzie can show me to the room." Jordan finished hanging his gray-checked Burberry scarf and looked at me expectantly. "That is, unless he'd prefer me to bed down in the barn."

I tamped down the embers of my own temper. He wasn't exactly innocent here. He hadn't exactly gone out of his way to convince me we were a sure thing. Besides, he *wished* he could bed down in the barn. After a week of being apart and thusly, self-imposed celibacy, we were going to have sex. Well, first we were going to argue, and *then* we were going to have sex—I really didn't care if it was angry sex or not.

"Follow me," I gritted out, brushing past him hard enough to make him move a step.

I made extra noise on the staircase to vent my frustration, and I could hear Jordan on my heels.

"Real mature," he said, (of course not out of breath) as I huffed up the stairs.

"Can it," I snapped. Yeah, it was going to be angry sex.

When we reached the top of the stairs, I unlocked the door and blew right in, slamming the door. Which of course he reopened a second later and slammed behind *him*.

"Nice," he said. "Real nice. Let me guess, you're not ready to be an adult?"

We seemed to be of the same mind as he yanked his shirt out of his jeans and over his head. I was made briefly stupid by the sight of his bare chest, but his fingers on his belt buckle made me hurry and speak. If I didn't get it out now, I wouldn't be able to. God, there was something about the authoritative way he took off that belt buckle, eyes locked on mine. Something that said we were about to *fuck*.

"Someone's fairly horny," I said. My voice sounded thick. Funny.

"Of course I'm horny," he said, grabbing me by the belt loops and pulling me against him. He rubbed his cock into mine, and I felt the haze of lust lick at my consciousness. "We haven't had sex in a week," he muttered against my mouth.

"Well, whose fault was that?"

"Yours!" he said, frustrated, working to pull up my shirt.

I felt like I had cotton in my head, and I pushed him back a few steps, tangled in my shirt. Blinked to clear the sexual haze as I pulled it back down. Tried to remember what virus had cracked my mind's software to make me leave all this behind in Florida. *Ah. Yes.*

"You said *see ya*," I growled in his direction. I tried to point, but my hand was shaking a bit. No matter. He knew what the hell I meant. "I was upset and frustrated, and all you could offer me was a flip 'see ya'?"

He bit his lip. Gave me a miserable look. "I wanted to hurt you. Hurt you as badly as you were hurting me."

"You succeeded."

He ran his hand through his hair and then down over his face, exhaling strongly. "So let's talk about it. Like two adults. Minus the hurting one another."

"I never wanted to hurt you."

His eyes almost approached wolflike intensity. "By giving up on me? Us? Goddamn it, can you give me ten fucking seconds to get used to the idea that everything has changed? You know, without leaving the state?"

I looked down at my hands. We'd already established that was a fault of mine. When something went wrong in a relationship, I reacted. I reacted badly. We should have had this conversation that day, back in his kitchen. Maybe we could have if I hadn't acted like a big ole Moe and taken off. I sighed. Might as well put all my cards on the table. *If* we got past this—and that was a big if—I didn't want to go over it ever again.

"You were back a day early," I said evenly. "And you didn't tell me."

"More PI business?" His tone was laced with a trace of bitterness. "Do you pay yourself a retainer, or is that just pro bono?"

"I'm sorry. I shouldn't know that you were, but now that I do...." I lifted my shoulders helplessly. "I have to know."

"I had the taxi take me straight from the airport to your office, I was so excited to see you. I was waiting in your office—you can ask your secretary. Thin? Kind of a habitual frowner? She brought me coffee. And then Rachel called. She was crying, said she had to talk to me. I knew she and I had some important things to talk about, and I didn't know how long it would take. It wouldn't be fair to her to drop her like a hot potato because I wanted to be with you. It could wait a day. I didn't think you'd understand."

I ignored the feelings fighting for superiority in my chest: Relief blooming because I knew he told the truth. Happiness because he was as excited to see me as I'd been to see him. Delight that he'd come straight from the airport just to be with me. And as always, the surety that none of those feelings could last.

"I thought you were having second thoughts. That you weren't sure of me. Us."

He sighed. "How can you be sure of how anything is going to turn out? I can only promise that I want to be with you. More than I've ever wanted anything in my whole life." The corner of his mouth lifted. "And I was the kid that asked Santa for a Huffy bike ten times."

"And when you get tired of me? Tired of this experiment?" I looked back at him. "Ten times? For real? What were your parents, Nazis?"

He ignored the latter half of my question. "You don't get tired of people that you lo—"

I slammed my hand over his mouth. "Don't say that right now. Not in the same sentence as you not being sure about us."

He licked my palm leisurely, and I shivered. Finger by finger, his tongue paid absolute attention to every digit. By the time I released his mouth I was a shivery mess.

"How can I convince you if you won't let me tell you how I feel?" When my eyes lifted to his, there was nothing but truth there. So I felt the punch clear to my stomach when he said, "I love you."

I wanted those words. I needed those words. I squeezed my eyes shut. Wished I could believe those words.

"Look at me."

I shook my head.

"You don't want to see me?"

My heart squeezed at the sadness in his voice, and my eyes flew open. "Of course I want to see you. I love to look at you. I would look at you all day if I…." I trailed off to see the amusement in his eyes.

"What can I say to make you believe me?"

I didn't actually know. I should be ecstatic, over the moon happy. But part of me, the part of me that I had only become recently aware of, told me that it couldn't be real. It couldn't last. Why should I get exactly what I want with who I wanted?

"Can I ask you something?"

"Anything," he said. "What do you want to know?"

"The baby. What if it's—"

"Mine? We'll deal with that then. She's pretty sure it's his, though, because we weren't really intimate at the end there. But you know Rache. She just wanted to cover all her bases and let everyone know about every *possible* outcome. I swear, she's going to have that kid a day planner before he's two."

I had to smile a little at that. He was probably right.

"So you. You and Rachel. Are you—"

"We're over. There's nothing there, Mac. But she's a nice person, a good friend. I owed it to her to break it off gently."

"Even though she cheated on you?"

"I can hardly blame her." He spread his hands. "I haven't been there for her… mentally, for a long time. She found someone who would pay her the attention she deserves."

"Yeah?"

"Yeah." He smiled a crooked half smile. This time when he reached for me, I let him pull me close. "Besides. I'm kind of into wise-cracking, sun-worshipping surfer dudes who jump to conclusions now. It's taking up a lot of my time."

He kissed me then, so thoroughly that it actually curled my toes. His tongue worked through my mouth slow and deep, leaving my nerves sensitized and frenetic. My cock throbbed in response, and I was tired of pretending I wasn't affected by his nearness. My hands slid down to his waist, then to his behind, and I pulled him flush against my body. Undulating against him. Grinding.

"So we're okay," he said. One of his broad hands slid under my shirt, rubbing the sensitive skin of my stomach.

"We're okay," I said, unresisting as his other hand tangled in my hair.

He held my head still as his tongue swept through my mouth, and I felt the jolt clear to my knees. His mouth trailed down my neck, pressing kisses against the skin there.

"We should take this slow, though," I managed, baring my neck for better access. "Slower than we have been."

He cocked his head in confusion, and I hastened to explain. "So that we'll both be okay when... if things don't—"

"Asshole," he whispered. He gave me a push, and I staggered back. He swallowed a few times. His voice was stronger when he spoke again. "I tell you that I love you, and this is how you respond?"

"What do you expect me to say, Jordan?" I speared my hair with my fingertips, knowing I was screwing this up so badly. "I'm trying to be understanding. Supportive. All that crap. Give you an out."

"What about anything that I said indicated I wanted an out?"

"Last I saw, you were cuddled up with your fiancée—"

"Yes, and then I bought a rather expensive, last minute ticket here to prove that you're important to me. Thanks for that, by the way."

"I didn't ask you to come." The moment the words flew out of my mouth, I wanted them back. His mouth went tight and his eyes went flinty.

He folded his arms. "I'm done chasing you. I've chased you to your apartment, to your office, and now halfway across the damn country. One thousand four hundred eighty-seven miles." The gap between us had never seemed so wide. "You're going to have to make up those last few feet."

Dammit, it was just so simple. Why couldn't I trust and believe that anything good could last? I felt the sting of tears at the back of my eyes. The hurricane my mother had sent through my life was still thrashing and spinning anything in its path, throwing both tangibles and intangibles in its wake. Destruction. Furniture and trees. Love. Happiness. Trust. *She fucking broke me.*

And I knew then that I couldn't do it. I couldn't take that last step. As I spun on my heel, I knew I was about to make the biggest mistake of my life.

Despite his words, he grabbed my arm when I would have fled and whirled me around to face him. I struggled against his hold for a moment, realizing with a little bit of shock that it was futile. I was strong but obviously no match for him. Apparently he took working out as seriously as he did everything else.

"You're not leaving me that easily. Not this time."

"Move," I ground out. "Or I'll move you."

He twisted my arm up behind my back—not hard enough to hurt, but certainly enough to show who was in charge. "You and what army?"

I growled furiously, helpless. I would rather he hurt me than treat me like a wayward child. Maybe that's why I was determined to let my past win. On some level, I was still hurt, and I wasn't done hurting him back, despite my agreement to do so. It was cowardly, and I hid the shame with anger. "Get. Off!"

"Mackenzie," he began warningly.

I worked one of my hands loose and took a swipe at him, which he blocked and recaptured my hands. Fingers deftly shoved my flimsy belt through the loops of my khakis and began working my button one handed. His fingers brushed my aching dick through the worn material, and I hissed.

"What are you doing?" My voice wasn't nearly as authoritative as I wanted it to be.

"I should think that would be obvious."

My pants fell around my knees, restricting my movement. I bucked against him, but I couldn't deny what he and I *both* knew—I was as turned on as he was. Even without the visual of my dripping cock, bobbing in the air. I felt him throbbing against my leg. Thick. Insistent. The combined scent of our arousal was heady. Made my vision blur. I wanted him to shove me down and have his way with me, had wanted that from the moment I laid eyes on him, all icy and distant in the cold. And as I felt the sudden pressure on my lower back driving me to my knees, I realized with certain clarity that I was about to get my wish.

I was exposed, my most sensitive areas bare to his gaze. I should have been trying to hide. But when I felt those fingers working the ring of my muscle I only sighed. He must have felt my acquiescence because he let my arms fall gently. My spine dipped, and he ran his hands up and down my back, following the arch. I braced my elbows on the floor and let my head fall slack between my tense shoulders.

The sudden scent of apples hit my nose, and I squawked briefly as he inserted his finger, slick with what I could only imagine was the Sugar Valley lotion Nick had left in my goodie basket. "I was going to use that... for something else," I managed.

"Better than this?" He was close to my ear as another delving digit joined the first.

No, I couldn't say that applying lotion to my knobby knees while hopping foot to foot was better than this. But he was sure taking his slow-ass sweet time, and I had already waited too long. Even as irritated as he was, he was clearly going to make sure I was good and ready.

I smacked his hand away. "Just do it," I said through gritted teeth.

He tried to go back to loosening me up, and I slapped him again. He finally bit down, hard, on the hollow of my neck. The pleasure/pain made me go stiff and still as he slowly twisted and rotated those two fingers, pumping them in and out slowly. A whimper escaped my throat, and he groaned in response.

"My luggage," he ground out. "I need... condom."

Despite his statement, he added a third finger, making me huff out a breath. I knew it was wrong, but I pushed my ass back at him, daring him to take it, begging him wordlessly.

"We can't," he said, but somehow his cock had tunneled its way between my asscheeks and was leaking a copious amount of fluid there. I clenched and pushed back against him, causing him to grip my hips tensely.

"Just a little," I whispered, and I knew the magnitude of what I was asking him to do. I didn't bareback, but damn if I didn't want him buried balls deep in me, filling me, pounding me clear into the goddamned floor.

The thick, mushroomed head popped in, just enough to make us both groan. And then he was gone, leaving me empty and frustrated.

"We'll get tested," he ground out. "And then God help you." He anchored his hand in my hair and pulled my head back, taking my mouth roughly. "I can't believe you let me do that," he scolded when we came up for air.

"I trust you," I said, and I was surprised to find it was true. We shouldn't have done it, and I briefly had lost my mind, but I *did* trust him. When we finally did come together with nothing but skin on skin, it would be absolutely worth the wait.

"'Bout time," he muttered. "Now where the hell is my bag?"

Mercifully, he found the condom and was back inside of me before I could even voice a complaint. He entered me with no preamble, his length dragging across every sensitized nerve on the way in.

"Shit," I managed, my hands clawing for traction on the smooth floor.

"Mine," he ground out as he stroked, long and smooth.

"Who else's would it be?" I managed. I swore fluently as he pulled out and drilled me again.

God, no one could fuck me like Jordan did. There was no point in denying that. I was mad, not crazy. He was it for me.

"I love you," I blurted and then wished the floor could open up and eat me whole.

He stilled. "Say it again."

I shook my head, and he pulled back, nearly all the way to the head, and then even more slowly pushed back in. His grinding had me groaning, making noises that ripped from my throat like a feral animal forced into a cage.

"Say it," he growled, and finally I did.

"I love you, *goddammit*," I swore, pushing a wild tangle of hair out of my eyes. "Now fuck me."

I could feel his grin against my neck. "I love the way you talk to me so pretty, baby." And then he complied, pinning me down and fucking me into the floor.

"Yesssss," I hissed, pushing back onto him, meeting his hard thrusts. "That's. Fucking. It. Don't stop." I could feel the pressure building in my core, the tingles spreading through my extremities. "Don't you dare fucking stop."

"You feel so fucking... good," he managed, mouth flush against my neck. "I don't know how much... how much longer...."

There was something just fundamentally different about making love to someone who loved you back. Every move, every touch was meaningful. Fingers lingered and stroked. Lips caressed, and words were whispered. We found each other's rhythm—moved in perfect synchronicity without any effort at all.

His hand took control of my bobbing cock and began a firm stroke, base to tip, that mirrored his thrusts in my ass. When his thumb dug into the slit, I gasped, my back going rigid. I yelled as I spurted over his hand, coming so hard I saw stars, forgetting that I was at a bed-and-breakfast with vanilla guests and very thin walls. Dimly I was aware of Jordan groaning in my ear, his thrusts taking on an erratic rhythm. He convulsed against my back, and I felt him swell inside me, his hand falling off my sensitive cock. He came for quite some time, shivery and jerking there, heavy on my back as I braced us both against the storm, my breath still coming harsh and fast in my ears.

My knees hurt a little, and my leg was starting to cramp, but I would stay there as long as he wanted me to, as long as he needed me to. His weight finally powered me flat to the floor, and I collapsed there silently, his body heavy and welcome on my back. I didn't yet care that I was lying face-first on a strange floor. Or that I had just screamed the walls down in the most intense orgasm of my life.

I briefly spared a prayer that my fellow guests had attended the Thursday night hayride and wondered how I was going to get my brains back on the inside of my head.

"You think they heard that?" Jordan's voice, sleepy and quiet, echoed my own thoughts.

"Wonder if we'll get a refund if the guests demand our removal."

"You got a check from this inn in the mail," he said, yawning. I felt bereft as Jordan slipped out of me. I heard him disposing of the condom but couldn't be bothered to open my eyes yet.

A check in the mail? My eyes flew open. "What?"

"Peyton must have sent you a refund. I assumed you knew. That's how I knew the exact address."

I popped up like a jack-in-the-box. "That sneaky little mountain man. He knew I wouldn't get it until I got back."

Jordan flopped onto the bed. "Get up here. I have activities planned for you that don't involve a crick in your neck and a sore back. At least not until after."

My eyes went wide, but I was revitalized enough to scramble up and join him in bed. Sounded promising. And Jordan always kept his promises.

32

I woke up alone. Cold. Instinctively, I snuggled into the blankets, gradually awakening. I looked around, getting my bearings, fighting the softness of the bed that threatened to pull me back into dreamland. The dying firelight was low and lazy, sending dark patterns flitting across the walls. Despite the lure of the cozy bed, I got up, sticking my bare feet in a pair of Sugar Valley slippers. I pulled on a pair of jeans and padded to the deck. When I slid the door open, cold air rustled through the room, and I wished I'd bothered to find a shirt.

He was sprawled in one of the Adirondack chairs, one of the custom white Sugar Valley blankets on his lap. I stood there on one foot, the other scratching my leg, wondering how to approach him. We hadn't exactly ended on a sour note, but we'd both said some harsh things.

As if he'd felt my presence, he looked back at me, and we stared at each other wordlessly. After a moment, he snorted and lifted the edge of his blanket.

I dove under, suddenly aware that I had been unconsciously asking to do so, and settled my chilly body against his heat. He re-tucked the blanket around me and locked his arms around that. The cold was as good as toast.

"You make eyes like a deer," he informed me.

I snuggled against him, fitting my head in the hollow between his chin and his neck. "You just say that because my eyes are brown."

"They're hazel. And they're beautiful. Everything about you is beautiful. And I can't believe you're mine."

I stroked the back of his hand, adding to my mental scrapbook the map of his hand—memorizing every curve, every scar, every groove of the man I loved and only important to me. "You say that like you mean it."

"I rarely say things I don't mean."

The wind whistled through the tall trees in a sweet symphony of sound that only nature could make. I heard laughter somewhere below us and the sound of the front door opening and closing to the warm inn. I snuggled closer. We would go back home, sure, but we would take this moment (and a few Sugar Valley robes) with us.

"Do you think it will snow?"

"Probably." He tightened his arms around me. "You cold?"

I shook my head. "I meant what I said, you know."

"About what?"

"About taking this slow."

He stiffened beneath me, and I rubbed my hand across his chest in a manner that could only be described as soothing.

"Not to give us an out, but to make sure we do it right. I don't want to shut you out to protect myself. I never did. It was just too hard to think about you leaving me and too hard to let you in." I drew an imaginary circle on his shirt. Added eyes and a smiley. "I spend the greater portion of every day picking through the curdled remains of love that was. Despite my protests to the contrary, I don't know if I even believed it truly existed. Until now." I half smiled. "You defined my love. Short of holding a boom box over my head and singing "Don't wanna miss a thing," that's the best way I can describe it."

"God no, please don't ruin it."

My hands slid into his hair as I angled my mouth over his. It'd been too long since we'd kissed like this... three hours? Too long since I'd felt his mouth take absolute possession of mine and too long since I'd felt the mind-emptying indulgence of his kiss.

"Say it again," I murmured.

He didn't hesitate, and his eyes, big-sky-country blue, seared my soul with intensity. "I love you." After a moment, his affronted voice broke the stillness. "Don't you have something to say in return?"

I pretended to think. "You'd better?"

I closed my eyes, a smile creeping across my face. I enjoyed my sassiness for two seconds before he dug his fingers in my ribs, causing me to laugh and shriek. "All right, all right! I love you too."

We listened to the sounds of the inn shutting down for the night. Lights going off. Doors closing softly.

"Good night, John-Boy," I said, and Jordan elbowed me.

"Too bad I didn't know we'd resolve this amicably. I used up my grand gesture."

"Yeah?" I yawned. "What is that?"

"I was going to invite my parents here and declare my love for you. Trust me, with their gossipy nature, that's like taking out an ad in the Sun Sentinel. People I know. Not just random people seeing me hold your hand." He picked up said hand and kissed it gently.

"Too bad," I laughed. "I might have enjoyed that spectacle. So glad you didn't really invite your parents here." When he didn't join my laughter, I looked back at his innocent face.

"You didn't. Right?"

"My dad loves fishing. You love fishing. That's something you guys can enjoy together."

I groaned. "Argh! I have no desire to visit with your parents and perfect family and watch you all reenact it's a wonderful life being a Channing."

"Have you even seen *It's a Wonderful Life*?" he accused.

"No, why? It's not about a wonderful life?"

"God, Mac." He set squinty eyes on me. "You will meet my parents, and you will be your loving, charming self. Except minus the blasphemy and sex jokes."

"That's all I have." I shook my head. "The things I do for love."

"What kind of things?"

I tossed back the blanket and stood, holding out my hand. "I show better than I tell."

He grinned and took it, letting me pull him to a standing position. "Baby, I kind of like your style."

AFTERWORD

Thank you for reading about Mac and Jordan! Drew finds the love of his life in the second book in the PI Guys series, *So Into You*.

If you're interested in reading more by yours truly, you can follow me on Facebook, Amazon, or Bookbub, so you'll be notified of new releases. You can also join my Facebook group, Harmon's Hideout, if you'd like to chat.

I'll see you on our next fictional journey.

S.E. Harmon

ACKNOWLEDGMENTS

I would like to thank Sam, my most stalwart champion. You are my sister because of genetics, but my best friend by choice. I would choose
you again and again. I couldn't have done it without you, so...thank you.

ABOUT THE AUTHOR

S.E. Harmon has had a lifelong love affair with writing. It's been both wonderful and rocky (they've divorced several times), but they always manage to come back together. She's a native Floridian with a Bachelor of Arts and a Masters in Fine Arts, and now splits her days between voraciously reading romance novels and squirreling away someplace to write them. Her current beta reader is a nosy American Eskimo who begrudgingly accepts payment in the form of dog biscuits.

Website: https://seharmon.weebly.com/

Email: silkguitar2011@comcast.net

ALSO BY S.E. HARMON

So Into You

The Blueprint

A Deeper Blue

Blitzed

P.S. I Spook You

Principles of Spookology

Spooky Business

The Spooky Life

Coddiwomple

Chrysalis

Cross

Addicted to Ellis D.

The First and Last Adventure of Kit Sawyer

Love Is

Printed in Great Britain
by Amazon